salt

salt

A novel

Earl Lovelace

persea books   new york

Salt was first published in the United States in 1997 by Persea Books, Inc., New York; originally published by Faber & Faber Ltd., London, in 1996.

Persea Books, Inc.
171 Madison Avenue
New York, New York 10010

Library of Congress Cataloging-in-Publication Data
Lovelace, Earl, 1935-
        Salt / Earl Lovelace
            p.   cm.
        ISBN 0-89255-226-3 (hardcover : alk. paper)
        I. Title
    PR9272.9.L6S25   1997   96-50266
        813–dc21   CIP

Printed and bound by Haddon Craftsmen, Scranton, Pennsylvania

First U. S. Edition

For
Tiy, Maya, Lulu, Che, Walt

With thanks to Margaret
and to Bob and to Ken and to Lillian and Lyris
and to Lawrence and Jenny and to all the marchers
who have brought us to this place

BOOK ONE

1

Bango

Two months after they hanged his brother Gregoire, king of the Dreadnoughts band, and Louis and Nanton and Man Man, the other three leaders of African secret societies, who Hislop the governor claimed to be ringleaders of an insurrection that had a plan, according to the testimony of a mad white woman, to use the cover of the festivities of Christmas day to massacre the white and free coloured people of the island, Jo-Jo's great-grandfather, Guinea John, with his black jacket on and a price of two hundred pounds sterling on his head, made his way to the East Coast, mounted the cliff at Manzanilla, put two corn cobs under his armpits and flew away to Africa, taking with him the mysteries of levitation and flight, leaving the rest of his family still in captivity mourning over his selfishness, everybody putting in their mouth and saying, 'You see! You see! That is why Black-people children doomed to suffer: their own parents refuse to pass on the knowledge that they know to them.'

And some of them only stopped badmouthing the old man when just over a year later he appeared to his eldest daughter Titi in a dream to let her know that the reason he left so abruptly wasn't because he was a wanted man, was because his first wife who he had been dragged away from in Abeokuta, when they captured him and brought him enslaved to this island, was sick unto death and wanted to see him before she died. He really wasn't happy hearing his children cursing him. It wasn't a good sign. He knew they had a heavy load to carry; but when a people begin to curse their elders, the next step they take is to curse their gods. He loved his children. It was their living that would make him an ancestor. His wisdom was theirs to have; but they had eaten salt and made themselves too heavy to fly. So, because now their future would be in the islands, he preferred not to place temptation in their way by revealing to them the mysteries of flight.

This was one of the beginnings of the story that Uncle Bango sat down that year to tell, that had me looking out for him to complete each Saturday when he stopped by our house on his way from the market where he went to sell the toy steeldrum sets he made from bits of wire and condensed-milk tins and the heads he sculptured out of dried coconuts, the bare brown fibres for the face, the eyes red beads, the moustaches and eyebrows painted green or black or red as his fancy, each head wearing a crown or an arrangement of feathers fabricated from the images of the warriors and kings that he said had come to him in his dreams. His women were all queens, each face with the high cheekbones of Miss Myrtle and her full-mouthed heart-shaped lips. His clear celebrating of Miss Myrtle's beauty the only reason my mother could see for her to stomach the craziness he give her to put up with.

That year I watched him come into our front yard with the brawling parrot-toed sure-footed walk with which I had seen him step on to the cricket field and into the stickfight ring, grand and compelling, making my mother step back, draw away as in the face of some danger, drawing me and my brother to her when she saw him coming, releasing us only when he was in the yard, glad to have our dogs barking at him, shooing them away from attacking him, only reluctantly, and then, only after he had marched disdainfully past them with an arrogance that even the dogs respected, the three animals quieting down resentfully, one to growl and the other two to whimper whenever there was a sudden move from him, as if they too were aware of the danger he carried in his person.

I watch my father's uncomfortable smile as he looks on at the scene, wanting a better welcome for his brother, but neglecting to intervene for fear of offending my mother and giving her the excuse he suspects she is looking for to extend her hostility to him.

I look to see what kind of danger Uncle Bango brought with him into our front yard on those Saturdays, but there was nothing I could identify as threatening. And I knew of no possession of his, or of any previous differences between either my mother and him, or him and my father, no family quarrel. All that I could see separating him from my other uncles was this story that he was ever willing to tell. So it had to be his story.

4

'Watch the landscape of this island,' he began with the self-assured conviction that my mother couldn't stand in him. 'And you know that they coulda never hold people here surrendered to unfreedom.' The sky, the sea, every green leaf and tangle of vines sing freedom. Birds frisk and flitter and whistle and sing. Just so a yard cock will draw up his chest and crow. Things here have their own mind. The rain decide when it going to fall. Sometimes in the middle of the day, the sky clear, you hear a rushing swooping sound and voops it fall down. Other times it set up whole day and then you sure that now, yes, it going to fall, it just clear away. It had no brooding inscrutable wilderness here. There was no wild and passionate uproar to make people feel they is beast, to stir this great evil wickedness in their blood to make them want to go out and murder people. Maybe that madness seized Columbus and the first set of conquerors when they land here and wanted the Carib people to believe that they was gods; but, afterwards, after they settle in the island and decide that, yes, is here we going to live now, they begin to discover how hard it was to be gods.

The heat, the diseases, the weight of armour they had to carry in the hot sun, the imperial poses they had to strike, the powdered wigs to wear, the churches to build, the heathen to baptize, the illiterates to educate, the animals to tame, the numerous species of plants to name, history to write, flags to plant, parades to make, the militia to assemble, letters to write home. And all around them, this rousing greenness bursting in the wet season and another quieter shade perspiring in the dry.

On top of that they had to put up with the noise from Blackpeople. Whole night Blackpeople have their drums going as they dance in the bush. All those dances. All those lascivious bodies leaping and bending down. They couldn't see them in the dark among the shadows and trees; but, they could hear. They had to listen to them dance the Bamboula Bamboula, the Quelbay, the Manding, the Juba, the Ibo, the Pique, the Halicord, the Coromanti, the Congo, the Chiffon, the Banda, the Pencow, the Cherrup, the Kalinda, the Bongo. It was hard for Whitepeople. It had days they wanted to just sit down under a breadfruit tree and cool off, to reach up and pick a ripe mango off the tree and eat it. It had times they just wanted to jump into the sea and take a sea

5

bath, to romp with a girl on a bed of dead leaves underneath the umbrella of cocoa trees. They try, but they had it very hard. They walk a little distance and then they had to stop, perspiration soaking them, sticking their clothes to their bodies. It was so hot. They had to get these big roomy cork hats to wear to keep their brains cool. They had to get people to fan them. People to carry their swords, people to carry cushions for them to sit down on. They had to get people to beat people for them, people to dish out lashes – seventy-five, thirty-five, eighty-five. But, what else to do? People had to get licks to keep them in line. How else they coulda carry on The Work, feeding all those people, giving them rations, putting clothes on their back. And it was hard. It was very hard to mould the Negro character, to stamp out his savage tendencies.

They tried to make provisions for allowing him innocent amusement after Mass and until evening prayers, to see that he didn't cohabit without benefit of matrimony, to lay out the work for him to do, to pass around later to see that he do it. No, really, they try. They reduced the number of lashes to twenty-five. They tried in administering the floggings to make sure and not to cause the effusion of blood or contusion; but, what else to do?

There was no natural subservience here. Nobody didn't bow down to nobody just so. To get a man to follow your instructions you had to pen him and beat him and cut off his ears or his foot when he run away. You had was to take away his woman from him and his child. And still that fellow stand up and oppose you.

But these fellars here. These fellars was the most lawless and rebellious set of fellars they had in the Caribbean, the majority of them dangerous rebels exiled here from the other islands, men that had no cure, fellars whose sport was to bust one another head, fellars who make up their mind to dead, who land on the wharf from Martinique and Grenada and St Lucia and from wherever they bring them singing:

> *Mooma, Mooma, your son in the grave already,*
> *Your son in the grave already,*
> *Take a towel and band your belly . . .*

singing:

> *Thousand*
> *Ten thousand to bar me one*
> *Me one, me one . . .*

singing:

> *When I dead bury my clothes,*
> *I don't want no sweetman to wear my clothes.*

And it wasn't just men alone. It had women there that was even more terrible. They had to ban them from talking. They had to ban them from walking and from raising up their dresstail and shaking their melodious backsides. They wasn't easy. The plantation people couldn't handle them. They beat them. They hold them down and turn them over and do them whatever wickedness they could manage; but they couldn't break them.

And then it dawn on them that you can't defeat people. Then they find out that people too stupid to be defeated. They too harden. They don't learn what you try to teach them. They don't hear you. They forget. You tell a man to do something and he tell you he forget. You tell him to shoot and he forget to load the rifle. You tell him to get up at five, and nine o'clock he now yawning and stretching: he didn't hear you; or, he hear something different to what you tell him. You is the expert, but he believe that he know better than you what it is you want him to do, and he do it and he mess it up.

Four hundred years it take them to find out that you can't keep people in captivity. Four hundred years! And it didn't happen just so. People had to revolt. People had to poison people. Port-of-Spain had to burn down. A hurricane had to hit the island. Haiti had to defeat Napoleon. People had to run away up the mountains. People had to fight. And then they agree, yes. We can't hold people in captivity here.

But now they had another problem: it was not how to keep people in captivity. It was how to set people at liberty.

7

2

Under the Immortelle Tree

On the morning of the day that Alford George was to discover that he wasn't going to be leaving the island, Miss May parted the curtains at the front door of the wood house on top the hill, gathered up her strength and stepped down into the speckled sunlight filtering through the overhanging branches of the immortelle tree, her small black Bible gripped in one hand, a finger between its pages marking her place. And with the laborious delicacy choreographed by her pains eased herself down unto the step where the sun was brightest and rested there, her eyes shut, her breath inhaled, the metronome of her mind keeping time to the rhythm of her distress, trying to find within the music of her pain a space in which to breathe. And when she did, she opened eyes sparkling with gratitude to chuckle with reproachful admiration for the pain, saying softly, 'Like is kill you really come to kill me,' in her mind glancing at it sidelong, as at an acquaintance sitting there beside her.

With a new, laboured care, she bent over and lifted one nearly lifeless foot, placed it next to the other, spread and smoothed the cloth of her skirt over her knees, and in a weak, strangled voice that she wanted to sound rejoicing in order to hide from him her pain, she called out to him to 'Come and read this psalm for me,' and watched with pride this son come forward, broadshouldered to this ceremony that she had initiated since he was a child – in order to monitor his progress in reading – grown now to render the texts of her pleas, of her prayers, of the reaffirmation of her faith, the sight of him bringing water to her eyes, pitching her back to Lawd! Just yesterday! This child drawing back awestruck before miracles that his brothers took to be ordinary, back before the cooing of doves and the grave-hopping of toads, back before the miracle of raindrops, the architecture of shadows, the curl and drift and spin of smoke, reverential even then to a world he expected soon to make his own.

Sometimes she would find him sitting naked in the yard, trying with his tiny fingers to grab hold of the tail of a chicken or to scoop up the light patterning the ground under the immortelle tree, dirt on his face, dirt in his hair, dirt between his teeth, in his eyes bafflement and the surprise that these mysteries did not stand still for him.

At first it frightened her, the thought that this infant should believe that this world could ever belong to him. And she tried to think of ways of breaking to him the more cautionary truth, that for all the noises that his brothers made, and the weight with which his father walked their world, they were tenants in the very house in which they lived; but, witnessing the stubbornness of his optimism in the marvelling breadth of a smile that invited complicity in his adventure, she decided to become his ally, to make herself a child, to share in his sense of discovering and to watch the world take precious shape in his eyes. She began to point things out to him: 'Look! Rain!' and allow him to slip outside to let it soak him; 'Look, a butterfly,' and watch him smile and slide behind it in patient hopeful pursuit, refreshed each time by the treasured wonder and hope as yet indomitable in his eyes; until she and all began to believe that, yes, with patience, reverence and delight he could really make this world his own.

'Yes. Take yer time,' she said, not aware that she had fallen into the habit of speaking aloud the thoughts she was thinking. 'Take your time,' thankful that she was able to allow this one child, her last, if she was lucky, the luxury of his infancy; since the other four, boys too, had been issued into the world all in a rush, one after the other, with hardly a year between them: a litter of Georges, same height, gait and combativeness, with the deep-chested stance of their father, his swimming walk and the cocked bottom that made him look like a duckling; with the narrow forehead and half-shut left eyelid, that gave to each face the comical and trusting wisdom of an innocent who suspects he has been tricked, all of them so much alike that Cascadu had baptized them all with the single name, Breeze. And quite appropriately, she thought, because from the moment they could walk, they had all gone off racing into the vast serene smallness of the landscape, traversing the tiny rivers, scaling the little hills, exploring the forest, setting traps for crabs, for doves, for singing

9

birds, capturing with gleeful ingeniousness fish and iguana and small game, their weapons slingshots from tube rubber, harpoons from sharpened bicycle spokes and knives from flattened nails, to return at dusk with the harsh tangle of their speech and the grenades of their laughter and the yelping of their dogs in the stillness and noise and heat of that irritating hour when the world was closing in upon her and she couldn't get enough air to breathe.

'Take up a book! Take up a book!' That used to be her cry. But she didn't make it any more as she watched their thickening necks and chests and thighs, their trickster faces wise, already affecting the satisfied swagger of conquerors with no vision of a larger world and with no grander enemy in sight, sinking into the village's aimless ease, learning blind support for its cricket team, looking beneath each phrase spoken or sung for its other meanings, running the gauntlet of ridicule to emerge toughened to an indifference that made it fun for them to tease the cripple and mock the weak, hardly a day passing without somebody coming to her house to make a complaint about their mischief so that it was only her own courage that made her try again.

The more they flourished, the more she seemed to wilt, and she walked around the house, baked aloes tied to her swollen feet, her limbs greased with a mixture of nutmeg and soft candle and coconut oil, her head bound with a cloth soaked in the juice of fresh limes, wearing two, sometimes three dresses, one over the other, and one of Dixon's old jackets over them all to keep from freezing.

'Take your time. Take yer time,' triumphantly, happy to keep him infant and human and potential a week or a month or a year longer, thinking of the others, that she would like to have them all over again, birth them all afresh, with time and strength for them to nurse at individual breasts and to be weaned singly and to be alone longer and to spend a longer time as her children.

'But I not well,' she said, thinking that she was still thinking. 'This house here under the immortelle tree too damp for me. Look at my foot how it swell.' And she would draw up the hem of her ankle-length dress and look down at her swollen feet encased in any number of old socks, not expecting any response from the child but the look in his eyes. And she did not realize that he was six years old and that anything was wrong until one afternoon Dixon, at the table wolfing down his food while the estate jeep waited to take him back to work, paused and cocked his head sideways, as if he was trying to catch the disappearing note of a song, a sound, and with his mouth still full said,

'Hey! You know I never hear this boy talk. Come, boy. Come and say something. Come!'

And Dixon swallow the mouthful of food and get up and go to the corner where the boy was sitting and he squat down beside the child, 'Say something, boy. Say something.' And even as he, Dixon, turned with alarm in his eyes towards her, it hit her same time he said it: 'This boy *mumu*. He can't talk.'

'He can't talk?' She heard her voice like it was some stranger's talking. 'He can't talk?' Her stomach turning over and cold sweat breaking out on her skin. 'He can't talk?'

'Well, yes,' Dixon said, getting to his feet with the sense of weariness, of affliction, that he managed now whenever he thought he had her to blame for something. 'Well, yes,' pressing together the sides of his head with both hands as if he were sticking its split halves back together.

'Say it,' she said, with the calm aggression she had begun to cultivate as her protection against the tormenting certitude of his own self-righteousness. 'Say what you thinking, Dixon. Say it!'

'Say what, May?'

'Say it: a mad woman for a wife and a dumb boy for a child. Say it, Dixon.'

'Is all this dirt you allow him to eat, May, and all the water you let him play in.'

And she had said serenely then, 'You should cut down the immortelle tree, you know, Dixon. The dampness going to kill us here.'

'And his hair, May?' Dixon pleaded, looking almost comical in his earnestness. 'May, why you cut his hair for? You don't know you have to wait until a child start to talk before you cut his hair? Eh, May? You don't know this, May? Everything I have to explain you? Is six years this child have and he can't talk! Six years!'

'What he have to say?' she asked, angry now. 'What revelation it is you waiting to hear him make? Everybody so hurry. Every-

11

thing must have so much speed. What it is you waiting to hear him say? I know you busy, Dixon,' her voice theatrical, still subduing the tears she never used, 'and the immortelle flowers pretty, but if you don't cut it down, it will kill us here.'

'May,' and she could see him straining to be calm, 'I tell you already is not my tree. I tell you already; we could live on the land. We could grow things, but we can't cut down the trees. That is the agreement Mr Carabon make with me. We can live on his land, we could grow things, but we can't cut down the trees.'

'Trees? Dixon, is this one tree that hanging over the house.'

'I make an agreement.'

'Yes,' she said. 'You make an agreement. *You*.'

'I tell you already. When I buy the land I will cut down the tree.'

'When you buy the land?' she asked. 'Well, you coulda very well fool me. I thought you did buy the land already.'

'May, ain't I tell you the agreement?'

'And the bricks?' Now it was her turn. 'You make an agreement to buy bricks too? Eh, Dixon? Eh?' And at his silence: 'What you buying bricks for? If the land is not yours, what you buying bricks for? People right to laugh at you.'

'Laugh? At me?' he repeated scornfully.

'Yes. And at me. They laugh.'

'At me? They? Those jackass could laugh at me? They? Them?'

'And why not? Blackman killing himself working on White-man land. For what?'

'Yes. For what?' he challenged. 'For what?' And when she made no reply, he added: 'So I wrong to buy bricks? I wrong to want to build a house?'

'You not wrong. You never wrong. You right,' her irony by then a habit of speech, ineffectual for any other purpose than to underline her helplessness. 'You right.'

'Is the agreement.'

'And you wouldn't try to change it even though you know it killing me?'

'May.'

'Don't may me.' For right at that moment the truth had hit her: Dixon was prepared to honour that agreement, not out

12

of any wonderful feeling for its legality as out of the greater stubbornness and spite and pride that debarred him, even as she died, from appearing to ask Carabon for anything that could remotely be deemed a favour, lest it be granted and corrupt his own male and vainglorious martyrdom.

It was that same martyrdom that had placed him at odds with the men on the estate from the very first day he arrived, a stranger, asking for work, odd-looking beside the labouring men in raggedy work clothes, with the hair on his head cut low to the bone of his skull, his luxuriant sideburns, shaped and out-lined with the mark of a razor, taking up half his face, looking like a sweetman from the city, wearing the black ruffle-fronted shirt and the white flannel trousers and the two-toned shoes that three days earlier she had seen him in at the two-to-ten foxtrot dancing competition at the Cunaripo Government School, even then set apart from the other young men who had come from the surrounding villages of Cascadu and Cushe and Mile End and Maloney, with their low-cut hair and shining shoes and pants seams cutting, neither because he was shorter nor taller than the rest, more that he had chosen his costume deliberately to challenge and confront and emphasize that he was more man, more person than would have otherwise been gleaned; and yet beneath this she could see the uncertainty, as if he was not quite happy, was almost apologetic of the persona that the style and newness of his clothes had invented, giving off a sickly grin in an effort to countermand the spectacle of his apparel and to reveal the real true person that was he.

It was the sense of his unease that had touched May, had made her feel for him, since she herself, at her first dance, in new dress, new shoes and her hair pressed, was sweating in self-consciousness.

He must have spied in her that very quality of vulnerability that she had glimpsed in him, and this had encouraged him to think that she could be his partner for one dance at least. As the music struck up, she watched him set out for the corner where she was standing with her two sisters and Marva Balandra in a row of the most stylishly dressed girls from the town, each one with her hair fashioned in the same style, the same expression on each face, the whole preened and self-important gaggle of them swamped in the potent chemistry of cheap perfume, rose-mary, Limacol, Pond's baby powder and freshly ironed hair, each one masticating chewing-gum with the intimidating power of her indifference to any but the prince she was awaiting.

She thought that he would come directly to her, and she was surprised when, with the overbearing formality that, before she knew him better, she thought was shyness, he bowed before the first girl in the line, Marva Balandra, a 'red girl', the dancing queen, winner of the jitterbug and foxtrot competitions, and the most vain girl in the whole of the county.

And he remained there, holding his pose of entreaty with the same deliberate and challenging gesture that left him vulnerable and exposed while from her lofty and remote pity Marva Balan-dra looked him over from head to toe. Without missing a beat of the rhythm to which she was chewing gum, she began shaking her head over and over again as if to uproot completely whatever hope he might have cherished of dancing with her.

She watched him go on to the next girl in line, who, without bothering to look at his face, turned her head away. On to the next her sister, and the next. He continued down the row of them, with the utmost politeness, the solemn bow, the martyred smile, holding himself with a pained haughtiness as each one turned away, not as if he was the one rejected, was the one doing them a favour, or was it putting them to a test?

May was the last in line. She was going to follow the example of the other girls and refuse him as well, but when she saw behind his sickly smile the wound, the bleeding, his desperate appeal and shield against the devastation of his faith, she realized that what had fallen to her was not just a decision about dancing. She was certain that she was the last person through whom womankind and for that matter mankind might be redeemed. Although she knew she would appear a traitor to the imperial sisterhood that had dismissed him so comprehensively, she took the hand he offered and went on to the floor with him.

After the set, he walked her back to where she had been standing. Electing to protect her from dangers she herself had not even thought existed, he took up guard over the little space in front of her, so that fellows approaching her to dance felt it necessary first to ask his permission. Her sisters were outraged.

14

'May, what jail is this you put yourself in? And you don't even know the man name.'

He was too pushy. They didn't like his clothes. They didn't like his looks. Where it is he say he come from again? May found herself having to defend him. But their attack had made her so self-conscious that when he left his post and returned with a beer for himself and a sweet drink for her, she felt bound to refuse it.

With the arrogance that refused to accept rejection and the persistence that she had seen so much evidence of already, he wanted to know what he had done wrong. Before she could give her answer, the music struck up and thirsty fellows pressed in from all sides to ask her to dance. It was then that Dixon, requiring her reply, made the announcement that her sisters would tease her with for years after: 'She not dancing.'

Cowed by the resolute nature of his declaration, some of the fellows turned away. Carlton didn't. He wanted to know who had given such authority to this stranger.

'You is her owner?' Carlton asked. 'You own her?'

'Yes,' grumbled one of Carlton's pardners, known as Rat, 'you own her?' tapping Dixon on the shoulder for Dixon to turn now and face Carlton, Rat and the other fella who was with them.

With the wordless tension of a performance he had made before, very calmly, Dixon first took off his silver chain, then began to roll up the sleeves of his long-sleeved shirt, the other fellows mirroring him, except Rat who was unbuttoning his shirt.

'They going and fight,' Marva Balandra prophesied.

'They going and fight!' May's big sister screamed.

People around began giving them room. Rat was about to slip his shirt off his shoulders when May's big sister left the fellow she was dancing with and with both hands held Carlton in an embrace, Carlton standing loose and rubbery in a heroic surrender. May, aware of the threat of that posture, with an action that she was to wonder about for years, because it wasn't as if she really liked the man, grabbed Dixon's hand and dragged him on to the floor to dance, only to have him make another memorable announcement: 'You shoulda leave me. I woulda handle them.'

Over the years at odd times the scene would replay itself to her and she would think, 'You right. Yes. I shoulda leave you

15

right there.' Instead, for some reason that May never worked out, as if this incident had given them their introduction, she yielded to the pressure of his hand on her back, moved closer to him and when he asked her her name she told it to him. So this time when he came with a sweet drink she took it and at the next set as he looked at her, she stepped forward to dance with him.

And that would be the basis on which three days later he would appear on the street where she lived. In the roundabout way in which he did most things, he set out to get her to come to her door without his going up and knocking. And that was how he came to be riding his bicycle and purposely throwing himself down, trying to make a loud enough noise to draw her outside so that she would see him on the ground, come to render assistance to him. And he would get to talk to her. It didn't happen that way. Who saw him was her father. He called her and her sisters to the window and together they watched this madman riding up and down the street and throwing himself and his bicycle down, lying on the ground, groaning in pretended hurt, picking himself up and going through the same routine again. No, they didn't know him, the girls said, though May thought she recognized the ruffle-fronted shirt. Her father had strapped on his cutlass and gone outside into the street to discover that it was Dixon come to visit his daughter May. Out of admiration for his inventiveness, pity because he was so much in love, and politeness, because Dixon was not from the village, her father invited him to come in. It was out of that same politeness that he was to endure Dixon's visits for the three years it would take for Dixon to convince May that she should marry him, even though he already had a job.

In the story that Dixon told her later, from the very first night he see her, he decide that he not going to leave Cascadu without her. He had no idea of where he was going to stay. The morning after the dance he was standing by the bus-stand when someone hailed out to him. It was Carlton, in his glee because his heroics of the night before had brought him closer to May's sister. There were no hard feelings. Indeed, it was Carlton who told him of the abandoned government house down by the railway where, if he wanted, he could stay. He knew he had to get a job right away; and that was how he came the following morning to be standing in the yard of Carabon's estate, asking for work, until at last they handed him a spade and sent him down to the cocoa field where the men were digging trenches to drain the beds of cocoa, wearing the same clothes he had on in the dance since they were the only clothes in his possession.

Rain had been heavy that whole week and he walked down to the fields in his two-tone shoes, picking his way through the thick clinging clay, his trousers rolled up to his knees, the spade held across his shoulder like the balancing pole of a tightrope walker, to be greeted with jeers of amusement by the men already in the field. He didn't say nothing. He set to work digging along the line already stretched out for him, working all through his lunch hour while the others took a rest, the men watching the ruffle-fronted shirt and the slim-hipped pants he was wearing, sizing him up as a smart-man, a schemer, an impressionist, a man from the town come to the country, making a grand show on his first day just to curry favour with the foreman. Without letting on that it was the first time he was doing this kind of work and that his hands were blistered and bleeding, Dixon had gone on digging with the spade, water-bladders forming and bursting on his hands, knowing that if he took a rest at all the pain would make it impossible for him to recommence working. That day they left him in the field still digging, his task still not complete. And next day he was back again, working while the others took a rest, the men waiting to see when he would get fed up of the pretence and be human like everybody else. He didn't stop, not because he didn't want to but because on the second day his hands were in worse condition than they had been on the first. He had kept on working that whole week, his hands blistered and bleeding.

It was then that he had made a covenant with the pain that lifted him above the men and the estate, that took him to a high place past the pain where the sound of the jeers began to fade and he began to feel that he had a power over the work and a kinship with the trees and the land and the mud and the drains that was to remain the source of his strength. Working there, he would discover that his life was with life, with the trees and the grass and the rain, each doing its work, fulfilling its mission

17

without reference to whatever was done by anybody. He began to think of himself as the grass, as the mud, as the rain. The workers couldn't understand him. They felt the power from him. They grew suspicious, wondering what was he profiting. On evenings now one or two of them would deliberately stay around to see what it was he was taking away from the estate; and when they couldn't discover that he was gaining any advantage that they could detect, that all he was doing was the work, they decided that he was a spy, someone planted by the overseer to demonstrate that they could produce more for the same pay. Dixon had nothing to say to them.

In time he mastered the arts of cultivation, of cutlassing, of digging drains, of pruning, and he began to work on the estate as if it belonged to him, content not only to do the tasks assigned to him but attending to any other chore that he saw required attention, addressing the work with such implacable devotion that it reached a state where the foreman didn't even bother to direct him where he should work or what he should do, or how much; and in time, he would become on a labourer's pay perhaps the man most important to the estate.

He knew where every key was, where the tools were, what field was to be pruned, what field needed to be reaped, what produce was sold and for how much and the condition of every animal. Sometimes on the single day of the week when he did not have to report to the estate, the overseer or Mr Knott or Carson the foreman would drive the jeep down the muddy trace deep in the Cascadu settlement to the place where he was renting to ask him some question concerning the estate to which he alone had the answer, his only profit, as far as May could see, that he could say to her and to the world, victoriously, 'They can't do without me.'

'Work-Jumbie Dixon' the men called him, implying still that there was some madness in his soul or something subversive in his behaviour: 'You will get your reward for all this work you working. Carabon will give you a piece of his estate. Wait.' 'They can't do without me' no longer simply an empty boast; because by now he was a law unto himself, the estate his own in everything but title and reward counted in money, his industry and devotion such a challenge that the very men who knew that there was no profit to them in doing more than a day's work felt the need at least to show their own mettle and so the work of the estate was carried forward without no raise in pay. And this must have been brought to the attention of Mr Carabon, the owner, that there was this man taking away his estate, and that must have been what brought Carabon one morning into the fields walking with more uprightness and a forced sprightliness so that the men, clearing the drains, seeing him coming had whispered to themselves, 'The big boss himself,' and had set about working more diligently. He had walked past them and came to stand in front where Dixon was working, silent for a while, about him the aura of one who had come to reclaim, with a kind of grandeur and a kind of envy, as if he regretted not being himself the muscular man perspiring there, had the need to make himself taller in order to be his equal, Dixon himself feeling his own power, his hand moving as a bandmaster's as he expertly lopped the excess suckers from the tree, Carabon speaking eventually, saying in his hoarse voice, a pitch or two louder, the way some big people talk to a horse or a child, 'How'd you like to be my foreman?'

And I look at him and I say, 'Boss, leave me as a labourer.'

'Leave you as a – ' And he watch me. 'You don't want the responsibility? What happen, you can't read?' his voice suddenly gaining the correct pitch. 'We could get somebody to make up the time sheets for you.'

'Read, sir? Read?' Dixon chuckled. 'Sir. Leave me as a labourer.' When the men listening nearby hear what I tell him, they nearly piss theyself. They nearly pee – 'Let me work for the work, for the plants, for the animals, for the land. Leave me so. Leave me just so.'

When Dixon told May the story, May said, 'Leave you just so? Leave you as a labourer? That is what you tell him? That is what you say?' *And, we?* But she didn't say it. She didn't have the heart to tell him how much of a fool he was. For she knew by then that his way to feel himself the equal of if not the superior to anybody was to give more and more of himself, this giving making him more martyred and heroic.

For the three years he had courted her, bringing gifts he could not afford, bangles, bracelets, dresses, making promises that were

19

hard to keep, she had seen this side of him and she wasn't
certain, really, if he loved her seriously or if she provided the
audience before whom he could appear to be the man he felt he
needed to be. It took her three years to make up her mind and
in that time she asked him over and over again, 'You sure you
want to married me? You sure you know what you doing?' It
was a question she should have asked herself.

'Leave you as a labourer?' And Carabon who thought he had
heard everything from these people looked Dixon from head to
toe – the men listening peeing on their own self – and shake his
head. 'Well,' Carabon said, 'it look like you don't want to be my
foreman, but I want you closer to me. I like how you working.
I like the interest you showing. I was planning to put you in the
house the watchman used to live in. It closer to the estate. You
could live in it. You have family now, not so?' For by then the
rush of children had started.

Dixon was going to say no to that too, but somehow he
detected in the offer a challenge and heard in it the respect he felt
was his due.

'You don't have to take it if you don't want to,' Carabon said.
'But it will be good for your family. You can live in the house,
you can pick the fruit and keep the place clean; but one thing: I
don't want you to cut down any of the trees. That is the only
condition.'

And Dixon, not to be outdone, not wanting to be beholden to
Carabon, not for house or land or anything, said, as if he really
was Carabon's equal, man to man, said, 'I will want to buy the
land to build my own house on, Boss.'

'Is two acres and a half,' Carabon said.

'I will want to buy it, Chief.'

And, Carabon, the heart of magnanimity, as if he was also
talking to an equal, although he must have known full well
that with the pay Dixon was getting it would take him another
generation to buy the land, said, 'Yes, yes, yes. When you ready,
just come to me.'

So that was the bargain Dixon had to keep and the challenge
he had to meet. That is the spot he get himself into.

So Dixon moved with them into the old house on the edge of
the estate where the watchman used to stay and where Alford

would be born and where May's own troubles would begin. Because a good six months hadn't passed, living in the house, there under the immortelle tree, when the dampness started to penetrate her bones and she began to be ill. And Dixon, instead of getting her to a good doctor, in order to fulfil his declaration and boast of wanting to buy the land to build his house on, began to pinch off money from his next-to-nothing pay to stock up on bricks in order to establish publicly, for everybody to see, the material evidence of his intention to build his own house.

And that was the furthest he would reach: a stack of bricks growing in the yard, there to maintain the fiction of a construction that he could not advance until he bought the land. And he couldn't buy the land because his money was going in bricks. And he couldn't stop buying bricks because to do so was to suggest that he had abandoned his mission of building his house. And although the dampness was killing her, he couldn't cut down the immortelle tree, because to face Carabon with such a request was to give to Carabon a power that he, Dixon, was unwilling to concede and expose the very shame he was seeking to disguise.

'So this is where we is,' she had said, reaching out to draw the child to her, not even realizing that the sound of the jeep had long died away and that she had been talking to the child all this time.

'Nothing ain't wrong with you,' she said to him now. 'You not dumb. You will talk. You just not hurry.'

Then she felt herself tremble as a terrible fright took hold of her at the thought of this son remaining dumb, and she knelt down and began to pray; and she dragged herself through the remainder of that day, singing hymns from her childhood that she had not allowed herself to remember since moving with Dixon up this hill.

That night she lay awake for endless hours, hearing the intermittent hoot of owls and the creaking cries of bamboos, thinking how she had allowed herself to turn her back on her mother and the church and the people, how she had come to this better place with this friendless man, to fall sick, alone, with nobody around her to help, to awaken next morning with her night clothes heavy with sweat from toiling in her sleep, and with the memory of a dream in which her grandmother was frightened and crying in a forest where the trees made no sound and where the sun was shining and she herself was freezing; and she felt how deeply alone she was and she decided to put aside her shame and go to Mother Ethel, the Shango woman down the hill in Warden Trace, to see if she could get a cure at least for the boy.

'How you know to come to me now?' asked Mother Ethel, pushing herself up from the bench facing the shrine in the yard, with the calabash tree and the pomegranate tree with the iron for Ogun and the conch shell for Yemanja and the sugarcane plant, for Damballah, the snake.

'You and Dixon living up there on that hill for yourself alone, thinking about nobody but yourself and your children. What we do you, Maybelle? Why you wait till trouble take you to come? And you don't know you must baptize? Nobody ain't tell you you must come home to your nation?', speaking to her as to a child, while May bowed her head. 'And this child,' said Mother Ethel, taking Alford's hands in hers, 'care this child. He have a big work to do. Wash down your front steps. Sweep in front your yard where this child does play. People who come inside your yard bring things that is not all good. Come,' and she held Alford by the hand, and she closed her eyes, saying a prayer, May shutting her eyes too, opening them only when she heard Mother Ethel speak: 'You have to hold a thanksgiving feast, offer up a young ram, invite people, let them eat. Nine days from the end of the week, I having my feast. That is a good time.'

She agreed at once, not only out of desperation to see the boy cured. This sacrifice would be for her too. It would bring her back to a self that had been drifting, unrooted. It would give her the opportunity to connect herself to a past that she had neglected, to place herself within the shelter of a new and ancient force that would take her into a new space and meaning. She found herself crying; but it wasn't sadness she felt as Mother Ethel held her to her bosom, it was a feeling of homecoming, of being found, being rescued. It was this feeling that had prompted her to give over one of Dixon's young rams for the feast. Knowing how he scoffed at such practices, she had said nothing to him about it.

When Dixon missed the goat, he had asked one of the boys

about it and was told that a man had come and taken it away. He assumed that May, with what he suspected to be her usual unthinking, had sold it to one of the butchers passing around buying animals for slaughter. Without even checking whether he was correct he had resorted to his patient martyred resignation, thinking to be generous, to be forgiving:

'May, you know I didn't want to sell that young ram. And you sell it?' And without waiting for her reply, 'So, how much they give you for it?'

She had to tell him: 'I didn't sell it. I give it to Mother Ethel for the feast. For Alford, so he will talk.'

Dixon couldn't believe it. 'You give it? To Mother Ethel? Well, yes,' Dixon cried, with an amazed and bitter chuckle. 'You give them my goat to eat? May, you think this stupidness could save anybody? Eh, May? Eh?' There were tears in his voice. 'All I could do is to try and to not get myself in trouble. I bring you up here. I keep you away from them. I leave The Settlement. I come up here. All I could do is try. That is all I could do.'

For the first time she saw how funny he looked. All her anxiety left her and she felt in such a state of repose that she had to bite her lip to prevent herself from laughing out loud.

From that day she had to listen to him moaning about the goat that was lost, ridiculing the backwardness of these superstitious people, until, refusing to take any more, she challenged him: 'Tell me, what you know about these people?'

'What I know?' It was then that he told of his childhood in Charuma, of his grandfather who was an Orisha priest and a bush doctor who all the village sick came to and who he treated with massages with soft candle and doses of medicinal herbs, how one day the police came to arrest him for practising obeah, how they took all his things, candles and the flags and the cloth and the oil and the brooms and the herbs he had gathered and lifted him up – he was eighty-three years – they lift him up and put him on his donkey. They put his head to face the tail of the donkey and they tie all the things, all the candles and the broom and the flags and everything they found in his possession and they rode him through the streets down to the courthouse. None of the people raised a hand.

'Is the first time you really tell me anything about yourself,'

23

she said. 'How much more things you have bottled up inside you?'

'That is why I stay alone,' he said. 'That is why I depend on my own self, on what I could do. I know these people.'

On what only later May realized was the twenty-first day since the feast had gone, she was sitting with Alford on the bench in front the kitchen thinking about Dixon, wondering what to do to make him see that she was lonely, that in punishing the people he was punishing himself and her.

'Talk to him.'

She looked around, in that moment wondering if she had herself answered the question posed by her own thinking. And then she saw the boy looking at her. Still not sure that it was he, she asked, 'What you say?'

'Talk to him, you tell me. That is how you begin talking. In full sentences, like a teacher: The dog is hungry. The flowers are pretty.' And that was when I know that you being dumb was a sign directed to me. My own son had to be made dumb so I could be brought home to the wonderful truth: Thy will be done. Yes, as surrender, not defeat, as the benediction she would employ in her life, patched with defeats and threaded through with illness, to meet her own set-backs, not so much to cushion the hurt of her disappointments as to acknowledge and salute a power wiser and grander than her will, to renew her faith in that wonderful mystery around which she knew her own life revolved.

'Ma,' Alford asked. 'Ma, why you telling me all this now?'

'Because,' she said, 'Carabon selling the land we living on. He have it up for sale. And your father don't have the money to buy it. And because you must go away. I sacrifice myself already in this life. I was the sacrifice. I miss my whole life. I forget my dreams. Don't let the same thing happen to you.'

'Ma . . .' tears were in his voice, 'Ma, why you didn't tell me this before?'

'I telling you now, not to put a burden on you. I just want you to go away, to leave this place and go.'

'Ma?'

'Don't speak. Come. Read this psalm for me,' she said, handing him the Bible. 'Read here,' showing him the place.

And he sat at her side in the bright morning, surrounded by the scent of guavas rotting on the ground beside the house, listening to the silence behind the cries of birds and the noise roaring inside the stillness of the trees.

And he took the Bible and held his tears and read the text of her prayer, of her plea, of her faith:

> Hear my cry, O God;
> Attend unto my prayer.
> From the end of the earth will I cry unto thee,
> When my heart is overwhelmed.
> Lead me to the rock that is higher than I.

And he had turned with the garland of his pain and faced the road.

3

The Umpire

Now he was a child again, trotting to school ahead of the chorus
of children leaving the lopsided landscape of Cascadu, with the
whitewashed estate barrack houses on the low side of the road,
and on the hillside, the squat houses, standing apart from each
other, their thatched roofs weighing them down like the overbur-
dened trays of market women who had paused on the steep part
of the hill to catch their breath and summon up their strength
before they moved on. He saw himself running, uphill first, then
down the hill through Deep Ravine past the gang of labourers
patching the road, with the staccato of their wheelbarrows and
the arc of their rakes as they laid gravel over beds of stone
and poured upon them boiling asphalt through the sieves of
steaming blackened glistening tins, past Hibiscus and another
set of workmen stinking up the morning with the burning scent
of cigarette smoke and the forbidding odour in the stale perspiration scent of their clothes, men bent from the waist over the
verge, their brushing cutlasses lifted like cricketers at bat and,
with the flourish of batsmen heaving cutlasses through the roadside grass, the cut grass, in showers, like bees swarming, flying
up and falling down in sparkling rainbows. Onwards, downhill,
under the piercing morning sun in this stretch of unshaded road,
past the stand of young teak with their broad stiff leaves and, in
the wind, scraping sounds, into the valley with its guard of
mahogany trees, dark and cool, and up this last hill past the
cemetery, for it to burst upon him, Cunaripo, the town: with
the police station and the Catholic church and the Warden's
office its major buildings, with a Scale House for weighing canes
and an Ice Box for selling ice and a Buying House where farmers
from surrounding estates brought bags of polished cocoa beans
and dried coffee to be weighed and exchanged for money and
then to be shipped by rail to Port-of-Spain, the port where they
all led, the train lines and the ribbons of road, streaming through
forest, along sea coasts, joining plantation to plantation, coconuts

and cocoa and cane, until they reached the port from which ships sailed out to England, out into the world, *the world*, already to him more than a place, a mission, a Sacred Order that brought him into meaning, into Life.

As a boy, Alford was already dreaming of one day going out into the vastness of that world. And, perched in the sunshine, on the lower branches of the mango tree at the back of the house, or at the table with the kerosene lamp when his mother wasn't ironing, with books he borrowed from the library van that came to Cunaripo on Thursdays and parked near the Scale House, he entered into the adventure of the legion of heroes spawned by that world – Perseus, Theseus, Atlas, Ulysses, Hercules, Tarzan, Phantom – to be awakened by one of his brothers calling him to wash the wares or fan the fire or graze the goats, to emerge dreamily from the trance of that world to the place where his body lived to hurry over the chores demanded of him, doing them still in a dream, so that a plate would crack, a glass would break, the goat he was minding would become entangled in the vines and rope; and his brothers would watch him and laugh at the mishaps his clumsiness produced, seeing them as punishment he deserved, since they were convinced that he was using his reading as a trick to escape the chores required of him.

He could feel his father watching him too, with the eyes of a probation officer, with the suspicion that he was harbouring a traitor, someone who was dissatisfied with what he had been able to provide, who wanted much more than he was able to give, whose reading had given him the idleness to plot and the distance for contempt and the wistfulness to dream, his father cautious with him as with a stranger, deliberately not asking him to do any work which would give the impression that he trusted him or depended on him. Sometimes on the one day when his father was home, Alford, eager to help, would stand around watching him fix the steps or carry out any of the number of minor repairs, waiting to be called to hand him the hammer or to get some nails or anything. Nothing.

His brothers were also part of the conspiracy. He watched them making flips, walking on their hands, sparring, swordfighting with sticks, wrestling, racing with breathtaking indifference over stone and broken bottle in the trace in front their house. He

27

entered their games with the intention to placate them by showing himself capable in their world; but all he managed was to disclose an ineptitude that confirmed for them that he was indeed an alien, an inferior, weakened by reading and the treason of his dreams, not quite fit for the rigours of the life they had mastered. And he felt forced back into dreams of the other world.

It was his mother who came to his aid, her allegiance prompted by her feeling that she was a fellow· sufferer, dwarfed also by the overpowering health and robustness of her husband and older sons.

'You musn't tease him,' she pleaded. 'He's your brother,' looking out at them from the window to the yard where they played their games, her intercession deepening an alienation that he was to endure even from the first day he went to school, that child of nine, dressed in the full regalia of the comic order into which the boychildren of Cascadu were inducted from infancy, wearing its perennial badges, the clean-headed trim, the uniform of khaki and blue, too new, too big, appropriate for the purpose of penance since it did not provide the arrogance of a proper fit, beside him, his mother, the two of them walking the two and a half miles from their home in Cascadu to Cunaripo, the town, followed all the way by a band of silent bug-eyed schoolchildren, fascinated by the uncommon sight of such a big boy with a slate on a string around his neck and clothes of such newness, captivated even more by the outrageous vision of this tall gaunt woman in high heels, and funeral clothes, ankle-length black and white polka-dot dress and broad-brimmed black hat edged with lace hanging over her forehead, talking loudly and incessantly to who at first they thought was the boy, about love and loneliness and pride: *leave it then if it will make you feel better, if it will make you more of a man, I can die anytime* . . . , telling him of a life lived to make a point, a life lived to show you are somebody. *How you could live a life to make a point? How you could live a life to show you is somebody?* The children, wordless, following behind them, declining every opportunity to overtake them, stopping when they stopped, starting again when they resumed walking, ignoring his mother's pleas to go on, to go ahead, to go to school. So that they had arrived at the school at the head of this procession, the two of them in front, the royalty section in a Carnival band that would disband finally only at the intervention of Miss Berisford, the teacher, who shooed away the children and led him and his mother into the office to enrol him in the Infants Department, and have him join the class of small children engaged in learning the words of the alphabet by heart and writing its letters on their slates.

He would sit quiet and uncommunicative through all the lessons until at the end of the first term Miss Berisford, her bosom right in front his face, took his slate and saw drawn on it the most artistically crafted A's she had seen in her career. No B's or C's or the other letters she had been teaching them to write. For a moment she was stumped, then illumination came. She must have recalled the image of his mother carrying on a conversation with herself. 'Oh-ho!' she cried, unable to stop herself from saying what she was thinking: *You must be half-cracked too.'*

But it was already said and somehow to lessen the blow she spoke to him with a careful gentleness, 'Come, boy, come, Alford,' stroking his head when he appeared: 'Go to the schoolmaster and ask him to send two sticks of chalk for me. You know what to say?' she encouraged. 'Say, "Miss say to send two sticks of chalk for me." '

'Miss say send two sticks of chalk for me,' he had repeated.

'Please,' she added.

'Please,' he said.

And that was how he grew up at school, running errands for his teachers, cleaning the blackboard, collecting homework assignments and maintaining silence in the teacher's absence. On some days he occupied the teacher's chair, surveying the class with strict humourless zeal, his eyes alert to discover the slightest breach of order so he could dutifully report it, so that by the time he entered Standard Two his classmates had already given him the nickname Sir.

It was his air of Sirness, his stiff, grave, wooden intensity, as much as his greater size, that in the beginning set him apart from his fellows and kept him an outsider for most of his school days.

He was older and bigger than almost every boy in his early classes. In their games his solemnity and awkwardness made him appear a bruising giant among them. Seeing how the tiny tots were bowled over by his charge, teachers and bigger boys cried shame on him. After a while, his very classmates, seeing him approach the playing-field, not even considering that they were in many cases more adept at games than he was, would withdraw to the sidelines complaining that, as they put it, 'We not playing any game with that man.'

Just a little ashamed and believing that they had made a mistake that they would want to rectify, he would walk away slowly, wanting to remain longer within earshot of them so they wouldn't have to shout to call him back. The call never came.

Among boys closer his own age, Alford didn't do any better. Their play was a rough, boisterous affair open to anyone with the ability to rush and push and bluff and bully, each man for himself. And Alford tried, but, inhibited by his reserve and lack of confidence in his talents, he handicapped himself from the beginning. He began to develop into someone tentative, ungainly and suspicious, never quite able to trust the competence of his natural instincts to get the hang of things, needed something less fallible, more guaranteeing of success than the blind imitative venturing of most of his fellows.

On the few occasions when he did get a kick of the ball or managed to get to bat, he addressed his opportunity with a solemnity that suggested that his very life was at stake and there to judge him was a tribunal of not only the players around him but all those who had mastered the game and, more than they, the very implements he was seeking to manipulate. Seeking the perfection that such an audience demanded, to the delight of the other boys, he failed. It must have been, he reasoned later, his ambition to be better than his gifts dictated that vexed them. They readily accommodated fellows who accepted their own limitations, who did not take themselves at all seriously, were content simply to get an opportunity to take a swing at the ball and hope to the gods that they connect. They cheered such fellows with as much gusto as they did the heroes, for what by luck and by chance and by enterprise they eventually were able to achieve. Alford's efforts irritated them. And they began to punish him. Even in scratch games the captains were reluctant to pick him and, rather than choose him, they would play with a man short or call to some indifferent boy passing and invite him over while Alford stood by dying for the opportunity to play.

He began to arrive at the playing-field earlier than anybody else. He began to provide the wickets and the ball or bat for the game, to sweep the pitch in preparation for cricket or put up poles for goal posts for football. He would go into the forest and cut lengths of wood, take them home and shape them into wickets. Occasionally, he produced a tennis ball which he taped over and polished until it bounced and looked nearly like a real cricket ball.

But even such contributions were not enough to guarantee his selection.

One day he arrived on the ground with his own wickets, a bat he had himself fashioned out of the root of a bois canot tree, one of his taped and polished tennis balls. He was setting up the wickets when the other boys arrived. One took up the bat, another the ball. He went behind the wicket and they began a game. Then more fellows came and it was decided to play a match. The two captains selected themselves and began to pick two teams, Alford looking on anxiously, counting the fellows to be sure that there would be an even number so that there would be no excuse for him not to be picked. There were eighteen boys, enough for each side to play with nine. Each captain had chosen eight, and left to be picked was Alford and a thin Indian boy who had proven before that he could neither bat nor bowl nor field and who didn't really care either. The boy was selected. Alford was already beginning to move to join the other team. Perhaps the eagerness in his eyes, in his gait, struck that team's captain. He held up a hand. He didn't want him.

'You take him,' he said to the other captain.

But the captain of the first team did not want to have any such advantage. They argued back and forth for several minutes and then the thin disinterested boy decided that his time was being wasted and left. That left seventeen players. Each team already had eight. Alford was out. He thought of taking his wickets and his bat and his ball and leaving, but he felt that to be too easy. He wanted them to think, to feel guilty. He wanted somebody to remind them that it was his ball and bat and wickets.

'Keep the implements for me,' he said to Victory, one of the three fellows who had begun the game. Then he turned to leave.

'Wait!' Victory said. Alford stood and waited for Victory's intercession. 'Why we don't let Alford umpire?'

Alford couldn't move. He couldn't look at anybody.

'You want to umpire?' one of the fellows enquired, impatient to get on with the game.

Alford was surprised that his voice carried any sound; he heard himself answering, 'Yes. I will umpire.'

From that day and for the duration of his time at Cunaripo Government School, Alford became the umpire at cricket matches and, as an extension, the referee at football games. Later, it would be forgotten by everyone but himself that he had any other ambition.

It was here, in this role, that for the first time in his life he had a taste of the exercise of power. There were those who, thinking him still the diffident apologetic Alford, wanted to challenge his decisions; and for a time he tried his best to please. He wanted to be fair, to give correct decisions. And in the beginning, what errors he made stemmed from this concern, but then he discovered that he was the power, that his was the final authority. He established his control by his recitation of the rules which nobody else had read and by an inflexibility of will. All timidity left him. He penalized for the most minor infringements, delivering his judgments not as an upholder of the law but as an angel of vengeance victoriously punishing sin. Sometimes he would wait long seconds deliberating after an appeal had been made, while the player over whose fate he was about to adjudicate did his best not to look up lest he see the sword of Alford's index finger pointing him back to the pavilion.

He worked himself into the drama of the game, signalling boundaries with the elegance of a dancer, redrawing the bowling crease, calling no-balls, turning down appeals, making a theatre of his adjudication until he became as much of an attraction as the star batsman or bowler at school. He so impressed that captains of adult clubs asked him to stand in their games; and the schoolmaster, delighted to have in his school a young man with such a sense of force, invited him at sixteen to become a Pupil Teacher. It was this apprenticeship that would begin his career as a school teacher and allow him to place another firm foot on the steps to the world.

There was so much to learn. He needed to improve his vocabulary, to get the correct pronunciation of words, to have quotations at his fingertips. He needed to be able to talk of novels, the theatre, opera, to know what wines to choose when he went to restaurants in England. And he had to begin alone. He knew of no one else journeying to that world.

At times, though, the language defeated him. His thinking was in another language and he had to translate. He began to speak more and more slowly to make sure that his verbs agreed with his subjects, to cull out words of unsure origin and replace them with ones more familiarly English. Caribbean words like jook, mamaguy and obzocky all had to be substituted. He felt his meanings slipping away as he surrendered his vocabulary. But, he had to surrender meanings; he couldn't take his words out into the world. There was no help for it. As soon as he could afford it he bought *The Concise Oxford Dictionary*, opened it at 'A' and began to write down five new words every day and, as one of his books advised, to use them in sentences. He would say to a child, 'What has so acidulated you today? The abnegation of our friendship is final. Aren't you convivial today!' he sometimes greeted the children, or he would say: 'The presentation you are making is so convoluted that my conviviality is assuaged.' For better elocution he began to speak with pebbles under his tongue. For the correct pronunciation of words, he put his radio on the BBC. He bought a book called *Improve Your Word Power*. He bought a notebook in which he recorded the new words of his expanding vocabulary and striking statements that he felt he needed to remember. He wrote, 'Man is the only animal that laughs and weeps because he is the only animal that is stuck with the difference between what things are and what they ought to be.' He wrote down: Facts do not cease to exist because they are ignored. He wrote down: Problems exist to be overcome. He wrote: beauty is truth, truth beauty. He read the sonnets of Shakespeare. He read the novels of Marie Corelli, *The Decline and Fall of the Roman Empire*, *Of Human Bondage*, the essays of William Hazlitt. He bought an umbrella. He began to develop a new walk – gait would be the word – slower, more leisurely steps that gave him more time in which to work out his translations from his thinking into what he saw now as proper English.

By and by, he began to feel himself bound for *the world* and to look at his stay in Cunaripo as temporary, as a state from which he would graduate in the same effortless way in which one grew old, as a stop, a halt, a station to refine and purify himself and straighten out his defects, ever conscious that it was never to be his final home. And he waited, preparing for his departure into that other world, the world, watching the seasons change and the deluge of rain turn the cracked savannah into pools of mud; and he continued to call out spelling and work sums with the children; and sometimes, feeling himself a stranger far from home, feeling surrounded by the cocoa and the canes, watching the forest peeping through its window-panes of sunlight, or sometimes on an evening when darkness covered the town and all that was alive was the cinema, and the gambling club that he had never been brave enough to enter, he would sit and listen halfway across the island for the sound of the sea and the rush of waves dying on their barricade of foam and in his mind picture the ships, the planes, and he would sound upon his lips as if to taste them and be refreshed, revived, those words, names, Thebes, Athens, Mesopotamia, Constantinople, Great Britain, Ulysses, Bellum, New York, London, sometimes calling them out suddenly among pauses in his teaching, surrounding them with a halo of timelessness and space, as a shipwreck might call out the name of his distant country or an absent lover whisper his woman's name. And he began to walk through the town, filled with his sense of the magnificent world, about him his own heartfelt grandeur, expressing himself in cool, contained, almost shy gestures, afraid to extend himself lest he should give the impression that he had accepted this island as his home.

His resolve faltered briefly, one time only, when the National Party arrived to promise a new world and to present its candidates for the elections: doctors of medicine, of dentistry, of theology, of philosophy, winners of public speaking contests, attorneys at law, masters of debate, historians, archaeologists. Like a troupe of magicians, each one with a top hat, a black cape, a silver-topped cane, a briefcase, eyes shielded from the light by a pair of dark shades, and one ear wired with a hearing-aid, they came to ascend platforms decorated with palm and bamboo leaves and photographs of The Leader, to present over loud-speakers their theses on Aristotle and Freedom, on Plato and the Greek City States, on Wilberforce and 'The Emancipation of Slaves', to pontificate on The Indenture of Indians, while below them in the streets steel bands from behind the Bridge played calypso music and big-bottomed women and gnashy men danced bongo on the graves of the colonialism whose death they had come to celebrate. Mesmerized by the shining silver of their speeches, he followed them through the villages with sonorous names, Caratal, Platanal, Mundo Nuevo, Carapichaima, Tabaquite, Siparia, to soak in their gestures, their er-er pauses, to listen to the cadence of their speeches as they chanted the mantras that were to unchain them, Socrates, Tacitus, Timbuktu, Tagore, Delhi, Nkrumah, Nehru, Gandhi, Senghor, Toussaint, Césaire; and for a moment it occurred to him that he didn't have to go anywhere to get to the world, that maybe the world was right here. Then he saw the grand smiles swiping at his brothers' faces as they whispered in conniving tones of the chance they had to get a house lot of land from the government, a job as a watchman, a passport. He had felt ashamed, saddened to watch these men who had once commanded the landscape, who knew the rivers, the hills, exuding now this sense of satisfaction, of arrival at what he sensed was another secondclassness, the fire gone from them so early, all the irreverence of their youth, their sense of battle tamed by the small grandiose promises that had to do with the idea of Nation. And where was the world?

He watched his father who had also fallen under the spell of the Party, large with his fictional power, standing beside his columns of dinged and mossy bricks, the evidence of the house that he was going to build, talking about the house, how many rooms, how many toilets, with the sense of a small promise renewed, revived. And Alford had left for Teachers' Training College with a sense of relief, of escape, glad to be away from this settlement and compromise, his belief renewed that the world was elsewhere.

Free to prepare for the world, he began to lift weights, to pull strands under the correspondence tutelage of Charles Atlas, the universal strongman. He acquired the habit of drinking raw eggs

35

beaten in with Guinness stout and condensed milk. Brimming with a sense of the world, he began to walk slow, patient, like a man nailing himself down so he wouldn't fly away.

When he left Training College after his two-year stay, he had developed his shoulders, had reached 'C' in his dictionary, had performed the role of Othello in the Training College production, had taken part in the formation of a steelband, had sung in the choir and acted as a back-up singer to one of the singers in the annual calypso competition, had tried his hand at writing poetry and had represented the indifferent Training College team a few times in cricket and football. And even if his speech was still painfully slow, his verbs were in more frequent agreement with his subjects.

As luck would have it, a Government quarters became vacant in Cunaripo and, wanting to test the bonafides of his new status and also to leave home at least for a time, he applied for it. It was granted and he moved in next door to two young ward officers, bachelors both, Ashton and Floyd, who were planning to leave for Canada and were enjoying their last few months in the island, Ashton using his after-work hours for drinking rum and Floyd his for running down a procession of young women from the town who entered the Quarters giggly and shy and left with the fumbly grace of newly hatched chickens. They expected him to join them and when he didn't they began to complain that he was giving The Slaughtery, as they called the quarters, a bad name.

He had joined Wanderers Cricket Club and used his afternoons to attend the practice. After school he dressed himself in the full cricket outfit from cap to shoes and walked through the town to the ground, the first man to be there once again. They made him vice-captain partly, he believed, because they knew he was going away and they would soon be rid of him. He was wrong. It would be Vera who would come and make him understand that he was more than that to them, that they saw him as not so much leaving them as taking them with him.

He had first seen her four years earlier when he went jogging past The Settlement of Cascadu, standing with who he took to be a few of the neighbourhood boys, younger than she or the same age. They would wait for him to appear, then they would join him, running a distance with him and then racing each other flat out and then stopping, leaving him to go on. She continued among the runners even as she grew, her parts rumbling and bouncing as the boys allowed her to match them. Later, as if to acknowledge the changes that were taking place in her body, she would stand by and look at him a little shyly and wave as the boys continued their running; he would wave back.

When he returned from Training College she was a woman, attending Cosmos Business Academy, in her uniform of blue and blue, her books cradled in the crook of her arms, carrying the scent of green wood-fire smoke and forest moss under her armpits and on her skin, no longer surging forth with the careless, leaping exuberant rhythm of the bush and the cocoa fields of The Settlement, that rhythm abandoned – that under the unsettling gaze of taxi drivers and young police constables idling in front the Public Works building across from the bus stand made her feel that she had no clothes on – exchanged for more careful steps that controlled the victorious roll of her buttocks and calmed the round soft curves of her flesh. Her efforts at concealment reveal something more modest and provoking and rousing and tall. Seeing her going by, the women in the market wonder what madness had provoked her mother to waste money to send such a big young lady to a school where the girls go to learn shorthand and typing and come out with a belly. Vera doesn't listen. She is pleasant enough as she walks through the town. She dismisses with a smile the entreaties of police constables and shakes her head at the offer of rides from taxi drivers, and goes down Main Street to the school with a calm sense of her own desirability, carrying about her the aura of defensiveness that makes her appear a little abrupt, a little brittle, the books in her hands adding to that quality of pathos that undermines the awkward assuredness of the struggling poor, guarding herself with a kind of proper upright blindness, indifferent to the advances of any but the perfect man of her imagination. So that already, among The Settlement people and those who watched her in the town, she had gained a reputation for haughtiness, and slick young men accustomed to easy conquests, and gossips, seeing her not linked to any man, had begun to speculate about the true nature of her sex.

At the dances held in the Roman Catholic school, she went outfitted in the most expensive dresses her mother could afford. Fellows lined up to dance with her and she danced with a vague warm modesty, encouraging no one, choosing scrupulously from among the throng who, if any, would partner her in a slow dance; and even then, as if to emphasize that preference did not mean welcome, she placed a hand on the shoulder of the lucky one to keep him from pressing against her body, while she absently hummed the tune to which they danced.

Alford held her at a distance from the start, more concerned with executing the correct dance steps than with her body, exaggerating the distance he believed she wanted between herself and her partner. It was she who had moved close. And pressed her body to his. Suddenly everywhere he turned he was seeing her. They began talking. One day he found her waiting on his street. She walked with him to his quarters.

'What you waiting on? Hit it,' Floyd said to him. But it wasn't like that. She talked to him about her home, about her brother, her parents, school. She didn't really like this shorthand and typing. She was terrified that she would not fulfil the hopes her mother had for her. She felt a sense of emptiness, as someone in a dark place, stumbling.

'What do you want?' he asked her.

She wasn't certain. She wished she was going away, travelling. She loved travelling. The furthest she had gone to was San Fernando.

'Do you believe in God?' she asked him.

They talked about religion, cricket, marriage, love, her body. Before she came to school in Cunaripo she had not thought of her body. Before she could think of what she wanted or anything, she had to think of it now. Sometimes she felt it was not really hers at all, but something she carried, or something that carried her, that she felt herself following, not knowing where it would take her, ever alert to the danger into which she expected herself to be led. Sometimes she said, 'Yes, let it take me, let it go,' as if to do otherwise was to make a futile gesture, to escape a path she would be led along anyway.

He was going away, he told her. It was something that she knew. She was happy for him. She wished she was going too.

'Will you miss me?' she asked.

'I will miss you,' he said.

'Why will you miss me?'

He said, 'Because people miss people they leave behind when they go away.'

'But will you? Will you miss me? I will miss you.'

'And I will miss you.'

'You see, you had to wait until I said it before you said it. Why do you let me come here?'

'Let you?'

'No. You do not let me. I come on my own.'

'I care for you,' he said.

'Why do you care for me?'

'I care for you.'

'Why?'

'Because I just care.'

'Because you just care? What does it mean to care?'

Like that they toyed with each other, and between them lay their bodies, their sex, his caution, her care.

When she first came she sat out in the living-room, the two of them pretending to be talking about the Marie Corelli book she had borrowed and had come to return. She came again. They read each other's palms, they related their dreams to each other. Then he kissed her. She spat it out as something bitter and dangerous. He didn't expect her to return after that. When she did come back, he was cautious, playing their little games, smoothing out her fingers, caressing her fingertips, taking deep breaths to escape the young womansmell of her. They sang together, '*Oh, my love, my darling, I hunger for your touch*'. They sang, '*I bless the day I found you*'.

'The girl just waiting for the opportunity to give you a piece,' Ashton said. 'But like you don't want it.'

She came in at odd hours, through the door he left open for her. She never tired of talking of his leaving, of the world that he was going into, 'You will see Buckingham Palace! You will see the Queen!' she cried. It was of Vera that Alford was thinking as he listened to his mother. What would he say to her?

'So Pa didn't know that the land was not his own? He didn't know that he had to buy it? Why he didn't tell me anything?

39

Why?' He tried to keep the pleading out of his voice. 'And the Party? The government? They can't do something?'

'You know him. He too proud to ask anybody for anything. He was always a man bigger than he really could afford to be.'

And it was true. His father had pretended to be bigger than the person he could really afford to be because he really was bigger than what he could afford. His pretence wasn't deception, really, it was a man playing out the wish of what he felt he ought to be.

'You have to go,' his mother said.

'Ma, you know I can't leave things so,' he said.

'Leave your father. He will be all right. Just shut your eyes to everything around you and go. Don't even look around you. Don't listen to anybody. Just go. You is all we have to show. You is all that produce out of this. I begging you, go.'

'And you?'

'Me? Don't worry with me. I ain't going to be here long.'

'You hear your stupidness,' Alford said. 'You hear you?'

'And don't shout at me,' she said. 'I tired. Look,' she said, 'look at the immortelle blossoms how they pretty,' lifting her head to the sunshine and the overhanging tree. 'The flowers will look nice on a wreath.'

'Ma, what you talking about death for?'

She leaned on him, 'I should baptize, you know. I should do it soon. Every night I see it in my dreams. I am down by the river and the Leader is there in white and he is coming to dip me in the water. And a man is standing on the other side looking at me with his arms folded and a frown on his face . . . I suppose that is your father . . . And this is the hymn I hear them singing.'

And she began to sing this hymn with a voice that had forgotten the melody. 'Come,' she said, 'come and sing it with me.'

Hearing her, he asked, 'This is the hymn in your dream?' frightened, because he realized that it was not a hymn of baptism, but a hymn of burial.

'Sing the hymn, boy,' she commanded. And she began it again and he joined in, steering her into the right key, this hymn:

> *Come, O thou traveller unknown,*
> *Whom still I know but cannot see,*

My company before me is gone
And I am left alone with thee.

'*And I am left alone with thee.*' And he knew, Alford knew that that was not the time to leave her. He knew also that he couldn't leave his father in that predicament in which he had found himself and go.

One day in the following week, he came out of the shower to find Vera in his bedroom taking off her clothes. It was the first time she was taking off all her clothes. And she was doing it now with great care and modesty, not looking at him, folding each garment as if she had completed ironing it and laying it out on the back of a chair, with the same wistful, deliberate ceremony as if she were laying herself down. The other times had been different; then, her yielding had been the result of his seduction rather than her surrender and those times she had kept her dress on, thinking that if she kept her body hidden she had not fully given herself. Now it was different. She had come to yield up herself and she wanted to do it properly, with taste and unambiguity, the way she would give a present that she wanted treasured, as an act that required no help from him.

With her thumbs hooked inside the elastic band at her waist Vera stood tall, long-legged, knees together, her wonderfully curved buttocks out-jutting, poised to make that soft curtsying movement that would accommodate the sliding of the garment down her hips and thighs and knees and ankles.

She had avoided looking at him while she undressed, but now her eyelids flew up and she watched him sitting back on the bed, relaxed-looking, he hoped, but in fact afraid to breathe out lest he disturb the flow of this ceremony, too still, he felt, to appear sincere, feeling that anything he did would disturb the mood of her giving, remembering how once in the forest he had watched a deer wander close to where they waited and then calmly, as if sensing the danger, stood there and as if it was part of the pattern of its movements, just a step away from capture, scrambled away. Almost as if he felt himself unable to bear the tension and waiting in the moment, he reached out a hand to draw her towards him; but the very gesture of his wanting disturbed the mood, pitched her into a new doubt and concern

41

and fear, as if all at once she realized that this last garment even more than what lay between it was the last barrier to her pride and self.

As if she had awakened in her the value of herself as person, requiring now out of her to surrender more than the act of generosity, more respect and honour and acknowledgement of her worth, so that her generosity would not be just the surrendering and giving away of herself, but also an act for her, she asked, 'You love me, Alford? – the words surprising even her. Love was the last thing she had expected herself to mention. She had come freely on her own, expecting nothing from him in the way of lasting commitment, knowing that there was no future here, that he was going away, and that it was because he was going away she was making this gift of herself, and by that means not only giving of herself but of binding herself to him, so that she herself would be taken out into the world when he went there; so she had wanted to make no demand, but suddenly, his gesture of impatience, of wanting, had placed in doubt his valuation of her. She did not want him to interpret the ease of her offering as a sign of her worthlessness. All this, she didn't know how to tell him.

'I never do this before, you know,' she said quickly, before he could speak.

'Do what?'

'Take off my clothes in front a man.'

He wanted to caress her, to calm her.

'Don't answer,' she said. 'I mean about love. Don't answer. I don't know where that stupidness come from.'

'What you mean?'

'I mean, that is not what I really mean.' She sat beside him, she took his hand and parted his fingers, her tone changed, 'When you go to England you will think of me?'

Alford felt himself grow cold. He took away his hand.

Something in his face made her apprehensive, 'You angry?'

'I better tell you this,' he said.

His tone alerted her. 'No,' she said. 'Don't tell me nothing.'

'I'm not going to England. At least not now.'

'I don't believe you,' she said.

'Believe me,' he said. 'Believe me.'

42

She sat on the bed naked. After a while he looked and saw tears streaming down her face.

'Why you crying?' he asked. He was getting irritated.

'I love you,' she said, choking.

'You don't have to say that,' he said. Because he knew that those words were meant for herself. He put his arms around her.

'God,' she said, trembling. 'I feel so unclean.'

He could feel her mind withdrawing and her skin growing colder. Suddenly he felt himself swelling, wanting her.

'Let me go,' she said, removing his hand from her shoulder.

Alford let her up. He watched her gather her clothes and take them with her to the bathroom. After a while he heard the toilet flush then the sound of water filling the tank. He heard the door open. 'Vera,' he called softly, 'Vera!' There was no answer. He went and looked outside.

He saw her going down the street with her dainty stretching walk. He knew that he had betrayed her. And all at once the world was a different place. He felt jolted back to the island. He put on his short pants, thinking he would go for a run. Suddenly his heart wasn't in it. He knew that the fellars were probably down at Khandan's shop drinking beers. He dressed himself. He would go and have a Guinness.

That must have been the time when my mother saw him.

4

Eye

That time I am a child in this same penitential island, in this
town where every street corner is a rumshop where we have five
churches, a Hindu temple, a mosque, two cricket teams and a
single steelband that we make from oil drums – that is the part
of the oil that we get: the steel – drums that have no use again
except for rubbish, bins that we take and fire and shape and beat
to make a music to coax into the daylight present those rhythms
that issue from the goatskin drums and the chanting voices in
the Shango palais where they kill unspotted ramgoats and
wring the neck of white and red cockerels and drink their blood
and cook their flesh and eat it without salt and dance till morning
to gods that drag them down into a deep deep darkness where
they froth and suffocate and perspire and groan and spin until
their senses leave them; my mother thankful to her God that we
not living next door to them, not by those drums that would
giddy your head and full you up with a power African and
useless that point you back to a backward people that can hardly
help theyself, far more help you, can only make you shame, can
only drag you down deeper into the dark.

To her the onliest thing to save us is the education that she
begging me to learn.

Because without it you have to dance below the limbo pole.
You have to bend down low and flex your spine and bend your
back and try to come out on the other side of the stick without
your knees touching the ground.

'You could do that?' she asks with an error of tenderness that
slips out of her before she can catch it and twist it into the
instrument of fright that she believes would better discipline me.
'Eh? You could do it?' trying to sound tough now to compensate
for the startling stroke of tenderness that had escaped the prison
of her emotions.

And I chuckle and smile. 'No, Ma, I can't dance the limbo.'

'Good. Well, learn your lesson and don't let people mislead

you,' her reference clearly to Uncle Bango, whom she believes I have too much admiration for. 'Look at where he living and he know so much,' hinting at the land that is not his own and his house that is in need of repairs, in her voice a note of triumph that somehow she had been able to do a little better by my father than Miss Myrtle had been able to do by Bango, though not enough to please her, not with my father taking up his cuatro and going for days from house to house to sing and serenade the village for Christmas, bringing back with him a fleet of half-drunken men to eat the ham and drink out the rum before they leave to go again; not with his leaving for Carnival with the stickfighters and the most he returning with is a bandage where somebody bust his head.

No. There was no blame for Myrtle; is Bango. It is that curse on him, that *light* that pass down to him from his great-great-grandfather JoJo, who was one of thirty persons they arrest and flog when on Emancipation Day he stand up in Brunswick Square and curse the governor for granting him a half-way freedom instead of giving him the liberation that was his due, and who out of his own spite and pride refused the opportunity that others take to run away to squat a piece of land in Arouca, remaining instead working on Carabon plantation, deciding not to leave and not to dead until they compensate him for the more than seventy years they had him held in unlawful captivity, doing everything within the power of his outraged anger to keep both Carabon and the work alive, not missing a day of labour, refusing to be part of any strike or any sabotage or any subterfuge that would destroy the prosperity of the plantation, so that he became to Carabon more brother than enemy.

'I just lucky,' she says. 'Is just that I refuse to let love rule me as it rule Myrtle. Just lucky that I know how to set my mind against my feelings and say no,' vexed still as much with my father as with Uncle Bango who, as she explained to Aunt Florence, take it upon himself that first Independence Day to drill and outfit, from the district, forty boys, my brother Michael and me included, to give us red berets and khaki uniforms and pieces of wood that he shaped out to look like guns and to lead us the two and a half miles from Cascadu to Cunaripo and to march us through the town and down to the recreation ground where they were holding the March Past ceremony, with the government representative and the religious leaders and the County Councillors and the important people of Cunaripo and Cascadu.

'Nobody didn't invite him in. Nobody ask him to come. The government have their business fixed. They have their programme, with the Police and the Red Cross and the St John Ambulance Brigade and the Volunteer Firemen. Bango fall in behind them, decked out in the admiral's suit that some years before he had played sailor in for Carnival in City Syncopators steelband, when another one of his brothers, Sam, the badJohn, was captaining that band, his chest weighed down with medals, gold braid looped over his shoulder, in his hands the flag. And behind him, these poor little boys, their hands swinging in every direction, some heads turned to the left, some heads to the right, people applauding because they so astonished and amazed that this man with nothing to his name, no house, no land, the little money that he get coming from sculpting heads from dry coconuts and little trinkets from dried coconut shells, would from his own pocket outfit these boys and bring them, uninvited, into this big Independence march. But that had passed and his extravagance forgotten and she had made the sign of the cross.

Now, this year, Uncle Bango had come to tell her that he was going to do it again. This time he proposed to add to his presentation four boys, each to represent one of the major races in the island. He was going to deck them out in his idea of the appropriate ethnic wear: the Indian in dhoti and turban; the European in Scottish kilt; the Chinese to have on a big Cantonese hat and two false plaits of long hair; and the African a grass skirt on, beads around his neck and a spear in his hand. And he was serious. Lochan was going to provide one of his sons to be the Indian, Carabon was going to get a grandson or a nephew to be the European, and Loy the shopkeeper was expected to provide the Chinese. He wanted her to let my brother Michael be the African. And she had agreed. For the sake of peace, I agree to let Michael be an African.

Now, with Independence Day nearly upon us, Uncle Bango had come to report that neither Lochan nor Carabon nor Loy was willing to provide their children for this march. He wasn't

46

going to let that stop him. He had managed to get Miss Dorothy's albino son to be the European; Chance's half-Indian son was going to be the Indian; he counted on Michael to be the African; and if it was not too much trouble he wanted her to allow me to portray the Chinese.

'Help me,' my mother said to Aunt Florence. 'Help me to understand the craziness that would cause this man to want to take Blackpeople children and put them in the Independence Day hot sun to portray people who living right here in this district, who if they wanted anybody to represent them have their own children to do it.'

And didn't my mother see the beauty of what Uncle Bango was doing, Aunt Florence asked, with the largeness of understanding that she had begun to affect since she began waiting for the appearance of her future husband.

'You don't see the wonderful welcome he is making to each and every race of people in this island? You don't see it, Pearl? You don't see it? The Indian, the Whitepeople, the Chinese: to have all of them in his band, the whole world together? You don't see it?'

'What I see is people going crazy,' my mother said, and with a backward glance as she flounced away: 'You better watch yourself.'

Aunt Florence was going good. She had her hairdressing business in Port-of-Spain. She had her friends, Valerie and Roger. She had her family to come up to on weekends. She would go to a fête, she would go to church, she would go to the beach, whatever she wanted. Anything she want to do she could do. She had no chick, no child. She was even thinking about going to England just to see the place. She had a gold bracelet that she buy with the first real money she worked for. Just so the gold bracelet disappear. The bracelet was not in the pawn shop. It was not on the dresser where she rested it when she took it off to clean it. Bernice, her single assistant in the hairdressing salon, did not see it. Then the fifteen dollars that she draw from her susu hand disappeared from the drawer where she put it. Then Bernice get herself pregnant and had to leave the work. One day just so in the road a woman come up and ask her if her name is Florence and when she say yes, the woman start abusing her

47

about Reynold. She had talked to Reynold one time. One single time. Business start slacking. Poor she don't know what it is was wrong until her friend Valerie pick her up one Sunday morning and take her in a taxi to La Seiva to see Papa Cochon the famous obeah man, who could call birds out of the forest by whistling through his fingers, who had pointed out the location of buried treasures to the Whitepeople of Maraval, had found husbands for women and secured election victories for politicians.

She had returned reeking of scented oils and a new awareness of the spiritual and the unseen. Her eyes were wide open. She could not believe, as the years went by, how she could have functioned in the world in such innocence of the need for protection from evil forces, from people with devious heart and wicked designs, without her candles lighting in churches and priests offering novenas for her safety, without her own small thanksgivings and daily prayers. Now that she had become a convert to the presence and value of that other world, she didn't let a month pass without paying a visit to Papa Cochon and, as time went on, other seers recommended to her to see what was unfolding in her future. It was on one of these visits that she learned that her success in business was linked with her quest for love and that the man that was going to marry her would find her there on the veranda of her sister's house.

This was information that had my mother amused at first and alarmed later as Aunt Florence began to appear every weekend to sit on the veranda fully dressed, with high-heeled shoes and stockings and her most elegant clothes, sipping iced tea and leafing through one of the fashion books on the side table or turning the pages of the single copy of *Ebony* magazine that my father had bought in Port-of-Spain from a street vendor who had come back from the war because it contained pictures of Jack Johnson, Sugar Ray Robinson and Joe Louis, letting herself be observed by the parade of eligible males, some of whom had heard of the prediction and dressed in their best clothes so as to make a proper presentation of themselves to her; but others in whatever they were wearing from the fields or halfway barbering tugged there by the irresistible aroma of the scented oils with which Aunt Florence daubed her body, that had cocks crowing in the middle of the afternoon and male animals for miles around barking and baaing and neighing in a cacophony of confusion over their unexplained arousal whenever she was in the town. Owners had to tie up their animals and parents send their teenaged sons to soak in the river. When eventually it was ascertained that Florence was the origin of the discomfort of the males, a delegation of mothers set out to bar her from the town, but this was opposed by the older men who did not want to surrender their own feelings of rejuvenation. The women came up with the tactic of burning incense to permeate the air of their houses, the scent so strong that the fathers left their homes to go down to the cricket ground, where they would be safe from the stifling scent of incense and could inhale to their satisfaction the aroma of Florence's scented oils.

So when my mother – with all this craziness around her, feeling herself alone the only sane person in the family, if not in the world, in that mood my father steering clear of her, refusing to be drawn into a discussion that he knew would inevitably end up with an attack on him – when my mother, anchored in the swamp of her anxiety, on this edge, believing that the world was poised and waiting for us just to make a false step to drag us down into the deep from which she struggled daily to keep us, by herself. By myself, let me say it again and loud. Without support or help from anybody except my God, since your father who shoulda been the one to spearhead the escape and progress of his children is following his brother to dredge up a past that everybody gone past. Everybody seeing about theirself and their family, and he and his brother preparing to march.

When my mother, on the look-out now for that limb of rescue that would heave us upwards into a brighter day, worried that despite her threats and warnings, I now, the one next in line, the last hope, Jesus! Hallelujah! Boy, like if your hearing stop up and your eyes can't see, would take the opportunity that you get, this chance, luck, the prayer of a hope you have to win a College Exhibition and squander it because of that male and aimless rebellion, the disease that afflict the menfolk of our family, that had already claimed her other son, my brother Michael, who at fifteen had kept on going to school in order to play cricket and be with his friends doing school gardening, taking time out from these important exercises at the appointed day each year to

49

sit the school-leaving examination and fail it with a calm that announced and emphasized that his future lay elsewhere, that he was Bango's nephew and the grandson of Pappy King Durity who up to the age of eighty-one was still going from district to district to dance bongo and to sing hymns at the occasion of a death and who, according to my mother, didn't care if Good Friday fall on Christmas Eve once he had a rum to drink and a cuatro to play and a woman to caress, the yield of his adventures, fourteen boychildren with eleven different women scattered from Toco to Icacos, each male child beaming with the cheerful air of festivals, his handsomeness something male and careless and dangerous that other men wanted to fight him for and women wanted to save in him, the best, the loveliest women drawn to them, these good-for-nothings, like moths to fire. My mother confessing herself one of those fools, those *backsides* who see the beast and believe she could tame him and save him so that they could have a life, now find herself fighting to save herself not to go down in the pit with him and not to let the pit swallow down her boychildren.

When my mother see Alford George in Cunaripo, near Khandan shop, surrounded now with an aura of vacantness, gazing at the town with the wounded melancholy of a shipwreck, and on the horizon not a sail, when she see him there with this sense that something in him was betrayed, that there was a wound there that had to heal, that there was a fury there in need of an outlet, she said, 'Yes!' softly as the taste of the thought coursed sweetly through her body: 'Yes. He's the one to straighten you out when you get to that Exhibition class,' triumphant, almost with an exultation she would replay for me in front my father who had come in from work in the forest a few moments before her and was there still sitting on the bench in front the kitchen, taking off his talltops. 'Yes! He's the one to straighten you out when you get to that Exhibition class,' her triumph almost vengeful, uttered with glee, with the extravagance of respect she showered on strangers who met her approval, and in whom she was ready to repose her trust, with an undertone of censure directed at my father who through some default they both knew of had long lost the genius to merit her applause, her dissatisfaction in him deriving, I imagined, not from any deception on his part as from her own disappointment that she had not managed to change him.

'To be the man you want him to be?' Aunt Florence once asked her.

'I? What I want? Me? No, dearie.'

'You should listen to him, Pearl. Listen what he trying to say.'

'Listen? And let him believe that I agree with him?'

'But if you don't listen, Pearl, how you will know what he thinking? How you will know what he feeling?'

'Look at Myrtle,' my mother said. 'Myrtle listen. You see that change anything? All it do is make Bango believe that she agree with him. If wasn't for me, we would be still paying a rent. You see me, I can't live like Myrtle. If Bertie want to live like Bango, I can't live like Myrtle.'

'But I thought he was going away,' my father said.

'Wrong. He decide to stay here and teach the children. He making a big sacrifice. England was where he was going. Now he will be here to straighten you out, to turn you to something more serious and sensible than the stupidness your Uncle Bango encouraging you in,' looking at me but really talking to my father who sat on the bench in the kitchen, one huge woodcutter's hand resting in the other, not with the opposition she anticipated and perhaps wanted to evoke, but listening with bemusement to an enthusiasm that he had heard from her before, when she had presented her other champions whose promise had evaporated with each passing season, each failure leaving her more vexed with Bango as if whatever it was he stood for emerged more dangerous and compelling, had to be resisted even if it meant that she had to invent another hero to pit against the belief my father had in his brother, my father left with only his patience and his unsurrendered insistence on the valuing of his brother, holding on more stubbornly to that thing that left him unsurrendered, that kept himself himself, dredging up stories of her heroes, and of their fall from her own grace: Ethelbert B. Tannis, who as president of the Village Council and chairman of the PTA she had expected to pull the village together so that people could have a say in the affairs that affected them, and who because of his fierce support for the National Party had turned the village into two opposing political camps, so that people who had a real interest in the village, who had worked for it without thinking about politics, had withdrawn and left it for Ethelbert B. Tannis and his crew to finish mash up; Father Cliffie Dick, the English priest who wanted to administer to the needs of his people, put on a costume and join them to play masquerade for Carnival, inspiring the calypsonian Cypher to sing:

> *If the priest could play,*
> *Who is we,*

who come and start up a choir that was to take the children of Cunaripo and Cascadu to sing in music festivals in Arima, in San Fernando, in Port-of-Spain, their voices coming over the radio, until they find out what he really wanted the children to do, they had to run him out of Cascadu. The police were coming to arrest him when just like that he disappear off the face of the island. Somebody say they see him in Bermuda. Somebody say they see him playing Carnival in St Lucia; Doctor Courtney L. Bobb, the false doctor who come with this wonderful plan for everybody to put up money to form a co-operative that will buy goods and sell them back to the people for less money, and buy land for planting, and who her sister Irene was saved from marrying because her son Ronnie didn't like him, take people money, put advertisement in the newspaper, organize a big sod-turning ceremony, invite the Minister of Commerce to give the feature address, the priest to bless the spot and the school choir to sing for the dignitaries. Everybody turn up except Doctor Bobb, because —Doctor Courtney L. Bobb is not Doctor Courtney L. Bobb at all, is really a fella called Lesandro O'Kieff whose business it is to go about and get poor people money away from them. He would pursue his vocation under different names, nobody able to trace him until years later they found him living down the islands under the name of Porvell Priest, showing tourists around the caves and the reefs until one afternoon, diving for the treasure that was rumoured to be buried there by Blackbeard the Pirate, he disappeared and was never seen again.

Now here was another one.

'So he staying? Here? In this island?' my father asked, trying to keep the smile from spreading across his face.

'Right here in Cunaripo.'

'Good,' satisfied that he himself could have fashioned no sterner test for anyone who would be a hero.

5

Becoming a Madman

In the last few years everything Alford had done was devoted to preparing himself for his mission to the world. His attention to his jogging, his elocution, his vocabulary, his grammar had produced a performed refinement that many in the town took to be comical and they had put up with him with a sense of amusement, chuckling under their breath, 'This boy mad, yes,' thankful that the exercise of his madness was something intended for another world.

Now, with his departure uncertain, postponed, as he walked through the town, his long sleeves buttoned down over his muscles, he began to feel the absurdity that he had become. His elocution, his vocabulary, the agreement of his subjects and his verbs, his Hazlitt, his Keats, his Shelley, his Browning, his knowledge of wines seemed to be of little use here.

He tried not to see it as effort gone to waste. He tried to feel himself bigger than the place. Nobody was taking him on. Ashton and Floyd had not managed to leave the island either. They had intensified their programme of rum drinking and womanizing. Vera had disappeared, he knew not where to. He made no effort to find her, and he found himself either jogging or playing cricket with the Wanderers team. His mother was vexed that he had used his money to go away to study towards the purchase of the land, but after a while she came around to accepting it as another chapter in the mysterious cosmic plan where 'Everything that happen happen for the best.'

His father approached him shyly in the beginning, grateful for his sacrifice, then he began to discuss with him the angle from which he needed to approach the immortelle tree so that when he cut it down it wouldn't fall on the house. He spoke to him of his plans for the house, how many bedrooms, how many toilets – everybody would have a room – of the esteem in which he was held in the Party, of the need for young leaders to lead these backward people of Cascadu. Even if you go away, you will still have a place in the Party, his father said. There were chapters of the Party in England, in Canada, in America. You don't have to be living here all the time. You could come from America or England one day and go up for election next day.

'Yes, join,' his brothers urged. 'With your education you could go far.'

A fear seized him. Then came a rage that surprised him because he had grown up believing that he did not have the right to feelings of outrage, since the world did not owe him anything and the little that it offered he had to be thankful for.

He became angry with everything and with everybody, with his mother's surrendering faith, with the quiet submissiveness of his brothers, with the accommodation of his father and the threat of the idea of himself settling into this little world outside the world. To hit back, he took off his tie. He grew his beard. He let his hair grow. He wanted to mash up the place. He set himself apart from everything and everybody, withdrawing his gentleness and understanding from those around him, as something they did not merit. He became abrupt, insulting, feeling a small triumph when he heard that people didn't like him. That was exactly what he needed, not to be accommodated, to not belong to their little world.

And he walked with his buttoned-down sleeves, a stern vexed melancholy surrounding him, using the words he had learnt, the bigger the better, recalling the quotations he had memorized, becoming something of a spectacle in the town, until the headmaster Mr Penco, wanting, as he told Alford, to put to use the expertise he had acquired at Training College, asked him to teach the College Exhibition class. At first Alford was reluctant to accept, believing that it would identify him too closely with permanence at a time when he was still unwilling to give up the idea of going abroad; but he took it, as a project for the focus of his energies, his force, his anger, as a challenge that would give more meaning to his waiting and allow him to help at least a few children escape the humbling terror of the island.

From the very first day he took charge of the class, he gave notice of the seriousness with which he intended to pursue this new, if temporary, mission.

First he insisted that the children in the class be exempted from the school's gardening programme. He wasn't there to produce farmers but to produce scholars. Secondly, he put aside the educational psychology they had taught him at Training College for a clear, firm voice, the habit of repeating things over and over again, a random questioning of the class to make sure that what he said was understood. Finally, he hung, on a nail next to the blackboard in plain sight for everybody to see, a leather strap that he called Betsy, whose weight and flexibility he let us believe resulted from being soaked in urine, and a simple statement of philosophy, Do, Die or Runaway, that he soon changed to Do or Die, since he realized that we had no place to escape to. 'Do or Die,' my mother intoned, lifting up her hands in thanksgiving, 'Praise God, Hallelujah! At last we have a saviour. Look, carry for him these two avocados and this half a dozen eggs to build up his strength. And don't come home here and tell me he had to beat you, because I will give you my share of licks too.'

Over the road from us, our neighbour Miss Jane, a small busy wasp of a woman struggling with a single son, was not delighted: 'The day that madman touch my child. The day he touch Treasure, they going to have to jail me,' she cried. Inevitably the day came. She tied an old dress under her belly, tied her head with a red cloth and holding Treasure by the hand she set off for the school, announcing to the neighbourhood that she was going down today, 'Today, O Lord, they going to jail me!'

When she stepped into the school Alford George met her with such a fearsome righteousness that she returned home trembling, satisfied that she could do nothing better for Treasure than to leave him in Mr George's hands. After that we would hear her in her attempts at discipline threatening: 'Treasure! Treasure! You want me to report you to Mr George?'

Still, everybody was not so easily won over to his methods of teaching and discipline. He would have his greatest test the day Big Jonah Jones and a noisy band of villagers from Hibiscus led by Miss Mildred, the mother of Little Jonah, land up in the school to get an explanation as to why their son get beaten.

'That is all we want to know,' said Mildred the mother, arms akimbo, legs spread open in the stance of a stickfighter. 'The boy come home with these marks on his body and say that his teacher beat him, and when I ask him why the teacher beat him, he tell me he don't know why.

'Look at him there,' she said, 'if you think I lying.' And to the boy: 'Why the teacher beat you? Eh, why?' The boy was silent. 'You see,' she said. 'That is why I ask his father to leave off his work in the quarry to come with me to find out why,' looking at Big Jonah, a stout solid, awkward iron of a man, with thick forearms, about him the sense of a vocation missed. He had been in and out of jail for fighting; but he could easily have been a light heavyweight boxer. But all that was behind him. That stupidness was when he was younger. Now he did not look for trouble; he just liked right things to be right. He didn't want anybody to take advantage of his children, so that was why he lose a whole half-day of work to come to the school to find out why the teacher beat his son.

The headmaster wanted everybody to be reasonable. Discipline was one of the levers by which children were induced to learn. Nobody was there to harm the children. In school as a child he the schoolmaster had to take his own share of floggings, 'and look at where I am today. Look at me.'

'Sir, I appreciate everything you say,' Jonah said. 'I just want to know why he beat the boy.' He did not look once at Mr George, who had been standing quietly in the small room, observing the sparring going on between the schoolmaster and the parents of the child.

'Is I who beat your son. I beat him. Me.'

And for the first time Jonah looked at him as he spoke.

'I beat him because I don't want him to grow up to be a jackass like you. I beat him because I want him to know that he has a brain and if he doesn't use it he will catch his backside like you, slaving in a quarry breaking stone, or like some of your friends outside idle on the side of the road. I cut his arse because I want him to prepare himself for a future, for life, for a world brighter and bigger and more grand than the rumshop and the icebox by the corner. I beat him because he is my responsibility once he sit down in the class I teaching. That is the general. The specific is because while I trying to get this boy to put some sense in his head he trying to find out what cause the bruise between Emelda Farrell's legs.

'And, Mr Gentleman, Sir, if you were a little boy in my class and refuse to listen and to learn after I explain and explain and explain and you still can't tell me the answer, I woulda cut your arse too. You want to know why I beat him, well, I have told you.'

And, turning to the schoolmaster, he said, 'Mr Penco, do you need me for anything more? I have children waiting. I have a class to teach.'

The schoolmaster, soaked in perspiration, looked blankly at Mr George, who now more sternly said, 'Sir, do you need anything further?'

It was Jonah Jones who recovered first. Mr George, he realized, had established by his very intensity a stronger claim to the child than any he could make.

'I think I understand your feelings, Teacher,' he said, stretching out a hand to Mr George. 'I glad to meet you, Teacher.'

'Don't meet me yet,' Mr George said, ignoring the hand. 'When you come into this school in the proper fashion to enquire after the progress of your son, you will meet me then.'

Even then Jonah didn't think of doing anything; but Mildred looked at him and sucked her teeth in disdain. It was in that moment that Jonah felt obliged to punch him: a left just above his belt that doubled him over so that he didn't even see the right hand. When he regained consciousness he was not angry with Jonah. He realized that he had omitted an important aspect of his development that was as essential here as it would be in England. Self-defence. The schoolmaster wanted to call in the police. But, no; Alford wanted no outside intervention. At the end of that same month, he took up boxing, all alone, as he had done everything else, buying two pairs of boxing gloves and sewing the mouth of a canvas bag filled with sawdust and setting it up to swing on one of the flooring joists below the house and giving a little money to one of the boys who came around to clean the yards of the quarters to spar with him. The rest he did himself, jogging, shadow-boxing, punching the bag and working out with weights. The villagers, already convinced that his standing up to Jonah was a sign of madness, were now sure that he was not a man to tangle with. Nobody took him seriously until he came

one day and told Floyd and Ashton that he was training for a
fight.

'You must have a manager,' Ashton told him.

'Who?'

'You looking at him.'

So Ashton bought a book on boxing, draped a towel over his
neck, and became his manager/trainer, adding another dimen-
sion to what the villagers always thought was a comedy, people
glad to have Ashton to belabour:

'Your fighter start to cut down any trees yet?'

'What is his boxing name?'

'He don't have a boxing name? Every boxer must have a
boxing name – Joe Louis, Battling Freddie . . . If he don't have
a boxing name he's not a real boxer.'

So they named him Kid. And when they saw him jogging on
evenings or met him in the street they would say, 'Hey, Kid,
what you doing? How the training?' and then kill themselves
laughing behind his back.

'When he fighting ?' they asked Ashton.

'You have everything in place? Don't forget the towel. A fella
went one night to a fight and his trainer forgot the towel. The
fella getting bad licks, lefts and rights, uppercuts to his chin, the
trainer looking all about for the towel to throw it in the ring, he
can't find the towel.'

'So what happened?' Ashton asked. 'In case something like
that should happen.'

'Oh, the trainer had to shout to the fighter, 'Lie down! Lie
down! I forget the towel.' '

Alford fought two three-round fights as an amateur in the
middleweight division, the first against Battling Billy a tall, rangy
left-hander from Coalmine near Sangre Grande, and the other
against Easy Boy Docks from Marabella. He outpointed Battling
Billy, and got a small cut on his left cheek in losing to Easy
Boy, who showed the class eventually to become middleweight
champion of Trinidad and Tobago and go on to fight in Venezuela
and Columbia. After that, Alford never fought publicly. He continued to train and to jog and to spar and gained the reputation
of being clumsy but a hard hitter.

With the children now left completely in his hands, Alford set out to make us champions. On the blackboard he wrote down what he wanted us to accept as our new slogan: 'Best or Dead', which he made us repeat in chorus as every morning he erased and rewrote it. Each one of us was required to run at least one mile a day, and to ensure that we did it, he would take us jogging in the school ground or set the boys to sparring with each other and the girls to skipping rope. Our parents' involvement and support was essential to our success and he wrote to parents advising on the need to provide a good home environment, to exempt us from everyday domestic chores, to give us incentives (for example, the offer of a bicycle if we won a College Exhibition) and most importantly they needed to give us the proper diet. Not all those starches, not all that carbohydrate. He gave each student a typed sheet with details of the proper diet.

BREAKFAST:
Two eggs
2 slices of toast
wheatgerm
Quaker oats, 1 teacup
1 slice of cheese
1 glass of milk

ADDITIVES:
Cod liver oil, nerve tonics

LUNCH:
Fish or Meat 4 ounces
Rice
Provisions
Salad
Avocado
Fruit

DINNER:
Steak
Chocolate (hot)
Rice or Potatoes

It was his expectation that we follow this diet that raised

questions of his sanity in my mother's mind. 'But then,' she said, 'all great people must be a little crazy.'

When at the end of that year Emelda Farrell won an exhibition to go to Bishop Anstey High School in Port-of-Spain, the district erupted in thanksgiving. In the fifty years of the College Exhibition system, it was the first win by not only the school but by the county. Alford George became a hero. At the function held to honour him, the headmaster Mr Penco gave a speech and there were votes of thanks from our neighbour Miss Jane whose Treasure she declared was now as straight as a pin and from Jonah Jones who used the occasion to make a public apology for the little misunderstanding we had before and who now invited parents to stand behind Alford George. 'Wherever you going, we with you, Sir.' And he offered Alford George his hand to shake. This time Alford George did not refuse it.

'Yes,' my mother said, as she joined in the applause. 'Give him time and he will straighten out the whole district.'

Parents brought him gifts of eggs, of fowl, of fruit, of fish and someone gave him a live bird, a singing bird in a cage, a semp, a vieux mal which was to become his pet and which he called by his own name, Alford. That was his season. Past pupils boasted of their encounters with him and children who had the good fortune to be in his class that year boasted of the floggings he gave them. They swapped recollections of his sayings and the more adept at mimicry outdid each other in imitating his gestures, his widened eyes when he was astonished at their answer, his eyes blinking, as he raked his fingers through his hair when angry, and the sudden smile of mockery and astonishment when they failed to grasp a concept that he thought so easy.

Alford George accepted the accolades with great caution. And while he had grown to have a little more sympathy for the people of the town, he continued to keep his distance from them, feeling the need to guard that life, that hope and ambition that he had not surrendered. He did not want to become too accessible. The children alone remained real to him. He took them on excursions to see how newspapers were run, to watch the machines on which news came in from the world. What was sent out, he wondered.

He took them to spend a day in the shade of the botanical

61

gardens among the hundreds of rare and foreign trees that he told us Sir Ralph Woodford had directed his gardener David Lockhart to plant back in the year 1816. He took them to the pitch lake where Sir Walter Raleigh stopped to caulk his ships on his way to El Dorado, and had us standing in terrified awe at the thought that a whole village of Arawak Indians, their animals and dwelling places had been swallowed in one night many years ago by an eruption of the lake. He took them to the oil refinery at Point–Pierre and the dragon breathing out fire and smoke and to the sugar refinery at Saint Madeline. This was the world of the island; but there was another world. He filled them with the idea of the bigness of that world, with the idea of escape. His heart grew large when later he heard a child in the accent of the village say the words, ideas, Mesopotamia, Ulysses, Thebes, Exeter, Los Angeles, or he read in the essay of a child the simple sentence, 'He flew away' or, 'He flexed his muscles.' Then he would scratch his head and begin to feel that his efforts were being repaid, that the children were beginning to feel the flavour of the world, of the grandness of space, of the bigness of time and the possibility of escape and he would get frightened all over again that he was getting too close to these children, and to think with alarm that in concentrating on them he was burying himself and forgetting his own escape. Sometimes, he would read of a fellow returning from England with his BA and he would feel a knife twisting inside him; or, in the cinema he would see a British newsreel – not American, British. The States did not touch him in the same way Britain did. It was still too young, too raw, too huge, too loud. He would see this newsreel and he would look at the scenes and identify the landmarks of London and say the words, their names: Thames, Buckingham Palace, Number Ten Downing Street – though here and there with America a word could get him – Los Angeles, Chattanooga, Ithaca, Utah – and the old pain of homesickness would sink into the flute of his bones and he would rise in a temper, anxious about time passing, his life passing. Suddenly, desperate for something to show for his time, he would charge at the class, frantic for success, berating, bullying, hitting at himself and everybody as he uncurled Betsy and lifted it over his shoulder, to terrorize the children into learning, this passion sweeping

62

through the whole small school, trembling it, making it hum, galvanizing everybody to greater effort by his intense demanding: his class, the cricket team, the netball team, children competing in the school gardening competition, the teachers rushing around busy busy, on their toes, as if they had to lift their own work to merit being in the same place with him. And he was left at the end feeling that this place was becoming too much his own.

As if to unshackle himself from this bondage, to advertise to himself that he was not sinking into the routine of the school, that he remained unsurrendered, he began to look to see how far along he was in the payments on the land, to check applications to schools in England and the schedule of ships sailing to Britain.

At home with the land secure, the house was going up slowly. The foundation had been cast, the walls put up and it stood uncovered, a shell of concrete, ugly, cramped, the tiny rooms like little cells, with the opening for windows and doors, looking like a public urinal. But it was on its way. As it grew, he felt torn between embarrassment and relief as he watched his father stretch into a new self-importance, careful now about little things, with a sense of ownership, of achievement at last, telling him over and over again, 'This is your room, that is the kitchen, that is the bedroom,' as if he had not told him all that before. He saw its faults: Where was the guest room, the library? Where would they put little children? It seemed so small. All this time and what a conception! And he had to remind himself that this house was his father's achievement, not his own. And he realized that for himself he had to renew his commitment to the world. The world!

Then suddenly one day he awoke to find that time had gone; the house completed, the immortelle tree cut down, his mother dead, Ashton transferred with promotion to Cedros, Floyd married and gone, and he, Alford, thirty-three years old still in the island, at Cunaripo Government School, standing in front his class watching coming towards him, leading a boy by the hand, this young woman, Gloria Ollivera, who had joined the staff just two months before, pounding down the corridor between the classes with quick hard mincing steps, her head tilted birdlike to one side, about her the breathlessness of announcement and triumph and on her face the full blossoming of a mischievous smile, as if finding herself the focus of all eyes was its own joke and she had a mind to stop and burst out a big laugh just so and horrify the pious congregation her walking with the boy had transformed pupils and teachers into. For two months, from his own scowling face that he believed gave no clue to the disturbing effect she had on his breathing, he had watched her, her hair unstraightened, her droopy skirts, her large eyes in that funny face, saying nothing more than the obligatory 'Good morning.' Now he watched her come onward magnetic and suspenseful, her face half-turned to the boy she was leading, carrying in her step and sway the dizzying sense of her outrageous potential, the thought of laughing not yet dismissed, playing tantalizingly at her mind, bearing down upon him as if her intention was less to bring the boy to him than to bring him alive to her presence, walking directly at him with her gait unslackened so that he had to step back a pace to prevent himself becoming a party to their colliding.

And when he looked up, boiling with anger and surprise, it was to find himself looking into the large laughing and mischievous eyes of that woman that he had given up expecting to find in this island. And he stood before her shaken, alarmed, breathless, charmed, already beginning even before he said a word to puzzle out why, what was it that had brought her into his life at that moment. For he saw it as no accident, her appearing then there at Cunaripo Government School, but as something well within the framework of his understanding of the cosmic plan where no gesture was without a larger meaning, where for anyone to be at a given place at a given time was itself an act, a presentness that had to be accounted for. So he stood there wondering with a touch of astonishment and gratefulness and fear, with a sense of his own mischief, whether she had come to be with him, had been sent as the gift for his enduring.

The school Inspector, before departing that morning, had instructed her to put the boy in Standard Six because he was too big to be among the small Standard Four children. This she explained to Alford George, in her throaty lulling voice, her large eyes pools of smoke, her slender hands sculpturing soft waterfalls and waves and vases as she talked, so that Alford George, regarding with new wisdom and his own terror this young woman who had forced him to step back a pace, now felt it necessary to fix his eyes firmly upon her, leaning forward wary and alert as if also wanting to alert her to the danger she had released with the breathlessness and lace and perfume of her coming; and it was not until she left, her eyelids downfluttering, her chin upthrust, a mysterious female provocation and entice-ment and challenge communicated from her to him, bringing the faint outbreath of a smile to his lips, that he exhaled, awoke in the aftertaste of her presence and turned to discover that the boy standing there was the one a few months earlier he had refused entry into his class because he was over-age. He got angry again, really at the Inspector whom he felt had used her to instruct him. He was not going to be instructed. He sent one of the boys to call her.

This time he watched her come towards his class with her droopy skirt, her white bodice edged with lace, slower now with a tramping slanted left-handed walk, almost with the apology of one who had conquered where she had hoped to surrender, with a little smile to put him at his ease and not to tease him as she had done before.

It was she, she confessed, who had suggested to the Inspector that the boy be put in the Exhibition class, even though he was over-age. 'At least he'd get a chance to learn something.'

'Why didn't you come directly to me?' he asked with his most intimidating frown.

'I was afraid . . .'

'Of me?' he asked.

'Was,' she said, the suppressed laughing in her eyes sending him reeling, scrambling in his mind to hold on to what he was saying.

And then he had turned to the boy who during Miss Ollivera's timeless presence had remained before the blackboard where she had released him, sturdy, placid, heavy-limbed, with the dumb enquiring and defenceless eyes of a young goat. His calves glist-ened from being rubbed with coconut oil and his hammer-shaped head was trimmed down to the scalp, a low, uneven trim, splayed with erratic furrows, each occupying its own highway, criss-

65

crossing his head in those severe patterns we called zugs. His short-sleeved blue shirt was buttoned right up to his chin, his khaki pants, too tight already and a bit too short for his growing frame, gripped his thighs and strained against his buttocks, and he wore socks, limp frail slips of netting that barely reached his ankles, were contending instead with his feet for a place inside his shoes.

For a moment Alford George felt that he had been transported back in time and was looking into his own face. This boy was the image of the kind of clown that as a schoolboy he, Alford, must have presented to the world. He wanted to turn him away immediately. But she was there, her scent in his nostrils.

'OK,' he said to Miss Ollivera, relenting; in that moment deciding that, yes, she was the one sent to rescue him. 'Next time it would be better if you have any dealings with my class to come directly to me.'

Now, Alford George found himself at school early on mornings in time to watch her come in, sweep into the building with her long-limbed left-handed dancer's grace and the cheerful mischief of her countenance as if she had encountered something delightful on the way and was holding back the laughter until she met him to share it with: 'Good morning, Mr George,' and for him to answer, 'Good morning, Miss Ollivera,' sometimes their eyes meeting and catching and knitting, enclosing them both, as conspirators joined in regarding a slightly ridiculous world; and against every practice of his own, his own smile would spread outwards from his eyes and relax his own face so that sometimes in order to maintain his image of aloofness he would bite it off lest it be shown how easily he was destroyed.

At home he sang 'Unchained Melody' by was it Al Hibbler or Brook Benton?

> Oh, my love, my darling,
> I hunger for your touch . . .

Sometimes at home, hearing the semp, the bird in the cage, break out in song, its tiny breast trembling, its soul poured out, he would feel pass over him, through him, wave after wave of what felt like his heart folding, and he would find in his nostrils the smell of her perfume, or, turning the pages of a book, he would hear in the scraping of the paper the rustle of her dress and know that he was lost.

And then, as if it was the most natural thing in the world, he found himself in those timeless afternoons pushing his bicycle alongside her as she walked from school to the taxi stand along the quiet street past the little jalousied wooden houses in their gardens fenced with hibiscus or sweet lime. It was natural too that on the days he gave lessons to his class she would remain in school to write out her programme for the next day, completing it just as he finished his lessons so he could say, 'You're leaving, Miss Ollivera?'

And for her to answer, 'Oh, yes, Mr George.' And for them to walk out of the school together.

Abruptly one day she made him stop the bicycle. 'This is foolishness,' she said, and hopped sideways on to the bar of the bicycle. 'Ride,' she said, folding her skirt over her legs. 'Why couldn't you think of this?' letting her body sink against his chest. 'You're a coward, you know, Alford.'

'Yes,' Alford said to his bird as he changed the water and fed it, 'she has come to save me.'

He invited her to see him play a cricket match. He took her to dances, to the beach. He performed for her. One night they left the dance in Mayaro Government School and sat on the beach. He held her and when he felt the tremor of her body and the yielding in her voice, he was so touched that he felt he would save her. He would not allow her to be the sacrifice. She had too much promise for this place.

'You must go away,' he said. 'Get out into the world.'

'Yes,' she said. Then she told him that it had been her intention to come to the school, to work there, to save enough money and go to meet her brother who was already in London. All the arrangements were made.

'So you had it worked out all the time. Congrats,' he said.

She saw that he was hurt and she tried to hold him. He let her hold him. She knew that she should have told him. She had meant to tell him, 'But I felt I would be warning you and I didn't want to warn you because I did not know where it would lead. I wanted things to develop naturally.'

'Well, they have. Now you will see snow,' he said. But he was hurt. 'Everybody,' he mused, 'has everything worked out. Except me. '

'You make me sound like a traitor.'

'You are not a traitor.'

'You can change everything,' she said. 'All you have to do is to ask me to stay.'

'There is nothing here for you,' he said.

'Ask me! Ask me to stay.'

'Don't tempt me,' he said.

'Well, it's settled,' Alford George said to his bird. 'It's settled,' he said to the wind and the trees and the hills and the pain in his soul. But it wasn't really.

On her last Friday in school, he was sitting below the tamarind tree in the schoolyard, watching the children let loose for their afternoon games, their rejoicing limbs and screams imposing upon him a sense of age, the pain of loss. Mr Lyons, the sports master, was teaching the bigger girls netball, coaching them, straightening their shoulders, fixing their arms: how to shoot, how to jump, how to pass, how to guard. 'Guard me!' he says, taking the ball, holding it high above his head as they leap impossibly in what is partly play, their bodies pressing against his, to take the ball from him. 'Jump! Shoot!' The girls' starched skirts, limp from the week's wearing, swirling around their lean thighs, their breasts trembling as they show Lyons how well they are learning. There is this one girl, taller than the others, whose elegance sets her apart, her plaited hair, sculptured face, perspiring nose, one back-flung leg, eyes on the hoop, a statue of fluency as she freezes to shoot: ballerina of Cunaripo. Ballerina in the Bush. He turns away. Around the cricket pitch in the middle of the playing-field, a troop of boys waiting to begin their game are putting up wickets and dividing themselves into two teams. Nearby, the girls are skipping rope, screaming, as they turn the rope faster and faster: 'Salt . . . Vinegar . . . Mustard . . . Pepper . . . Pepper, pepper!' Miss Ollivera, her shoes in one hand, enters their game. She jumps barefooted, shrieking like a child in terrified delight, holding down her skirt with the other hand as the rope is turned faster, faster. And then she is coming towards him, her shoes in her hands, on her face that laughing

68

mischievous look that made even the children declare, 'Miss crazy, yes,' her eyes flashing the secret of their intimacy as if suddenly she didn't care who knew, who saw, looking down on him sitting there, her eyes alight as if just in that moment there was the temptation to fling herself atop him and embrace him in full view of teachers and children.

It was he who reached for her hand and drew her down beside him. Still breathless, she said, 'You see me? I've been skipping rope!' delighted, bending her head over her knees, wiping her face with her dresstail. He handed her his handkerchief and she patted her face with it, then her neck and chest, little pats – pat pat pat – that he would remember. The boys had put up their wickets. The schoolmaster passed through the yard by the pipes and the toilets, his strap slung over his shoulder, right-handed sleeve rolled up above the elbow, head down, body crouched, looking for scraps of paper thrown on the ground, stopping at each scrap either to pick it up himself or to say to the child nearest to it, 'Pick it up! Pick it up!' his hand touching the strap without removing it and then moving on, nodding his head briskly, jerkily, with the solemn insipidity of a turkey cock. He watched the boys picking their teams. He saw Peter standing, watching them. He saw the tall girl, Miss Elegance – Ballerina of the Bush – poised to shoot.

'Yes,' he said. 'You must go away.'

'So you have decided.'

It was he who felt like embracing her. Later that evening at the party he held for her at his quarters, she said, 'So you won't marry me,' like she was joking.

'And keep you here?'

She said in another, a graver tone, 'Alford, why don't you go away?'

'I am part of this now.' The words had slipped out.

It was the first time that he was admitting to himself that he was now part of the island. 'You go. I must stay with the children.'

'To save them?'

'If you put it like that.'

'Save them for what?'

He had been thinking of that question for a long time and he had an answer: 'Not save them *for*; save them *from*.'

'Alford, what are we saved for?'

'What are we saved for?' He repeated her question. 'That is what we must find out, Gloria.'

On the day that she was leaving, he went down to the ship, to the port in Port-of-Spain to see her off; and all the time to calm his racing mind he kept saying to himself, Saved. Saved. She is going to be saved, cheerful-looking on the outside, polite with all her friends and family there, everybody making the expected fuss over her and he a little on the edge of everybody, watching with a kind of uselessness, glancing at her and she casting an eye on him every now and then to find out if he was OK or if with all these people there she needed to come to his assistance and he glancing back that it was OK, was she all right and she nodding in her eyes yes, she was OK until at last it was time to say goodbye, for friends were leaving already and it was just the closest of family left and he went over to her and stood with this goodbye in his body, watching the almost comic strangeness of her, with her droopy skirt and a hat set upon her hair – a concession to fashion? to the cold? to the winter she was going into? – he, making a joke of it, saying, 'You cold already?' and her eyes filling with the distance that had already sprung between them crowding out the laughter. He put his arms around her and she faced him, each one looking into the eyes of the other, their bodies touching ever so slightly, and then she put her head on his shoulder and let him hold her, their bodies pressed together in that last forever embrace, and then her body stiffened and she drew herself away carefully and then she fiercely said, 'You could have changed all this.' And he looked at her, in his mind thinking: *I? I could have changed all this?* Wondering where he had been; thinking, *Where was I?* 'Goodbye,' as if she had been waiting to deliver this wound and blow before she left and he took it, it pierced him and he left not seeing anybody, his mind in a blur and went down the gangplank and off the ship and out of his hurt looked back to wave at her and to feel the coolness as she waved goodbye, Take that! and he put his hands in his pockets and walked a distance out of sight of her and stood alone by himself and waited until they pulled up the gangplank and the ship eased out the harbour, taking her.

It had remained a clear day, with the sky blue; and the sky was still as blue all the way back to Cunaripo. Though now, of course, she wasn't there. Everything was as it was: the slow dogs stretched out in the lazy street, the wooden houses surrounded by their flower gardens hedged from the road by hibiscus and sweetlime fences. All of it was there but nothing had substance. It was as if they were all shadows, as if her leaving had taken the life out of living things and left them shadows. He himself was a shadow. He felt no weight to his step, no sound to his voice, no solidity to his gestures. He forgot time. He felt the ache of a pain whose depth he could not fathom nor whose end anticipate.

'Now I know where nowhere is,' he said to the bird, as he sat at home on his couch. And when he looked up to see if the bird had heard him, wondering whether he had spoken aloud at all, it was to see the creature, its head flattened, its body stiffened, the neck and shoulders squeezed halfway between the bars of the cage, a covering of ants over its body, ants soldiering its feathers, the feathers rocking like sails as the ants toted them away. He felt a scream in his brain. He looked in the cage. The pans for food and water were dry. The bird had died of starvation. In its agony it had tried with no luck to squeeze through the bars of the cage. He buried the remains of the bird. He thought of burning the cage, but he didn't. He left it to hang empty on its nail.

I would be there sitting in his class to see him when in the new term he appeared before us that first day, his bearded face the colour of ashes, his trousers almost folded round his legs, the cloth puffed out and tuckered about the loops, his belt tightened to keep it on his waist, his white shirt buttoned all the way up his throat, with the thin stiff air of a sick bird, its feathers starched with death and with that bird's angular stillness, his eyes gleaming bright and glassy like that bird's eyes, with the bones of his face pressing against the skin and a mournful tiredness about his shoulders as if it would take all his strength to lift up his hands.

'Good morning, Sir!' chorused the children.

We watched him stand before our class, the fingers of his right hand clutching a rolled-up length of paper, the fingers of the other hand balled into a fist, looking out at us for that eternity, his Adam's apple bobbing up and down as if he was testing his throat for sound; then, with a voice scraped up with all his strength from the depths of his toes, he said hoarsely, 'Good morning!'

And so relieved were we to hear him speak we shouted again, 'Good morning, Sir!'

He unfurled the length of paper. It was a map of the world. He hung it over the blackboard. He opened his drawer and took out an eighteen-inch ruler.

'This,' he said, his hoarse whispery voice coming from the grave of his belly, pointing with the ruler, 'this is the world. The world. These are the Alps. Here are the Himalayas. This is Kilimanjaro. This is London,' all of it done in slow motion. He spoke to us about mountains, about rivers, about civilizations, about cities. He pointed out New York, he showed us Timbuktu. He spoke of tides, of currents. He showed us the Gulf Stream. Then, with his voice choking and the ruler trembling in his hand, he came down the archipelago of the Caribbean: 'This . . . this dot. This is your island.'

His armpits were soaking. He wiped the perspiration from his face and hands. He talked about dots, of points, of lines, of infinity, of zero. He told us of the death of his bird. He spoke of cul-de-sacs, of escape, of bars. He moved from one subject to another, forgetful of time, deaf to the sounding of the recess bell and we of the class awed, cowed by his powerful remoteness, afraid to interrupt and tell him that it had rung.

In the weeks that followed we couldn't tell for sure what subject he was teaching and not one of us felt bold enough to ask him. We sat intimidated, amazed at the sorrowful explosive potential that tick-tocked in him. His voice became louder as he went on and the whole school more subdued, the teachers pretending not to hear him, going ahead with their lessons until even that became impossible and the children from other classes turned to listen to him and the teachers from those classes with contrived casualness strolled by the class in the hope of awakening him to the fact that he was disturbing them.

Many times the schoolmaster strode resolutely towards our

class and we thought that now, yes, he was going to do something; but, confronted by the brilliant gleam in Mr George's eyes and the sorrowful slump of his shoulders, he shrank away, wiping his face with his handkerchief.

Mr George was talking about the capture of Trinidad from the Spanish by the British. Instead of giving battle, Chacon, the Spanish governor, had ordered the Spaniards to burn their ships. To Chacon's shame, the island was taken without the firing of a shot. Mr George stopped and looked at us.

'What?' he shot at us suddenly. 'What are we saved for?

'You?' he asked, moving from desk to desk. 'You? You?' his index finger slashing the air, his body supple and feminine as he bristled with anger derived from we knew not where.

'All stand!' he commanded, for no one among us had even attempted an answer.

We stood. He looked at us in one grand eternal magnetic pause, then tears welled in his eyes as he returned to his senses. 'Sit. Sit down!' biting his lips, turning his back so we wouldn't see his face.

One morning after recess, he asked us to take out our copybooks, clasped his hands behind his back, and, pacing backwards and forwards before us began to call out words: 'Infinitude, boundless, constellation...' the pitch of his voice mounting, then falling, when a word called forth a particular softness, to a whisper: 'Felicity, elegance, svelte...' We did not know whether he meant for us to spell the words or give their meanings. Not daring to question him, we began writing, some of us putting down meanings, others trying to spell, all of us racing hopelessly against the rapidity of his dictation, until unable to keep up, we stopped, some to doodle, others to make paper aeroplanes to sail across the class when his back was turned. I began a game of tick-tack-toe with the boy next to me. His words went on, 'Epoch, galaxies, archipelago, illuminate, alluring...'

The lunch bell rang, the rest of the school went out, he went on. We remained seated, looking at him now as he went on with clear allusive rhythm. The school bell rang again. Other children returned, still he went on, through the afternoon, past recess. The bell rang for school to be dismissed for the day. The rest of the school recited the evening prayer. Then they left. None of us

73

said anything, but now all tick-tack-toe, all plane-making, all doodling stopped. The schoolmaster came up behind him on a couple of occasions since the dismissal of school, but turned back, thinking perhaps we were engaged in some special project. Some of the braver boys now began to look down at their wrists and their imaginary watches. The whole class had stopped writing. Suddenly, as if catapulted into the present, Mr George stopped. He looked us over.

He roared, 'Why is Peter alone writing?'

And then I, we, all of us turned to look at Peter scribbling frantically.

'All stand!' Mr George commanded.

He marched to the blackboard. We watched him take down Betsy and fold one end over his fist, then snake out the fearful length of its body. He began with the front of the class, each child individually, 'You? Why were you not writing?' his eyes filled with the unreasoning anger that at times consumed him, his mouth tightening, his lips trembling. He came to me. He lifted the strap. I watched him silently, half tensing my body because in that situation I did not want to insult him by putting out my hand. The strap curled over his shoulder. I heard the schoolmaster's scream: 'Mr George!'

The lash fell limply on my shoulder.

'Mr George,' the schoolmaster said, speaking soothingly now, almost with apology. 'I think I should let you know that school is over.'

Dazed, groggy, the strap still held in his fist, his eyes blinking him back into presentness, Mr George looked around him and perhaps for the first time realized that the rest of the school was empty. He straightened himself, his hands falling limply at his sides, 'Dismiss!' he said, his voice nearly inaudible, turning and walking to his table and sinking into his chair.

Softly we took up our books and filed out of the classroom, our heads bowed so as not to have to look at his face, that is, all of us except Peter, who broke the line and went to Mr George's table and held out to him the stack of copybooks into which he had spent nearly the whole day writing.

Mr George was flabbergasted, 'What are you giving me this for?' making no move to accept them.

74

'The spelling, Sir,' Peter said.

'The spelling?'

'The words you just finished calling out, Sir.'

Mr George looked at him disbelieving. 'Sit down,' he said, taking the copybooks, suddenly sober, feeling in that moment a new strange burden. 'I will look at them.'

As Alford George would explain in the foreword to the book that was at that time not even a thought in his head (but that was very much on its way), he was always aware of Peter in a special way from the day Gloria Ollivera brought him to his class. And while he felt grateful to the boy for being an instrument in bringing them together, he had kept his distance because, as much as reminding him of Gloria Ollivera, the boy reminded him of himself, his hesitancy, his awkwardness, his plodding, his futile efforts to establish himself among his fellows. It was a self that he was never proud of, that he had always been trying to escape or forget, and seeing it in the boy, he had kept the boy at arm's length.

As he looked at the copybooks filled with misspelt words, he had felt himself grow almost angry: 'Why did you do it?'

The boy seemed genuinely surprised, 'Do what, Sir?'

'The others had stopped, why did you continue writing?'

'I want to learn, Sir.'

It was an answer he should have expected. Of course. Of course, what else? Even in the most absurd situation, this boy had pressed on. For what? He wasn't even eligible for the College Exhibition examination.

'For what? What did you keep on for? Don't you know that you are too old to sit the College Exhibition examination? Didn't you know?' His words had come out with a sternness that neither had expected, and the boy had answered defensively: 'Yes, Sir.'

' "Yes, Sir?" Then why . . .?' And even as he was saying the words, it hit him: How can a child of thirteen be too old to learn? It was as if a light had been turned on in my head. It was not the boy who should be embarrassed, it was I, me, the teacher. And as the terrible import of such thoughts hit me, I felt my entire body grow numb. I realized that I was a traitor to my own self. I had led the children astray.

75

'OK,' he said, more to himself than to the boy. 'OK.' He was choking.

Nineteen years as a teacher. And he had spent them contributing to a system that gave all its rewards, put all its prestige towards training a few students for escape. Failure was to not escape. To fail to escape was defeat; defeat even before you began. And that was why you could accept the secondclassness of the place. Secondclassness was · the punishment for the defeated, the failures. What redeemed this system? How many did escape? How many did in fact win a College Exhibition? In all the years the school had been preparing students for the examination, three of them had won College Exhibitions. Those left behind were the failures, the dregs. He realized that saving the two or three, if you could call it saving, was not enough for his life's vocation. If he was to go on, he would have to begin afresh to prepare children for living in the island.

'You keeping the copybooks, Sir?' It was as if the boy has sensed his conversion.

'Yes. Leave these with me. Look!' And Alford put a hand in his pocket and drew out some money. 'Here! Buy yourself some new ones.'

That same evening Alford came to the barbershop by Victory and sit down in the chair. He didn't say anything. He didn't tell me what to do or anything. He just sit down there like if he half dead and don't care anything and is only here he could come to see if a trim could cool his brains and help him start his life again. I get up and I myself ain't say nothing and I take up the cloth and tie it round his neck and I start on his head and when I finish, I trim his beard and his moustache neat and smooth-looking. And when I finish I take off the cloth and dust it off plop! plop! plop! and he get up from where he was sitting and push his hand in his pocket and pay me my money and he leave the shop as smooth and soft as he come in. And not a word. He just halfway look in the mirror and kinda nod at me. He didn't say anything. And I wouldn't'ta been surprised to hear that just so he go out and do something crazy.

And this was the thought Mr Penco, the schoolmaster, had when Alford came into his office the next morning, not, as Penco expected, to make an apology, but to tell him of the terrible damage the College Exhibition system was wreaking on the nation's children under the guise of educating them and to ask, not ask, demand that he put an immediate stop to it.

Mr Penco had listened with growing alarm. He had known of the relationship Alford had with Miss Ollivera and had some suspicion of the effect her departure had on him.

'Maybe you should take a rest.'

Mr Penco himself was prepared to take the more demanding Exhibition class and let Alford teach the Sixth and Seventh standards he, Mr Penco, was then teaching.

Such an exchange would not solve the problem. What he wanted the schoolmaster to do was to abolish the College Exhibition class and reorient the entire teaching programme to give every child that came to school an education.

'But I do not have the authority to do anything of the kind,' Mr Penco pleaded. 'That is a decision for the Ministry.'

'Very well, I'll go to the Ministry.'

'You will have to take leave,' Mr Penco said. He didn't want to threaten, but he felt the need to safeguard himself.

'Then I'll take leave,' Alford said.

For the remainder of the day the school was in confusion. The schoolmaster called a staff meeting to see if he could get other teachers to convince Alford George of the folly of what he was attempting.

Alford did not change his position. Mr Penco neither condemned him nor supported him. 'In principle,' he said. As a teacher, his task was not to make policy but to follow the policy made by the Department. He couldn't prevent his staff from thinking. He couldn't prevent fresh ideas emerging, but his job was to ensure that the policy was upheld. The other teachers were not as ambiguous. Some of them blamed it on the departure of Gloria Ollivera, others on Alford's too intense involvement with the children. They had always been afraid for him. Now, poor fellow, he gone. He gone off.

Mr Lyons, one of the more senior teachers, a married man with an abundance of children, who had made a career out of his frustration over not getting the promotion he felt he deserved, angry at what he saw as another loss, found this the occasion to

77

justify his own lack of enthusiasm for the job: 'You see me?' said Mr Lyons. 'You see me? This school will never send me crazy, like Don Quixote. And you know why? I don't take them on. They could do what they want, I don't take them on.'

Before he left for Port-of-Spain, Alford George came to the Exhibition class and stood before us with the paleness of the resurrected, his beard shaved off, his head trimmed, to tell us that he would be no longer teaching us. He was sorry to disappoint those of us who had begun with him, but he really couldn't go on as it was. There had to be changes made and he was going to Port-of-Spain to the Ministry to see that they were made.

We were all very moved, we of the Exhibition class. And I remember feeling very sad about the rumours already circulating that Alford George had gone off his head. 'Goodbye, Sir,' we chorused. 'Goodbye, Sir!' And he waved to us as if he was really off to another world.

In Port-of-Spain, Alford went directly to the Director of Education. The Director wouldn't see him. His secretary came out to say that the director was engaged.

'Could he make an appointment, then?'

Yes. The Director could see him . . . er . . . er . . . on the 17th of June. It was then the 27th of March.

'It is urgent,' Alford told her.

She took pity on him. 'You could wait here until he come out and see if he will see you. Boy, that man always busy.'

Alford decided to wait. At one o'clock the secretary looked around and saw him and said, 'Boy, you still here? I don't think you will see him today. If you really want to see somebody, maybe you should try to see the Minister. He does talk to people.'

Alford went to the office of the Minister. He wasn't available on such short notice without an appointment. What was his business? the secretary wanted to know. Alford told her. She promised to get back to him. That entire week, he went from official's office to official's office; but found nobody of a rank capable of making a decision available to him. There was one remaining recourse: the public, the newspapers.

It was while he was at *The Standard* waiting to speak to a reporter who had broken off listening to his story to answer the telephone that his eyes fell on the newspaper lying on the desk. On the front page was an article on the Civil Rights struggles of Dr Martin Luther King, Jr., with photographs of Martin Luther King and his inspiration, Mahatma Gandhi. And, just like that, it became clear to him what he would do to get the attention of the authorities. He would go on a fast, like Mahatma Gandhi. He had never fasted before. And up to that time he had no idea of how he would go about it. The details would be drawn out of him by the reporter.

'Where you going to be doing this fasting?' the reporter asked tiredly. He was not a real reporter but the leading poet of the island, of the country, of the region, a caustic man by name Shabine Villaroel, who was angry with the country for the neglect that had forced him to do reporting to help out with his own living.

'You going to be eating anything?' Villaroel asked him.

'Did Mahatma Gandhi eat anything?' Alford asked.

'Just like a Trinidadian,' Villaroel scolded. 'Gandhi didn't eat nothing and you will eat nothing. Great as Mahatma Gandhi and you ain't even start to not eat yet.'

Alford was immediately apologetic. He had no intention of comparing himself to the great Mahatma. He just wanted to gauge what he should do. Maybe if Gandhi drank only water, then he would drink only orange juice. It was just guidelines he was trying to establish.

'OK, OK,' Villaroel said. 'Drink orange juice. What you wearing?'

'My ordinary clothes,' Alford said.

'Listen, man,' Villaroel was uncharacteristically sympathetic, 'how you going to wear your ordinary clothes? Did Mahatma wear ordinary clothes? This is a performance. You doing this to gain attention. You have to dress the part.'

'You think I should put on a suit, then?'

'A suit? In this hot sun? You want to dead or what?'

'You right,' Alford said. 'You right. I think I have just the clothes for the occasion.'

'So when you starting?'

Alford was going to start this fast the same way he had started everything else, alone and uncertain. He was going to begin his fast next morning at seven. He was going to sit in front of the building of the Ministry of Education. He was going to fast until some official of some rank talk to him.

'Until they talk to you?' Villaroel asked him. 'What happen? You want to fast until you dead? Listen, man, if you fasting, fast for something. Fast until they change the system. That way at least you will die for something. Don't die just for them to talk to you. Die for the idea.'

'Write that then,' Alford said to him. 'Write that I will fast until they change the College Exhibition system.'

'Or until death,' said the poet.

'Or death,' said Alford.

'Good,' said the poet. 'And you better go and give the story to the other newspaper, because I don't know if these jokers here will print this story when I done with it.'

Alford thanked Villaroel and left for the other daily paper, *The Guardian*. He need not have worried. Not only did *The Standard* print the story under Villaroel's byline, they put it on the front page:

SCHOOLTEACHER BEGINS FAST TO THE DEATH,
BLASTS COLLEGE EXHIBITION EXAMINATION.

Next morning Alford arrived under the samaan tree in the front of the offices of the Ministry of Education, dressed in the long white gown and turban that he had retained from a Christmas play he had done with the children, a cushion to sit on, a Thermos flask of hot water to drink – he was having water and fruit juice during the fast – and a placard that read: STOP THE COLLEGE EXHIBITION EXAMINATION. He was totally unknown in Port-of-Spain and people gathered at the Ministry did not know what to make of him. Some had been drawn there by the newspaper headline; and others, struck by the spectacle he presented, as he walked from the taxi stand at Independence Square through the city, had followed him, the majority exhilarated by the exciting possibility of another young man gone mad doing something crazy, a lesser number, on the look-out for signs and wonders as they waited for Armageddon, waiting to give support when he stopped to deliver his message to sinners to repent. Alford sat under the samaan tree, his legs crossed in the lotus position, when it began to rain. In order to establish his resolve before the assembled people and the cameramen and reporters who were just then arriving, he decided to remain seated while it rained.

Seeing that the rain would wet him, Sunita Ramnarine, a typist who travelled daily from her home in Arouca to her job at the Education Ministry and whom Alford was to celebrate in one of his poems from the book he would write, *Poems of Fasting*, rushed out of her office with an open umbrella and placed it over his head. It was this photograph, capturing the stoicism of Alford and the concern of Sunita, that appeared in both daily papers next morning. Along with it was the poem that he had written even as the rain fell:

> *Rain didn't wet me,*
> *The sun didn't burn me,*
> *Just was my cause.*
> *Angels sent Sunita . . .*

Every day Alford George appeared dressed in white, wearing variously, the loose cotton wrap of the Indian, the dhoti, the loose cotton gown of the Shouters, Nehru jackets and baggy trousers and baggy shirts and different styles of cloth caps and head wraps provided by fashion designers who, seeing how well he looked in the picture with Sunita, had rushed to outfit him. He came at seven in the morning and left at five in the evening. He brought with him the same cushion, the Thermos and each day a fresh placard:

EDUCATE NOT DISCRIMINATE – SAVE THE CHILDREN – HOW MANY FAILURES FOR ONE SUCCESS???

From the very start there were people who accused him of trying to embarrass the government and who seized upon his choice of Hindu clothes and Orisha turbans to accuse him of seeking cheap publicity. These came out to heckle him; but there were others who had no special feeling for his cause but who had come to give support to him based just on the fact that he was protesting. It was to these he felt a growing responsibility. All at once he had the sense of the whole world watching him, of the need to be careful and calm and to husband his strength for a long fast. In this cause, he began now to speak more slowly and more softly and with the sincerity and posture of saintliness that made some people make the sign of the cross when he was finished addressing them.

Each day more and more people came: bands of schoolchildren running away from school to stand across the road from him in little groups chewing gum and exchanging whispers; housewives with loaves of bread and baskets of fruit; shouters trailing incense smoke from censers made of condensed-milk tins with holes punched into their sides; shifts of hefty women from the Shango Baptist faith coming to pray with him, sanctifying the ground on which he sat with graceful dances as they curtsied and poured libation of holy water from brass vases; Catholic nuns counting the beads of rosaries; Hindu pundits with their greying hair parted and the red dots painted on their foreheads, pious men in their own right, giving him tips on posture and teaching him how to breathe; self-styled revolutionaries asking him questions to see if he was the leader they wanted for, as they called it, The Next Round. Members of trades unions came; guerrillas who had remained underground since 1969 resurfaced; members of Masonic lodges; a group of unemployed youths came to him with a constitution for a new political party to which they had already elected him leader. Mother Earth, a woman who fifteen years earlier had left the city to go alone into the forest of Matelot to live naked with nature, came out with fifteen of her followers dressed in skirts made of plantain leaves to tell him not to waste his time trying to change the system, leave it. Leave Babylon and come back with us to the land, to the forest, to nature, where the lion will lie down with the lamb. Calvin Small, a badJohn who had provided the muscle for the National Party in earlier election campaigns and who was rewarded with the job of foreman on government-run Crash Programmes and was now disaffected because of their ingratitude. They had fired him, he said, without so much as a Thankyou. He did not remember to mention that he was the man who was responsible for drawing the wages of a hundred and fifteen fictitious names. Calvin Salandy, a political has-been from the cobwebs of the West Indian National Party of the 1950s, who each election wandered from party to party, going up for election for six of them in the thirty years of his involvement in politics. Calvin Rodriguez with the green fatigues and black beret and a beard to make him look like a Cuban revolutionary, preferably Che Guevara. Members of the Orisha worshippers, who after years of supporting the National Party had not been granted legal status in the country. From Carapichaima came Indians who wanted him to be their leader because they would have a better chance of gaining political power than they would have contesting under an Indian leader. Nurses from the St Ann's mental home, with patients in cast-off jackets, ancient ties and tight-fitting trousers, came to get him to intercede with the government for more beds in the hospital; cooks from the same institution wanting sanitary equipment with which to prepare egg-nog; people who were tired waiting on the National Party for a programme of land reform; Rosco Bishop and his organization of seven persons who wanted more from democracy than voting once every five years; artists who were in need of recognition, not to mention support, led by John De John who had been writing novels and poems for thirty-five years and wanted a publishing company formed so that he and other writers would get their fiction out into the world. University scientists came with plans and programmes for feeding the people of the nation from the coconut palm, and from bananas, banana rice, banana flour, banana sugar; squatters from the heights of Lady Young Road, wanting squatting to be regularized and roads constructed so they could transport the materials to build their houses; people wanting roads repaired; people wanting water in their taps in Trou Macaque. And there was Angela Vialva, almost apologetic, her hunched shoulders, her large eyes droopy, wandering over his body. She had come to plead the plight of domestics and to see if he would be interested in becoming involved in a programme to educate them and help with setting up pre- schooling centres for their children in Laventille, Caroni and The Beetham.

For the duration of his fast, Angela was never far from his side. She took upon herself the duty to protect him from those other women who would gobble him up if he was left unattended, persistent women who would be the last ones to leave on an evening, remaining in earnest conversation with

83

some intense political activist while he closed off his own discussions, then, at exactly the right moment, turning to ask him if he wanted a ride to where he was going. The weaker he seemed, the more nurturing the women affected and he accepted their support in front of Angela's open and challenging eyes, with the hypocrisy of his discretion, finding his way into houses where he was given a bed for the night, to emerge next morning, dropped off in shiny motor cars, leaning on the arm of the solicitous women. Some people had felt that he wouldn't last, but after two weeks it became clear that he was serious and determined and, just from that, those who had held back came to see him before he was swept to power and they were left out. Now came Adolphe Carabon, whose father owned nearly all the lands in Cascadu, apologetic, timid, standing apart from the crowd around him until Alford beckoned to him with the tired gesture of an exhausted master and he came forward with his countenance suddenly changed to a kind of instinctive aliveness to ask, 'How you going?' and what Alford thought was the more curious question: 'You think you could go through with this, boy? Eh? You think you could go through with this, not eating?' Alford wasn't sure that he answered him. And there were teachers from the school in Cunaripo, Mr Lyons, ragged from the journey by bus from Cunaripo, bringing him up to date on the domestic issues of the school, fixated still on his own problems, whispering, what had obviously become his anthem, 'You see me. That school. That school will never send me crazy like Don Quixote. And you know why? I don't take them on.' There was Mr Penco with his new wife, an Indian woman nearly half his height, nervously fingering his necktie and saying what he must have given much thought to, 'We miss you at the school. We are very proud of you up there.' Sonan Lochan came too with his dark shades on to make a vague promise to help in his campaign when he was ready to launch his political party. And there were his friends Ashton and Floyd, Ashton asking over and over again in voices of deep concern and with a suppressed smile, as if the whole thing was not to be taken too seriously, 'What happen to you, boy? What happen?' as if they were talking to a con man; Floyd holding his crotch and saying, 'You must be getting a set of woman from all this, eh?' He didn't know how to answer

84

them. And yet it would be Ashton who would bring him the most surprising visitor of all. With an air of mystery, Ashton presented him: 'You know who this is?'

Alford felt he was on trial. He looked at the slim Indian man, with his brightly flowered shirt and the even more brightly flowered tie that took up nearly the whole of his chest. 'You are . . .? Lenny? Kenny. Lennos!'

'Kennos,' said Kennos, passing a hand over his slicked-down hair, fingering the spot where it was thinning.

'Yes, Kennos.' It was Lochan's nephew, Kenwyn, the boy who back when Alford was in Standard Five had been chosen to play instead of him, and whose walking away had caused Alford to be left out and later to be chosen to umpire. Kenwyn had left to go to El Dorado Presbyterian School, sat and won a College Exhibition there and had gone on to Queen's Royal College and then, through another scholarship, to Cambridge University where he had studied philosophy and religion. He went next to Winnipeg in Canada for his PhD and his wife – Ha-ha! – had come back to form the Church of Fellowship and Joy.

'There is a world we need to inhabit together, all the people,' said Kennos. He had a radio programme on Sunday mornings and was now planning a crusade to encompass the whole island, where all God's children would come together under the one sky: 'I have come,' he said, 'to offer my services to your new, our new party and government. I believe that working together we can really save this country.' He was prepared to accept the portfolio of Minister of Education and Culture, or Planning and Development, or Foreign Minister. He didn't want Trade.

Alford was cautious, 'If we do have a political party, we shall need to go to the people.'

'Agreed,' Kennos said. 'Just as soon as we select the Cabinet. Once we have selected the Cabinet we can then go to the people. Once they see that they are represented by good people they will give us their support.'

Kennos left a little disappointed at Alford's lack of enthusiasm, of passion. 'Look, if you not sure of . . .'

'Of what?'

'I mean if you are reluctant to take decisions . . . No. Never mind. You be Prime Minister.' And Kennos left him his telephone numbers, one for his home in Tacarigua, the other for the church.

The next day Angela broached the same subject. 'Your fast coming to an end. We have to organize these people before everything dissipate. You know Trinidad, how fast we forget.'

His days of fasting had weakened him and he did not totally trust his own judgement. He wanted to wait till he was stronger. There was also the very essential matter. He wanted to go and talk first to the people.

'The people, the people, the people,' Angela said. 'Who do you think we are? We are the people. The people that you waiting on waiting on you.'

The push for Alford to form a political Party intensified. Businessmen came offering him loudspeakers and suggesting venues for his election meetings. One of them sent a letter in which he proposed a name for the Party and a list of names of persons to form the cabinet and one to be speaker. The secessionist movement in Tobago sent to let him know that they would throw in their lot with him if he would grant Tobago independence from Trinidad. In Woodford Square, Aldwyn Primus, resident preacher, philosopher, revolutionary and mystic, was revealing to his spellbound lunch-time audience the signs that pointed to the inevitable victory of the yet unformed party. At his home in Tacarigua, Kennos had decided to move things along by himself preparing the manifesto for the Party.

By the time Alford had fasted for thirty-two days, it was impossible for the politicians to further ignore him. The Leader of the Opposition, who had sent out signals to Alford that they could work together, now moved a motion to have the College Exhibition examination debated in the Parliament. In response, the Leader of Government Business countered that such a debate would be premature because the government had already set up a One-Man Commission of Enquiry into all aspects of the College Exhibition Examination and were then awaiting his findings. Anxious to bring to an end a story that had peaked already, the newspapers interpreted this action by the government as a victory for Alford's vigilance, temperance, courage and steadfastness, and urged him in nearly identical editorials to bring his fast to a dignified end and not to go and risk his health. The nation was certain that the qualities which he had displayed so admirably in the cause of education would serve him well in the important role they believed he was destined to play in the greater affairs of the nation.

At a press conference organized by Angela Vialva, Alford George, surrounded by Dr Kennos, Mother Earth, Calvin Salandy and Calvin Rodriguez, thanked the people for their support.

This was not his victory alone, he said. It was a people's victory and if it says anything to the authorities it is that the voice of the people will be heard. Most of the people had come to hear him announce the formation of his political party and Dr Kennos had come armed with his manifesto as well as a set of application forms to give out to people who wanted to join the Party. All of them were disappointed. Whether through caution or principle or fear, Alford wanted to first speak to the people. This produced the first rift in the unformed party, Calvin Rodriguez grumbling that if Alford couldn't make up his mind about the Party, it was better Dr Kennos take over as leader. Alford refused to be rushed. If the others felt he was too slow, then he would be happy to withdraw entirely and they could go on and form their party.

Alford returned to Cunaripo with the sainted aura of celebrity to the discovery of another problem. He had been suspended indefinitely and without pay for abandoning his post of teacher without official permission. Calvin Rodriguez who had identified himself publicly with the new political party, on his own initiative called a press conference to say that what the government was doing was cowardly. It was a crude attempt to separate Alford George from his political base and take away the means of his livelihood. Be assured, he said, that nothing like that would stop the onward march of the progressive forces. Be assured, he said, that the population would not be hoodwinked by the gymnastics of reactionary bloodsuckers who have defined their duty as standing to bar the doorway to a people's liberation. The villagers, my mother included, took an entirely different course. In spite of the publicity on radio, television and the newspapers given to Alford George's objection to the College Exhibition examination, they listened to their own imagination and came up with the idea that behind Alford George's suspension was the attempt by people in high places to take him away from our little village school and send him to teach the children of the rich in Port-of-Spain.

'They find he too good to be teaching poor countrypeople children,' my mother declared. I tried to point her to the newspaper reports and to what Alford George himself had said. My father tried to add his bit; but my mother was not taking us on.

'We not going to take this sitting down,' she warned. True to her word, she rallied the villagers to what they saw as their cause. They held up placards, sang songs, chanted slogans in a demonstration in front the school, calling for Alford George to stay. Their victory did not take long. Alford had become a national figure and the media were set to martyr him. After just three days of demonstrations, the Ministry decided to settle for a mild reprimand and reinstated him with full pay for the period of his absence, the Minister of Education himself appearing on the radio and television to dispel any insinuation that Alford was in any way victimized by his Ministry.

My mother and the villagers were joyful. Dr Kennos and Calvin Rodriguez were clear that this was the most auspicious moment for them to announce the Party. Alford himself was thinking of holding a public meeting in Cunaripo to explain his objection to the College Exhibition examination. But, recognizing the political potential of the villagers' support and believing that he would profit from the prevailing confusion, he kept his mouth shut and let them see him as the martyred schoolteacher prepared to stand up for the people against a bullying ministry. It was the logic of this appeal that led him to make the promise that he would give private lessons to those of their children in that year's Exhibition class. So in the end it was as a hero that Alford George resumed his career as teacher. He had come home now with renewed energy, enthusiasm and passion. Once again he postponed the formation of the party.

He turned his attention to the Post Primary class now assigned to him, his objective now to root them in their world. He introduced his class to literature by having his students tell and discuss Anancy stories. He made them sing and discuss the structure and content of calypso. He got his footballers and cricketers to chart and calculate the angles of their passes and strokes. He discussed with them the circle, the globe, the ball, leather, thread. He moved from geography into history into civics. He took them hiking past the rivers along the tracts that as a child he had so cautiously travelled with his brothers. He took them to a motor car garage and got the mechanic to talk to them about engines. He got villagers to come and talk to them about medicinal herbs and plants.

For Christmas he put on a Christmas play. He invited a Shango leader to come in and talk to them about the Orishas. He had a pundit come and talk to them about Hinduism and an Imam explain Islam. He took them to Shango ceremonies and to the Muslim ceremony of Hosay and encouraged them to light deyas for the Indian festival of Divali. In addition, he wrote letters to the newspapers under the *nom de plume* of 'Cascadu' on subjects ranging from cricket to Anancy as a moral guide. In that period also, he completed the writing of his book of poetry, *Poems of Fasting*. He published it himself, with a photograph of himself on the cover, one hand holding a telephone to one ear while he used the other one to lightly prop up his chin. In the book, he used a full page to acknowledge all who helped to make the book possible, from Miss Berisford, his primary school teacher, to the boy Peter, the mirror of himself who had said, 'I want to learn, Sir,' Sunita Ramnarine who had lent him her umbrella, and Angela Vialva who symbolized the people who stuck with him through the fast. He had an Introduction by Mr John De John, the novelist from Matura, and a foreword by himself of fifteen pages, half the book, which gave a substantial portion of his life's story, from his childhood to the occasion of The Fast.

Angela Vialva organized a launching of the book in Port-of-Spain and a dramatic reading of his poems at the Anglican Cathedral. It featured the Malick Folk Performers doing the dances while actors from the Trinidad Theatre Company did the drama and narration. She had publicized it well and the Cathedral was full to capacity with people from every creed and ethnic origin. Dressed in the dhoti and turban that had been his favourite wear during the Fast, Alford thanked the people for their support and goodwill and read the poem that he hoped would become another national anthem:

Many races equal stand
Voices blended raised to sing
The goodwill of our blessed land
The beauty of our daughters
The bravery of our worthy sons
The talents of our people proud

Break asunder old worthless chains
Forge new ones of love
Raise high your hands, La Trinity
With new strong chains
Of fellowship, freedom, unity and love.

The response of the audience was overwhelming. Alford felt, as he looked out at them from where he stood on the pulpit, that the goodwill of people alone demonstrated that they all required a place. And it came to him afresh that he had to work to make this island a place where people didn't have to leave to find the world. He had to redouble his efforts with the children. The first major project that suggested itself to him was the organization of a band for Carnival.

The band he would organize would involve parents and children. It would depict the beauty and the promise of the people of the island. It would portray the Amerindians, the coming of Columbus, the importation of Africans, the arrival of Indians, of Chinese, of Portuguese, Europeans, Syrians. In order for people to understand one another he wanted them to take on the role of the other: Africans were to be the Conquistadores, the Buccaneers, the Pirates; Europeans were to be African warriors; Indians were to be Amerindians; and Chinese and Syrians were to be enslaved on sugar plantations. To make the band a success, Alford knew he had a lot of work to do to get people to support it and he set out to pay personal visits to those parents who had not traditionally been involved in Carnival. Everybody was interested, and the white families especially glad that neither they nor their children would be required to portray Columbus or any other European.

Three weeks before Carnival, disaster struck. Pastor Peter Prue of the Tabernacle of Righteousness and Light, fresh from an evangelical crusade across the island, appeared on television condemning Carnival as devil worship and calling on all true Christians to keep their distance from it if they did not want to put their souls at peril.

In the beginning, nobody took him on; but in a series of paid advertisements he continued his mischief. Fired by his own enthusiasm for what he was attempting, Alford, as the national figure he had become, decided to respond. In an article published in *The Standard*, he claimed Carnival as the future religion of the island, because it was the single celebration in which disparate races and classes of people could come with whatever was their contribution to celebrate freedom and fellowship without a feeling of patronage or alienation.

Pastor Peter Prue was delighted to have someone so prominent to take on. In a transparent attempt at publicizing himself in a field that was very competitive, with new churches springing up every day, he condemned the indoctrination of children into this lewd and heathen worship. He wanted teachers who promoted this to be instructed to stop or to be removed from teaching Christian people children. Week after week Pastor Prue pounded away in his paid advertisements until eventually the cracks began to show. Suddenly, every religious body wanted publicly to give the impression of its own piety. The Maha Sabha called for Indians to support their traditional festivals which promoted chastity and strong family values. Muslims called for self-respect. Adventists renewed their call for their members to go to Toco for their annual Carnival retreat. Every day there was something about it in the papers. To the responses that threatened to separate people by race and religion, a few people started to hit back. Mrs Glenda Dubisette-Carabon – who signed herself poet/actress – wrote that Carnival was really a fun thing that gives us all the occasion to come together even for two days to show what is possible in the other three hundred and sixty-three. Let us, she said, leave the past in the past and press on. She ended with the plaintive cry, 'Why can't we get along, people?' Letters came in from all over the world. Dhanraj Gool wrote from Toronto to say it was time the squabbling stopped. 'Up here if you not white you black. You giving a bad impression to the foreigners. People up here asking me, That is the sweet Trinidad you talk about? All you making me shame.' From Bayreuth, Germany, Sylvie Kohl wrote to say that she found the discussion in the papers very enlightening, but that Dhanraj Gool need not worry. She had been to Carnival, she had a ball and was coming back to play with the Burrokeets band.

But Pastor Prue wouldn't let up. The publicity that he was receiving over the issue had been good for him. His crusade was flourishing. And he had forced the major churches, the Catholics and Anglicans, into virtual silence. Dr Kennos, the same Kennos of the Church of Fellowship and Joy, ordinarily would not have thought it necessary to respond but was forced to do so as his patriotic duty to save the country from this avalanching hysteria that was threatening to put brother against brother and sister against sister, to put Indians against Africans and Whites against Blacks and Hindus against Christians.

Dr Kennos was of the view that Carnival belonged to all the peoples of the islands. Living as we were so close to one another, any creation or practice by any group in the island achieved its character because of the presence of the others in their midst, that in a way we all share in the creations and practices done by everyone in this island. Each one of us needs to understand that he runs the risk of denying his own self and presence when he looks at the creations or practices produced in his presence, in his place and time, as if he had nothing to do with them. The problem, he argued, is not with the practices. Nothing is wrong with Carnival or Phagwa or Easter. It is clear that there is a sense of insecurity in every sector of this nation. Instead of exploiting it for their narrow purposes, leaders need to help with the healing.

'For my part,' he wrote, 'Carnival must be claimed by all of us, just as we must all claim all that has been created in our presence.

'As far as I am concerned,' he wrote, 'I find the idea of Carnival, its indigenous character, its embracing fellowship, its sense of celebration of art, of life, of creativity, worthy to be given the kind of appreciation reserved for religion. Let us put it to the test. Get a costume for everybody, bring in tassa, tabla to join the steel band, teach the children how to play these instruments and to make them harmonize. Put the thing in the schools. We have the teachers here, designers, pan players, singers, wire benders, sculptors. I am willing to give my full support. I can't teach steel band and I can't teach tabla, I will be more than willing to show them how to *wine.'*

The religious community was shocked, but Dr Kennos Lochan had, as he had anticipated, stolen the limelight. The point was made. Alford George was saved. But the band that Alford had dreamed of had to be abandoned. The children were in tears. Some had already sewn their costumes, some had worked on dance and dramatic routines. A number of parents wanted him to still bring out the band, *just to show them*, if only with a few of the sections; but to do so, Alford knew, was to give the wrong message. No, the band couldn't play. But he had learned an important lesson. People were wounded. Goodwill was not enough to heal the nation.

'No. Goodwill is not enough,' said Angela Vialva. 'You have to form the political party. People in this island need a fresh start. Everybody feel he is a victim. African, Indian, European, everybody feel wronged by everybody else.'

'The trouble,' said Kennos, 'is that we are all strangers. What we need is someone to make the others welcome.' He was looking at Alford.

Until that time Alford had not been sure of the political party, now he knew he could not postpone it any longer. He had to find the one to make the welcome.

6

Florence

It was in that time, Easter Sunday to be exact, that Aunt Florence, sitting on our veranda, looked up from *The Universal Book of Dreams* she was reading and saw Alford George passing in the road in front our house. Rightaway a chill raced through her body and her left eye started jumping so vigorously that she knew with an uncanny certainty that her destiny had found her. For a moment, it was a puzzle. How could she not have been expecting him? Just three days ago on Good Friday, in order to get a peek into her future, she had poured the whites of an egg into a glass of water and left it to sit to form the shape that would guide her. What it had formed, she recognized now, was not a ship as she had then insisted, but the church that my mother and the rest of us had seen. Since it was a church, it meant that it was marriage, not travel, that was in her future.

'Oh, gosh,' she cried out, alarmed and awed by the realization. 'It is not a ship!' so that my mother, indoors at the time, rushed out:

'Florence, what happen?'

'It is not a ship!'

'What it is you talking about?'

'Look!' and she pointed outside where Alford George was going past our house. 'Look him going there. That is the man. Is he, is him!'

'That man?' my mother struggling to understand, then it dawned upon her what Florence was suggesting. 'Him? No!' my mother said. 'No, Florence, not he. Not him.'

'Yes,' Florence said. 'Look at my left eye how it jumping. Yes.'

'That is a sign of trouble, of tears,' my mother said.

'I know. But what to do? The future is there already. Remember is you who see a church.'

And there it was. After the years of waiting, the numerous false alarms that went off each time a new man talked to her, after the hopes, the preparations, the bush baths from Shango

94

Mothers, the oils of charm, the bracelets for good fortune, so many candles burning in so many churches, so many priests saying novenas for her, she had begun to believe that if the man foretold in her future did come at all it would be so late in her life that she would not be able to enjoy the quality of ecstasy she had associated with his coming but would have to settle simply for his companionship in her old age. Now he was here.

Years before, when Mother Mabel told Florence that her future husband would find her on the veranda of her sister's house in Cunaripo, she had taken the prediction with more than a pinch of salt. To start with, she lived in Port-of-Spain and saw so many men there that it seemed to her a little unlikely that she would find the man to marry her in the little town of Cunaripo; still, the thought that there was someone in her home town waiting for her made her feel good, feel nice, feel charmed, deepened her sense of her own desirability. She didn't feel rushed; and it was with this quality of self-confidence that in the beginning she stretched out, relaxed on our veranda, under the shade of the cedar tree, watching the iguanas change their skin, the cedar seeds burst open, spread out their wings and set sail on the wind, not at all concerned that, from the way the chair was placed, it was possible for people passing in the road to see her face only in profile, thinking with the same humour and the not inconsiderable pride with which she approached the exercise that in the event that this man turned up there in front our house he would find her minding her own business and not scanning the horizon desperately on the look-out for him.

Florence had never really taken to Port-of-Spain, never felt quite at home there. She had been there already since she was seventeen when she ran away from Equilimado Millette, a young carpenter, a boy, really, whose mother was too hurry for him to marry her. She had battled her way though tough times to have a little hairdressing salon on the edge of the southern outskirts of Belmont, and a rented apartment deeper in the same Belmont district. And she had Valerie and Peter and a few friends she could depend on to bail her out if she got in any trouble. For years Port-of-Spain remained remote, and she continued to go back to Cunaripo not only to see her family but to continue to present herself on what was still for her, her stage, the place where her dresses, her fashions, her successes were to be paraded, and where she wanted to be acclaimed; and it was not until the year Valerie and Peter encouraged her to play mas' with them in George Bailey band, 'Back to Africa', that she softened to the place. The morning when she set out from Belmont with Valerie and George to go and meet the band in Woodbrook, she had felt naked with her short skirt, short hair, her standard, her ridiculous little crown. She felt people's eyes on her and she kept her head straight and her eyes down looking. It was only when she looked up, looked again at the spectators, that she saw in their eyes their admiration, their acknowledgement and their granting of a right that she had claimed by the display of herself. She recognized then that this city was a place that granted you only what you were willing to claim. Tramping the streets those two days marked the place as her own. She felt joined to every masquerader, not only the ones playing in her band, but to all, everywhere. For the first time she felt the holiness of the town and saw the beauty of its people and that it was hers, the city. She was no longer an alien in it, no longer intimidated by it. She felt brought to a new sense of freedom and a sense of peace and at last she felt herself herself, that self she had always suspected was herself, that even she herself was only then seeing.

She had played a Nubian princess, with her hair cut short and ringed with coloured beads and a tiara of gold. The sun had tanned her so that the rich velvety blackness of her skin glistened and she had felt so much herself on those days of Carnival, soaked so deeply with a sense of her own beauty, that after the festival, she continued to keep her hair in the same fashion and to wear her skin with the same pride, the result being that men took her for a foreign woman.

'African!' they called. 'Darkie!', admiring and flirtatious, until she spoke and they realized that she was from right here in the island. For some reason this broke the spell. She couldn't understand why until she met Elvis Thom, calypsonian and postman, who had stood together with her for her friend Valerie's child, she as godmother and he godfather. He was so certain she was from some other place.

'So where Valerie know you from? How long you in Trinidad for?'

And when she said that she was from right here, living in Port-of-Spain seven years already, he had looked sideways at her, stuck, checked. He didn't know how to go on. It was as if the new pride and beauty and confidence she exuded had made her somehow more chaste and forbidding, had turned something off in him. She thought he would regain his ease with time; but he did not see it as his problem. It was she who was deviant, was strange, odd, pretentious. And his feelings about her would come out a month later when they were on the beach together, Valerie and Peter and the child and she and Elvis, when he said, 'Florence, why don't you just be yourself? Be a Trinidadian.'

'Be myself? Be myself? What self? This is myself.' And it was then that she realized that there was some idea of herself that she wasn't fulfilling. It wasn't about beauty or that she was afraid to fuck or anything. Something from her had taken him into a new unaccustomed area. He didn't know how to handle it. He didn't know, she thought afterwards, after she had puzzled over it a long time, how to respect her and still try to take her to bed. He required from her an ordinariness that would guarantee her surrender. What was she to do? She didn't know what it was he wanted done, and they drifted away. This became her experience with Adalbert as well. An insurance salesman, he came to her with his insurance voice and his calculating manner until he discovered that hers was not a performance too. He didn't know what to say. And she turned away from them, glad for the prediction that there was a man who would find her on the veranda of her sister's house in Cunaripo. More deliberate now, she dressed herself up in her latest fashion and turned her chair increasingly to face the road so that whoever was passing would get a full view of her face.

For thirteen years she had looked out on that road to see who among the men passing fit the description of her prospective husband. As if they knew she was looking, they passed in a parade, without concern for their own matrimonial status, men working on the sea, sailors from the inter-island ferry, men from the oilfields over in Guayaguayare, fellars working in the telephone company, policemen and prison guards, men in electricity,

97

men from the fire services and in the County Council, tradesmen, cabinet makers and motor car mechanics, saga boys with their yellow shirts and green pants with polka-dot handkerchiefs sticking out of their back pockets, men in suits, men in dark blue jackets with brass buttons, men with Panama hats and two-tone shoes. There was so much traffic that Miss Jane opened up a little parlour where the men could refresh themselves with sweet drinks and mauby and, although she didn't have a licence to sell it, a little under-the-counter rum. Later she provided a draughts board, which gave them the excuse to appear occupied, but they were looking at her. She tried to look interested and to send little signals, little eye-flutterings or other gestures of interest to those to whom she was most attracted and when they didn't respond in the way she wanted, she sat on the veranda under the mottled sunlight and the leaves falling from our cedar tree and picked them apart with merciless candour, amusing herself with the details of their defects, of height, of dress, of manners and, out of her own spite, as if to rub salt into their wounds, she decided just to be nice, just to nice them to death, just to be herself, this outrageously elegant woman, out of reach, causing even the most conceited of the men to turn and look with pure admiration at the breadth of her style and say the single word, Woman! She went on excursions and she wouldn't fraternize with strangers. She went to dances and she wouldn't dance. She moved about with a superior and forbidding beauty and all the time there were tears inside her. All the time she was wishing even for a fool, bold enough to challenge this sense of dignity that she could not relinquish. Nobody saw this.

'You frightening the men,' Pearl told her.

'Then tell me what brand of toothpaste to use.' Because by then she had grown tougher. One day she listened to the harshness of her voice, talking with Valerie and she realized, No, this is not me. No. I not going to let these people sour and harden me. No, sir; not me. That was now the battle, the fight with her own toughness: between her toughness and her vulnerability. She tried to soften and to still hold on to herself. She would go on the beach with suntan lotion and stretch out on a towel in the sun. Who ever hear of Blackpeople tanning? Blackpeople place is in the shade, but she lay there till her skin glowed purple, people watching her with amazement. She must be a foreigner, she must be a madwoman. Beachbums would come over to chat her up and she would want to talk to them, but would remain silent until they had finished their spiel before she spoke and then when they heard her accent they would catch themselves, scratch their heads and drift away. Still, she played mas' and she burnt her candles, praying not now so much that the man would come but that when he did she wouldn't be too sour to give him a proper greeting.

Now, this Easter Sunday he had come. Good Friday she had broken the egg as was the tradition and poured the white into a glass of water and let it sit to form into the shape that would tell her of her future. And what made her so sure now, two days later, that it was marriage really in her future was because the man passing there was someone she had known for years but had never seen on this road before.

That morning Florence had been wearing the clothes she had come with from church so she knew she was looking good and that from where she was sitting he was certain to see her face. She had expected him at least to say Goodmorning. But no word came from him as he went on his way. She left the veranda, fuming.

'Pearl! Pearl!' she called my mother. 'You know the man pass and say not a word.' She went inside and looked at herself in the mirror. She refreshed her lipstick. She changed into shorts. She began to worry about the authenticity of the prediction and was carrying on in such disconsolation that my mother had to shout at her:

'Florence, the prediction say the man would see you on the veranda, it didn't say he would say anything.'

Florence decided right then to take things into her own hands. She did not feel herself getting any younger and from her own experience she knew that timidity did not pay off. She felt insulted and challenged by the fact that the man had looked at her and not said a word. She decided right then not to wait for her future sitting down. Bad as it was, it was better if this thing was to happen for it to begin early so as to allow time for the long struggle. The sooner she began, the sooner it would be over; and that was how a week later, the next Sunday, instead of going directly home from church, she found herself on the veranda of his house knocking on the open door and calling out his name, softly at first as the lover with whom he was expecting to rendez-vous and louder when after a few knocks he did not appear.

She had shouted his name once already and was about to shout it again when she saw him standing just inside the door-way looking forbiddingly at her. The first thing that came to her mind to say she blurted out, 'I come for you to give me some private lessons.'

He responded firmly, 'I don't give private lessons here. You have to come to the school on Monday evening.'

She answered with almost reflexive authority and sternness, 'Well, I can't come to the school for them. I'm a big woman. And it can't be during the week. I working in Port-of-Spain. It will have to be on weekends.'

So he told her to come in, still formal, still wary. 'Come in.'

He asked, 'In what?'

'In what what?' She was still nettled.

'What it is you want these lessons in?' said with such innocence that she had to still the mischief of her own suddenly inappropriate laughter. But he was wary still.

'You does read a lot of books,' she said, as she removed some books from the only other chair in the room in order to sit down.

'Yes, I read a lot of books,' he said, sounding irritated, so that she said:

'Don't rough me, you know. I don't like people to rough me.'

She saw that she had gained his attention. He said, 'Sit down, please.' She sat down and looking up saw the empty bird cage.

'You mind birds?'

'No. I do not mind birds. But I had a bird.'

She watched his face twist with pain: 'What I say wrong again? Eh?'

She saw his confusion. 'No,' she said. 'Correct me. Tell me if I wrong. You's the teacher.'

He looked at her again, still deciding.

Softening, she asked, 'You don't want another bird to put in the cage, seeing that you have a cage already?'

'What you want these lessons in?'

'You know what I really want to learn? I want to learn how

to be me, how to be myself. I don't know a damn thing. Like I miss something, or something miss me.'

Tears were flowing silently down her cheek and she felt like a fool. And she smiled through her tears when she looked and saw that he was looking at her knees and the bit of her thigh that was showing.

Carefully, she arranged her skirt around her knees, hearing him say, 'I will see what I can do.' He didn't have to say anything more. It was foretold.

'I'm glad,' she said, 'that I follow my mind and come here,' trying to get the feeling back on track, trying to reintroduce the spirit of romance, but it had slipped away, if it ever was there, into the kind of politeness that was to endure for nearly a year between them.

From that very first day she knew that she would have to wait. He was busy. He was writing a play. He was working on his second volume of poems. He was meeting with Angela Vialva, Sonan Lochan, Adolphe Carabon and Dr Kennos on the formation of their political party.

Kennos was convinced that they had to move quickly, now that Alford had the attention of the public and his utterances were newsworthy.

'Let's go to the population and tell them that right away,' he said. 'So that they will know we not after power, but that our concern is with their welfare, the national welfare. We are here to set things right. Once we put this country in order, we should all resign.'

Alford was concerned about the practical things like a symbol, an office, a secretary, a name, before going public.

'We don't have to burden the people with these matters,' said Dr Kennos. 'These are things we ourselves can do. We already have a manifesto. Then we hold a convention and bring in the people.'

It was agreed. Alford's quarters became their meeting place, Dr Kennos' office address became their mailing address. Angela Vialva was elected secretary, but was finding it hard to come up from Port-of-Spain for every meeting, so Florence was appointed to take minutes and to send out correspondence.

People's Unity Movement was the name proposed by Carabon, and the symbol offered by Alford was a length of chain.

'Wait, I smelling something,' Kennos declared. 'Look at this name: PUM? That is what we want to call ourselves? And this symbol, you think people will want to identify with chains?'

They had to rethink the entire business. In the meantime, they agreed to call themselves The Group and accepted the offer from Dr Kennos to have correspondence sent out on stationery from his church. So the first correspondence Florence sent out from The Group to invite people to their first public meeting in Cunaripo was in care of the Congregation of Righteousness and Joy. That meeting, they all decided, had to be grand. It had to have a wide cross-section of people, and it had to present to the population the one, symbolically at least, to make the welcome to the others.

'Who will be the welcomer? The Amerindians welcomed Columbus. They are not here now to welcome anyone,' Lochan said. 'Who here has the authority to welcome anyone? Who here can say, come in, you're welcome?'

Carabon couldn't do it. Everybody was agreed on that. For all his personal goodwill, he was from a family that was seen as a beneficiary of enslavement, indenture and colonialism. He couldn't come now to welcome people.

'You already welcome us, boy,' Dr Kennos said. 'Alford as nigger and me and Sonan as coolie. So you can't take this role again. You lose your chance.'

'You, then?' Adolphe Carabon asked.

'I? I?' continued Kennos, speaking as if he was already on the platform. 'As well prepared as I am personally to do it, I would be a little reluctant at this time to put forward either Sonan or myself to take up that role. The principal reason being that we see ourselves as the more recent arrivals here. Before East Indians came, there were others here before us, people who faced the brutality and the promise, who had the task of responding to the reality of a landscape new to them, who set the tone of the new language we would use and the new gods we would worship, whose struggle against enslavement set down the cornerstone of the new society that is to be constructed . . . I am talking of the African. I could go on and on . . .' He was looking at Alford. 'So, Alford, old man, the one to welcome must be

African. The lot fall on you. You is the one in Cunaripo to make this welcome.'

And, yes, Alford agreed, if one had to choose from among them, yes, he would be the one to make this welcome. Still, he found himself hesitating.

It was Florence who brought Bango to the attention of the Group.

In the beginning Alford wasn't so sure he was their man. He recalled seeing him at the very first Independence Day parade marching with fussy grandeur at the head of his troop of little soldiers going down Main Street. On that occasion Alford was tempted to laugh; but when he learnt that that man on his own authority had outfitted the boys and at his own expense put four of them in costumes to represent the different ethnic groups of the nation, he had felt humbled, embarrassed, elated. He had felt that truly this man was making a statement of welcome to them all. Later that same day, after the march, he saw Bango again, this time at the bus station, surrounded by the boys, checking his money to see if he had enough for the bus fares to take the children back to Cascadu. The scene didn't look at all grand. While it moved him to an even greater appreciation of Bango's efforts, he had noted that alone and by himself, Bango did not seem to have the means to make the welcome. Why was he doing it, then? Alford had not dwelt too long upon that question. That kind of sacrifice was not unfamiliar to him. His own father had provided a wonderful example of a person's pretence of power he did not possess. He had tried to see Bango's effort as a beginning. He hoped that others would join in. It did not happen.

In the years that followed there was in Cunaripo no further official Independence Day parade. To cut down on expenses, Government centralized the parade in the city of Port-of-Spain. In Cunaripo and Cascadu people used the day to go to the beach or to attend the big cricket fête match between Bachelors and Married Men. Bango, however, had kept on. His own march now involved the Picoplat steel orchestra, his little soldiers with him at the head and before them the costumed children representing the many races of people in the land.

Sonan Lochan remembered standing as a boy in front his

103

grandfather's hardware store and watching the marchers. He did not see their poverty. What he saw was something powerful and rhythmic and grand from which he and his brothers were excluded. That was the memory that remained with him. It never occurred to him that there was a place for him in the march, or that even if there were his father would allow him to join it.

'It frightened me,' Carabon said. 'All these Blackpeople marching with the flag as if it belonged to them, as if we had no place here, as if the country belonged to them. We just watched them.'

'He was depicting Chinese, Europeans and Indians in his band.' Alford sounded hurt. 'And you didn't feel that you were welcome?'

'It didn't seem to have anything to do with us,' said Carabon.

'What you feel now?' Alford asked.

'We don't need to go into history,' Kennos said. 'This is the man to make the welcome.'

'And the means?' Alford asked.

'Of course,' Carabon said. 'We could get new uniforms for the children. We could organize some sandwiches for them and make a contribution to the bus fares to take them back home after they finish marching.'

Florence had held her peace during the discussion. After Lochan and Kennos and Carabon left, trying to keep her vexation under control, she turned on Alford:

'How you could do that to Bango? How you could ask him to welcome people when he is the one that needs the welcome?'

'Wait! But I thought that you were the one that proposed him.' Alford's puzzlement angered her even more.

Florence was going on. 'You think a new uniform and a few sandwiches is what Bango want to make him make the welcome?'

'What does he want then?'

'Why you don't ask him?' She was sitting opposite him. She got up, 'Look, I better go. But I don't see how you could value your welcome and put no value on the welcomer. I better go.'

'Wait!' It was as if something dropped, revealed her to him for the first time, a depth of softness and luxuriance of feeling. 'Wait!' looking at her again, in that moment for the first time seeing her, the woman, everything in one glance, the edge of her teeth, the frilly lace at the tail of her dress, the curve of her arms, the stretch of her neck. 'Wait.'

'Don't touch me,' she said.

'And can we give it to him? Whatever it is he wants?'

'That is for you to answer. You are the teacher.'

'How are we going to find a way to welcome the one who we want to welcome everybody? How?' he asked. And in that moment she too was looking at him, sensing his vulnerability, his uncertainty.

She sat down once more. He came and knelt beside her chair. He held her hands. For a moment they gazed upon each other.

'You asking us to begin a whole new world,' gravely, uncertainly, the weight of the challenge in his voice so that Florence herself grew suddenly frightened, as if she had stumbled upon something too enormous for them to handle. He had put his arms around her. And it was with her own sense of caution that she leant to his embrace as they rose together to their feet. In unison almost they released each other and looked again to see that, yes, yes, it was she, her own eyes looking out saying: Yes. Yes. Is me. Yes, smiling all at once her teeth filling her mouth, her eyes sparkling with mischief, with the pleasure that after these months at last he had seen her. The door was open. He looked towards it and back to her. Yes. Close it, she breathed.

A week later they were lying in bed after the exertions of their lovemaking. With one arm still around her, he talked of his father, of his pretence of a power he didn't have, of the bricks and the land. Then he drew himself up into a sitting position and took up a book from the bedhead.

'Listen,' he said. 'This is from the *Royal Gazette* on the occasion of the first anniversary of Emancipation. Listen.'

'Em-hmm,' she breathed, her spirit and body in a cocoon elsewhere. She heard him turning pages: 'Wait, what it is you doing?'

'I have been looking into the history.'

She couldn't believe it. Alford was reading:

We look forward too with some confidence to more settled habits on the part of the labourers, for as they advance in the paths of civilization, the more will they become acquainted with duties and obligations, and be sensible that it is by sober steady habits alone that they can improve their condition and render themselves comfortable if not independent. The great truth that it is by labour alone – continuous and unremitting labour – that the great majority of mankind obtains the means of sustenance will surely, though perhaps slowly, make itself felt by the most dissipated and improvident amongst them . . . The old notion that freedom meant merely a cessation from labour, generally maintained as we believe it was by those whom the first year of freedom has just closed, is, we have heard, obliterated from their minds for ever . . .

He read:

How far it may be possible to check it effectually (labour going to independent agriculture, planting not for export and the consequent fall back of society) it will be necessary to prevent the occupation of any Crown lands by persons not possessing a proprietary title to them: and to fix such a price upon all Crown lands as may place them out of reach of persons without capital . . .

'So as you can see,' said Alford, to the Group at their next meeting, 'Bango is a victim of this deliberate plan set down from the beginning to prevent people working their way out of enslavement.'

'What you talking about is reparation,' Dr Kennos said.

'How can anybody make up for those years?' Carabon asked.

'This is what we must address. Let's talk about it,' said Alford.

The talks didn't go well. Everyone was a little uncomfortable. Bango wasn't the only one in our history to suffer. Giving compensation to him alone would raise more questions than they could answer. Who going to give him what? And what about others, what about Indian people who were indentured? What about the Caribs and Arawaks, the aboriginal inhabitants? And would they now take away Whitepeople property? And wouldn't that frighten away people and split up the country?

Kennos believed that whatever reparation was decided on could only be symbolic. His suggestion was that what was needed was two houses and two plots of land, one for Bango and another for an Indian.

'And the Amerindians?'

'Okay, three houses. But you'll have to go to Dominica to find the Caribs.'

The best thing to do was to give nobody nothing. Let us enter into socialism and that will ensure freedom and equality for all. This from Calvin Rodriguez, who had begun to journey up from Port-of-Spain for the meetings. The Group was going forward, only slowly. The date of its grand meeting was forever being postponed. Members started to slack off. Calvin Rodriguez began talks with George Correia and Andrew Chin to form the People's Revolutionary Party.

It was at this time that Alford received a letter from The Concerned Citizens of Cunaripo/Cascadu inviting him to a meeting at the Cunaripo Business Academy to discuss urgent business of the community. Alford was not afraid to go any-where. He believed himself to be on an ongoing campaign to recruit new people to the cause of his Party then in formation. It wasn't until he got there that he discovered that he had been invited to the Annual General Meeting of the National Party. He stood up to leave. As he was about to do so, Ethelbert Tannis, the Chairman of the Party Group, stopped him: 'No. It is not a mistake. We are inviting you to lead us.'

It was totally unexpected. Alford didn't know what to do. Every argument he presented was countered. They were having their elections and they were unanimous in wanting him as general secretary.

To all his uncertainties they were prepared to offer him the option to resign at any time after one week. Just give us this time, think it over and come back to us.

As he told Dr Kennos and Lochan and Carabon – Angela Vialva was not present that day: 'I didn't know what to do, so I simply accepted.'

'You talking as if you wasn't there,' Dr Kennos said. 'As if you didn't have any say, as if they bathe you down with this nomination.'

'And what about our programmes?' Carabon asked.

Alford had given the entire matter serious thought. If they all together joined the National Party then they would have a powerful force to work from the inside. They were all young

107

people and, if they were determined, they could influence the party.

'What about ideological differences?' Kennos asked. 'I never wanted to be in this just for power, you know. I'm here only because we have no other institution through which to make a serious contribution to this nation.'

'That was exactly the point,' Alford agreed. None of them really wanted power, what they wanted was the opportunity to make this a better country. They had a chance to work from inside the governing party. They had the ideas to influence them, to truly involve the people in democracy.'

Of the three of them, only Carabon agreed to go along and join the National Party. Sonan had much more to consider. Although his grandfather had fought two elections as an Independent, his family had always supported the Democratic Party. He was not certain what he would do. Dr Kennos reserved his decision, not because he had any doubt as to what it would be but because: 'I don't want it to look like the Indians against you. I am sorry though that we are so hastily abandoning a possibility into which we have already put so much work, and I must urge you all to reconsider. We still have time.'

But from the tone of his voice it was clear that the enthusiasm he had started with was gone.

A month later Dr Kennos would write Alford a letter in which he would talk of the hopes they had for the country, the purity of their consciences, and the belief in his integrity. 'And, that, rather fortunately is most of what you have,' he said. 'You may think of yourself as a politician; I am not so certain. Like me, you are a crusader, a patriot. With perhaps your greatest attribute your good heart and your integrity. If I am correct and it endures – your integrity, that is – as I expect it to, you will have a shorter stay in this party than you now anticipate.

'In a way,' he continued, 'this has been a good thing, because it has clarified for me my own position. I have done a lot of soul-searching. Do I want really to become involved in politics, or was politics an attraction because it is the only area of power at our disposal today? '

'We need new institutions in this country. I have a vocation at

which I am more than moderately good. I will stay here and campaign for what I want for this country as a preacher. Farewell,
'Your friend, Kennos.'

Alford felt so touched that he framed the letter and put it up on the wall of his living-room. Later when he got elected to the parliament he would put it up in his office, on the wall facing his chair. He would read it many, many times in the few years that he was to remain there.

BOOK TWO

7

Vera's Eyes

On a sweaty afternoon in that July, with dark clouds hanging low over Port-of-Spain, stirring up a heat that had policemen unbuttoning their tunics and passengers begging taxi drivers to turn down their music, as if less noise would mean less heat, the Prime Minister who earlier that week had thrown his telephone into the Gulf of Paria to protest at its being tapped by foreign agents spying on him from their station in the upside-down Hilton Hotel, was in his office dictating a letter to his secretary, when the heat wrestled the air-conditioning unit into uselessness, penetrated the drapes of the room and reached him at his desk.

He undid the polka-dot neckerchief that had added some gaiety to his attire since he put away the party tie at the height of the events that had come down to us as The Black Power Revolution, that time of his greatest political testing, with the army in revolt and mischief everywhere: with students and unemployed marching the streets for Black Power, Black Love and Black Justice, but with no clear plan as to how these were to be achieved beyond the rhythmic performances of Mau Mau drummers in Woodford Square and thunderous choruses of 'Power To the People' punctuating the grandiloquent denunciations of speakers celebrating in the extravagant robes of our reclaimed Africanness; so that in the end, when we were hoarse from shouting and exhausted from marching, he was left so firmly in power that he could choose to be benevolent. Nobody was put to death, nobody was killed, and he rose triumphantly from the ashes of a revolt that he wanted desperately to believe that he had inspired, to forgive the excesses of a generation that rightly had rejected the subservience of their fathers, ready to go again and take them to the sweetness of the land promised in the manifesto of his Party.

The heat persisted and it occurred to the Prime Minister that he would have either to remove his jacket or open a window.

He chose to open a window. This ought to have been an easy thing to do, but the building that housed his offices had been constructed in 1904 and the cord of the pulley operating the window had been so thickened by the numerous coats of paint put on the building in the more than seventy years of its existence that it couldn't slide through the groove of the pulley as was expected.

The Prime Minister noticed this only after he had strained with all˙the strength of his muscles and the insistence of a will that had long practice in being obeyed. The window didn't open and when the Prime Minister looked at his hands they were plastered with dust and grime. The Prime Minister didn't say nothing. He had nothing to say. He had talked already about the leaks in the roof of the building, about silverfish that were destroying his books, about the unreliability of the air-conditioning unit, about the slackness of the workers, about the mess the place was becoming. He had threatened to fire people, to leave the pack of them and go home and write his books. They didn't take him on. No. No. They wanted him to get blasted vex and resign again.

The last time he sent in his letter of resignation to the President, all of them, the whole country, lined up to beg him to come back. Editorials in every newspaper, pleas from the Catholic Archbishop, the Anglican Bishop, the Muslim League, the Ecclesiastical Congress of Spiritual Baptists, the Calypsonians' Association, the Congress of Trades Unions, the Carnival Players' Association, the Women's League, the Manufacturers' Association, the Chamber of Commerce, the Parent-Teachers' Association, the Association of Village Councils, 255 party groups of the National Party, the Youth League, the Women's Auxiliary Arm, the Salvation Army, the Seventh-day Adventist Churches.

It was a little child that saved them. He was ready to ignore every last one of them. He was ready to go. But it was that little girl, seven years old, Kathleen Hope from Prizgar Lands, from the Laventille slums in the heart of his constituency, who wrote to him, who ask him this simple question that open up his heart:

'Right Honourable, Mister Prime Minister, what will become of us if you go?'

He couldn't leave again. He couldn't do it. For all the fed up he was fed up: for all his fed-upness – because he wanted nothing, no honours, no statue, nothing from them, neither in his life nor at his death; he wanted nothing – he girded his loins and set out again upon this thankless journey, knowing this time that he had a mandate to govern from the Future, from the Young, and 'Who don't like it,' he said – because he was ready for their arse now: all the back-stabbers, all the slackers, he was ready for their backside – 'who don't like it could get the hell out of here.'

And he went into Woodford Square, where every three years he came to tear up before the populace the invitations to professorships at universities from Berlin to Ife because I have decided to let my bucket down right here among my people. He went into Woodford Square, walking through the grandest guard of honour ever assembled for anybody in this country, the line stretching from the Singer entrance on Frederick Street right up to the podium, the whole country gathered there, the place looking and smelling like Trinidad and Tobago, market women in Shouters' headdress, smelling of red lavender and rosewater, vendors of paratha roti in orhnis, about them the scent of fresh coconut oil and burnt geera, clapping hands and shaking tambourines; stevedores with flags in their huge fists and towels draped over their formidable shoulders, nurses in grey stockings and starched aproned uniforms, vagrants in their Sunday best, soapbox politicians with their fingers on their lips, choirs of schoolchildren, oyster vendors and sugarcane workers, and a contingent of supporters from the opposition parties. Yes, men in dhotis, beating tassa drums and ringing tabla, all of them standing together, John De John and Trou Macaque and Mundo Nuevo and Carapichaima and Oropouche and Brazil, du-dups and dholak beating and flags and heliconias waving and doves and balloons in the air, in an outpouring of support that so overwhelmed him that when he went to talk, when he went to read out his prepared speech, the acceptance again of the mantle of Leader – three times he tried to begin it three times – his eyes filled with water and he couldn't go on. 'Good Lord!' he said.

And he threw open his arms and cried, 'If loving you is wrong, I don't want to be right.'

And he tell them, talking not from no paper now, talking from his belly, talking from his stones. He tell them that they was the people. 'You are the people who have to make this place what it could become.' He tell them of the difficulties he had, of how hard it was to turn back the hands of time when there are interests that don't want you to progress. They don't want it at all, *at all*. What they want is a dolly-house government that they could tell how high to jump. What they want is an overseer to oversee things for them as they used to have on their plantations. But I want to let them know: those days are done. Massa day done! Why don't they listen? He tell them how hard it is to make them a people – the intrigue, the set-ups, the interest groups, my God! What you need is political education. And who will do the educating? He had so much to do already. He had so much to do. In addition to leading this government, giving direction to the party, captaining the General Council, organizing the Ministries, he had his writings. People at Oxford, at Cambridge, Harvard University, the University of Tokyo, people from all over are sending for him. They want him to come and teach their young people. But he was only one man.

He tell them about democracy, about the need for eternal vigilance. You can't trust everybody. You have to know who to trust. You have, as Bob Marley say, to know who to trust and that was why he had to depend on new people. Fresh blood. That was why he had to start looking now outside of those who were elected. They mean well. They are good National Party candidates; but the colonial education system didn't prepare them for this epoch. What to do?

You have to bring in new talent, fresh people, not those set in their ways, new blood. And after that speech he went into action. He reshuffled his cabinet to get rid of the millstones and to bring in persons who had arrived into the twentieth century and he made it mandatory that anybody who he decided to make a Minister in his government had to give him a signed undated letter of resignation so that in the event of any dissatisfaction on his own part we could part company promptly, right away, without jeopardizing the work of the country. Yes. Because what was important was not the careers of would-be Caesars, not the pathetic sight of millstones there in the House warming up the back benches unencumbered by the need to make any

116

contribution beyond a dubious maiden speech, it was the work of the country.

That was now how it was going to be; and who don't like it . . . Yes, he said. *Yes.* Because the crowd itself finished the sentence for him: . . . could get the hell out of here.

He had brought in women from the Women's League. He had brought in a young man from the Youth Arm to broaden and rejuvenate the government and to give an image of discipline to the youth, in response to the disorganization and sloganeering of the so-called political parties. But you can't change people overnight. The millstones and hangers-on were still there drawing a salary and standing in the way of progress. To get anything done he had personally to bring it under his supervision. Now the nonsense was starting up again. But he had talked enough. He had nothing more to say. Nothing. I will not spend another moment in this blasted building.

He pulled out a tissue from the box on his desk and wiped some of the grime off his hands, packed up his papers, took up his briefcase, directed his secretary to call his chauffeur and to get another of the drivers to take her and to follow him. And he rode to his residence where he soaped and washed his hands, put his pipe, unlighted, between his teeth, sat at his own desk and resumed dictating the letter that had been interrupted. He then called his Minister of State and outlined to him plans for the construction of proper offices for the Prime Minister. And he didn't want any air-conditioning. No damn air-conditioning. He wanted windows that could open and architecture that could circulate the air. 'People here are getting too damn soft,' he said. 'That was how they built them long ago. They had no air-conditioning, but the place was cool.'

Anticipating that his Minister of State would point out to him the obvious – that things had changed, the population had grown, that houses had been constructed in the path of the wind – he said, 'Build it high. I don't care if it is the tallest building in the island.'

He next directed his secretary to have the books and the papers he had left in that place to be sent to the Residence and to alert the Cabinet that its next meeting would he held in, yes, the Cocrico Room of the Hilton Hotel. Yes!

'And,' he said, 'arrange a press conference. There is to be a reshuffle of Cabinet.'

As the secretary was getting up, the telephone rang and she answered it.

'It is for you, Sir,' she said. 'Scholasticus P. Nelson, the member for Cascadu.'

'Scholasticus who?'

'The member for Cunaripo/Cascadu.'

'Oh! The Minister of Silence. Well, what does he want? Eleven years in office and he has not said a word. '

'He is dead, Sir.'

'You see,' he said to the secretary. 'I haven't opened my mouth yet and they start to drop down. Take the message. '

At one-thirty that afternoon, Scholasticus P. Nelson, representative of the District of Cunaripo/Cascadu for nineteen years, was at home eating a meal of coocoo and red fish when a bone stuck in his throat. He began to cough and splutter and choke. His wife, who was not eating with him, and who had stopped waiting for him to turn up at the table on time ages ago, was at that very moment going down the stairway that led into the living-room, plastered on her face the green mud mask that she wore about the house every Thursday afternoon – to clean and nourish her skin, she said, though Scholasticus and Evangelina, her helper, thought that it was the better to intimidate the household – she believed that he was trying to tell her something while his mouth was full. Since his ascension to public office, she had taken upon herself to direct him in matters of etiquette, to choose his clothes and to buy the dye for his hair. She walked right past him, giving him a sidelong look of disapproval, saying, as she went by, 'Scholasticus, how many times must I tell you not to talk while you eating. One of these days you are going to choke and dead.' And she continued on to the telephone to call a friend, Priscilla Gordon, to find out the day and the hour of the meeting of the Divine Circle of Prayer that she had stopped attending then for nearly two years but that she felt she needed now to help her with her breathing and to recharge her spiritual battery.

As soon as she picked up the phone to dial, she heard a gurgling sound from Scholasticus. Exasperated, she hurried over to him to find him in the throes of what she did not recognize to be his death. She gave him three hard slaps on his back – for your stupidness, she said – and when his eyes started to roll and his skin to turn purple, she steupsed and hurried back to the telephone, this time to call Dr Mahabir. Then she returned to him and lay him on his back and despite the awful fish smell on his breath tried to give him mouth-to-mouth resuscitation. She still had the green mask on and was kneeling over him, her mouth on his and her hands pressing down on his chest, when Dr Mahabir arrived, felt his pulse, listened for a heartbeat and pronounced him dead.

'Of fright?' the Prime Minister asked. Without waiting for a reply, he went on, 'My God, the man cannot even eat a piece of fish properly. Damn! Get Ethelbert Tannis for me. And cancel the press conference. It wouldn't do to make so many changes at this death and then to go into a by-election. And inform the Minister of Festivals. He handles funerals as well, doesn't he? And, get hold of that fella from Cascadu, that young illiterate who's been shooting off his mouth about democracy, about change – flooding the Prime Minister's office with a set of reports – George. Yes, Alford George. I want him close to me where I could see him.'

From the moment Alford took up duties as General Secretary of the Party Group, he had focused on building the Party as a democratic institution to serve the people. Information and involvement were his key instruments. He noted and pursued every idea that the Group agreed upon, letting the central Party know of its activities and calling upon them for assistance of every kind. So that in addition to fund-raising and outings and attendance of General meetings there were discussions on the Party Manifesto, the constitution of the nation, discussions on their own vision of the Party, as well as criticism and commendation of parliamentarians.

In this connection he began to make of the minutes a forum for his own opinions on race relations, the education system, decision-making for the ordinary people and the role of Parliamentarians as representatives of the people, not their bosses. He encouraged the Group to buy a Gestetner machine and he had it smoking, running off his minutes and the reports from their various committees, and sending copies to each Member of Parliament, copies to the Party leadership, but most importantly to other Party groups to let them know what his group was doing. It was as if the Party groups were waiting for someone to show them the way.

They began to flood the centre with so many documents and demands and opinions that together they threatened to change the relationship between the parliamentarians and the rank and file, to the delight of the Leader, who saw this as a weapon that at his choosing could keep either group in line. And a major confrontation between the various arms of the Party was only averted by the threat posed to it by the formation of a new party assembled from traitors so hungry for power as to join up with the French Creoles and the worst of the most power-hungry of the Indians.

For this diversion Ethelbert B. Tannis was glad. Alford had a bright future in politics and he didn't want to see him throw it away by getting on the wrong side of the PM. Ethelbert B. himself had no hope for parliamentary honours. He had come into politics with a background in the Police Force. He had spent eight years there, had left to become an insurance salesman, selling insurance in the day and working as a Casa in a gambling club at nights. His experiences had given him an insight into people, and a knowledge of the underworld of the city. Later he would turn his talents to selling encyclopaedias and Yardley products. He was selling encyclopaedias when he met the man who was to become Prime Minister. He recognized him instantly, as the scholar who had debated with a Jamaican professor of anthropology at the Public Library the merits of Democracy in Athens, Atlantis and the Caribbean. With his hustler's instinct for a winner, he approached the man who from the very first he called Chief, and said to him: 'Chief, you better form your political party. I will help to make you the next Prime Minister.'

'Where you from?' the future Prime Minister asked him.

'I born in Cascadu but I living now in Laventille. I can deliver Laventille, Morvant, San Juan.'

'I believe I have the entire Port-of-Spain area covered, I want you to work in Cascadu,' the Chief told him.

The very next day Tannis called his woman who was then

living separately from him, asked her to marry him, packed his belongings and headed for Cascadu, where he opened a school teaching shorthand and typing in which he had received certificates while on the police force. In less than a month he had launched the Cunaripo-Cascadu party group of the National Party with a membership of sixty-five persons.

And it was due principally to him that the National Party inveigled its way into every business place, every Village Council, every government department in the district of Cascadu/ Cunaripo. The only worry Ethelbert B. had was his growing obesity and the fear of heart disease. He had for some time been unhappy with Scholasticus P. Nelson. Not only did he hardly ever say a thing in Parliament, for a politician representing rural folk he was always too well dressed and the black shiny dyed hair made him look a bit like a comic. He had wanted to groom someone substantial from the Party Group to take Scholasticus P. Nelson's place and only reached outside for Alford when he saw that the one coming forward from the Party Group was Rattan Ramjattan, a poultry farmer from Cunaripo who it was rumoured also held membership in the Democratic Party, Liberal Party and the Party of Political Progress and who was ready to go to any side that would nominate him to fight a parliamentary election. He was pleased with his selection. Alford didn't let him down.

With no idea of the good fortune that was soon to befall him, Alford was at the funeral of Scholasticus Nelson, beside Ethelbert B., in the line walking from the church to the cemetery, when Ethelbert B. tapped him on the shoulder and asked him to look behind him. Together they saw the multitude in black and white and mauve that had come out to pay their last respects to Scholasticus P. Nelson.

'I hope you get this kind of turn-out when your turn comes,' Ethelbert B. Tannis said.

There was a streak of superstition in Alford and for a moment he thought that Ethelbert B. Tannis's statement was a blight foretelling his death. He had answered sharply, 'Take your time. I not ready to die. . . . Why you telling me this anyway?'

'We putting you up to take Scholasticus Nelson's place. Next three months is the by-election.'

Alford changed gear instantly, 'Then I should be giving the eulogy.'

'No,' Ethelbert B. Tannis said. 'I arrange it already. You will say a prayer at the graveside.'

There was strong support from the Hibiscus and Deep Ravine groups for Rattan Ramjattan; but it was Alford's name that went forward from the constituency. Once it became clear to Rattan Ramjattan that Alford was the candidate for the by-election, Rattan Ramjattan became Alford's principal support. He provided Alford with the loan of his truck and a loudspeaker. He saw that handbills were printed, and sent one of his workers out to stick them up all over the constituency. And when Alford won the election, he organized a victory party for him at his home.

'Watch him,' Ethelbert B. Tannis had said. That was all. Alford, to his shame, didn't even ask why.

Some people are born great, some achieve greatness, some have greatness thrust upon them. Alford George was guided to greatness: his childhood dumbness, his efforts to leave the island, the Exhibition class, his mental breakdown, the method of his entry into the National Party, the circumstances that gave rise to his nomination mapped a trail of events that couldn't have *just happened* and he was convinced that he had a great work ahead of him.

For his election campaign he had chosen a simple theme: Seeing Ourselves Afresh. In this he argued that because enslavement and indenture had brought our peoples to these islands, we had continued to see ourselves from the perspectives of our loss, characterizing ourselves as ex-enslaved, ex-indentured. In reality we would better address our future if we saw ourselves as a new people brought together and created anew by our struggles against enslavement, indenture and colonialism.

As he said to Florence, now snuggled under his armpit, in one of the speeches that he sat up in bed to make after one of their love-making sessions:

'What we need to counteract the three, four hundred years of colonial propaganda is a tourism thrust of our own. We need to look at ourselves afresh. We need to look at ourselves with a new curiosity. The truth is that we do not know who we are. And we will never know until we see ourselves with new eyes.'

He prepared a single sheet folded in the middle. On the front page was a photograph of himself and the Party's symbol. On the back page was a listing of his experience and accomplishments. Taking up the middle page was a map of Trinidad and Tobago with information on the numerous rebellions attempted by the enslaved, the laws passed against them (to show what they were up against), the riots (note the characterization, he said) of the indentured. He gave population figures, the breakdown by race, location of population, major resources, the beaches. He listed steel bands and steel-band yards and calypso tents and calypsonians and masquerade camps and poets and painters, the mango tree in Matura under which the novelist John De John went each day to sit and write out in longhand his thirty-seven unpublished novels, Shango churches, Hindu temples, mosques, friendly societies, sporting clubs, best village groups, choirs, dance groups, village councils, their chairmen and secretaries.

And it was partly through these maps that he recorded the highest number of votes ever polled for a candidate in the elections, because everywhere schoolchildren wanted to get hold of these maps, village councils wanted them, teachers, agricultural officers. Long after the campaign was over he kept receiving requests for those maps.

In his speeches, pursuing his central theme of people looking at themselves and their islands afresh, he called for people exchanges, between rich and poor; Indian and African and Chinese and French Creole and Syrian; between Caroni and Laventille, Morvant and Goodwood Park, Elleslie Park and John John; Morvant and Carapichaima; Trou Macaque and Rio Claro; Roxborough and Cascadu; Canaan and Matura.

Victorious in the by-election, Alford to his surprise was given the portfolio of Minister of Social and Environmental Rehabilitation in the Office of The Prime Minister. As he told Florence, 'This is a job for a visionary.' And he was made to feel even more favoured when the Prime Minister, congratulating him at his swearing-in ceremony, in a show of warmth that surprised Alford, directed him to make use of the office he, the Prime Minister, had vacated. 'You may start your rehabilitating from there. I hope you have better luck than I have had in cleaning up that pigpen. Yes,' he said, when Alford looked to see if he was serious, because the new offices for the Prime Minister were still under construction. 'Go ahead. I have no intention of ever setting foot again in that building.'

Favoured as he felt himself to be, Alford felt a sense of the steely wilfulness of this man and the need for caution.

The chaos and dilapidation that Alford had expected to find in the Prime Minister's office were not there. Instead, he found a surprising order and nobody aware that the Prime Minister had removed his office to elsewhere. Cars were organized in the car park, a receptionist was at the entrance at the bottom of the stairs, everybody seemed alert and employed. Perhaps the one thing that gave Alford an indication that the Prime Minister was not going to be in that day was, when he rode through the gate at ten in the morning, the sentries were seated in their little green hut playing what at a glance he thought was a game of single-hand rummy.

Inside, the Prime Minister's office was polished, its drapes in good condition, everything was in shape as if they expected the PM to turn up at any time. The only problem was that the air-conditioning was on too high and the room freezing. Just to make sure that all was well, Alford held the handles of the window and heaved. The window took off so smoothly it nearly flew away with his shoulders. The cords had been replaced.

From the very start Alford George knew that this office was not him. He had a bad feeling about occupying it; but the Prime Minister had asked him to use it.

'And you going to use it?' Ethelbert Tannis asked him, in shock.

'But the Prime Minister say . . .'

Ethelbert Tannis cut him off: 'The Prime Minister say plenty things. Be careful what you hear him saying. Listen.'

This was in accord with Alford's own instincts. So, for himself, he selected a small room that had served as a small meeting-room. It had a good table. And he ordered a new chair, brought in a map of Trinidad and Tobago, his Oxford dictionary and his *Roget's Thesaurus* and a photograph of himself with his left hand under his chin and his right hand holding the telephone into which he was speaking. In regard to the Prime Minister's office, what he did was to hang a huge photograph of the Prime Minister above everything else on the walls, and, as protocol required, an equally sized one of the President of the Republic alongside it and to leave the office otherwise just as he had met it. It was in that room, however, he went sometimes to do his thinking, believing that there he would be able to access the vast experience and the prodigious intelligence of the Prime Minister and tap into the aura of history that emanated from it. Sometimes, too, in his fits of thinking, lest his ideas evaporate before he could get them down, he would call Miss Baldeosing, his secretary, and sit there on the sofa, never on the PM's chair, and dictate his letters and his speeches. He liked the room, the huge polished table, the chairs, the leather sofa, the feel of it, the walls with the portraits of colonial governors, all of whom would become familiar to him: from the first one, the Spaniard, Antonio Sedeno, who in 1530 had arrived in Trinidad to colonize it with a few followers armed with swords, shields and crossbows, from Santo Domingo to discover that the Indians here in Trinidad were not as defenceless as those the Spaniards had encountered in St Domingo, Puerto Rico and Cuba but were a warlike and dangerous foe; Don Antonio De Berrio, who took possession of the island to settle it as a port and principal base from which to enter and settle El Dorado and who Sir Walter Raleigh would capture and later release just to demonstrate his power and contempt; Don Maria Chacon, the final Spanish governor, who would surrender the island to the British without firing a shot; Hislop, who in order to act swiftly against what was rumoured to be the intended insurrection of the enslaved Africans invoked the Spanish law that empowered the Governor in council to act judicially and on 19 December 1806 tried and found guilty four Africans and condemned them to be hanged the next day at twelve noon, their heads to be exposed after death on poles erected for the purpose, and their bodies to be hung in chains on the seaside near the district where they resided. Picton, Woodford, the English governors to Sir Hubert Rance: this was their history, he felt, not his. *And where was ours?* he thought.

And there it was. On another wall, the mural commissioned by the government at the time of Independence, to give our citizens a sense of themselves, the various races and cultures and diverse traditions out of which we are springing, done by an artist selected as a result of a Caribbean-wide contest, the winner a West Indian living then in London, who had done a mural for Jamaica for its Independence, and who would later do ones for Barbados, for Antigua, for St Lucia when their turn came, each one similarly titled, New Day in Jamaica; New Horizons in Trinidad; New Dawn in Barbados, each one with the three ships of Columbus, each with the crucified leader of what they called a slave rebellion, the rebel leader, arms outstretched like a Carnival sailor doing a movement of the King Sailor dance, dying heroic-ally for Freedom. There it was. Native Indians in a ballet of welcome offering gifts to Columbus, who stands with imperial nonchalance, one hand on his hip, the other holding a lance as if deciding whether he should accept their offering. Behind him his soldiers heave into position for planting a gigantic cross that will surely weigh down and drown the small island. Las Casas, his hair almost all gone, his shoulders sagging under the grief of murders, is penning another plea to the conscience of his king. Africans are dancing to their jungle tom-toms. Sir Francis Drake, sleek like a pigeon and alert as a hawk, surveys the burning wreckage of Spanish galleons. Ladies in lace petticoats and bon-nets of silk are having tea on the cool veranda while Black maids with abundant bosoms and willing hands hold the trays. Blood is oozing from the bleeding sugar. Toussaint L'Ouverture in the dress of a general is on horseback at the head of a ragged army swooping down upon burning plantations.

Governor Don Maria Chacon supervises the flogging of an African obeah man, while in another corner Asian women with red and saffron orhnis and with rings weighing down their hands curtsy on the quay of this small island. And in its easy, its simple resolution there stand, in the foreground, a tall white child and next to him a shorter Black girl and an Indian boy and a Chinese girl, so comfortable, so easy. Off to the right of them, looking sideways at them, is a woman, a Black woman with the mop, the broom, the accoutrements of service, with an ironic acquiesc-ence and the stance of rebellion. Alford recognizes her. She is Vera from Cascadu, whom to his surprise he came upon one day in her apparel of cleaning, cap and apron, as he was leaving the office late and recognized her too late, because he had not expected to see her there and she had looked at him with a half-smile of recognition that more resembled accusation. *What is he doing here?* is the question in her eyes. Her power is her belief that he would like to pretend not to know her since the knowledge of their relationship would be an embarrassment to him. Her grace is that she will also pretend not to know him.

'Good evening, Mister Alford,' she had said.

He had answered, 'Good evening.' But just as he recognizes who she really is, the Ambassador to Guyana whom he was going to meet comes walking towards him and when he turns back from greeting him, Vera had disappeared, and he had to leave without letting her know that she was recognized by him.

The whole evening that episode bothered him, and he had made it his business to wait next evening so he could see her. When he sees her, he believes that he owes her an apology.

'Vera,' he says. 'I didn't know you working here.'

'Yes, Mister Alford,' she says. 'I here five years now.'

He wants to ask her why she was addressing him as Mister but he is ashamed. He wants to ask her what about the shorthand and typing? What about the dreams, the travelling? As if she had heard the questions, she shrugs. He understands that that is the distance she feels, from him. Is it from him?

'I saw you yesterday but I didn't make you out,' he tells her, trying to sound familiar.

'I know, I see you was busy.'

'Busy? Yes. That was the Guyanese Ambassador.' He does not know whether she has forgiven him. He doesn't know whether he needs forgiveness. What he is guilty of? He feels this guilt over Vera, over his brothers. Somehow the power he is supposed to have is not enough to banish his guilt. Instead, it ties him up. Why does he feel the need to apologize? And what is he apologizing for? He has the feeling that she believes that they share a secret, rather, that she is holding a secret for him.

Alford believed his portfolio to be important. It had given him the opportunity – no, the mandate to pursue the theme he believed to be crucial for development of his people and his islands. And he continued with unabating enthusiasm to trumpet his vision. The newspapers followed him to the various lunches and dinners he was asked to address and reported him speaking to the Chambers of Commerce, the Rotary Clubs, the Credit Unions, Friendly Societies and later as he became more popular at schools' graduations and installation of officers at village councils.

See these islands with new eyes, he encouraged. See past the slums, see past the racial divisions, see past the present ownership of resources, see a people who have been thrown together and are working to make this a new world place. Look not at what has been done to you, look at what you are doing, look at what you have done. He wanted to make the steel band the central symbol of the nation, an icon encapsulating our struggle for freedom to express ourselves in our own idiom. He wanted the Laventille slums transformed into a shrine to the steel band, with art galleries and restaurants and a theatre. He wanted the Carnival arts placed at the centre of the educational system. There is no profit in imitation, he said. What we have to do is to see ourselves with new eyes, see a land where it is possible to create a new people and a culture of prosperity and dignity and freedom.

With applause ringing in his ears, he walked through the city with the stride of a man who had a mission, a little self-conscious that everywhere he was recognized.

Early on mornings he jogged around the Savannah in a red, white and black tracksuit marked Trinidad & Tobago, stopping at the completion of his run at a coconut cart to drink a coconut water, light jelly, standing there jumping on the spot as his coconut was cut and other early-morning joggers pointed him out slyly, 'That is him, the Minister,' bathing in the attention, watching a fellow watching him in puzzlement, divining that he was saying to himself, 'Where I know this fella from?' and then the sudden flash of recognition, 'Ah-ha! Is he! Is him!' And then the fella coming over to shake his hand or to say Goodmorning. Or to make a comment or to ask him a question. He enjoyed this attention. It was his little weakness and he went all about where people were gathered, not only at cricket test matches or calypso tents and at Carnival shows. With his wider interests and experience in matters of art, of culture, of sport, he would drop in any night at the finals of the Best Village Folk Theatre competition; and for years he was the only government minister

128

or, for that matter, Member of Parliament at a play. He dressed up in jeans and a jersey marked *Desperadoes* and went to listen to steelband at Panorama. Carnival Sunday he sampled the fêtes, moving from the one in St Ann's to one in Goodwood Park and settling finally at one at the home of the actor Errol Jones with the literary and theatre and dance people, dancing until his whole body was soaked down with perspiration. From there he would leave and go to Calypso and Carnival costume finals, change and from there head out to the Oval fête.

For J'Ouvert he would daub his body with mud and later on Monday play whatever kind of African warrior Burrokeets was playing. On Tuesday he played with Minshall, a big important mas', a statement mas', jumping up with three four women around him.

And of course he paid attention to his clothes, his shirts, his track suits, his lounge wear, his rings, one with the good mark of the phantom and the other a plain gold band, his chains, his hair, his nails. And he moved about at cricket and football with that athletic ease out of his years of fitness, of clean living, no smoking, healthy eating. He appeared in the social columns as The Best Dressed Minister, The Most Eligible Bachelor in Parliament. He began to run ten-k races, five ks, and was urged to try the marathon.

One morning Alford had finished jogging and was at the coconut cart waiting for the coconutman to cut a light jelly for him when a fellow there also waiting to be served turned to him and said, 'You is the Minister, not so?'

'I am,' Alford said.

'Good,' said the fellow. 'Well, they pappyshowing you, you hear, pardner. You is the biggest pappyshow in this town.' And as if to make sure that Alford made no mistake as to his meaning, he said again, 'They making you a arse, you hear, pardner. All you do is end up talking and talking just like them.'

It wasn't beyond Alford to cuff him down. Instead he answered with a presence of mind that surprised both of them, 'Thank you, brother. Thank you.'

He meant it. Somewhere along the way his mission had got away from him. He said nothing to anybody, and Florence only got to know of it after transcribing the tapes of his musing after their lovemaking that Wednesday. For after observing that he did his most lucid thinking in his talks after their lovemaking, she had made him a gift of a tape recorder for his birthday and a chain to tie it to his bedhead so he could capture his own thoughts in their post-coital bed.

'I have forgotten my mission. I have become part of the tapestry of pretence at power. I who ought to have been the one to disturb this numbing peace have now become keeper of that peace. I have joined the gang of overseers that help to keep this place a plantation. Thank you, brother man. Thank you. Words that had easily slipped off my tongue – African, revolution, reparation, land distribution, decision-making – are now all coated with explosives and I no longer want the explosion. Not a new statue had been raised, not an old one razed.'

'This is a poem,' Florence said, when she was finished transcribing it. 'I don't understand what it saying.'

Alford thought of his earlier poetry. He thought of his teaching. He wondered if he had really made the best choice of a vocation. He began complaining; not big complaints, just little questions to his colleagues. What you think? How you feeling? He wanted to know if he was the only one feeling this sense of irrelevance.

And then he turned around to find that, just like that, the three years of his term nearly up, the country getting ready to have another General Election, and Ethelbert B. Tannis who knew all things telling him that there were whispers that in view of the need to give a more multiracial image to the Party the PM was thinking of replacing him with Rattan Ramjattan to contest the upcoming elections.

Alford was disappointed. He felt he had done nothing. He had let the people down. Ethelbert B. Tannis was philosophical.

'There is a power about time,' he said. 'What you have to do is just stay there and change will come. Stay in the wicket and runs will come. Win the election and stay there. This time you'll have five years for your mission.'

But first he had to win the nomination. And that is when he turned his mind back to Cascadu and Cunaripo, to present himself as theirs again, their candidate, their son of the soil. He thought to start with the village councils. But they couldn't get a quorum for meetings, far more a large enough membership for him to speak to. The established churches didn't want to have anything to do with him since his talk about Carnival as religion; but he got the leaders of the Shouters' churches in the area to invite him to attend a joint thanksgiving. He got the newspapers to come and there was a picture of him in the newspapers kneeling with the mothers of the Church, surrounded by lighted candles and flowers without thorns, marigold and croton and ginger lilies and chaconia and fern. He attended the schools in his constituency, their sports meetings, their graduation, their prize-giving. He himself offered up prizes to both the cricket team and the school, and a prize also for the best umpire. 'We have to train those who have to control the game.' Through Floyd, he got Wanderers Cricket Club to invite him to the annual Bachelors vs. Married Men fête match. He bowled the first ball to open the match and he played one innings with Bachelors and the other with Married Men.

He went to the women. He went to the market with his basket and did his shopping. He opened a constituency office in a room below the house he had bought and was renovating to live in. He set aside Thursdays for people of the district to come to see him. He still kept Mondays and Wednesdays for Florence. And he fed it all, every activity, to the newspapers with photographs of himself and texts of his speeches. And all at once he was nearly every day in the newspapers: Minister Opens Constituency Office; Minister Kicks Off Football Final; Minister Distributes Prizes; Minister Cooks for Needy in His District; Minister Promises New Day for Youths. He was shown bowling, kicking ball, handing out prizes, running races or, more often, on the telephone with one hand under his chin.

And then – hallelujah! – out of the blue it came, the invitation that when he received it he knew was the ticket to his salvation. It was a request from Bango, real name Emmanuel Durity, to take the salute at the March Past at the Independence Day Parade in Cunaripo and to deliver the Feature Address on that occasion.

As he said in another of his post-coital musings, 'I have to believe that there is a Divine hand guiding me. Who would have thought that I would be forced to address this subject of Bango's reparation in this fashion? Who would have thought . . .'

And it was this that brought him to his office at seven-thirty that Thursday morning along with the cleaners so that he could clear up the work he had for the day, and leave early for his constituency office and on the way pass through Cascadu and see Bango and accept his invitation in person. And he had done most of the work by three o'clock. He had gone to the sitting of the Commission of Enquiry into the State of Forest Products. He had attended the meeting on the Seismic Aeromagnetic Survey. Environmentalists had come to see him. The Society for Transcendental Meditation had come to see him. He had attended to some Party business. As soon as he was about to go to lunch some Sisters and Brothers of the Church of Fellowship and Joy, Dr Kennos' church, concerned about his spiritual well-being had come to pray with him. And finally, Ethelbert B. Tannis, his campaign manager, who had been in Port-of-Spain for the day, arrived to travel with him back to Cunaripo and to show him the photographs and the proofs of the handbill that he was thinking of using in the election campaign.

Ethelbert B. Tannis had come up with the idea that since he, Alford, was a champion of the indigenous, it would be appropriate for him to present himself in calypso. There were limits to the calypso, but Alford would welcome a calypsonian singing in his campaign. Ethelbert B. Tannis, who counted among his accomplishments writing calypso lyrics, had undertaken to write the calypso and had brought him one verse and the chorus:

> *I am sure you heard of Alford George,*
> *The man in the council we have is ours.*
> *He do everything we say and want to do,*
> *Georgie is a real dou-dou.*
>
> *Vote for him on election day,*
> *Don't let any other appeal get you tootoolbay,*
> *Son of the soil, man of the people,*
> *Alford George is the man for you.*

For the first time for the day Alford found himself laughing: 'You make this up?' he asked Ethelbert Tannis.

Tannis looked at him and smiled, 'You like it?'

'When you put the music to it I will tell you.'

'I was thinking that maybe I could change the line that says 'Georgie is a real dou dou' to something else. Like, for example, 'Georgie is the real man for you.' '

'Wait for the music,' Alford said. He was relaxed.

Alford had intended to drop off Ethelbert B. Tannis in Cunaripo and go on alone to see Bango in Cascadu. Because he was running a little late, he decided to stop at the constituency office to see if anyone was waiting, deal with the person and then go to Cascadu and see Bango. There was a woman sitting on the steps, waiting. It was Bango's wife, Miss Myrtle. She had come to ask Alford not to accept the invitation Bango had sent him to take the March Past because in her view his involvement would do more harm than good to Bango.

'And how will my refusal help Bango?' he asked.

'It will make him know that is time for him to stop this marching. If you don't hold it up now, he will never stop.'

'And you want him to stop?'

'Yes. I want him to stop. That is what I want.'

'But why?'

'It's a long story. You don't have the time to hear it now.'

'I have the time,' Alford said. 'I have the time.'

8

Miss Myrtle's Story

The evening the National Party land in Cascadu, Miss Myrtle in Lorenzo Rumshop & Grocery to make the fortnightly miracle of stretching the little money she had into a supply of food for her family, was watching Miss Esme heap the parcels and tins and bottles of her purchases on to the counter, her heart stopping each time Miss Esme take up her list to write in a cost and then starting to beat again when she put it back down, secure underneath the rusty six-pound weight that Miss Esme hardly had any cause to use since what she had to weigh rarely went beyond that number; and where it wasn't going to go this evening either; at least not for her, not even for the flour.

Miss Myrtle had finished selling for the day. She had packed away her coalpot and sent it and the table and stool across the road to be put underneath Miss Alice house where she left them for the night, placed the iron pot in the basket with the remainder of the coals outside the shop for when Tall Boy and his half-dead Zephyr limp back from Cunaripo to pick her up and carry her home to the Settlement.

Next door, in the rumshop section, the juke-box was playing 'Jean and Dinah', this calypso that she detested from the first time she hear it:

> *Yankees gone*
> *And Sparrow take over now . . .*

Take over what? Take over how? And everybody singing it, everybody dancing to it . . .

Above the music, Constable Stephen Aguillera, his police tunic unbuttoned at the neck and his cap on the counter next to the bottle of white rum, was arguing cricket with Fats Alexis, a County Council worker who never play a stroke of cricket in his life but had himself down as an authority on the game because Cascadu cricket team carry him everywhere as their umpire, Fats saying that it was time for them to make Frank Worrell captain of the West Indies cricket team, and Aguillera talking about a Jamaican fella they call Alexander. They was two good ones together: Fats who knows everything and this long-eyed, don't-care young fella who for the three months they post him from Matura to Cascadu, at four o'clock every day put on his dress uniform and come and sit down in the rumshop to drink rum, argue cricket and watch Miss Esme daughters. He was the one, this fella, who they leave in charge of the police station in Matura on Carnival Tuesday and who, as nine o'clock Tuesday morning reach, lock up the police station and release the single prisoner who he make agree to return to the station by eleven that night, the same time he Constable Aguillera was expected to come back, leaving for the prisoner, the key to his cell underneath a stone in the big concrete trough where they had some ornamental palms growing, in case he, Constable Aguillera, didn't make it back in time, take the same taxi with the prisoner and had him dropped off at Sangre Grande where he (the prisoner) wanted to stay and where it was easier for him to get back from since it was only nine miles away, he, Constable Aguillera, continuing onward to Port-of-Spain, to Belmont where he had to go to take off his uniform and put on his masquerade costume and then leave from there to go and look for the band where he had a woman waiting for him to play mas with her. They was two *good* ones, he and Fats Alexis. But she wasn't looking at them.

Miss Myrtle was watching Miss Esme's stylish daughter, the red, womanish one, with the rude mouth and bottom big already, moving slack-waisted behind the counter, with her own drowsy and female grace, idle, victorious, invincible, as if the youth she was carrying was a fashion that she alone had a right to model, weighing the goods she was selling, with her face pained, her polished fingernails held away from her hands like she just finish play the piano and was holding herself ready to lift off into the world of the calendar on the nail above her head where another girl, this one glamorous and white, with a bold stare and a bit of bare thigh already revealed, was stepping out of her négligé for an evening of romance in the brilliantly lighted city she could touch through her window. Miss Myrtle didn't even realize that she had a smile on her face until she heard the girl saying, in a tone that for the first time made her (the girl) seem human and vulnerable and shy,

'Miss Myrtle, you looking at me and smiling. What it is you thinking?'

Miss Myrtle was thinking how time does fly and pass and go away. She was thinking of the red anthurium lilies in the flower garden she was tending the evening she look up and see Durity in the road in front her mother house, tall and all in white, with a red handkerchief tied across his forehead, making him look more like a young Shango priest than the cricketer he was, astraddle a battered bicycle that she thought too small for him to be its owner, gazing out of the most startled and appealing eyes that had ever met her own, and saw in the clear mirror of his face how really beautiful she was. It frightened her, this vision of her own beauty, and she kept on staring into his face to make sure that it was really she who was there, and that the soft astonished wonder of his countenance was not created by a trick of the sunlight glinting in his eyes.

'Good evening,' he said; and at his voice the sweet trouble flashed from the earth, up through the flute of her knees and thighs and spread tingling through her loins and she felt, Lord! What trouble is this for me now? And she thought almost with vexation, I hope you have a house to put me and my child in; knowing, in a flash of wisdom, just from the set of his shoulders and the clear bold innocence of his eyes that such a man owned nothing but himself, that he had stumbled upon himself in her just so, with no preparation, no warning, very much as she had spied herself in him.

And we stand up there, he and me, the two of us alone in the great wide world, gazing at each other with the sense of recognition and amazement and an awkward fear, exhausted by their effort to say everything by speaking nothing, and she was struck by the sudden softness of the day and by her awareness of millions of years of time and the greenness in the green leaves of the lilies and by the sweet smell of the earth, and the stubborn strength and frailty of grass, and she felt herself tumbling into a new space and danger and excitement and peace, with the need to hold herself from spinning and the wish to step backwards to look at him again, to see if I could spy out in him something that I mighta missed earlier, some flaw that would diminish him in my eyes, make him less invincible and vulnerable and handsome and dazzling than he appeared. For if he was not going to be what he was, if this was not how the world was going to stay, if things was going to go back to the ordinary way they was, then it was better he leave me in peace to take care of my child and to not bring more grief to my mother and pain to myself by having to take on another set of man-troubles in my young life. So she stood up there with a fresh alertness, feeling the perspiration forming on the button of her nose and a tightness pulling at the corners of her lips, waiting for him to get fresh or say something stupid; so I could say, OK. Goodbye! But instead when he open his mouth, it was to praise the beauty of the anthuriums and to wonder about the care that make the flower garden so pretty, so that I, like this big fool, out of the generosity and eagerness that always get me in trouble, ask him if he want one of the flowers. And, yes, he wanted one to give to a special somebody. And, I again so stupid, not thinking. For how could a young man on his way to a cricket match just so ride up and be interested in flower garden, not thinking of any trickery, had believed without asking him or his saying who the flower was for, though I guess I musta been thinking that he wanted it to carry for his mother, because at that time I myself was thinking of my own mother how she had shielded me against the anger and shame of my father and ask no questions when I leave Benny and his stifling band of saints, with my belly big and his ring off my finger and come back home feeling more ugly and stupid than when I went, cut for him the most perfect lily, one red and smooth and glassy, and made the few steps to him where he was there still half-sitting on his bicycle and give it to him, the last thing I expecting is for this boy to take the flower that I give him and stick it in my hair.

So lovely it feel and so true and so real, I didn't care if is something he see somebody do in a picture, though in the pictures the boy would bring his own flower and come and stand up in front my door and I would have on a long dress and would now be coming down the stair. Months later I was to hear that as I leaned forward to hand him the flower and he leaned over to take it, through the open neck of my bodice the scamp

137

look and see down inside my bosom my bare breasts since I wasn't wearing a brassiere. That was it. That is what get you? I didn't know if I was vexed or pleased. 'Was my body you wanted?' But from the way he answered, she was never sure if it was the sight of her breasts that moved him to put the flower in her hair or if the moment he see me he fall for me the same way I fall for him.

'Come to the cricket match?' he crooned, his voice in the same tune of innocence that he sang about the flowers, and she was glad when later he tell me how I put him in his place, how I say, 'No, sir. I have a child to see about. I can't just pick up myself and run down to the cricket ground.'

'Bring him with you,' he said, taking one foot off the ground, setting it on the pedal and remaining for an eternity balanced there, his eyes bathing me in my own beauty.

'Him? Is a girl.'

'Well, bring her,' stepping down on the pedal of the bicycle and pushing it into motion and starting to ride away, all in one fluid stroke of fluent male and balanced nonchalance, looking back to smile and wave assuringly like a man who had been in my life for years and not for the less than half an hour that we stand up talking to one another, leaving her as she watched the loose ease of his pedalling, growing into her tallness, beginning to feel glad that I am me, happy and a little sad that this trouble that she had feared and wished for had overtaken her in this man, breathing, as much with defiance as with resignation, as her mind pitched her into the future and she watched him disappear, 'Well, I will just have to help him build the mansion.'

'So you went to the cricket match?' her sister Shirley asked, in the astonished and outraged and saved Pentecostal tone of a recent convert carrying also the motherly authority of someone freshly engaged to marry Paul who was also saved.

'Yes.'

'And see him?'

'Yes, I see him.'

'Myrtle! Myrtle! Don't tell me you go and get catch again. This man you talking about is Bango Durity, you say? Tall, big-eyed with his two lips like two cushions, the top one bigger than the one below and his eyes always watching you.'

'Yes. In them a light soft like a blessing. Yes. Is he, is him.'

'Get in with him and you getting in with the most backward tribe of people in this island. His family there everybody on the same level. Nobody to help you. All of them renting from Mr Carabon who own the whole settlement. Fête is all those people know to do. They start fêting for Christmas in September and they go right through to Ash Wednesday. The only thing they have is a cricket team and a steel band and this Durity is the captain of the both of them. What time he will have for you? The priest curse the place. They say nothing can't progress there. Once you start to live there you start to sink into a pit. They living there on the plantation where they used to work. It used to employ everybody back in slavery times and they still there waiting. The plantation run down now the cocoa gone, the sugar ain't have no price. They don't want to hear that. They don't want to hear that at all. They waiting for some miracle to save them. They have this belief. They believe that somebody owe them something. It have something to do with land that they waiting on Government to give them; but they have no papers and no claim. I not sure about it, if is true or is something they make up just to explain their laziness and to hide their shame.'

'And you smiling?' Shirley asking, her voice changed as if beginning to see in me the change that I didn't know was showing already. 'What happen to you?' Looking at me suspicious like I pregnant again.

'What happen to me? You see something happen to me? I looking saved?'

'You change your hair or what?'

'Change my hair?' And I run my fingers through my hair. And I know is not that my hair change or anything.

'Your nose?'

Was just me, my hair my own, the cushion of my lips soft on my mouth. Was just me.

'You have to be careful with that fella, you hear. Something about him I don't trust. He too good-looking. You leave a good good man like Benny, a decent Christian man like Benny. Pappy don't like this, you know.'

'You tell Pappy bout him.'

'I didn't have to tell Pappy. Pappy see you, how you looking and he ask me.'

'And you tell him?'

'Pappy know them. He know his father and his grandfather King Durity. He used to work with them long ago before he start to drive bus. He was driving truck for Noreiga, going up in the mora forest behind Cascadu.'

'And what Pappy have against him?'

'Proud, Pappy say. Proud and they don't have nothing. Is you Pappy thinking about, your future. He don't want to see you make another mistake. He still can't understand how you could leave Benny. He still don't believe you try. He see you just wanting to have your own way. And, girl, you have a child. You not single.'

Then one day in the big three o'clock sun he come home to the house where she living and nearly meet her father home – 'Boy, you crazy! You know you nearly meet my father home' – to take her to go to see where he living and lift her up and set her balanced on the handle of his bicycle and rode with her through the bumpy settlement roads until they reached this little two-roomed house, good enough looking from the road, but when she went in with him, it was to find that the treaders to the front steps were missing and to get into the house you had to jump up and to get back out you had to jump down. 'This is where you get your exercise?' she asked him. The back door was an open space, the front door swung on a single hinge and to open or shut it you had to lift it into place.

One of the windows, the wooden one, was nailed shut and the other, hanging from two strands of wire, was the aluminium door from the wreck of an airplane he had found in the forest.

The front room had two Morris chairs, each with one cushion, and a centre table with a photograph album, and his bed and clothes. The other room, the back room, dark from the windows being boarded up, had scattered about it cricket bats and pads and balls. Even the matting they played cricket on was rolled up in one corner of the floor. And on a table in another corner was his pitch-oil stove and pots and plates and pans for cooking and eating.

'And this is the storeroom for the cricket implements?'

He grinned, 'I just keeping them here. I have to clean out the place.'

'I shoulda been a prophet,' she said. This? And she was watching him full in his face. 'This is the place where you want me to come and live?'

'I ain't ask you yet,' he say smiling.

'Good,' she said. 'Because before you do any asking you have to do some fixing.'

'True,' he said. 'I will start tomorrow morning. I getting hinges for the windows and the doors and work out a way to get that airplane door to swing. I cutlassing the yard and I building an outside kitchen. Afterwards, I will extend the whole building. But come outside! Come outside and see the place, how it looking. Come!'

Outside the yard was planted with bougainvillea trees and red hibiscus fencing, orchids were growing on tree stumps, ixora plants, a calabash tree and two coconut trees near enough to string a hammock in between, guava tree near the latrine and some julie mango trees. She looked back at the house. 'It could fix,' she said.

'We?' he asked.

She nodded.

'Good.' He made to hold her. She let him. And still in his embrace, she let him know: 'One more thing. Before we go too far together, you have to talk to my father. I get burn already. Don't think I coming here just so and live with you. My family doesn't trust you. My sister find you too good-looking.'

'And your father?'

'He ain't say nothing, but I know him. He watch the gold teeth you have in your mouth and he wonder if it mean that you intend to be a sweetman with three four woman to mind you, or if you want to settle down. He know your grandfather.'

'And you?' he asked. 'What about you?'

'Me? You don't see me here with you.'

'They have no electric lights in Cascadu,' Shirley said. 'You have to tote water from a pipe by the roadside. You have to go down in the river to wash clothes. And bathe there with everybody. And where you going to send your daughter Vera to school? The school in Cascadu don't even have one good teacher.

141

And the environment. As soon as a girl have fifteen years she make a baby. The one or two who lucky, who escape, bolt, run and never look back. And the people. They look like they together, but the only thing they together in is not to co-operate with one another. The Indian off by himself, the Chinese you don't see at all. Carabon up there on his estate, trying to fence it round. All his children in town. He don't want them live there. You have no family near. You will be alone, with all his family round you.'

She had to laugh, 'Shirley, where you think I going? Africa?'

'Miss Myrtle?'

It was the Red Girl, her head bowed, her eyelids lifted, on her face a half-smile of suspicion. 'Like you don't want to tell me what it is you thinking.'

'Girl,' Miss Myrtle said, 'I don't know where to begin.' Same time she heard the heavy screech of a bus stopping and she turn to look outside, one part of her mind seeing back to that time those years before, a time after Christmas, a few days before the new year, the heavy screech of another bus and Bango wiping his feet on the fibre mat at the front door of the room made darker by the weather outside, by the curtains and the potted plants inside. She had invited him to meet her family and he had arrived with the same bus her father was waiting to leave by; her father, his shaved head and his thick neck, one piece, like a turtle's, his bus driver's uniform on and his cap in his hand, in front a row of greetings cards strung against the wall, all of them clean and new-looking as at the time of their issue, holding the arms of the chair and pushing himself up in silence, and going to the door and shaking Bango's hand and looking him over before he left to catch the bus that was at that very moment outside waiting to take him to the bus station where he would take charge of the bus that he was driver of. 'Sorry. I have to go. But another time, eh,' he said to Bango. And she knew then that it could not have suited him better if he had timed the whole thing himself, making her sure now that he had given her up, that as far as he was concerned her having a child of her own had made her a woman on her own, and it saddened her not to have him there as father on this day when she felt most like a little girl.

Shirley hadn't come either and she was left with Bango and her mother who, with her excited self, even before the boy could sit down had come sailing into the room with a tray with sweetbread and a glass of gingerbeer, Myrtle thinking, 'Ma, what you bringing these things for him for? He not coming here for his belly. Why you don't wait for him to sit down?' and at the same time feeling a sad thankfulness, knowing that in her over-excited awkward way that her mother was making a gift to her, to them, of her presence and blessing, although she didn't know him either, showing her best face and making him feel welcome, so he could understand that she, Myrtle, had a home and a mother who knew how to treat people like human. Looking back, that little meeting of the three of them was the celebration of her wedding feast because early in the new year she would move in and live with him.

From the day she arrived in his house and see the bats and pads and other implements of Cascadu cricket club, Myrtle understood that she had to share Bango with the team and the village. Shirley was right. His life was not just his own. He was captain of the cricket team and that alone was not just authority, it was responsibility. He was the man to conduct the practice, to roll the cricket pitch before the match, to buy the cricket ball and pick the cricket team and find an umpire if Fats Alexis wasn't there, to get somebody to keep score; and when they had to play outside of the village to make arrangements for the transportation of the players. Everything. Nothing was done without him.

But it was worth it. She would feel tears just watching him on a Saturday afternoon lead the Cascadu team on to the field, all of them in baptismal white, leisurely like princes dismounted from horses, throwing the ball and catching it and flinging it backwards and flinging it high into the air, time belonging to them, time to check the direction of the wind, the hardness of the pitch to be concerned whether it suited pace or spin, time for tea – really a drink of water or a cup of juice or an ice cream from one of the ladies selling around the ground – this space and stage creating out of estate labourers and watchmen on government projects, cutlassmen and stonebreakers, knights of the weekend.

She would feel full full to see him set the field, the players shifting into their positions like kites in the sky of the field moved by the invisible strings that he was holding to crouch like hunters around the batsman, this huge gloved and padded medieval beast himself waiting with his own breathlessness for their attack. Things wasn't all right but it was all right.

Because already she had realized that in taking her to live with him he was not taking a wife as something to put aside and adore as much as a mate, a pardner, someone who would do for him what he was doing for the village. He didn't even see her as someone separate to him. What he expected of himself is what he expected of her. She was a part of him and he expected her to give herself with the same completeness that he gave himself to the village. For his part he had fixed the house. He had put hinges on the doors and windows and after countless hours had managed to set up a mechanism of wire by which the airplane door that he had insisted on keeping as window could swing. He built an outdoor kitchen on a level lower than the house. He had walled it with a latticework of bamboo strips, temporarily ('Until I get the proper kind of grass and mud to plaster it with').

After nearly a year, when the wet season come around and the wind start to blow the rain inside the kitchen, he was reminded of the need to wall up the kitchen. A vaps hit him and just before the sun went down he start busy busy digging trenches all over the yard to get a suitable soil to mix with grass to make the plaster. Next evening he was back digging until night stopped him. Finally he located a spot with a satisfactory texture of soil. By now the yard was a set of holes and trenches, left to repair itself by the action of rain and sun. Two months later, he went looking for the grass. In a clearing in the forest he had found a huge field overrun with pangola grass. He made three trips with that grass. Proudly, he piled it up in a huge bundle behind the latrine where it remained unused until days later Boyie from the cricket team revealed to him that it was not the correct kind of grass for plastering. He never tried again to plaster the kitchen. Over the years the grass sprouted and spread in every direction, appearing in the wet season and seeming to disappear in the dry, until finally it established itself over the land, overpowering weeds, climbing trees, moving over every bit of unprotected ground, running down the hill to the roadside. Bango tried cutting it. He tried rooting it up. It was so tough and matted that it broke cutlasses. He tried weedicide. He tried fire. But it continued. Over the years she would get a guilty feeling as she saw it growing along the roadside through the gravel and stones. It travelled miles. She saw clumps of it in Deep Ravine, overpowering a field of grapefruit trees, covering an old wooden house in Hibiscus and weighing down a field of dried corn and pigeon peas, and she kept looking to see when it would reach the streets of Cunaripo, giving up with a smile the idea of Bango ever plastering the walls of the kitchen. With him nothing was permanent.

Nothing was permanent.

On top the house, the sheets of galvanize, instead of being nailed down, were held in place by pieces of lumber and an assortment of stones and bricks so that when the wind was strong it would blow the galvanize out of position and expose them to the sky. The first time this happened was in the night and in the rain. He took up the ladder and placed it against the building and climbed unto the roof. She remained in the house to shine the torchlight and, with a broomstick, tap the place in the roof where it was leaking. Rain coming, wind blowing and, inside, the house soaking and he on the roof, trying to locate the leak, shouting, 'Where, Myrtle? Where?' And she inside the house, jabbing with the end of the broomstick the place she thought was leaking, shouting, 'Here, Bango! Here!'

Every time it rained that was the drill.

'Nail down the galvanize, please, Bango. Nail it down,' she begged him. 'I don't want you falling through the roof. I don't want a piece of galvanize flying off and cutting off my child head.' But each time he rearranged the wood and bricks into more efficient formations or he would take up with him on the shaky ladder a plank of wood or some other bricks and stones to lay on the roof, but he never put a nail in the galvanize.

'Not yet,' he said. 'I don't want to get holes in the galvanize. I will nail it down proper when we expand the house.' That was his promise. That was his commitment that he was to repeat and reaffirm, not so much in words, in a look, a smile, a hug to put

145

her at her ease, to ward off her anxiety. And she accepted them, the gestures. They were together. She was there with him, close to life, feeling invincible, needing nothing once she was with him. And around them the village, with the weekend excursions to play cricket in the villages and towns in Manzanilla, in Biche, in Guaico, in Valencia, everybody pack up in Mackie old van and some travelling with Mister Trusse: with the holiday trips that the club made sometimes to the beach, to Toco, to Mayaro, to Los Iros.

She was soon one with the villagers, sharing her life with them, for Carnival Monday dressing up herself and taking a taxi with the children, dressed up too, their faces made up with powder and rouge, on their heads the peaked little paper caps marked BATA SHOES made of the same thin cardboard of almanacs that they got at Christmas from Lorenzo Rumshop & Grocery, with coloured jerseys, each one a different colour, with the creases of their newness, and go to Cunaripo and watch the bands and buy snowballs and balloons and windmills, and on Tuesday she and Bango would leave Vera with Miss Pearl and put on their sailor suit and with their big tin of white powder and their pretty sticks and a flask of rum secure in the pocket in front by the crotch of their pants and go down Port-of-Spain by Columbus Square to meet with City Syncopators Steel Band where Bango brother Sam was the captain, and all of them the whole family gather, Merle and Gloria and Bertie, everybody except Pearl who prefer to stay home with the children and Shirley who since she join the church believe that Carnival is a festival of the devil.

'You good,' Shirley said to her when she came to invite her to her own child's christening and meet me big-belly and coming up from the river with a load of washing. 'This is how this man have you? Working hard and making children? He giving himself to the village; you giving yourself to him: who giving theirself to you? Who giving theirself to Myrtle? You does go to church?'

'Yes, Shirley.'

'Yes? Well, at least you ain't forget God. At least you is still a Christian. At least you ain't turn away from Him, like you turn away from everything else you learn at home. At least that is one thing you still keep up,' making her pronouncements with an imperious, self-satisfied confidence as if she had full certainty of what life was and what one had to do and what was happiness and what was success, her certainty deriving from what her husband Paul say, or what Pastor Prue say or what she, Shirley, knew.

So even though Myrtle knew her own life, its quality, she felt the need for something concrete that was her own to show. All that they possessed, she and Bango, was what they had given and were giving, not what they had received, not what they had bought. They were what they were becoming. Maybe the people of Cascadu knew their value, but still, it was hard to face Shirley with nothing solid to show.

It worried her, this feeling that Shirley brought out in her, because, really, it didn't matter that the house wasn't the best and the land was not their own. This was their mission, this was what they were cut out to do. Other people had so little and they had come to look to Bango as the one to serve them and lead them and he had accepted it as his lot and she had joined him in his mission. Still, it embarrassed her.

More than fifteen times they save up money to start to pay down on a piece of land but some problem always come up that he had to solve with it, somebody had to bury his father, somebody house burn down; somebody child sick, something. And always he was there as if he believe he could put off doing for himself until everybody else business fix, like the captain of a sinking ship, the last one to leave until everybody else safe, until I began to believe that he didn't want to get off. He want to stay with them to the last. And that woulda been all right if people pull together and share the responsibility; but like the knowledge that he was there leave them free to do as they please. The only effect it had on him was that the weakness of others demanded from him greater strength. The extravagance of others required from him greater sacrifice. She was his support. And she found herself having to keep on believing in this thing that she herself didn't quite know how to explain, but that without explanation she had to keep believing in and holding on to.

They had plenty ideas: a co-operative store, a land-buying and a house-building programme. They tried plenty things to raise money: raffles, excursions, dances that didn't score because they

147

managed to keep them on the most rainy night of the year. Fitz-Vaughn Bryan band playing up a storm in the Community Centre, tickets gone out, people coming up by car, by bus, from Princes Town and Rio Claro and Sangre Grande and Biche, people coming by train from Brasso and Tabaquite. People reach Cunaripo. They reach. They could hear the music. Then right there at the bus stop and the train station, rain. Rain! So heavy that they can't even walk the few yards to The Centre, and when the rain look like it tired fall, it going to stop now, the wind begin to blow and bawl and big drops of rain begin again to hammer the galvanize roof of The Centre and on and on it rain and blow until the band pack up their instruments and people waiting at home change back their clothes; and when the rain sure that now everybody home, and there ain't no chance for the dance again, it stop. People leave the train station and the taxi stand and they walk up to the centre to the fête, just to see, because the place clear now, the sky clear and cool, and they meet the band leaving The Centre going home.

The one night when God smile on them and hold the rain and they get a good crowd at the dance and they thought now they will make some money, Johnny who was by the door with Francis disappear and when they open the box it just had enough money to pay the band. 'Blackpeople!' Pearl said. 'Me and Blackpeople!' And she tell Bertie, 'This is the time now for every tub to sit on its own bottom,' and she pull Bertie aside from the village to, as she say, see about her own two boychildren. Another brother, Mano, who used to play music in the parang band, put down his cuatro and take up a dougla girl from in the back of Princes Town and gone in the forest to build a house and squat a piece of land and plant watermelon and make children. And now Myrtle feel that is she and Bango alone. Now she begin to suspect that all that was keeping the people together was because they couldn't do better. She start to feel that as soon a people head reach above water and they could make a way for theirself, they gone. And she now in two minds: whether to battle the imposs- ible or just to let everything go. She tell this to Bango. As usual, he had an answer:

'What you expect? What keep people together is not the

148

principle but the need. What keep people human is because they don't get the chance to be beast.'

'And what you killing yourself for then?'

'Because what save us, what save the world is the one or two who hold on to the belief that we is more. More than beast.'

'The fools,' she said.

'The fools,' he said.

'Like you,' she said.

'Like both of we.'

And they went down that afternoon to the river under the cocoa trees, the two of them alone and went naked in the water and that night she felt a chill, a fear when they loved each other, and she didn't know what to tell him. Because right at time she know they had to leave these people. They had to go on their own.

She had watched Moon come on a day when the rain that was falling whole week let up a little. They hear this noise of cutlass-ing and at first they thought it was one of the boys cutting a track to set out his birdcage, but when they looked, it was to see this thin Indian man, bareheaded, with long-sleeved shirt buttoned right up to his neck like he just come out from working in the sugar-cane field, swinging his cutlass patient and quick through the bush and in the other hand is his crookstick heaping up the cut bush:

'Aye, Man!' Bango called out to him. 'What it is you doing? Man, what it is you doing? You don't see people living here. You just come and start to clean. You ain't ask nobody a question? Go and squat somewhere where it ain't have nobody.'

Moon had this smile on his face all the time Bango talking, and when Bango finish, Moon say, 'Neighbour, I think you make a mistake.'

'What mistake I make?' Bango talking in the falsetto of author-ity, as if the land was his own.

'This land is mine. I buy it.'

'You buy it? Forty acres?'

'No. I buy five. I have my paper right here.'

'You sure about this, that is this land?'

But even as he was questioning Moon, he realize that he had been tricked.

149

'Look!' and Moon brought out his deed. 'The boss sell it to me.'

'I didn't know they was selling no five acres. I thought it was only forty-acre blocks they was selling,' Bango said.

'Well, he sell me it. I was going way to another estate to work, but the boss say stay, you will get land, so I stay. And this is the land. Don't vex with me, neighbour.'

'I can't vex with him. Is not his fault,' Bango said to me.

Even she could feel that something was being betrayed, that they were being robbed of something.

'Leave these people,' Shirley said. 'Watch it they don't drag you down in the pit with them.'

'You have too much courage,' Pearl tell her. And though the last person I want to listen to is Shirley, it strike me: We have to leave these people, Bango. So by the time the National Party come, the truth is, she was ready to go on.

'Miss Myrtle,' the Red Girl, said, 'like you don't want to tell me what you thinking.'

'Girl . . . ,' I begin and before I could answer a car horn blow and I turn and look outside to see if was Tall Boy come with his taxi to take me home; it was to see two cars pulling up one behind the other across the road and five men, visitors, well dressed, in shirt sleeves and loosened ties getting out shaking the journey out of their limbs, moving towards the rumshop with the tall breezy satisfaction of men who just finished burying a dead, the first thing to come in my head is that they come from a funeral in one of the villages further along the road and was stopping at the rumshop to have a drink before moving on. As I open my mouth to ask Miss Esme if she know who was dead, a third car with a loudspeaker atop it pull up. When I see the huge weighty figure of Ethelbert Tannis, principal of Cosmos Business Academy, in the cap and gown he alone was privileged to wear because he was the only man in Cunaripo with a BA, heaving himself out of one of its rear doors, with the grand and laborious importance that he had assumed now especially that he was Chairman of the Party Group of the National Party, she realized without anybody telling her anything, that the evil that Father D'Heureux had been warning about from his pulpit for the last five Sundays, and against which he encouraged them to pray, had at last reached Cascadu.

Instead of fleeing as he had advised the congregation to do, she took out from her bosom the handkerchief knotted with her money, put her goods in her basket, checked the goods list, paid Miss Esme and, whispering the twenty-third psalm under her breath, she stepped outside to get her other basket with her iron pot and the remainder of coals and to wait for Tall Boy to come and take her home.

And, Mister Gentleman, I stand up there with my own thrill and trembling, trying to be brave, a little apart from the little gathering of villagers hanging back like if we are strangers to the district that is our own, when this young fellar come and ask me if I know somebody who could lend him a table and two chairs, and so polite and soft spoken and with a part in his hair. I couldn't refuse him. He was too nice to refuse. So I ask Evelyn two boys who was near to go underneath Miss Alice house and bring back my table to lend them and I couldn't let them keep their meeting on a bare table, so I ask Miss Esme for a tablecloth borrow and a glass jug for water and a vase and I send by Bisente for a few flowers from his flower garden and when I finish fix up the table the young fella didn't have enough thanks to thank me. He say, don't frighten, stay and listen.

Same time he thanking me, Tall Boy taxi stop and blow and he open the trunk of the car and I put the two basket in it and as I go to go in the car, myself thinking to go and get Bango to come and hear them, not sure that I will meet him home at that hour on Friday, a mind tell me, Myrtle, you here already, you better stay and hear these people, what they have to say. And I glad I do it because I was there to see them in the black gowns, like Abyssinian priests, with the cap of the rank of their learning, and their little black magicians' wands and the black briefcases stuffed with papers and plans and charts.

'And, sweetheart, I hear Butler talk. And Butler could talk. I hear Gomes, Solomon, Bhadase, Bryan, all of them. But, Love, when this man talk, my hair rise on my head and little bumps start crawling all over my skin ... Look at my hands now and I only remembering. Look how my pores raising. Twenty years later. Look!' showing him her hands.

With Butler politics was a prayer meeting, people taking courage from one another, together singing hymns hard and clapping
and moaning and making a loud rejoicing noise and waving
palm leaves in the uncertainty of the dark.

This was a different thing. The National Party was like a
school, a university that come to give us our history. They had
a projector and they unfolded a screen. And on the screen they
put up a map of the world and a map of time. They showed
Europe where the ships set out from Bristol and Liverpool, from
Nantes, from Lisbon. They show Africa and the coast of Guinea
where the ships arrive to collect the people they capture and put
in chains. They show The West Indies, Barbados and Jamaica
where they land the cargo of these captive people and collect
the cargo of sugar and cotton and spices to take back to Europe
for sale. They show us the plantation and the mansions of the
Whitepeople and the barracks Blackpeople live in. They showed
us the ships that come back with another load of saltfish and
salt pork and smoke herring and tasso and salt: with khaki
and cotton cloth and cork hats and hoes and cutlass and soft
candle and rope.

That evening under Lorenzo Rumshop & Grocery in the bright
dark sparkle of speeches from the National Party, Miss Myrtle
began to see the world afresh and nearly five hundred years of
time. She see the Indians of the Indies in a ballet of welcome,
offering gifts to Columbus who stand up disguising his wonder
with a pose of imperial nonchalance, one hand on his hip, the
other holding a lance, behind him his soldier heaving into erec-
tion a gigantic cross that they are about to plunge and plant into
the earth of the small island. She see Friar Las Casas, his hair
almost all gone, his shoulders sagging under his grief over murders, penning another plea to the conscience of his king. She see
Africans in Demerara with lithe limbs of dancers and teeth of
ivory and torsos of gymnasts hanging on gibbets from their
waists, swinging in repose as they wait for Stedman to draw
their portraits, Sir Francis Drake, sleek like a pigeon and alert as
a hawk, surveying the wreckage of burning Spanish galleons.
She see Toussaint L'Ouverture in his dress of a general crouched
amid the smoke of Haiti's burning plantations. She saw them
all, adventurers and those in bondage, from every continent,

152

Europe, Asia, Africa here in this America, men with whips and women and men in chains, the grand explorations corrupted by mountains of murders, power degraded by the terrible sovereignty it blinded it from. What did they dream of in the beginning? she wondered. What were their dreams? She saw the naive pretence of colonists to avoid self-condemnation, the Amerindian Cacique, Hatuey being burnt alive by his conquerors while Spanish priests stand by trying to persuade him to take Extreme Unction for the safe repose of his soul. She witnessed the grand uprisings in Haiti with Toussaint L'Ouverture and Dessalines and the plague of freedom beginning to spread fear of retribution, planters leaving Grenada, St Lucia, Martinique, heading for Trinidad, with nothing learned except greater vigilance, more brutality. In Trinidad hundreds of Africans rounded up on a trumped up charge of planning a massacre of whites, ninety brought in guilty, sentenced to have ears cut off, floggings, exile, and four ringleaders to have their heads cut off and placed on poles in the main square of the town and their bodies hung in chains at the seaside in the villages from which they had come. She saw the greed, the brutality, the people in grief, the land carved up to claimants according to their colour and the number of captives they brought to the enterprise: whiteman so many captives multiplied by thirty acres of land; mulatto and Free Coloured, so many captives multiplied by fifteen acres. This was the New World planted here in this small island: black and white, enslaved and enslavers, indentured and indenturers, Venezuelans, loyalists and revolutionaries, French, German, Americans, African Americans, freedom fighters and those who wanted to keep people enslaved, Africans from Africa, 'free' and unfree, Chinese, Portuguese, Indians, each group embarked on its own adventure, each one of them driven out or dragged out of home by reason of poverty or politics or space. This was the new world puking blood, already, murky with corruption.

In the shop, people stop buying. Miss Esme come out in the road and start to cry. The Red Girl have the fingers of one hand in her mouth biting her fingernails as tears stream down her face, Constable Stephen Aguillera, calm like a snake, have one hand round her shoulders to comfort her and the other holding the handle of his baton, waiting for riot.

Mr Albert start to cuss, children run bawling to their mothers, cars stop. Science Man start to butt his head on the telephone post. Something crack. Priscilla cross her arms on her breasts and start to wine. She take she hand off her breast and put the two of them on her head and she wine right down and she come up again.

Miss Myrtle just stand up there. She felt her body tremble at the stories of the tortures, of the whips, of the chains and this great sorrow for the island, for people, for the world and a shame. She hear dogs howling. She hear grieving parrots rise up as one fleet, cawing and squealing.

'What is all this? What they bring up all this for?' Miss Norma who was working, ironing and servanting for Carabon ask. 'What they bringing up all these things for now? They want people to commit murder? They want us to fight?'

'They want us to know.'

'They giving us power.'

'They making us wise.'

'They making us remember in order for us to forget.'

'They purging us out.'

'Where am I?' Myrtle asked herself. 'Where is myself?'

And what now? What after all this?' cried the leader. 'More brutality, more inequality, more injustice, more degradation?'

'No. Oh, God, no!' cried Miss Myrtle. 'No!'

'No,' said the leader with finality. 'No.' These things were done in the dark ages of our past. These acts were done from a different vision of what is the world, of what is human, in a time when men and women did not have the right to vote, when there was no ideal of democracy by which to live. But today we have Democracy, Brotherhood, Unity. This land that belonged to a few now belongs to everybody. Now we will share together in the sacrifices and the profits. And we will achieve this only through Discipline as members of society, our Productivity as workers and our Tolerance, one for the other, as citizens.

'Come and join us!' he cried. 'Come and help us make this one nation. Show us your support by raising your hands.'

And before the words could leave his mouth Miss Myrtle had up her hand. And when the speaking finish she go and line up with the other people and get a form and full out her name and address and give them a dollar for subscription.

'So what you give them your dollar for?' Bango ask her when she tell him what happened. And is only then I realized that the reason was not so much for any promise they made to me. It was because of the sense of release that they bring. They had brought the sense of an end, that whatever they was waiting on had come and that it was now time for she and Bango to move on. 'It finish, Bango,' she said. 'The estate is now our own.'

'And how?' Bango ask her. 'How it could be our own and we don't own it?'

'You know,' she said, not able to hide her reproach, 'they was selling out bits of the estate all the time. Moon buy a piece. We coulda buy piece too.'

'Buy?'

And when she saw the astonishment on his face she realized that he had never thought of the plantation as property, as something you could buy or sell, that to him it was more of a monster to struggle against, to outwit and outlast and defeat. His struggle she understood then had been not to buy the land but to make the land witness to his undefeat.

And she was frightened to think it far more to ask Bango: what all these years were they fighting for? For what?

And it occurred to her that Bango himself didn't even know. He don't know, she thought, in amazement. He don't even know what he was fighting for.

Now she watched him carrying on, marshalling the cricket team, going to the Village Council meetings, going to steel band practice, as if nothing had changed. But, things had changed. Politics had come in. People were now going to the meetings of the Party group, attending political rallies, hiring the same old van that used to take them to excursions, decorated now with heliconias and palm leaves, they themselves dressed in the jerseys with the red and black lettering of the National Party. People were going on about their new business. She had to speak to Bango. She had to tell him, if not on her own behalf, on behalf of the children.

Before the coming of the National Party it had never occurred to Miss Myrtle that Vera might profit from education beyond

Standard Seven of Primary school. For a while when Vera was much younger, Miss Myrtle had dared to think of the possibility of her winning a scholarship, not because the girl was in any way exceptional but because it was a wish expected of every parent. But Vera wasn't bright and, apart from playing netball for the school and that on account of her height she had shown little interest in anything and had gone through most of her teen years with the suspicious charm of an orphan, the trigger of her smile at ready, her goodwill something she needed to establish, as if she believed that she subsisted in the world not as of right as by the beneficence of someone unknown, so she had to be careful and always to smile lest she frown at the person who had been her benefactor.

For three years after Vera completed primary school, Miss Myrtle left her at home to take care of the house and to mind the two children she had for Bango while she, Myrtle, battled with the market. In that time she had watched the child's penitence deepen, her eyes more downlooking, more sideways glancing as if she could not bear to look at people, not Miss Myrtle though out of fear now as out of shame, turning from people to the dogs and the chickens and the goats and things in nature as if they were her true companions, neglected and vulnerable and misunderstood, in need of a priestess, someone who would soothe them and show that she cared. Miss Myrtle had watched her fold herself into the drowsy mistiness of that priestess, cutting wild grasses and the blossoms of wild shrubs and mixing them with oddly shaped dry sticks and placing them in vases and putting them in corners, making them the centre piece of altars all about the house. She had watched her sinking into a radiant serene amazement at the rain and the blossoms and the beetles and the birds, comfortable with the holes in the roofing and the snakes that unfolded in the sunshine and slithered along the rafters of the thatched roof of the outdoor kitchen, unconscious of her body, continuing to run and jump and bathe half-naked in the river as if her childhood was a state she saw no point in growing beyond, Miss Myrtle watching on helpless as the girl settled deeper into that world from which she found herself increasingly unwilling to pluck her, continuing to make her dresses for someone younger, as if she also needed to keep her a child that much longer, giving her the cut halves of yellow lime to rub under her armpits to erase the wild perfume of greenwood-fire smoke and forest moss fermenting there and on her skin, to calm the wild leaping exuberance of her limbs that was bursting forth out of those dresses as part of the blossoming greenness of young trees and the mauve and the colours of the vegetation and the friskiness of the animals, suspicious that leaving her home alone was giving her opportunities for a kind of mischief she would rather not think about, consoling herself with the thought that everybody in the Settlement knew Bango's temper and would be careful not to get on the wrong side of him; that, her only consolation as she worked out in her mind what she would do for her future, shutting her eyes to the men looking at her height and thinking she was older than she really was, having to bear the sadness that this child's future would depend on the kind of man that would choose her.

From the evening Myrtle hear the National Party she felt she could hold back time no longer. The world was changing and Vera needed to be rescued from the danger of her own onrushing womanhood. And what would rescue her, she thought as she looked out the window of Tall Boy taxi at the breezy green settlement around her, the wisps of hibiscus squeezing through the mat of roadside Ti-Marle, their sparse stunted flowers splashes of red on the wreath of the Carabon plantation, at the boy, in the brilliance of this peace, barebacked, his solemn muscles polished by sweat, with the calm demeanour of a saint emerging from a thicket of cocoa with a slingshot and birdcage and bunch of bird-pecked bananas to pause shipwrecked before the ocean of road sailing away for miles under shimmering waves of heat, at the parrots that, at the beep of the vehicle, scatter screaming above their camouflage of trees, and from the stillness of the whitewashed wooden barrack houses overhung by the outflung branches of the giant immortelle shading the blighted cocoa, at a girl with unplaited hair peering out of the dark door of her windowless room, catching in her haunting eyes the bemused, enquiring shift and shine of a trapped animal that is no longer seeking rescue.

'And what will rescue her?' I ask myself as I pay Tall Boy his money and wave a hand at the shyly smiling figure who had

157

come to the doorway of her prison. The muscular boy panting to lead her under the shade of the cocoa trees unto a bed of dead leaves? The gentleman in the red motor car and the green mohair suit and dark shades and a white broad-brimmed hat who comes all the way from Port-of-Spain with his fingers sparkling and his mouth full of gold to tell her how pretty she is and how in the city is this palace where is her throne, all you have to do is come with me and you'll get presents and dresses and everything and somebody will show you how to walk and somebody will teach you how to talk and you'll be a candidate in the Miss Universe contest just leave everything to me. What will rescue her? The floors waiting to be made spotless in the Whitepeople kitchen in Cascade? Where we want a girl from the country, not too bright, not one of those bright bright ones who will bring man in my house and thief out my things and carry her freshness to my husband, a clean Christian girl with a head to learn and we'll show her how to cook the food the way we like it and how to clean and she'll have a uniform and her own room and a day off once a month so she could go home?

'Eh, Bango? What will rescue her?' she rehearsed with a sternness she knew she would have to temper if she was to get him to listen, thinking now not of the girl in the dark house underneath the tree but of her own child Vera, taking up her basket from the trunk of her car this noontime Saturday, shouting with vexation at the dog that had loped out to greet her, 'Bully!' the animal confused by her reprimand, approaching her from another angle, its eyes fixed sorrowfully upon her, its belly dragging along the ground, its tail wagging tentatively wounded and reproachful, moving her to say almost with apology, 'You don't see my two hands full? How you expect me to pat you?'

'What will rescue her?' she asked Bango. And while she had not expected him to oppose her proposal to send Vera to Cosmos Business Academy to do shorthand and typing, she was a little surprised at how readily he agreed, his only regret that they couldn't afford to send her perhaps to Port-of-Spain where they had better schools, had instead to settle for Tannis school whose pompous name, Cosmos Business Academy, was the most impressive thing about it.

For a time Bango tried with Cascadu, going himself to the

men who played cricket to get them to take a deeper interest, going to the parents of the boys in the steel band, talking to people in the Village Council asking for their support for things that were really theirs, but nobody could understand what he was saying, what he was getting on about. All they could sense from him was his anger, his dissatisfaction with things. They began to see him as a nuisance, as someone to avoid, escape from when they saw him coming, so that his voice became more strident, his very efforts making him appear loud and absurd; and then he did the thing that they might have secretly wished him to do. He began to withdraw. No more cricket, no more steel band, no more Village Council. He left it all up to them. He came home from work promptly and occupied himself with the making of his earrings, curios and jewellery from dried coconuts and dry coconut shells. For Carnival he didn't even go to see the masquerade in Cunaripo. He took her and the children to Port-of-Spain. They had their basket with pigeon peas and rice and chicken and they had an icebox with cool drinks and a bottle of rum and they spread a towel underneath one of the trees in the Memorial Park next to the Savannah, where the children had space to roam and had only to go to look over the railing on the Frederick Street side to see the bands entering the Savannah, or run across the Park in the opposite direction on Charlotte Street and see them when they were leaving. But he wasn't happy.

For nearly three years that was the way he lived up until the elections that would put the National Party back in power and send the Prime Minister and the Leader of the Opposition to England to have discussions on the Independence the country was soon to begin living under.

So when one evening she come home and see him outside in the street in front the house drilling twenty or so little boys, she made the sign of the cross in thanksgiving, glad that his vexation with the villagers had not extended to the children.

At first she thought he was trying to revive the Boys Scout troop that he had tried to raise in Cascadu maybe some three years earlier. It wasn't that. The island had gained Independence and Bango was preparing these boys to take part in the Independence Day parade in Cunaripo. And she only became alarmed when she realized that Bango was not only drilling these boys himself, he was not only going to shape out from wood the thirty or so imitation rifles they would shoulder, he was planning on his own to outfit them in the khaki trousers, khaki shirts and red berets that he had decided on for their uniform.

'Thirty khaki pants, thirty khaki shirts, thirty red berets. Where you getting all this from? Your factory?' trying with an attempt at humour to make him understand at least the financial implications of this large undertaking.

'Why you don't get some people to help you?' knowing, by the shrug of his shoulders that he intended to do it alone. It was a curious expression of pride and spite. She was tempted to leave him with his project to do all by himself. But one day she went to Cunaripo and saw the banners and the flags going up and the buildings being repainted and the flagstones in the police station being whitewashed and bunting hung across the streets and a stage built in the recreation ground for the March Past as the town readied itself for the grand occasion, it came to her that perhaps others were also planning their contributions and, knowing that her uninvolvement would cost them much more in the end, she decided to put aside her own pique and help him. So it was she who went around to the parents of the children to encourage them to use clothes already in their possession, and, in the end, they were able to have the boys turned out without the kind of expense they would have incurred if everything had to be new. They had to purchase just a few shirts and pants and to buy the cloth out of which she herself sewed the berets.

So she was there with nearly the whole of Cascadu to see Bango on the morning of Independence Day take up his position at the head of his troop of soldiers, in his admiral's uniform with epaulettes on his shoulders and medals on his chest with his white gloves on, holding aloft the long slender bamboo rod that he had painted silver and unto which he had sewn the nation's flag, set out to march the three miles to Cunaripo, behind him his little starched soldiers with their khaki pants, red berets and wooden guns.

She was there in Cunaripo to see them march through the decorated town down Main Street and outwards into the Recreation ground to join the Red Cross, the Volunteer Fire Brigade, the Police, the St John's Ambulance Brigade and a contingent of cadets and to hear the burst of cheering as Bango shouted out the 'Eyes right!' command and the boys with charming inexactitude brought their hands to their foreheads and puffed up their chests and jerked their heads in the direction of MP Scholasticus T. Nelson standing with other dignitaries on the rostrum to take the salute. She was satisfied. It was good. Whatever was his point Bango had made it alone, by himself. Everybody was witness. And right there he shoulda stop, invite other people in and if they wanted to carry it on, OK. He had done his part. But the next year he was back again, and every single year after that, each year with more expense. And then he started to march for not only Independence but for any and every cause, once The People were involved.

Some young people in Cascadu hear about the Flower Power movement in the USA, they bathe themselves in *flour* and ask Bango to bring out the boys and march. Bango do it. He march in the bus workers' strike. He march in the Black Power revolt of '70, not only in Cascadu, he take his troops to San Fernando, to Port-of-Spain, to Caroni, to San Juan. Every protest, every celebration, he was there until it wasn't an event if Bango wasn't there. And why is he marching? Nobody ever ask him a word. Sometimes they bring him on the stage with them like a clown, like a puppet show, on parade. They giving the speeches and not asking him to say a word.

Miss Myrtle watched his own suit, the admiral suit, grow tight, grow slack, grow frayed, grow thin. She patched it. Nobody give them a cent and neither he nor she ask anybody for any. After he use up his own money he started to borrow from her. Because now he couldn't stop this marching because now he was expected everywhere. It wasn't fair. They couldn't afford it, not by themselves. Sometimes she wondered what he was marching for, was it this show of Independence, this sense of nation? She didn't ask him anything. Then she realized that what she had to do was to leave him let it die on its own. But her heart was too soft.

Then this year, her sister Shirley, who had built over her own house into a upstairs mansion, came busy busy. She had to go to church. She had to do the catering for a big National Party meeting, she had to send her children to camp in Paramin. And wasn't it nice what Bango was doing. Paul say the government was thinking of giving him a medal for meritorious service to the nation. And Miss Myrtle was sure now, yes: Bango have to stop this marching.

'And that is why I come to you, Sir.'

'You want me to not accept his invitation?'

'I begging you, Sir. It is not fair for you to encourage him to continue. It not right for him to believe that he is the only man responsible for this community. It not fair.'

'And what,' asked Alford, for it was clear to him now what he had to do, 'what if we give him the support? What if we gave you the land for your house?'

Because Alford had some power still, he could talk to the Minister of Agriculture and Lands.

'I didn't come here for that, Sir. I come for you to help me to stop him.'

'I understand. You not against the marching. What you against is the cost to him, the cost to you.'

'Yes, Sir.'

Once again, Alford felt himself returned to the road of his mission. Giving Bango land would remove the shame from him. It would provide him with the security to make the welcome. He did not see a problem. This was a case that he could justify. He had not forgotten his history.

And now Alford knew what the subject of his address was going to be. It would be a call to unity, to creativity, to a new beginning. It would be a call that would be based this time not on mere words of goodwill but on his government's concrete efforts to elevate those who had been disadvantaged by history.

The idea that they were to be given the land they lived on seemed to Miss Myrtle not only fair but deserved and she congratulated herself that she had something to do with an offer that had come at a time when she was getting tired and when Bango himself was getting on in years. But when she gave the news to Bango, she found that instead of sharing her elation, there was from him that discomforting silence that fell over him when he was particularly wounded. She had to wait until later that night to hear him say, carefully, as if he had been thinking how to tell her what he had to say, 'You miss the point, Myrtle,' his voice soft, choking, his head down, the light from the gaslamp enclosing him, as he worked on the bangle he was making, sandpapering it now, slow and smooth as if he needed to calm himself to continue to give an answer that he knew she had come out there on the steps to get. What Myrtle heard was a tone of someone who felt himself betrayed and she had fallen silent too, seeking the same kind of space to shape her reply, watching him sand the bangle as the gaslamp dimmed. As if she needed that darkness to hide her hurt she said carefully, to hide her own emotion, because she felt it was so unfair that after all she had done he should think her a traitor:

'I? I miss the point?'

'I don't want anybody to feel sorry for me,' he said.

'That is what you 'fraid?' she asked. 'That people feel sorry for you?'

And when he said nothing, she said, again after some time, this time almost with accusation, 'This is what you call people feeling sorry for you? Giving you the land you want for so long? This is what you call people feeling sorry for you?' And when he still didn't say anything, 'What about me? You not sorry for me? Eh?' putting on a bantering tone and adding her smile to lead him away from his unhappy thinking. He didn't fall for it.

'Look,' he said. 'Don't let us argue,' his very attempt to soothe, to smooth it over, deepening her hurt.

'You think I will sit down and agree with people to feel sorry for you? That is what you think I will do?'

Then, what you do? Why they offering me land now? But he didn't say it. He said nothing. He held the gaslamp and pumped it into brightness once more. Then he turned back to working on the bangle.

And she sat there watching him work on one bangle after another, neither of them speaking. Eventually she spoke, in a new tone, not with reproach now, but in the amused tone of compromise they both employed after a quarrel, 'So I miss the point, eh? I marching with you for nearly twenty years. I sewing costume and defending you to people and I miss the point?'

'Is not you alone. Nearly everybody think I crazy or lazy or whatever.'

'And you see me as everybody?'

'This was never just about land,' he said.

'Just? Why you add the just?'

'I mean it was more. Just getting the land wasn't going to better our position.'

'It couldn't make it worse. You know,' she said, her tone stiffening, 'I really don't understand you.'

'If they give me the land they must do it openly. In front of everybody. People must know why they giving land to me. It must be public.'

'So why this publicity? Anyway, that is not what Alford George agree with me.'

'You see. I tell you you miss the point.'

'If I miss the point,' I tell him. And it was something I didn't want to have to tell him. It was something I thought that at last he woulda realize for his own self. 'If I miss the point, then why you don't tell me the point.'

'Why I don't . . .?' And I could see it hit him. For the first time. And he look at me in the new light of the gaslamp. And I could see his mind working, searching, recalling, questioning: I never tell her? I nevertell her? I nevertellher, 'I never tell you?'

'You begin plenty times to tell me,' and it was I now nearly crying. 'You talk about Guinea John your great-great-great-grandfather and about his grandson JoJo and about the others, but you never finish the story. To this day you never tell me why you marching this march every year. Everybody seeing about their own self. Even Pearl, your brother Bertie wife, feel is stupidness you doing. But you never tell me why? If somebody was to ask me, I wouldn't know what to say.'

'And you never think about it? You never ask yourself why?'

'Plenty times,' I tell him. 'And you know what I think? I think you do it for spite. For us to remain at this stage, having nothing. Because to have money, to have things will take you away from your struggle. It will make you too ordinary. You will be just like everybody. What else to think? But, man, you can't keep on struggling for something that everybody else forget. Let us say

Thank God and accept the land. Don't make this good thing another problem.'

He put down the bracelet he was polishing and he get up from where he was sitting and he come over to me and he sit down in front of me and he take my two hands, and he take my fingers one by one and touch them and smooth them out to take the wrinkles out, and he look in my eyes. And I myself looking at him, seeing the Bango who stand up balanced on his bicycle in front my mother house years ago. And is now he see me seeing him, seeing that Bango; he see me, that young, long ago Myrtle too. 'OK, OK, OK,' soft hushing me, drawing me to him and holding me to his chest. 'Thank you,' he tell me.

'Thank me for what?'

'Thank you.'

And they sit down holding on to one another in the gaslamp's glow with the insects buzzing and the call of the frogs and the hooting and sighing of the night. And what she felt was something that she wasn't expecting, because it was something that she wasn't even looking for. It was the sense of a new comfort and a strange and lovely triumphant peace because in one flash she could see that Bango had recognized her. He had made me out. All at once he realize that in the journey he thought that he had made alone, I had been with him the whole way.

He take a deep breath. 'Watch the landscape of this island,' he began.

'No,' I say, stopping him before he could go on.

'Don't tell me yet.' Because there was no way he could repay me. 'Tell the man who want to give us the land, why he must give it openly. Tell it to Alford George.'

9

Alford in the PM's Chair Listens to Bango

When my secretary, Miss Baldeosing, announced the arrival of Bango and Miss Myrtle – I had invited Ethelbert B. Tannis to be present as well – I was in the PM's office where I usually did my thinking, sitting on the sofa, going over the transcript of my post-coital musings from two nights before, working on the ideas for my Independence Day speech. I was thinking of the coming elections, wondering whether I should approach the PM, the Leader and confront him about the status of my nomination or whether I should do it through one of my parliamentary colleagues, which one I was not sure – it was hard, from day to day, to keep up with who was in his good books and who he was not talking to. Ethelbert B. usually had such information, but at the moment he was not enjoying the PM's ear. The other option was to not ask him anything, just to carry on doing what I was doing and let the success which I was sure to make when I took the rostrum to take the march-past and make my speech at the Independence Day celebrations show me to be the candidate the people wanted to represent them.

So when Miss Baldeosing announced the arrival of the three people, I was so engrossed in the task before me that I just lifted my head and asked her to show them in, not looking at her really, and, if looking, not seeing the surprise she must have expressed since she knew that I never received people in this office. The next thing I knew was that all three of them were at the door. I myself got up from the sofa and welcomed them in and showed them to the sofa, all of it done with a certain decorum that I thought was quite becoming, that confirmed for them the sense of my appreciation and respect for their dignity. I didn't want them to feel awed, or, what was worse, the need to put on airs and speak in that falsetto of an inferior trying to assume importance, but to be themselves. I mean, I had simply wanted to indicate my respect for them without appearing to be too chummy. Naturally, this necessitated keeping my own distance.

So, without even thinking, I had gone, after they were seated on the sofa, and stood beside his chair, and for a brief second, even as I was in the act of sitting, I caught the eyes of Ethelbert B. opening with alarm, and I am thinking: *Why is he looking at me like that? What is wrong here?* and then just as I sit down, I realize that I was sitting on the PM's chair. It was too late to unsit, though I suppose I could have got up and gone and sat with them there on the sofa and have us all look rather foolish, squeezed up together on the sofa while in front of us sits a big empty chair. So, yes, I sat down on his chair; yes, and I must say, quite at ease, since I might as well look ministerial to my people. Yes. But of course that is not the story. That was only made the story afterwards, when the hatchetmen of the Party embarked on their vicious campaign to discredit me, to make me seem a traitor, disloyal to The Prime Minister, suggesting that I had some pretensions to replace him. But that is another story that belongs to the politics of rumour, scandal, idleness. I am gone now, done with that now. My gaze has been turned elsewhere to the real story, Bango's story.

'I know I should be thankful for your offer of land,' Bango began, his voice straining to be polite, looking at Miss Myrtle with an appeal that made me feel that what he was saying was as much for her benefit as for mine.

Into my mind plopped a picture of my father standing pathetic and heroic before his column of dinged and mossy bricks, on land that was not his own. And I began to settle back for the falsetto of false modesty, of self-pity and martyrdom that I had come to recognize as the voice of my father's generation struggling with its victimhood and its pride. But that was not what I got from Bango.

'Understand from the start,' he said. 'I ain't come here to make the Whiteman the devil. I not here to make him into another creature inhabiting another world outside the human order. I grant him no licence to pursue wickedness and brutality. I come to call him to account, as a brother, to ask him to take responsibility for his humanness, just as I have to take responsibility for mine. And if you think it is easy for either one of us, then you making an error. This business of being human is tougher than

167

being the devil, or being God for that matter. And it doesn't matter whether in the role of brutalized or brutalizer.'

'How,' he went on, 'do you face in liberty a people who you organize a whole island to keep in prison? When you enlist every male resident of the island, being white, coloured and free persons from the age of fifteen to fifty-five to serve in any of the following: the regiment of light dragoons, the regiment of Hussars, the three regiments of infantry, one brigade of artillery, two corps of mounted Chasseurs in eight sections, two battalions of Sea Fencibles: when you have priests preaching obedience to your masters, preaching: Render unto Caesar the things that are Caesar's; preaching: Servants obey your masters; when you change the names of these people and put a wedge between them and their past: your name is Kosonibeye and they call you Mary; your name is Kanimba and they call you Ann; your name is Motonrinka and they call you Alfred; you can't walk carrying a stick, you can't walk in the night without carrying a light, because from a distance they want to see you coming, when they have the militia hunting you down when you run away (because, remember, people not taking it sitting down), burning your camps and stamping on your nests.

'How you going to live in liberty with a people whose bondage you make the basis of your land settlement policy? When the scramble for land is the scramble to hold people enslaved, when the law, your law, require that for every forty acres a whiteman have he have to have at least one man in bondage, and for every man bondaged a free coloured was entitled to fifteen acres of land. How you going to free a people who you root up from their homeland and force against their will to give their labour for three hundred years to you?'

These was the questions Whitepeople in this island had to answer.

There was never any magic about what they had to do. People know it already. In every part of the world. From time begin, people have always done each other wrong, not because one fella is so much more wicked than the next but because to be stupid is the principal part of what it is to be human. And unless we want to doom ourselves to remain forever locked into the terrors of the error of our stupidity, we try to repair the wrong by making reparation: so many cows, so much land, so you could face again yourself and restore for yourself and the one you injure the sense of what it is to be human.

That was what his grandfather JoJo felt entitled to expect when he hear that emancipation was coming. He was thirty years old, a single man, a roamer, a fella who spend one night by one woman and another night by a next one. He was a singer and a drumbeater and for all the noise that he made in ordinary life throughout the year, when he hear emancipation was coming, he just wanted to bawl out. He just wanted to shout and mash up the silence he had lived in.

He remembered his mother now who, because she was born with one foot shorter than the other, had escaped the work gang. Her job was to supervise the little children, to sing songs with them and lead them into the life of work, a little weeding, little sweeping, little tasks. He remembered her and his two brothers Hubert and Noble in that little barrack-room there on the Fondes Amandes estate, their life lived in a waiting silence, everything a whisper, the fear to breathe, to open your mouth and breathe. All around them this noise of trees, of minds thinking, of grief, birdsong louder than the human voice. He remembered himself at the age of four awakening to the silence of that world to hear that his grandfather Guinea John had flown back to Africa, to the feel of sorrow and the stifling of tears, everybody talking soft soft, the whole plantation quiet like a storm pass, not knowing then that the reason for their silence, their sadness, was their mourning for four men, the ringleaders of a supposed rebellion. Rounded up one day, tried the next and sentenced the evening of the same day to have their heads cut off and set on poles erected in front the Royal Jail and their headless bodies taken and hung on chains miles away on the seacoast in Carenage and Cocorite and Corbeaux Town for the vultures to feast upon. They were mourning for the ninety other women and men, some having their ears cut off, some flogged, some sentenced to work in chains and some to be banished for ever from the island. After that he remembered first, the storm and the flood, that washed away the five children of the overseer Frank Peschier into the swollen St Ann's river. Then the fire that burned down Port-of-Spain, the government house, the customs house, the hospital, the Anglican church, the jail, the town hall, part of the public archives, the treasurer's office, ninety-four fine houses. Then the diseases that start to afflict Whitepeople, fevers and fits and swellings, that his mother tell them was coming from the magic of his grandfather, his obeah, his juju that was sending punishments on to the whiteman from where he was in Africa.

He remembered the silence of the evening he saw his brother Noble, just sixteen, standing with this big straw hat on his head and the big soldier boots on his feet, his eyes huge and serene as if he was looking out a window at the whole huge world, and their mother sitting on the bed in the small room, smelling of coconut oil and rosemary, of ginger and sleep, saying as if to reassure herself, 'No, the boots all right. They not too big. Your foot growing.' And Noble standing before them, eyes front like a soldier on parade not looking down at the huge boats on his feet; then, taking off his hat after the inspection and sitting and taking off the boots and putting them in a sack, JoJo asking, 'Where he going, Ma?' and his mother saying nothing, just looking at him and subduing him into silence, speaking to Noble, saying quietly, 'When you get to Venezuela, don't let them feed you too much meat.'

Noble himself answering with his eyes, nodding his head at his mother, getting up and embracing her, and as if he believed he was a big man, patting JoJo on the shoulder and going on outside into the night to find his way to Cocorite and the boat that was to take him to Chacachacare to join the expedition led by Santiago Marino that was to take thirty-five men across the waters in two open boats to Guiria to fight in the liberation of South America, Noble getting the opportunity to go because the two hundred men who Marino had paid and outfitted and given rifles to go had taken the money and weapons and decided to stay at home, leaving Santiago Marino to scramble up thirty-five new people. Noble was one of the thirty-five who would cross the Gulf of Paria to Venezuela and take the city of Guiria that had been abandoned by Captain Juan Gavazzo and go on to further glory in the liberation of Columbia.

And another even deeper silence when his mother limped home one evening and sat herself down with her head in her hands and remained gazing through the open door. His brother

170

Hubert had run away to the forest of Tamana to join a maroon camp there, with him two women and another fella. One of the women had hit the overseer with a rock in his head and he Hubert had decided to make off with her.

He remembered his own silence at seventeen as he stood before the magistrate to hear himself sentenced to have one ear cut off for attempted escape, wanting to shout but not daring to breathe, standing there with an outrage whose calmness the magistrate said was insolence, unable to make any other plea but silence, since to argue was to give the impression that he did not believe that he was born free.

JoJo was on the estate of one George Beeston when he met Faustin Alfonsine, who some years earlier had been involved in a scam with Reginald Cadette, a planter who had settled here from Martinique. It involved Faustin presenting himself to the authorities as a newly arrived African consigned for Cadette's plantation, so enabling Cadette to claim an additional forty acres of land. Three times Faustin acted this role on behalf of Cadette. In return he was to be granted his freedom and five acres of land; but Cadette sold the plantation, Faustin with it, and migrated to France. Now Faustin convinced JoJo to impersonate a newly arrived African. They would get fifteen acres of land. JoJo would get new papers which would enable Faustin to free him, Faustin would get his land. It didn't work. They were caught and declared to have attempted escape.

Marked as a risk, JoJo tied a cloth across his forehead to cover his severed ear and entered into the life of the plantation. He had to learn how to conjure power out of his situation of power-lessness. He learnt the power of parody, of ridicule, of *double entendre*, of grand charge, of mamaguy, of pappyshow. He learned to divine the degree of vulnerability of a person. He learned the songs, the dances, beating drums and singing at wakes and at estate games. For the next thirteen years, he presented himself as a freeman, going through the most elaborate stratagems to get himself off work gangs, managing by his own luck and cunning to work as a bricklayer, a carpenter, a blacksmith, moving from woman to woman without anything to offer except the touch of his unconquerable spirit, his trickery, his flattery, his sham, his dreams, the women finding in him something they

171

wanted to nurture, to keep alive, to uphold and hold up, becoming coquettish and flirtatious around him, letting themselves go, surrendering themselves to his outrageous proposals to slip away into the bushes for the one moment in which they would love each other with the sense of no tomorrow, in the dawns of wakes, in the bush at feasts, restoring each other with the tenderest caresses they could wring from their own souls, women sighing with deep breaths when he left them, that this was it, until we meet again, eh, boy? knowing that he was not a man to live with, that living with him would spoil him, would be his defeat. He had to go on. And he went along with his dances and his singing and his loneliness, carrying in his bosom the treasure of all that tenderness, all that love, and only this way to give it. It was of these women and this love that he first thought when he heard that emancipation was coming, of the chance at last to make noise with them, to shout, to bawl.

Now, for this life that was coming, he had to prepare himself. It was not easy. He had to think of a place of his own now. He had to think of where his life had gone. He had to think of a new beginning. He had to think of forgiveness. He had to think of the scriptures, of the part that said, Lord, how many times shall my brother offend me? And try to understand the meaning of unto seventy everlasting times seven, to understand that his brother's and his own sin and forgiveness was an ongoing wrestling between human frailty and God's grace, a cycle of violation and restoration, of injury and healing as the lot of mankind. He had to think and work things out. He had to find meaning in his captivity, his enslavement, his enduring, to re-examine his relationship with women, his role as a man, he had to think of power, of what it was, of what must be its function. He had to think of the world, of life, what was it, was it a matter of domination by the strongest, what was man, what was tribe and people and race and country? He had to re-examine all the old questions, to look again at the old songs, the old sayings, the stories, —the meanings. And he had to be careful about looking back to what things might have been. He had to look towards the future. He had to find the elation, the zeal for this new life. For, what he had woken up into was a new world.

Around him people, the more recent captives, were talking

of returning to homes in Kano, in Congo, in Ghana. Some of Faustin's relatives were preparing to petition the queen to send them back. They knew where they would be going to; but for him, he had lost track of the exact place he had come from. His homeland was the whole continent. He was from Africa, not from a place in Africa.

'Look at that, eh,' he said to Faustin. 'Here am I, more African than any African and no place in Africa to go to. I don't know which part I come from.'

'This is your land now,' Faustin tell him. 'Your new home.'

'Home?'

'Home!'

He had no idea of the sky in that place, of the land, of the roads, of the shape of the leaves, of the smell of the earth, of his people in the setting of that home. He had no idea of their dances, of their songs, of the language. He had no idea of the loss he had lost. He had to try to put aside the depth of this loss he had lost and find a way in his mind to claim this new world as home. And he could claim it, he felt, out of having endured here, out of having planted the land without reward, out of having built houses without occupying them, out of having sown without reaping. He could claim it out of having made it a battleground for freedom. He was, he began to think, part of a new people whose sweat and blood had fertilized the soil of every plantation in every single island and over in South America where his brother Noble had gone with Santiago Domingo to fight in the war of liberation.

He could claim it not as a place to go back to, not as a place where he would find his past, but as a place in which he had to seek his future. And he had to do this in the midst of a new multitude. In the midst of new people: Africans who had fought against Napoleon, Africans who had fought on the side of the British in the American War of Independence, Africans captured on the high seas, men who had escaped the revolution in France, royalists and republicans from Spain, Buccaneers, owing allegiance to no king nor country, the remnants of Amerindians, survivors of European guns and diseases, now in settlements in Toco, in Arima, in the hills of Platanal; escaped black Caribs from St Vincent, peons from Venezuela, Barbadians, people implicated in all the rebellions and massacres in the neighbouring islands. All of them in an English colony ruled by Spanish law, run by French settlers. These were the people who he had to share this future with.

And what kind of future he could expect to share with the planters, these fellars whose blood get sweet, who get accustomed to cocking up their foot and lahaying while Blackpeople do the work, who as soon as they hear about freedom for Blackpeople all they could see is this bottomless well of labour drying up? All they could see is their investment jumping up in steel band.

'What will happen to our plantations? Our investment?' they start to bawl.

Is all right for you over there in England with your pious pretence and with your craw full to bursting to say is time to stop this thing, they tell the Englishman. Is all right for you, Mr Wilberforce, to send your saints out here to rile people up with your talk about humanity and freedom and justice and equality. Is all right for you. Just remember, when you sitting on your high seats of judgement, just remember that you are the ones who get us into this. Just remember that is you who tell us we could make a profit through this traffic in people, that is you, Britain, who set out the land settlement policy, is you who send the ships, is you who ruling this place . . . Is all right for you far over there where you don't have Blackpeople all around you to talk your arseness about humanity. We have to face them here. They not these innocent angels you making them out to be. We don't have a bed a roses here. We have our investments to protect, we have the banks to face.. If your belly full up now with profits, if you ready now to abandon us because you getting sugar from beet that you growing over there in England, give us the island to run. Change the constitution so we could put into effect the things we want to see in this island.

What kinda future you could have with planters who refuse the offer of a new constitution because they refuse to share power with the other so-called free people of the island – the mulattos and free people of colour who find themselves involved in the same criminal system?

This home, he tell Faustin, is the battleground for a new world.

*

The night before the announcement of Emancipation, JoJo was at the Nine Nights wake for Corliss McKnight who died from suffocation when digging a tunnel from underneath his cell in the Royal Jail so that he would be out in the open for Emancipation Day, and who somehow got himself stuck in the hole and was found with his knees drawn up to his chest, cramped with tons of earth around him, already dead: he was there dancing bongo and singing hymns at the wake when Faustin Alfonsine who had spent his life trying to effect a legal escape, malingering and pretending injury and illness so as not to work, going through the most elaborate exercises, feigning ignorance, feigning stupidity, stealing whatever he could put his hands on and not because he was so much in need of the items stolen as that it was the opportunity to strike a blow against the prosperity of their plantations, his whole life a contest with the drivers he worked under, to deceive them, to break something, to steal something. Fat and perspiring, his chest and thighs bursting out of clothes deliberately chosen because they were too small for him, his head round and sleek like that of a big tom-cat, Faustin Alphonsine came to tell him that on his way from St James to the wake he had seen the militia with their artillery pieces out in full force, a matter which, according to Faustin, supported the dream he had dreamed of losing his two front teeth. Faustin told him to look out for trouble on the morrow because he had heard that what the governor was going to announce was that they had to work ten more years for the planters before they really were set free.

Yes. This was trouble and JoJo got up from the log where he was sitting and he went into the ring where previously he had been dancing and he began in his hurt cracked plaintive voice not a bongo song but a stickfight chant, the song of a warrior with a battle before him:

> Joe Prengay, lend me your bois to play,
> Joe Prengay, lend me your bois to play,
> Aye ah yaye a yae, Joe Prengay, lend me your bois to play.

People watching him like if he gone crazy, everybody standing back and looking, until, drenched with sweat and ready to drop, they lead him staggering back to the log in the yard where, as he sat, the girl who was serving coffee, whom he had been looking at whole night, Evelina Rosales, Corliss McKnight's niece, with her big eyes and dancer's body, came up out of concern and stood beside him, the sense of her, her face and eyes for a moment blanking the hurt, the pain that he knew was awaiting him, she let him take her hand, thick-fleshed and heavy. He looked out in the darkness beyond the shadows, 'Come with me,' he pleaded, as if suddenly nothing else mattered.

'Why?' she asked, calmly taking her hand away.

'Because,' he said, 'tomorrow if I not free I feel I going to kill somebody.'

'And this is all I can offer? This is all I can be to you?'

And when she looked into his face for his reply she saw such desolation and impotence and sorrow, for right then he was thinking of what use was he to this woman, that nothing was changed, she took his hand and sat there with his hand resting in hers, then she looked at his face,

'Come,' she said, after a while, holding his hand and rising, her face turned to the bushes, and when he looked the question at her, she said: 'I don't want you to kill nobody.'

That night he left the wake with her and they walked into Port-of-Spain to Brunswick Square, there under the samaan trees and the little bandstand where the militia band played for the Port-of-Spain population the waltzes on a Saturday evening, near the Red House where the Whitepeople conducted the business of government. They found a place to stand by the fountain where a Grecian nymph was bathing forever in the water's constant stream, to wait for the announcement from Governor Hill, a man of seventy-three who was to die five years later, the first governor to die in the colony, waiting there in a silence highlighted by buzzes of whispered speech, in the midst of all these Blackpeople who had come from every part of the surrounding countryside to hear what he would eventually say that, yes, those who worked in the fields would be set free in six years and those who worked in the house would be freed in four. That was his Emancipation. And JoJo had looked around at the people, for the uprising, for the revolt that Faustin had promised, and all he was met with were the same astonished and outraged

176

faces of people who had learned to wait, of people who had learned to calculate. He was ready to dead. The square was clean, not a stone, not a stick. Around them the militia patrolled. He couldn't take it. He walked with Evelina out of the square down Clarence Street to see the same drifting and vacant and outraged people, and walked back up again into the same square to stand there with the people noisy now and jeering as the governor read on explaining what they had already understood and what they did not want to hear, that Emancipation was not to free them. Not that day or any other day for that matter, JoJo thought. What it had done was to manoeuvre them into accepting not freedom but the promise of being set at liberty, with no more attention given to their years of degradation and captivity and abuse than if they had been dogs that had been chained and were now going to be loosened to fend for themselves. And he knew that if they accepted these terms as freedom they would be forfeiting their own future and the future of this island. He knew now that, far from being the whiteman's burden, Blackpeople had to take responsibility for whatever new world was to be made. And he knew that world was not going to be created just by dreaming. It was the insult of the response that burned, that wounded him to the bone. And he realized that what they wanted was battle, what they wanted was some murder to bring them to their senses.

The chant was going on in his brain:

Joe Prengay, lend me your bois to play,
Joe Prengay, lend me your bois to play,
Aye ah yaye a yae, Joe Prengay, lend me your bois to play. . . .

'You better go home,' he said to Evelina, who had spent the day with him. For they had remained within distance of her relatives, who were also there from the wake. 'You better go home.'

'And when I will see you?' she asked him. 'When?'

And seeing how difficult it was for him to give an answer, the tears not far behind her voice, she said, 'Is not like we not in the same island.'

'No.' Tears were in his chest too, for what he knew he had to do. 'Is not like you in Toco and I in Icacos.'

'Or that they don't have horses.'

'Or roads.'

'Or like my foot sick.'

'Is not like I wouldn't be waiting.'

'Or like I wouldn't be coming.'

'On any day of the week.'

'On a Saturday.'

'Or Sunday.'

And he stood before her holding her hands and when he let them go, she fixed the collar of his shirt plastering her hands down his chest to feel the strength of his body, as in an anointing, tracing her hands palms down from his collar to his belly and she turned with that dancer's spin of her dancer's body and her eyes half hooded and her head upright. As she left him he saw Faustin coming, loose and disjointed with his clothes of a buffoon, to say simply, what he already knew, 'We have to fight.'

'We have to fight!'

And it was for that reason that he found himself two days later in the forest of Tamana searching for his brother Hubert, because he had decided that the solution to this matter was to begin the war all over again. This time they had to do like in Haiti and take over and rule the entire island.

It took him nine days to find his brother. He had climbed above the springs. He had walked in the heights of the forest where the monkeys howled and the snakes waited at the end of traces near fruit trees, where cut vines sprung water, high up where parrots feasted on balata trees, into this far peace where bands of wild hogs rooted among wild yams and up to the early paths of streams, high above the waterfall up among the guatacaire and mora trees, among the angelin and the perfumed laurier into a freedom precarious like the fern rooted on stone, all about it rooted itself anywhere it could hold, all about him, everywhere, breaking forth in the songs of birds, in the brilliance of flowers, ants crawling, with helicoptering honeybees, until after three days wandering, one morning with dawn breaking he saw at the side of a mora tree the huge eyes of a half-naked boy with his brother's face looking at him.

He had come too late. For more than twelve years his brother had roamed the forests of the Central Range, escaping the raids of Captain Taylor and the militia. Now he had a settlement of forty-five men, women and children and two wives both big-belly, the whole settlement living still in this silence, soundless like the forest, their footfall making no more noise than falling leaves.

'Is now you come? Now?' Hubert asked him, almost amused. 'When they give you freedom?'

'Freedom?'

JoJo tried to explain the disappointment, the deception, the insult. It was no use. Hubert wasn't really listening to him. He was listening to the silence of his children. He was listening to the lean black men who had their eyes glued to the traces and their ears tuned to the wind. He was listening to the eyes of the women hungering for peace, for rest, for a comfortable sleep.

'Look at my people, man. Look at my children. Look at my two wives both of them big-belly.'

And JoJo had looked at the ragged alert bunch and knew that it was unfair to ask them to take up arms again, to fight and run again. But he explained to them nevertheless what had happened, that Britain had declared an emancipation that would take place six years in the future, that would doom them to a secondclassness in a country that they more than any other people had brought to prosperity.

But the time had passed, Hubert felt. Months ago if they had come when Captain Taylor was terrorizing them. Nine years ago before they kill Carlo and Short and burn down the village.

'That is why I came here, to fight, not to run. But now, man? Now?'

JoJo couldn't argue.

'And you, brother,' Hubert said, 'why you don't just stay here. Leave them and their emancipation and use the opportunity and seize and settle a piece of land. It have land here. Nobody wouldn't bother you up here.'

Next day, after drinking the mountain dew and eating the meal of wild hog and white yam they offered, JoJo left, following as they led him through the maze of tracts that eventually put him on the main trace that would take him to the high road.

And he would arrive at the barracks where he lived to find the estate in turmoil with people missing, men run off never to return, some in total confusion brought on by the arrangements for their freedom and Faustin talking from two sides of his face, complaining that the men he could rely on had gone to Tunapuna and Arouca to seize lands of their own, that he also needed to seize a bit for himself because otherwise he would have to continue working for the same plantation. But now that you back, now that you here we could start again, we could go and talk to the men and explain them the position. And they had to get guns. If we have to fight, we have to have guns. He knew some of the fellars in the West India regiment, blackfellars who they catch and give a uniform and put a gun in their hands and make them soldiers.

'Faustin, man,' he said. 'Faustin, I was expecting you to round up the people. I was expecting to meet us fighting.'

'Greed and stupidity does affect everybody,' JoJo tell Evelina.

'Get a piece of land for yourself,' Evelina advised him.

'And what about the other people? You think everybody could go and get a piece of land?'

'You is not everybody. Well, Faustin do it.'

But JoJo saw the trap. Allowing the one or two to go and squat land was a way out for the authorities. It eased the frustration of the more adventurous people and made this scrambling for land appear to be the solution to the problems.

But everybody had worked. Everybody was entitled.

They had given the planters money for the losses they would suffer from having now to cease enslaving people, but for the enslaved who had lost their life, family, years, they had nothing to give. JoJo was clear: to squat their land now was to accept the status they had imposed upon him.

'So what you going to do, then?' Evelina wanted to know.

'I going back to the plantation.'

'Good luck,' Evelina told him, and he went to the estate of Carabon and reported for work. Carabon was surprised to see him,

'I thought you went away. I thought you abscond with those other fellars.'

'I come to work.'

'Well, at least you have come.'

Andre Carabon was hurt. As he told JoJo that morning, speaking loud so that the labourers nearby would hear, 'Call an estate where they treat you better than I do here. Call one. I have been godfather for your children, I come to your weddings, your christenings. I don't walk with a whip. If we have three floggings on this estate in any year we have plenty. I give everybody a plot of land for their own self. What you plant on it after you done work here is yours. Look at the number of people who work here and pay off for their freedom. I not against your freedom. I give you your rations. Each week every one of you get three pounds of salt meat and three pounds of salt fish. Everybody work half-day on Saturday. Sunday you free. From five in the morning till six in the evening that is the day work. Half an hour for breakfast, two hours for lunch so you will be out of the sun when it is at its hottest. I see about the sick and, after all that, people want to run away. The most contented set of people on this island. And that is my thanks, that is the gratitude I get.'

'I come to work, sir,' JoJo said.

'And what else?' asked Carabon, because JoJo still stood before him.

'This,' JoJo said, holding out the letter to him.

'What paper is this? You want me to read it?'

'To the Right Honourable Lord Baron Gleneagle, Her Majesty's Principal Secretary of State for the Colonial Department:

'The Memorial of the undersigned African Subjects of Her Most Gracious Majesty the Queen of Great Britain and Ireland humbly sheweth unto Your Lordship: That Your Memorialists are natives of Africa. That during the existence of the Slave Trade Your Memorialists were torn from their country, their friends, relations, delivered into the hands of Slave Merchants who imported Your Memorialists into the West Indies and sold them, that the names of Your Memorialists have been changed, that the work of the labour of Your Memorialists has gone not to their own advancement but to the upkeep of those who commanded unlawfully their labour.

As a result of the circumstances of their enslavement Your Memorialists have no other option now but to make this island their home, since

181

it is the place that many of them have been born into and it is the place that their labour has gone to build.

Your Memorialists believe that in the interest of justice, of humanity, of harmonious relationships existing in the future between those who have profited from our captivity and those of us who have been captives here, that Your Most Gracious Majesty do grant Your Memorialists relief in the form of land, in the form of amenities and such other means as Your Gracious Majesty might see fit as a form of reparation for wrong done to us and as an expression of regret from Your Most Gracious Majesty for the position your humble subjects have been placed in through no fault of their own and despite every effort on their part over the centuries to prevent Your Memorialists from being reduced in this most degrading fashion.'

And he had stood there and watched as Carabon read it and read it yet again, his moustaches trembling and his eyes getting red and a sickly look coming across his face, his whole body growing more calm, more amazed as his eyes went down the page, until at last he looked up with his now dangerous, now threatening calm: 'You joking with the Queen?'

'No, sir.'

'You joking with me, then?' with this half-sternness in his voice as if he was trying to come back from a limb he had stepped out on.

'No, Mr Carabon.'

'What you want me to do with this?'

'We just asking for a beginning, sir. A new start.'

'A new start for whom?' Carabon ask him.

'For both of us.'

'What you want me to do with this thing?' Carabon asked again, his anger almost mastering him.

'I would like you to support it.'

'You making a joke? Right?'

'You have been granted compensation for the loss of our labour, now we want compensation for the mashing up of our lives.'

'You expect the Queen to answer this? The governor will view it as insolence.'

JoJo take a deep breath, 'But if you support it. If you tell him of the justice of our claims.'

For a moment Carabon looked directly into his eyes, trying to force him to avert his gaze. But JoJo kept his eyes unblinking and his head straight.

'I see,' Carabon said, his eyes still fixed on JoJo's. 'You expecting a lot. Too much.' And it was then that JoJo saw in Carabon's eyes something like guilt and something like shame and something like rage and JoJo knew that Carabon knew that now he had either to carry forward JoJo's claim or to destroy him.

From that day Carabon tried his best to get JoJo to withdraw the letter. He wanted to rent him the plot of land he had been working on, then he wanted to sell it to him. He put the matter in the hands of his lawyers. They outlined the conditions to JoJo. He had to have cash to pay. JoJo didn't have money. Well, there has been a misunderstanding, the lawyers said. Perhaps you should apply to the government for other lands. Of course, JoJo knew that that was no solution to the matter and that in any event he didn't have the money to purchase and the land laws made it impossible for him to join with other people because the policy was to sell no less than eighty acres of land and that to a single buyer.

'You have money to buy eighty acres? If you have the money you could get the land in the morning,' the lawyer said, cynically, his face shining in a grin.

No. He didn't have the money. That is not what he was thinking. He was thinking that these people were forcing him into battle. They had brought enslavement to an end, but they had no new policy, no real new vision of how the plantations were to run and how people were to live in freedom.

Yes, there is a misunderstanding, JoJo tell him. And this time he went himself to talk to the people working still on the plantation about new plans for battle for their freedom. Faustin was having meetings with Daaga, the African prince who had been captured by the Portuguese and rescued by the British who baptized him into the Christian faith, named him Donald Stewart and put him in the West India Regiment stationed that time at St Joseph. They had a plan.

Daaga and his recruits were expected to seize the barracks at

St Joseph. Once it was secure they were to give a signal for the apprentices – that was the new name they gave them – from the estates nearby to join them. Together they were to march to Manzanilla, make connection with the African soldiers settled there since fighting on the side of the British against Napoleon. Here they were to set up a council which was to rule the land.

As it turned out, that was not to happen. Daaga and his two hundred-odd recruits botched the revolt by a set of singing, yelling and wild shooting. No signal went out. The apprentices never rose up to join him. Forty people were killed. And Daaga and some of his men were captured just outside of Arima. They were court-martialled and three of them sentenced to death by shooting, Daaga himself singled out and characterized as a madman leading a set of stupid fellows who, they were happy to report, planned to walk to Africa by way of the sea from the seacoast at Manzanilla. Daaga had been himself a seafarer and had come to the island by ship. He couldn't have believed he could walk to Africa. But that was the tactic of those in power. Every Black leader had to be seen as a madman. For Whitepeople to feel themselves human they had to make Blackpeople appear to be beasts. And they would push Blackpeople on the defensive by an unending programme of propaganda that would reinvent Blackpeople as demons largely unacceptable as proper humans on account of their blackness, their laziness, their cannibalism, their stupidity, their simplemindedness, their mimicry, their criminality, their immorality, their licentiousness, their unlawfulness, their childishness, their dancing and singing, their rhythm.

One year and one month after the Daaga fiasco, the authorities put an official end to Apprenticeship. JoJo was now officially free. The very next morning, he went to see Mr Carabon. With apprenticeship ended, he expected that the authorities would have no choice but to settle accounts with Africans whose labour they still needed for their plantations. Carabon looked tortured. Overnight, it seemed, he had become frail and JoJo was frightened that he would die before he settled with him and he was glad that Carabon that morning had two of his sons with him.

'You come to tell me you leaving now?' straining to appear in command.

184

But no, he wasn't leaving. He had come to remind Carabon of his petition he wanted forwarded to the Queen.

'Look,' Carabon said, turning to his sons, 'you boys will have to see about this now.'

That was the last time he spoke to Carabon. Four days later Carabon took ill, two weeks later he was dead.

It wasn't a good month afterwards when JoJo saw a group of strange people standing in the compound.

'Hey!' he said to Faustin. 'Where that band of oily-looking people come from?'

'India,' Faustin said.

'What they doing here?'

'They come to work here,' said Faustin. 'That is the answer to your claim for compensation.'

'You have to go to the Governor yourself about your petition,' Evelina said.

One morning JoJo was out in the yard, just about to go to the estate, when he heard the sound of cutlassing from the land nearby. He stopped for a moment in something between alarm and vexation. Grasping his own cutlass, JoJo moved to the sound and found himself looking at one of the Indian men cutting the bush. His anger grew even more. These people was bold. They come and take over the work and prevent the Governor from dealing with his petition, now, here was one of them squatting the government land.

'Hey,' JoJo called out, 'what is it you doing? You don't see people living here? How you could come in here just so and don't tell nobody nothing?'

The Indian man looked at him in sober outrage and when he spoke he was so choked up that his voice came out almost apologetic, 'This land is my own.'

'Your own?'

'Is because of my contract. I not going back to India.'

'Your contract? You have a contract? Who give you this contract?' JoJo interrogating him as if he was Protector of Crown Lands.

'What happen?' the Indian man ask him. 'You working here?'

'Yes, I working here,' JoJo answered.

'You working here and you don't know what a contract is?

185

I knew now what I had to do, and it felt appropriate that I should be in his office, sitting in his chair.

I felt strangely elated and strangely humbled. It was my turn now, my turn. I had not failed to see that the Colonial government, Britain, the authorities, however we called them, had had opportunities to make restitution and apology that would restore value and dignity and respect to our community and people. Each time they had backed away, out of fear, out of arrogance. The sadness was that the National Party had done no better.

Worse, we had left the problem unattended by not even acknowledging the presence of a problem. We had secured Blackpeople in their secondclassness. Now, it was up to me.

And I wasn't thinking even of nomination to fight the elections.

I picked up the telephone and called Miss Baldeosing to arrange a meeting with Lochan and Carabon. I would need their support. We together had to address this question. Yes, I would ask them to join me on the rostrum on Independence Day.

Ethelbert B. was hearing me. He was looking out those same big eyes at me.

'You think the PM would want this?' he ventured.

'Why wouldn't he? Why?'

Because I was not going to hide what I was doing from anybody. My action would make the Prime Minister and the Party aware of this great omission we had been guilty of. I was certain that Ethelbert B. Tannis having listened to Bango now better understood the task at hand. I couldn't understand why he was looking at me so forbiddingly. Could it be, I wondered, because I was sitting in the PM's chair.

10

Ethelbert B. Tannis

'I suppose that I could have tried harder to persuade Alford George to reconsider, to look again at the matter he was venturing into,' Ethelbert B. Tannis would tell me much later, in his voice a fresh anger and regret as he sat huge and unhappy in the little room that he called his office in the Cosmos Business Academy where he spent his mornings plotting a new career now that he had lost his place of influence with the PM.

I had gone to see him to try to clear up gaps in my understanding of the story; because up to that time I couldn't understand where Alford George had gone wrong. I couldn't understand why the Party would want to hound him out of power and represent him as a traitor. It didn't make sense to me, especially when it looked as if what Alford was attempting couldn't harm anybody, in fact could only redound to the benefit of the Party.

'I suppose I could have tried,' Ethelbert B. Tannis said. 'But Alford already had this gleam in his eyes, this sparkle about him that mesmerized me for a moment. It was as if his sitting there in the PM's chair had given him a new sense of power, so that in that moment there was no hesitation from him. He was going to do what he was going to do.

'I tell him: "Boy, you need time, you need power. This island seductive and sweet as it looks is a dangerous place, a minefield that you have to have experience to tread through. Coming alone to attack these problems just so, one man alone, independent, they going to stop you. Things look easy but nothing is simple here. You say you want to remove the fears from people. But people have a vested interest in their fears. They have a vested interest in their victimhood. And I not talking only about Blackpeople. It is everybody. Blackpeople know they get a raw deal. They see doors that closed to them opening up for everybody else. So they grumble and complain. Whitepeople feel guilty. They have the land, they have the money. Still they want people to feel sorry for them. So they start to cry out that Blackpeople is their burden. They lazy, they spending money they don't have, they having a good time. Indians jump in the brew, crying that Blackpeople keeping them from getting power. Everybody bawling. Everybody is a victim and that is what make everybody equal. That is the equality we have here: the equality of victims. And that is why people frighten to change. Everybody have a gang to belong to. Everybody have some cause to be righteous about. And the leaders don't want things to change because confusion keep them in power. Every one of them fraid of people who are free.'

'Things I shouldn't even talk about, things that I alone know and see, I tell him. But no. The man ain't listen to me. I not telling you not to do it, but if you want to give Bango land, if you want to involve Lochan and Carabon, at least go and discuss it with the PM, go and discuss it with some of the senior men of the Party.

'But he was already in motion.

'You think the PM ain't see what you think you see? You think you's the first person in the world that look at this situation, look at this island and realize that Blackpeople not free. But the mistake you making is to believe that the chief want Blackpeople to be free. Because when he free Blackpeople it would follow that everybody will be free. And how he will control people when they free? It frighten him. Freedom is a thing that frighten people.

'Look at the British! The British wanted to give Emancipation. They wanted to abolish their own system of enslaving people. The planters here in Trinidad is the first to oppose them. They get crazy. They was ready to commit murder to keep Blackpeople in captivity. They send to tell England: what all you doing going to take bread out the mouths of people here. We have plantations, we need people to work on them. They write to was it the Colonial Secretary, they write to the man, they say, Hey! This thing you planning to do here going to kill people. People going to dead, you hear. This shit all you doing going to kill the planters and we not taking it so. They say, Listen, Mr Englishman! Listen, you hypocrite, over there, all your talk about abolition and human rights and freedom and all that, you could afford to do because your business fixed. You put us in this and now you leaving us because you want to sound good to the world, because you want to sound good to yourself. Watch your arse, you know. Watch it. And what happen? The same British turn round and turn emancipation into imprisonment. They didn't think about freedom of Blackpeople, they think of Whitepeople security. Listen to Mr Brougham in the House of Commons in 1824: listen:

My opinion ever has been, that it is alike necessary to the security of our white brethren and just and even merciful to the Negroes – those victims of a long, continued system of cruelty, impolity and injustice – 'You hear him! You hear? THOSE VICTIMS OF LONG, CONTINUED SYSTEM OF CRUELTY, IMPOLITY AND INJUSTICE. The man knew. They knew!' – to maintain firmly the legal authorities, and, with this in view to avoid in our relations with the slaves, a wavering, uncertain policy keeping them in a position of doubt and solicitude, calculated to work to their own discomfort and the disquiet of their masters . . .

It is for the sake of the blacks themselves as subsidiary to their own improvement that the present state of things must for the time being be maintained. It is, because to them, the bulk of our fellow subjects in the Colonies, liberty, if suddenly given, and still more, if violently obtained, by men yet unprepared to receive it would be a curse and not a blessing, that emancipation must be the work of time . . .

'You hear him? Emancipation must be the work of time. Time!

'And so they turn round and give the same planters more than one million pounds compensation and not a penny for the Blackpeople they had under sufferation.

'You don't think that a man with the PM's brains know this, know it just from his knowledge of history, nothing else, not even his good will, not even himself being a Blackman. You don't think the PM understand? But the PM know that if he go and play the arse with Whitepeople property that is the last election he will win. Kith and kin, boy. Kith and bloody kin. You know what that is, eh? The PM see these things and didn't, couldn't. Yes, couldn't carry them through. You didn't read the speeches he make in '55? You didn't read the books he write? You didn't hear his lectures? You didn't hear him thumping his chest throughout the Caribbean? Greek city states! Athens of the Caribbean! Where is Athens now? Not a good library in the blasted island. Yes, he see the promised land, but when he visualize the pressure that will fall on him, he turn back at the gates. He turn back, otherwise he never sit on that chair you sitting on. You think it wasn't in his mind to change things? You think it wasn't in his mind to take us back to 1834 and say to everybody here, OK, people, we here now. We are here now and I am the boss now. When I talk, no damn dog bark. Who don't like it could get the hell out of here. Eh? They give the planters more than a million pounds compensation for loosening Blackpeople into a spurious freedom and they give the Blackpeople who they had enslaved nothing. Now is our turn. Let us fix this whole thing. Let us come together and fix up this whole rotten business. Let us bring to an end this long, continued *and continuing* system of cruelty, impolity and injustice. Let us find a way for justice and dignity and forgiveness and compassion to prevail, and go on together from here. You think he don't know that is action not time that does change things.

'Didn't he call people to action, to march to Chaguaramas and take back the base that the British lease to the Americans for ninety-nine years. We answered his call. We marched. We take back the base. The Americans give us. They say, OK, you want the base, look it. I give you. Here it is, your base. With all the amenities I build up from the time I here, from since 1939. Look it. And what he do? What happen to the Base? That was the time to talk about a new land development and land settlement policy, that was the time to tell people: Hey, look at us. Is just over a million of us in this green Godbeautiful island. From Columbus, all of us come here by chance. Look at us, we have the treasury of the world right here, of skill and language, but we can't get nowhere until we settle accounts with history. We can't do nothing until we liberate ourselves from the victimhood that is strangling all of us here.

'And is true, he say a few things. But then he end up giving slogans. He end up telling you about free secondary education, as if your problem was stupidity. He end up saying Massa Day done without taking the action that would bring Blackpeople liberation.

'Why I didn't say nothing? Why I only speaking out now?

Didn't I follow him for those more than twenty years? Well, I will tell you. I get trapped. I get trap following. I get trap with the belief that the way to keep Blackpeople together was to preach that we had a common victimhood. This history mash us up bad, you know. It scatter us according to which part they land us when they root us up from Africa, according to religion, to class, to colour. You was Grenadian, Barbadian, Tobagonian, from Belmont from St James, from San Fernando, you was Ibo, Yoruba, Coromanti, middle class, barrack class, you was Christian, Anglican, Catholic, Baptist Shango, Adventist Pentecostal. And the only thing to get you together was to make you remember that you all pass under the limbo pole of enslavement, every one of you, that of all the people in this island you alone dance that limbo dance. People didn't want to hear that. People didn't want to be together. People wanted to escape. People try – plenty people try, and with good reason because it had those who was free here while others were enslaved. It had Blackpeople owning Blackpeople, it had Blackpeople who had Blackpeople enslaved. Enslaved, not indentured. That was the error: joining up according to your sense of oppression, instead of looking at your world from the position of liberation. So we tried to draw the Indians in. We try to equate enslavement with indenture. Confused everybody. Was two different states – that was all he had. Your victimhood. To keep you together, otherwise you break up into factions and let the same whiteman come back and rule you. And that was the problem. The Indians didn't have that problem. And if they have it they don't show it at least not to other people. They is either Hindu or Moslem and those who is Christian is Presbyterian. They all together in one camp. You in a hundred. So that was the problem, to keep you victim and to free you.

'And that was why Alford George was so different. He stumble on the truth that to free yourself you have to free everybody. It is a situation in which you have no control over people. And how you going to carry out your work without that control? And that is why I was frighten.

'Everything I explained to him. And I thought he would listen; but he fooled me, this Alford fellar. He really wanted to be a hero. And that is when I knew that they had to stop him. The time wasn't ripe. The PM had things to do. He had his programme. He had to have time. Like the Mr Brougham in the House of Commons in 1824: Emancipation must be the work of time. We had to wait on the PM to guide us. He knew the way. Alford was too hurry. So they had to stop him.

'The very next morning after the talk with Bango and Myrtle, bright and early, the phone ring. The PM want to talk to me. He get the news already that we had this big discussion, that we were planning these great things. Me, Chief? I ask him.

' "I not taking this, you know, Tannis," he tell me.

' "Chief." And I try to talk to him. I try to tell him the boy young, that as a man of experience he should call him in and talk to him and make him see the dangers he was getting into.

'But the Chief wasn't listening to me: "I will not stand for this. I will not stand idly by and let this boy mash up the Party, mash up a country that I work so hard to get out of the doldrums of ignorance.'

' "But, Chief . . ."

' "Get him to stop his nonsense or he goes, and you with him."

'I call Alford, I talk to him. I tell him how the Chief feel. But he had come to his own decision. He would go on and work to get together with Lochan and Carabon and together they will get Bango the land as an example from his district for the whole nation.

' "You feel Carabon and Lochan will see this thing the same way you see it?" I ask him.

' "Well, we'll see, won't we?" That was the answer he give to me.

'All I could do is wish him well and wish that those two fellars Carabon and Lochan was also crazy.'

Adolphe Carabon: The Birthday Party

'We not giving them any blasted land. What the hell they take us for?' Michael said. And Adolphe Carabon chuckled because when he spoke to Alford George that had also been his first thought until he caught himself in alarm, realizing that he was not giving his own response but one he thought his family would make, expressed here now in the aggressive, bullying tone employed of late by his brother Michael, the lawyer, as if the whiteness of his skin and the correctness of his grammar and the substantiality of his arguments were not enough to give him the sense of authority he desired. He liked the idea of himself as Michael the lawyer, the badJohn from St Clair, as if such a persona made him less vulnerable, more native, more, if you want, animal, more man. 'If they want land they could buy it,' stretching out a hand to take the drink of rum Adolphe was offering. 'They will have to pay,' struggling to sit upright in the thickly upholstered chair, along whose velvety seat he had been sliding and righting himself all evening.

St Hilaire, their brother, the priest, the only man among them not clean-shaven, tugged at the hairs under his chin. He was saying in the diffident manner he employed as he fretted his way to the heart of a problem, 'That is clear. But that couldn't be what we gather here for. My impression is that they expect something more from us, some kind of gift . . .'

'Gift?' said Michael. 'Massa day done. What they asking for gift for? For marching? Eh? Is better we march too, eh, Ross?' turning to his nephew, Adolphe's son, Ross the bodybuilder, sitting on one of the straight-backed chairs next to him, dressed in denim overalls, the huge muscles of his arms and a portion of his chest on display. 'Eh, Ross? You want to march? Your body big enough. You could march for a long time. You could march for weeks, eh,' reaching across and throwing a punch at Ross.

'They not asking for anything for themselves,' Adolphe said, trying to cull from his tone the defensiveness he felt forced upon him.

'Then what we come here for?' asked the priest St Hilaire. 'What you call us here for, Adolphe?'

'Come and siddown, man. Leave the drinks, let somebody else serve. Everybody know where the grog is. Come and sit down, man, and tell us what you call us here for.' Michael was sitting upright now.

And Adolphe, still with the tray in his hands, trying to gain time, had said, 'You don't know is Daddy's birthday today?'

'Yes,' St Hilaire said. 'But you said there was something more. Sit down, man.'

'Why you don't tell them what you thinking, Addie,' Adolphe's wife Glenda encouraged.

He felt like a child. All their eyes were on him.

'You want a chair, Daddy?' his daughter asked. 'Get up, Ross,' she said to her brother. 'Ross! Gedupp!'

And Adolphe realized how alone he was and that once again he had over-reacted, that in his haste to bring them together for what he thought was a good cause he had exposed what they called his vagueness, a quality they condemned in him because it suggested carelessness, immaturity, an over-willingness to please that made him more plebeian than they felt he should be. Lamely, he said, 'I didn't know we were ready.' This time the defensiveness was in his voice.

'Ages ago,' said Michael, who Adolphe could see was taking the role of chairman. 'What is this urgent business that you invite us to here?' his tone light, jocular, tight, condescending the way Adolphe remembered him – and the rest of them too – always speaking to him, as to someone not quite all there, whose responses to the important business of the world could not be trusted, his decisions needing to be double-checked, corrected lest they allow him to involve them in some foolishness they were sure to regret, an attitude that imposed upon him a sense of inadequacy, and he began to sense that once again he had been defeated by his own best intentions, undermined by his own goodwill. With them there was no space for goodwill, everything had to be one two three, clear and concrete, an ability and attitude that he lacked, this lack in him vexing them, since what they saw as his vagueness, his carelessness had behind it his independence and indiscipline that went way back to the days of his boyhood when they were both afraid of him and repulsed and amused by him. That was his time.

He remembered that time, that one day, the beginning, his baptism, his confirmation, that day the master asked the class to name the Three Wise Men from the East and he, Adolphe Carabon, the youngest of brothers all of whom had gone to school here at St Mary's, put up his hand and in a voice of greatest confidence answered, 'Gold, Frankincense and Myrrh.' *Myrrh!* dumbfounding the class, who from that day baptized him with the nickname Myrrh, a name that was as outrageous and strong as he felt himself to be, that gave off a sound worthy of his toughness, that expressed itself in the challenges he accepted: who could eat the most hops bread or drink the most mauby, who could pee the farthest, who could stay longest under water, each event not so much won by him as contested and with such ferocious intensity that to beat him you had to really stay under water or eat or spit or pee. So that at the end his resolve was spoken of with an awe that left him more honoured and feared than the Victor Ludorum of the school, putting him on a plane above the athlete who could only run and jump and throw the discus, giving him the edge over fellars that were more talented and assured him a place on the football team, as right half for St Mary's, The Saints, when it is Intercol and the game is bloodansan, blood and sand against QRC and it just finish rain and the ground is wet and nice and skaty in front the Grand Stand in the Savannah and he in blue and white, sweeping ball and man on the slippery field, coming down behind Ming or Ancil Tobias, Toby the clown who could run from one end of the field to the next bouncing a ball on his head, the shouting stands full up with people chanting and blowing bugle and beating iron and old pan and shouting/chanting:

> *A bummalack a bummalah are who are we:*
> *We are the boys of St Mary's.*
> *St Mary's, we want a goal,*

in that call-and-response, breakaway jazz exchange, with QRC allowing St Mary's to hear their own noise until St Mary's, believing their noise had been heard long enough, stop to catch their breath and QRC start up with the same refrain, only the name changed, 'QRC, *we want a goal!*' And he would fly down the right wing even before the overlapping back became part of the modern game and leave Ming to cover for him and square the ball across the goalmouth for Gouveia or Selwyn or Pantin or Bleake, or make for the middle and lay it off for Ming coming down behind him and in the midst of the shouting, position himself for a rebound or a splice from any shaky QRC kick. And nothing in the world was sweeter. Nothing in the world. And after the bloodansan game to be the man to lift onto his shoulders Bleake or Pantin or Ming, to give the people their hero. And for fellars to pat him on his shoulder and call his name, Myrrh! Good game! GOOD GAME! Myrrhhh! The sweet hardness, the hard sweetness. Myrrh! That was when he was most needed, when it didn't matter what his colour was or who the fuck was his father, was just that the team wanted a goal or to prevent one from scoring and he was there, the man on spot. Just that. The man on spot.

And he did not know that really that was all. That was it. That was his whole life right there. Because that was when he had something to die for, people, a team to play for. That was his life right there. And for what? For at the end of the game to strip off his jersey and tie it round his forehead and go with the band round the Savannah and down Frederick Street when the girls from Convent with their turquoise skirts and their oh youngbodies would peek out through the gate with a show of fear that was not to believed and at a distance from him point him out with trepidation as if they were pointing at a funeral, Look him! That one. That is Myrrh! And he, so tough, so hard, so much male and pride and steel. But really, he was never the star. He was just the man on spot, the solidity that made other fellars shine, the awkward clawing do-or-die effort, that never-give-up, that fall-down and get-up-and-go-again fella, that if-you-beat-me-you-eat-me fella. He was the man whose name never get called when they was talking about the greats but who they couldn't leave out the team, who somehow when you review the story of the game was always there on the edge of the big play, making some little great last-minute touch or lunge that change defeat to victory. He was the fella they never had a chance to say they miss because he was always there. And he would add to his achievements the ability to sing any of the current calypsos and at least the chorus of the older ones, could play cuatro, and keep time playing a bass or keeping the rhythm, beating iron or hitting an old box or an old tin.

So already he found himself given a respect that set him apart from the crowd, not a real respect but a respect tinged with fear as if his gifts, these things he could do well, came to him too easily, linked him to the people at the roots, made him too black to be trusted with so much status. So already he discovered that those around him found the need to bring him down, to down-play his abilities so he wouldn't take himself too seriously and move away from them, because he was all they had: the man to represent them against all-comers, whatever the race or national-ity, wherever they went: Barbados, to play football and cricket, or down the islands among a set of shits. So they had to introduce him as an amuser, a shit-talk singer, which is what he came to accept himself as. He didn't feel he was no big thing, no grand important one, no big-shot musician or sportsman, no Sparrow or Kitchener. He couldn't read music, wasn't in their violin con-certo shit, their little pianoforte recital arseness, just a fella who could go anywhere and draw people to him with a cuatro or a guitar or a tabletop to beat on and a bottle and spoon to keep rhythm, and all the Beethoven and all them other fellars, all of them had to bow down in that moment when you finish bathe and you come out the sea and you fire down two three grog and you sit down there on the beach and the world is all there is and everybody naked with their self alone, with nothing, and all you have is you and the bottle you drinking from and the spoon you eat the pelau with, and you is your own instrument. In that situation it had nobody to touch him, nobody. And he could put himself up against anybody in the whole world, he with no cathedral choir with jacket and long dress on, just a few fellars to keep up the chorus, and he singing:

> Teena lost she Thermos flask
> And she mother find it,

199

Teena lost she Thermos flask
And she find it in a bunch of para grass,

singing:

Rum, glorious rum,
When I call you, you bound to come,
You was made from Caroni cane, extracted in Port-of-Spain,
I bring my scorpion to bite your santapee,
Sandimanitay

singing:

What you put in your sweetbread, Lillian,
That have it tasting so . . .

So if he was an amuser, that was OK. It was OK, because they knew the truth. They knew the guts and hearts he turned over and the tears he brought; they knew that without him they were just a few lost Whitepeople practising to be Tarzan without a jungle, jumping off the side of their boats in the waters of the Bocas down the islands, of Monos or Gasparee, fellars with the privilege to look shabby and talk loud and belch hard and fart free. So if it was as an amuser was the best way they could see him, so be it.

Because in a kinda way he knew that was the best they could do. That was their best. And it wasn't out of any despisement as out of a fear of feeling themselves inferior, out of the need, of failing to be the stars they felt they ought to be, that the propaganda of their privilege suggested they should be. So they would call him Myrrh with an undertone of condescension, setting him up as a mamaguy Captain Marvel, a pappyshow Tarzan, his talents making him the inferior, his earnestness making him a arse; and that is how it was. That was it. In this place you had to learn to be lessened because of your gifts, to be ruled by weakness, to be pappyshowed by shit. So he was Chief Backside, the chief arse.

So when he passed his Cambridge examination with marks low enough to let him know that he would be the one selected to go back to the land in Cascadu, one brother, Robert, would import and sell, another, St Hilaire, would become a priest and Michael, who had been cut out from birth to scheme, would be the one to make money as a lawyer, not only for the sake of the money but because there was nothing else; there was no greater cause or adversary to pit his wits and slickness and spite against. And he, Myrrh, stripped of the name he had gained for himself, would revert to being Adolphe Carabon and go back there to the land that they would want to sell and want to keep, and life would come to a stop at least for him. Everything would come crashing down.

Where was the life that he had intended to inhabit? Where was the football league that he had looked forward to starring in, where everybody had a place that was theirs already by race and colour? Where was Casuals and Shamrock and Maple and Notre-Dame and Cosmos and Malvern and Sporting Club and Providence? And the steel bands? Where was Dixie Land and Starland? Where was everybody? Independence had promised a freer, a bigger world somehow. Now, with colonialism ending, the places that had been made for him had begun to disappear and he was left with what? Instead of getting bigger, the world was getting smaller. Here every creed and race find an equal place, said the anthem. Where was his place?

In the beginning he would come down from Cascadu and go down the islands, drinking rum and playing all fours and having a good time and for Carnival he would take off his shirt and walk barebacked in Dixie Land Steel Band, a practice that when Dixie Land disappear he would continue in Invaders; for Port-of-Spain knew him. They still knew Myrrh, the hard crazy mud-derarse. But he couldn't touch their iron. He couldn't beat their iron. And for a time he and Toby and Bleake and some fellars would come out and black up theirself with grease or daub their body with mud and keep up their own rhythm section, they alone, with nobody following them, just five six, at most ten fellars and maybe one or two woman who had to be crazy or brave like a lion, just them and that was it.

The world was dying. His life was going fast and at twenty-three he would meet Glenda Dubisette in a Carnival fête at the Country Club, tall, with big hands and the hoarse voice of a man and young watchful and surrendering eyes, ill at ease, as if she knew that she was too beautiful, too elegant, too brilliant for this crowd and certainly too tall, needed to cut herself down to size to fit in, and he watched her trying to make her body smaller, the very effort giving her more height and grace, producing in her a kind of deformed beauty, making him think, That must be how I does look, that must be me, himself, deformed by his gifts. You are beautiful, he said to her. Beautiful? Where did that word come from? He was twenty-three. He had seen her before, down the island lying on a boat with her long limbs and her shapely thighs stretched out to her full length out there in the open where she could be herself, with an open book of poetry by her side. 'Oh, shit, a poet! What the hell is this?' he had said when he got to talking to her. She wrote poetry, she wanted to act. But at the moment she was stage-manager for a play then playing in the Little Carib Theatre. That night at the fête she spoke of her life, of the poetry she hoped to write, of the theatre, of meaning. Where are we going, Adolphe? she asked. And he grew awkward like the boy that had answered, Myrrh! And he felt shy that he wasn't more than the football, the shit talk, the iron. But what did other fellars have?

She brought out his gentleness, she echoed his questions. That night they danced every dance together, each of them shy, protective, as if each one understood the vulnerability of the other, happy, floating on the heights of the music, of the time, of Carnival, suddenly precious to each other, she gangly and awkward in the costume of a belly-dancer enveloping his shoulders with her long arms, he holding her, shielding her bare shoulders in his embrace. And after that night he would go with her to the theatre, but as a stranger, as a guard. So when they tell him, yes, he would have to go back to Cascadu and the hole opened in his heart and started to drip the pain at the thought of leaving her there in Port-of-Spain, he had wondered what was the best thing to do, what would Michael do? No, not Michael. Michael wouldn't let no woman interfere with his plans. Michael knew where he was going. What would St Hilaire do? So he asked her to marry him and they married, everybody thinking they too young. Her family thinking, 'He's a rango,' and his family thinking, 'She's a jamette.' He in steel band and calypso and she in the Blackpeople theatre. But it was all right, they would be hidden away in Cascadu. She was five years in Cascadu, just long enough to have the three children. But people were right: they were too young. At least he was. And she too bright and he was accustomed too much to surrendering out of his strength, too much the one given to retreat so that he would not wound the other; while she for her part had learnt to ignore criticism and go on doing whatever it was she was doing out of what she assumed to be her superiority. So they never really faced each other. So she would bear the children and with the same implacable resolve she would decide to go to live with them in the apartment in Port-of-Spain to be close to them while they went to school, because of course they couldn't go to school in Cascadu. Some weekends she would come up and he would go down to Port-of-Spain when there was a play to see or when they put on the annual ballet and the big pantomime for children that all the members of the tribe came out of their holes to see, people from down the islands, from school days in St Mary's. Then she got the position to do broadcasts on radio, to describe in her Holy Name voice the carnival costumes and the evening dresses worn by beauty queens. Her voice became known, her name, of course, too. In her little circle, she became a celebrity of sorts. He watched it from his distance of Cascadu, enduring it all, without the courage to tell her, 'Come home, Glenda. Come home, I need you. Come home, let's start our life here, this is not a life. This is not it.'

But, paralysed by his own uncertainty, he approached her in too much of a roundabout way that frightened her, that made her feel that the freedom she had grown used to was now under threat. And eventually when he did ask her, it was too late. She had begun to throw parties at her place. Patrons of the arts, artists, all of them knew her. She was now more properly a star.

'*You* come to Port-of-Spain,' she told him.

'And the land?'

'Leave somebody there. Get an overseer. What will I do in Cascadu? Fish? Hunt? Play patience? We're not having any more children, you know.'

'And Father?'

'Your father? You have seven brothers and sisters. Why you

have to be the one to take care of him? What about Michael and his big talk? What about St Hilaire and the others? Robert? What about Robert and your sister Margaret?'

She wouldn't come and he wouldn't leave.

The land forsook him too, like everything in that period. The cocoa and the sugar prices went tumbling down, labour disappeared. He had to work with his hands, not quite a peasant but he had to work, to be there to see after the citrus and the mangoes he had begun to plant. And then the land trapped him. He thought that he had never loved the land. It was just the property, just his duty to be there until Daddy died; now it began to claim him, not just the bearing trees but the old grapefruit trees with branches drying and breaking off and the fruit small and their skin thick and mottled with fungus, not just the grass, the weeds that appeared as out of nowhere, enduring and enduring cutlassing and ploughing and fire and weedicides that you could cut out and you turn around and they there. He knew he had wanted to change the entire pattern of production, that they had, to have fruit and vegetables for consumption right here, that the land now had to be geared to really feeding people. They had to have a good diet for the children, there had to be a concentration on themselves here, the people here. They had to change from export crops. That time was gone. They had not so much to find markets for the produce as to find a way to get the produce into the homes of the people right here.

'But wouldn't that mean that food would be cheaper? What money you could make so?' Michael asked, sneering.

'But the cheaper food would mean healthier people, it would mean better productivity elsewhere.'

'Your problem is that you too emotional. You spend too much time alone with these people. You starting to think like them.'

'House lots,' Michael said. 'Condominiums for the tourist. The beach just five miles from here. It have a group in Miami will take this estate and you wouldn't recognize it in a year. It have people with expertise.'

They couldn't come to a decision. And in this state of uncertainty over the future of the land, he kept things going as they used to go, making a little change here and there but nothing on the scale he knew would bring success. He felt himself weakening, not exerting himself on projects in which he did not believe and not breaking away and pursuing those he believed in. He began to accept the so-so yield of the land and the so-so work of the labourers on the estate and began to think more seriously of Michael's consortium. Nothing was created, nothing was ventured. The only thing that hadn't changed was the need for more security. Praedial larceny. You planting and tending and fellars coming in and reaping. So he began to put a fence round the house. What he was doing was not cultivating an estate, it was establishing a fortress, concerning himself with huge dogs and gates and keys until one day he stop and ask himself, what you barring round this place for so? What you protecting? And what was it? Your wife and children in Port-of-Spain and the old man going to dead anytime. What was it? The old man? The old house? The silver? The mahogany tables? That same weekend he went to Port-of-Spain to see a show, something from America that was passing through, a jazz concert or something or maybe it was whatever opera that was going on in Queen's Hall, and then to a shitty recital and a dance show where his daughter was dancing their little ballet, poor child, tough and round like a plum, more like a gymnast, not tall or elegant like her mother. Glenda, why you putting the child through this? And he met there the people from down the islands, the old lime, Whitepeople from his youth, the gathering of a withering species who got together at these events to talk about the same things, the women about their children and about Blackpeople children, the girls with no husbands making babies, all that breeding, the Indians making babies with husbands, the girls married from aged fifteen. Where all these people going? Where we going to put all these children? And the men talking about boxing and cricket and Blackpeople and Indians and Chinese and money, as if they were still in charge and what was right was what met their approval and safeguarded their interests. Even then there was something about him that they found changed, something that made him a kind of spy, someone who they couldn't quite trust to represent the race properly. Adolphe, what it is going on in your life? You have another woman or something? You looking . . . different. He watched Glenda. She had grown elegant and cold. She walked with not much of a slouch now and she wore heels to look even taller, and she knew everybody or everybody knew her even more than they knew the carnival queens and the contestants in the beauty pageants which she was called upon to describe.

After sixteen years of marriage he had come to accept the distance between them as a way of life, a challenge of enduring that had nothing to do with fidelity, so that he refused to have another woman and she refused to have another man, as if they had met in each other the best that the species had to offer, which was not good enough, yet they were afraid to look beyond the other for fear of meeting only deterioration; so they had continued with this living that each of them was totally dissatisfied with, but bound, each one by something, not so much by the vows of marriage as by a whole realm of fear, not knowing where was forward, what they wanted to do together, fearful that their coming together would reveal more deeply the emptiness around them and sink them into a more formidable pit.

The times when she was not too busy, they went out to a dance or to a restaurant and these times they approached each other like people who had met in another place, in an earlier time but had lost contact for so long that they had to be careful, on their best behaviour with each other lest they open the wound that had caused them to go asunder in the first place. Sometimes it ended up sweet with them going to bed together; at other times a shyness came between them or a boredom that no amount of small talk about relatives, friends, the theatre, the land, his father, could remove, and in a strange way this too drew them closer in their remoteness from each other. And what was there to do?

And how were the children going to live, he wondered, now that the old world was gone? They didn't even have a football team to play for, they didn't have the monopoly on winning the carnival queen or Miss Trinidad and Tobago. There was no separate world for them really, only a separate tomb. Where was life for them? His children didn't miss his world: they didn't know it. But where was their world? They had no separate football team, no steel band of their own, no Casuals, no Dixie Land. How were they to enter those that existed? On what terms? Were they interested? Or were they content to become spectators, keeping up the little ballet and the little recitals and playing mas' for Carnival? He realized suddenly that he had lost touch with the world, with his children. They never knew Myrrh. They never knew the shit-talk singer of oldtime calypso. Nor seen him beating iron in the band. They didn't know him. Then, what did they know?

So his talks with Kennos and Lochan and Alford made him think a life could be here for him.

He sold the dogs and he stopped the fence and he joined the National Party, becoming an ordinary member like anybody else, for Michael to tell him, 'You wasting your time. Your place is in the Senate. You will get a seat there as Business, as Plantocracy though we hardly have that any more, as clergy, na nah nah! It have plenty clergy now. Too much religion in this place now. You still have a place there as French Creole. That is your best bet: representing the interests of the old élite. That is your only chance, because you wasting your time in this Party. They won't even have the guts to put you up for election. They can't. Massa day done. And who will you represent? What constituency? Realistically, you believe it possible that you will ever represent Cascadu?'

So much of what Michael said was true. It was preposterous. They, his family had land here, had been here longer than the Blackpeople or Indians, but he felt himself an alien, walking on tiptoe.

'Numbers, boy,' Michael said. 'Numbers. Democracy. You out-numbered. Your time is up,' with a kind of vicious glee as if he was happy to be victim too like Blackpeople.

'These fellars in Miami, you think about their offer?'

There had to be something they could do.

'We emancipate them already,' Michael said. 'We ain't have anything more to do.'

'Except to emancipate ourselves.'

'Good,' Michael said. 'Emancipate yourself then come and tell me.'

The people in his constituency in Cascadu were so embarrassed to see him at their Group meetings that they elected him to the post of Treasurer. Still, he knew that there was something standing between them. On one level they seemed to respect and to be even deferential to what they saw as his power. Sometimes he felt that they were genuinely glad to have him with them as a sign of the togetherness preached to them; but more often he felt from them a kind of moral pity for him as if they were sad that such a fella as he had found himself in the predicament of what some would have said was his skin, but what with his own charity and knowledge he knew to be his history.

'So, what exactly it is that these people want?' St Hilaire asked now.

'Do they want us to give them land?'

'We had the land ready,' his father said, coming alive and speaking for the first time.

'Somebody see 'bout Daddy,' Michael said.

'Daddy,' Glenda said. 'Daddy, do you want anything? Daddy, do you want a brandy?'

'Daddy, do you want some ice cream?' Margaret said.

'He is not an imbecile, you know. Why is everybody patronizing him so?' his daughter Ann Marie said.

But the old man was speaking: 'It was always hard to be a whiteman in this place, to be an adventurer of sorts, following in the wake of the conquerors, the priests. Revolution in France, in Haiti. Come here from Martinique. Opportunity for land, for home, to be in charge of humans, to own humans . . .'

'Oh, shit,' said Michael. 'Oldman, we have to sit through this again?'

Adolphe said, 'Let him talk. Fuck it, Michael. Let him talk.'

'Talk, Daddy,' St Hilaire said.

'What does he want from you, eh? A contribution, something for his party, for his politics, for his poor?' the old man asked in his hoarse oldman voice, speaking with the sense of deafness, loud, as if to hear what he himself was saying.

'He is travelling! He is travelling!' Glenda said theatrically, wringing her hands. 'He's going back. He's back there in thirty-eight. Get a pillow for his head.'

'Oh, Gawd!' Michael said.

'Daddy, we are discussing the land,' Margaret said.

'He wants you to give him land?'

'Land. Yes. That is why we are meeting,' Margaret said.

'We should have settled this matter with him long ago. He came to me believing that he had been aggrieved. I said, I can't

208

do anything for you. He said, But you have kept me here in captivity for my whole life, my whole life up to now. I said, What do you want? What do I, he asked me, want? What do I want? You have to tell me. What do I want? You have kept me in captivity and now you asking me what do I want. You want an apology? You want an apology? I asked him straight out. He said: How can you ask me if I want an apology in that tone of superiority, as if it something I am begging for, as if it is not my due?'

'Who is he talking about?' St Hilaire asked.

'Does it matter?' Michael said. 'Does it really matter? I get a letter from the fellars from Miami. Where are the drinks? Ross!'

'He came, he said, to make a complaint. It was after the episode with Daaga. Waste of human life. He had a complaint to make, he said. Yes. I listened. I thought he had some problem with one of my workers, maybe somebody damage him or his belongings, something like that. I say, well, tell me the story, what happen, who damage you or your property and I will see what I can do about it, not promising nothing – you have to be firm with these people, set out your boundaries in advance so they would know exactly what they dealing with and you don't go beyond the boundaries. He wanted compensation and the person he want it from is me. He was thinking of taking the matter to court but he thought it would be better for all of us if I could settle without having to defend a position that was indefensible. Indefensible? I asked him. Yes, he said. You will have to argue that you had a legal right to me. You will have to argue that you have a right to me even now, say how you arrived at that right and why you have given it up, if you have given it up. Let us not carry on with this, I said. The person you want to speak to is the Governor, the Crown. But I have a little advice for you, if you will take it, because he looked very much his own man, you look like a bright enough fellow. We have the plot of land that you work on, I could really give that to you, just on my own, just as a sign of good faith, since we have to live together, you know. After this is over I shall still need your labour and you will need to work. But if I give you land, then everybody will want to get their plot of land and I don't know that I can afford it. Indians coming in from India soon, we have to pay them. This thing could mean the end of the plantation. Or the beginning of something new, he said.

'Yes, I said. Ruin. We are organized for plantation, for export crops. We need plantations, large plots, not little peasant plots. It was not something I should have said. I am not talking about land, Mr Carabon, he said. Look, a fellow like you have enough imagination to make this thing work for you. He said: You mean run away and squat a piece of land somewhere? You would like that. It would free you. It was the first note of insolence for the day. Look, I said, I will not brook your insolence. You will have to speak to the Governor, go and find your own way or stay on this estate and work for the wages we decide upon. Then I will stay, he said. He left. Next day he was back to work on the estate. He handed me a petition for the Queen that he wanted me to give to the Governor:

Your Memorialists: To the Right Honourable Lord Baron Gleneagle, Her Majesty's Principal Secretary of State for the Colonial Department:

The Memorial of the undersigned African Subjects of Her Most Gracious Majesty the Queen of Great Britain and Ireland humbly sheweth unto Your Lordship: That Your Memorialists are natives of Africa. That during the existence of the Slave Trade Your Memorialists were torn from their country, their friends, relations, delivered into the hands of Slave Merchants who imported Your Memorialists into the West Indies and sold them, that the names of Your Memorialists have been changed, that the work of the labour of Your Memorialists has gone not to their own advancement but to the upkeep of those who commanded unlawfully their labour.

As a result of the circumstances of their enslavement Your Memorialists have no other option now but to make this island their home, since it is the place that many of them have been born into and it is the place that their labour has gone to build.

Your Memorialists believe that in the interest of justice, of humanity, of harmonious relationships existing in the future between those who have profited from our captivity and those of us who have been captives here, that Your Most Gracious Majesty do grant Your Memorialists relief in the form of land, in the form of amenities and such other means as your Gracious Majesty might see fit as a form of reparation for wrong done to us and as an expression of regret from Your Most

Gracious Majesty for the position your humble subjects have been placed in through no fault of their own and despite every effort on their part over the centuries to prevent Your Memorialists from being reduced in this most degrading fashion.

'I have to seek advice. This is all very strange to me. I went around by the fellows, fellow planters. I floated the idea, what if we give these fellows the land they seem to want? If we enter a new relationship with them?

'Ruin, they said.

'Ruin? I argued with them. They wouldn't hear me. I looked to the coloured fellows. Philippe, Monsterin, Montbrum, fellows who had emancipated themselves, free coloureds. More European than we, more élite, more genteel. All the airs we were ready to give up, all the pretence that we had lived had found its way into them. Ruin, they said. He was a good worker, the best. I asked him, you want to be my foreman, and he turned me down, said he wanted to work for the land, for the trees. He had his cutlass in his hand. All these years and he is waiting on me. I wonder if he went to Philippe. I wonder what Philippe and Bertete and Crosbie and Beaubrun and Navet would have said. They didn't want to get involved. Their position was too precarious. They had just received more rights . . . Is he there? Tell him for me that we are meeting to discuss his matter. Tell him that we have put aside a piece of land for him. I am just waiting for him to ask. He must ask, mustn't he? Forty acres and a mule, the Americans said. Oh, in that wide expanse of land they could easily offer that. But the people didn't ask. They didn't ask.'

'Daddy, we have to interrupt you,' Michael said.

'I tell you he's travelling,' Glenda said. 'If you stop him too suddenly you could bring on a stroke. If you want to bring him out throw some water on his big toe.'

'Holy water.'

'St Hilaire, bless some water. Ross, get some water for your uncle to bless,' Robert said.

'Who will take off his shoes?' Michael asked, looking at Ross.

'Not me,' Ross said. 'I am learning a lot.'

'Listen, I don't know about you all, but I am not taking this guilt shit, you know,' Michael said. 'I not taking it at all. Give them land and what would happen? Will they plant it well, will they put it in cane? Will they be able to deal with the factories, the prices, the daily grind of labour without supervision, freed to be themselves. Will they take the country back to the dark ages, to this little patchwork slash-and-burn agriculture. What will happen to the place? What will happen? Will they build slums instead of mansions? What will happen?'

'That was a responsibility that we had to bear. It was our own, all this we had built. Could we give it up for some unknown nothing?

'And so we had to go on. Bring in the Indian, give him wages, get land to give him when he planned to go back, get the government to agree to give him lands too, bits and pieces of the estate here and there some of the same land they wanted us to give up.

'But I said no. No. That land is for Blackpeople, the African people. The time will come when they will ask for it. We are educating them now. Already they have people fitting into the system, imitating us, our music, our manners, our taste. They have trade unions, they have agitators, they have this fella there, this man, this doctor, the third most intelligent man in the world. They will ask us for a settlement. They will. So I made sure that the piece of land was still there, I began to work on an apology because I knew that when this fella took power he was going to come and ask us for some compensation.' The old man was talking again.

'Then Independence came and this time the land is a little less. We had to sell out a piece of it to keep things going, build house, give the Indians. And the fella is waiting. It always surprised me, why this fella, this bright one, didn't come to us and ask us for this land.'

'Pride,' St Hilaire said.

'They didn't want land, Daddy. They wanted to exhibit their pride, their power, to demonstrate their learning, their manners, their graces, their distance, their freedom,' Michael said. 'All that *zantaying*. All that nonsense about Massa day done when Massa was still here.'

'Robber talk.'

'And then 1970 came and we had another opportunity. All these Blackpeople marching, all this noise, all those drums. All their fucking airs: QRC, Belmont, Woodbrook. That was the time. And we waited for them to ask. All that marching. All those speeches . . .'

'But we are asking now,' Adolphe said.

'We?' they all chorused. 'We?'

'Well! Well! Well! Well!' Michael said. 'You better throw some water on his big toe too. Soak it in water. Adolphe, take off your shoe.'

'We'll have to draw up a balance sheet,' said Robert. 'This island has the most Crown lands in the Caribbean. Before we give them lands we have to see what they have done with what they have. We have to take an inventory of what we passed over to them.'

'Parliament,' St Hilaire said.

'The church,' said Adolphe.

'Look at the libraries we left them,' Robert said. 'Hospitals, a system of health service second to none. The schools. QRC, St Mary's. Intercol . . . Myrrh, you used to be a star in that system. Sweeter than fragrance, harder than fragrance,' Michael jeered. 'You can't take from the rich and give to the poor,' Michael said.

'Their treatment of their own people,' St Hilaire said. 'The corruption.'

'You, don't talk about corruption,' Adolphe said.

'Hey!' Margaret said. 'Daddy fall asleep.'

'No shame,' said Adolphe. 'No respect.'

'Apology for what?' Michael asked. 'For what? You don't see what's happening in Africa. This is a paradise here. If they want to go back, let them go. Like the Rastafarians. You hear any of them talking about Africa? You see any of them going back? Eh? Salt. Too much salt. Rastas don't eat salt. Too much salt meat.'

'All you, this is Daddy's birthday,' Margaret said. 'Glenda, Ann Marie, let's go and cut the cake. And let's wake Daddy up. Daddy! Daddy!' she shook him gently. 'Get up, Daddy.'

'You don't owe them anything. But you owe yourself. You owe the children.'

'Which children?'

'All the children,' said Adolphe. 'And these children?' he asked. 'These children?'

'What about these children?' Glenda asked, hope in her eyes. 'What about them?'

'The problem,' said his son, 'is that we don't believe in ourselves any more. We let those jokers bluff us.'

'Tell them, Ross,' Michael said.

Adolphe watched his son the bodybuilder, with his muscles and the torn knees of his jeans and the ripped-off sleeves of his shirt, trying to look like a caveman.

'And, you,' he said. 'You, what do you believe in?'

All these noises he was hearing. He watched his daughter Ann Marie, who for some reason he felt was sorry for him, who had some kind of softness for him, some pity as if she shared with him some of the thoughts that others did not. And you, what do you want? The question was in his eyes. And the answer in her smile. She couldn't even want. There was nothing she could even want. He had seen her one time appear in Phase Two Steel Band as a winer girl, in a shortpants carrying the banner, trying to wine. She was out of her league, but it was a nice try, a lovely try. It made him proud of her. It was like his beating iron in the band. She was trying. She was really trying. She was breaking new ground, but then it stopped, she couldn't go on.

As if he knew what Adolphe was thinking, Richard said, 'Time will change things.'

Time? Time has so much to take care of. He was thinking of his daughter at Panorama, on the stage in front of the steel band. He was thinking of Carnival, the ceremony of possession, of becoming, of joining. Of the beginning that was waiting.

'No, Myrrh! No, Myrrh,' Michael said.

'You know what the sin is? We have wronged them, that is the sin for which you want to give benediction.' He was looking at St Hilaire, the priest.

They were silent.

Adolphe said, 'St Hilaire, say something,' his voice threatening. 'Say something.'

'What can I say?' St Hilaire said.

'You know what to say. You know what to say,' Adolphe held him. 'You say it! Say it!'

'Look, you choking him,' Robert said. 'Adolphe!'

'Let him go. Daddy! Daddy!' Ann Marie screamed.

'Say it!'

The whole family, except his father, Michael and his son Ross, surrounded him, trying to pry him off St Hilaire.

'What the arse is this?' Michael said, from where he was sitting. 'Adolphe, you crazy. Let go the man.'

Adolphe took his hands off St Hilaire's neck.

'I'm sorry,' Adolphe said.

St Hilaire was fixing his clothes.

'I am sorry!' Adolphe shouted. He turned to them. 'There, I said it for you. I say it for all of fucking you: I am sorry. I am sorry! God!'

'Like this man really going off,' Michael said.

'We better than this, Michael,' Adolphe said. 'Michael, we are better than this.'

Glenda said, 'This is my father's birthday.' Quickly she added, 'Where is the champagne? Ross, open the bottle.'

'Wait! Let's have a toast,' said Robert. He looked around the room.

Robert said, 'Michael, you better give the toast.'

Michael struggled to his feet, fixing his trousers, wrestling the waist into place. 'Everybody have a glass? Is everybody ready?'

Ross held the bottle of champagne in one hand and worked out the cork with a great show of strength. They poured the champagne.

'To the most . . . No. He doesn't have to stand up. It is enough that he is awake . . . To the most . . .' It sounded like he was going to say something extravagant, something touching. He said, 'To the Oldman.'

'To the Oldman,' they chorused.

Adolphe looked at the old man at the old ways at the life dying and he thought of the theory that he had held that colonialism was a system of a dying power looking to ensure its life by penetrating another, seeking a host not so much to feast upon but to live in, to carry itself forward. It was a thought that did not make sense in the context of the present.

'Now we have to blow out the candles and sing Happy Birthday,' Ann Marie, Adolphe's daughter, said.

He watched the old man next to the cake, his lips pursed as if he was in another space, somewhere as a small boy whistling, holding himself there as if trying to remember where he was.

'Blow them out for him, Ross,' Glenda said.

With one big puff, with the same sense of his power that he had used to open the bottle of champagne, Ross blew out the candles. And as if he was really present to see it all, seeing it all from another time, the old man smiled as they sang 'Happy Birthday'.

St Hilaire looked across to Adolphe, 'Hey, man. You can't make reparation for a people, for a race. Is not your job alone. The whole society have to be involved.'

'We have to live here,' Adolphe said.

'You have a problem living here, Adolphe?' Michael asked. 'House, car, boat. Son, daughter, talented wife. Good family.' He chucked him playfully.

Later, the others were getting ready to leave. Michael looked across at Adolphe, as if he knew that the conversation was done. He said, 'You have anything more to say? Anything more to discuss? Because I have to push on. The early bird, you know.'

Glenda and the children were travelling back that night too. Ann Marie came over to him and he hugged her and she looked at him and kissed him. Ross came over and punched him lightly, then shook his hands. Eventually Glenda came and hugged him with arms that did not seem as long as he remembered them at their first embrace. He thought she was done hugging him and he made to break loose but she held him the way grieving people hold each other at a funeral, her body yielding he thought and he could smell her body scent, a smell of marigold, of yellow. And when she let him go the thought came to him that they were all leaving him here with the old man. It occurred to him that they had gone on to another life. They had adjusted. He was left with the old man in the old world, with the old hope, the two of them alone.

'You coming down Friday, eh? Independence. The play,' Glenda asked. 'Or you going and watch your Cascadu Independence march?'

'Watch?' exclaimed Michael. 'He going and march with his

people. Girl, your brother going and march. He going and march. He and his friend Lochan and his friend Alford George.'

And then as if he Michael wanted to soften the wound of what could have been construed a blow, he hugged Adolphe, 'Myrrh! Myrrh!' And he took hold of his shoulders and he shook him, 'Myrrh!' and held him again in an embrace that for all his bravado, his cynicism, his superiority, left Adolphe feeling the imprint of his fear, of the love that he was too afraid to give, of the shame in himself that he didn't dare to feel. So that he, Adolphe, Myrrh, held him too with the strength of his own worker's arms, 'Michael! Michael!' patting him on the shoulder, becoming in that instant the big, the elder brother.

12

Lochan

The first of his family to run for election was the grandfather
who they tell Sonan he take after, his father's father Moon, who
forty-nine years earlier had appeared in Cascadu from Poole
Sugar estate, with his wife Dularie and his sister Jasodra and his
five children, four boys and a daughter, walking through the
main street of the village, pushing a pushcart with all their
belongings: wire cages with chickens, wooden crates with two
dogs panting, a bag of flour, a bag of rice, their pots and pans
and other kitchen utensils, each black-haired, bright-eyed child
with the oiled wet glisten of a newly birthed calf, the smaller
ones suppressing giggles, Chote, who was to remember always
that morning, smiling, a hand held over his mouth to hide the
two front teeth missing, carrying the bag that contained most of
the children's clothing, the caravan stopping at each street corner
to ask the way to the five acres in The Bandon, the land that the
government had given him (his grandfather) in lieu of his return
passage to India, he, Moon, doing the talking, asking people
where The Bandon was, not so much because he needed direc-
tions as to make an announcement of his arrival into Cascadu,
the women who all the time had been walking behind him now
standing silently, not far behind him as most Indian men would
have them, but closer, more abreast of him, as if the old world
customs were behind them, exchanged for a new world freedom
in which they would have the chance to make themselves anew.

Sailing across the ocean of black water from India, the old
people told him, would make him go down a degree in caste. If
he accepted that edict he would be forced to consider himself a
chamar, the lowest of the castes. This did not seem deserved. In
fact he felt that his journey across the big stretch of salt water,
far from placing him lower ought really to have elevated him;
and that was the reason why, to give a more appropriate
expression of the value of his journey, he gave himself a Brahmin

name, making it clear that now he was not less than anybody even in the ancient orders of his motherland.

The change of name gave no immediate advantage to Moon beyond the consolidation of his own self-worth. The people who knew of the unilateral elevation of himself looked at him funny and were not unhappy to see him packing to leave Poole, convinced, most of them, as much by the merriment in his eyes as by the pose of importance he affected that he was off to something big, the whispers circulating saying that he was setting out for a district where as a stranger he would pass himself off as a pundit and start living easy. Instead of arguing with them, Moon produced his mischievous smile and let them believe what they would.

He found the land in The Bandon, half of it swampy and teeming with mosquitoes and sandflies. In the swampy part he planted dasheen, and on the rest he planted okro and corrailli and bodi beans. He made baskets. He made fishpots. He wove fishnets. He followed the swamp to the river and put down his fishpots. From them he harvested guabine and coscorob and taters. He went into the government forest and laid traps for doves. With his dogs, he hunted the wild animals he found there, the lappe and agouti and tatoo, selling most of it, but sending portions for the sergeant of police, the warden, the doctor and the Public Works' engineer. He talked the Engineer into giving him a job on the road. It was a nice work. By ten in the morning he was finished with that job and was ready now to go to do his own work. On the side of the road next to his house he set up a stall in which he sold fishpots and fishnets and fish as well as the produce from his garden. Seeing that people had to travel from Cascadu to the stores in Cunaripo to get household things, he stocked his roadside stall with brooms, with mats, with scrubbing brushes and useful household things, his wife doing the selling and he coming in to see what new had to be ordered and to talk to the people purchasing, to find out what they wanted. About him, at the beginning, was a sense of guilt, a need to establish his bona fides, that had him doing a lot of talking, about his own history, about India, about politics, about the stupidity of people, so that his wife, who was always the one with the business sense, had to come over and prise the customer

219

away from him otherwise they wouldn't have sold anything. The business grew. People watched him and marvelled at the speed of his progress. They were astonished at the ease with which he was getting through.

One night a government truck carrying a load of gravel, driven by a man named Emerald, who half an hour earlier had been drinking in Khandan rumshop in Cunaripo, ran off the road and crashed into his shop and flattened it. Neighbours who rushed out to drag Emerald out the truck looked to see who else was injured. They could find nobody so they pushed the truck back on to the road, placed Emerald in the driver's seat, advised him to go back to Cunaripo and make a report to the police, gave the truck a push start and went back to their homes. Next day Moon appeared heroically hobbling on crutches, one hand in a sling, his head bandaged. Cascadu who had taken its time making up its mind about him said, Yes. He is a smartman in truth.

With the money from the settlement he extracted from the government, he moved to Cunaripo, just off the main road, to an old building obliquely opposite the prosperous-looking establishment that was Gopisingh Hardware. He put his family upstairs and transferred everything from the old place into the downstairs, transformed now into a store, stocked with Coleman lamps and enamel pots and cups and buckets and cutlasses and garden implements and other useful things. He had his wife and his sister and his children selling. He took up his position on a chair at the entrance to the store, there to look across at Gopisingh and to plan the strategy for his own success. In the face of uncertainty from his wife, the first item he bought was a loud hailer which he put to use as soon as he got it, quickly bringing to the relatively quiet street the sound of his announcements advertising the articles he was selling, speaking variously in the refined accent of the radio broadcaster on 'The Indian Hour', the English peculiar to the Indian peasant, the African-inspired English of the town and a tone of voice that he had learned from British broadcasters doing commentaries on cricket. Shoppers hearing these different voices went into the store to look around to see who was talking. Seeing how successful he Moon was getting, Gopisingh bought a loud hailer as well and to get the edge, began to play music from the soundtrack of Indian films. Moon hit back with chutney singing from Trinidad Indians:

> *I see the young girl passing*
> *I tell she how de do*
> *She have a little garden*
> *And her pretty cow does moo.*

and when Gopisingh turned up the volume of his own hi-fi, Moon added calypso music to his arsenal of musical bombshells. Every Friday the street was a bedlam of chutney, calypso and songs from Indian films. Cunaripo started to be a real town.

Moon was always one step ahead of the opposition. He hired Ezekiel McKnight, a local layabout with a flair for the theatrical, to dress up in tall boots, in a raincoat with an umbrella over his head and a poniard case strapped around his waist to walk up and down in front the store to encourage people to come in and buy. And he was brave enough when Ezekiel McKnight, sleeping off his drunkenness, didn't turn up, to don the garments and do the parading himself. For Carnival, he encouraged stickfighting in the space in front his store and had a standing offer of five dollars for the first busthead, five dollars for the best drumming, five dollars for the best singer among the chantwels. On Carnival Mondays before the stickfighters assembled, the sidewalk in front his store was the stage for the carnival pantomimes of Police and Thief, Babydoll and Jabmalassie. Other businesses wanted to keep the sidewalk in front their stores free, but he encouraged people to come and display their wares. He loved the idea of craftsmanship, of work, of all the various wonderful stupid things that people made with their hands.

In the world, he felt, were so many delightful things to taste and do and he was really sorry he couldn't do them all. He loved the look of bamboo, the feel of it. He would say over and over again with regret, to his wife and children, If I wasn't in this business, I would make a million from bamboo. Bread too. He loved the smell of bread. He would go over himself by Miss Maud bakery and keep her in conversation just at the time when he knew they were taking bread out the big dirt oven, just to

watch and smell the bread. So many things to do, he felt, so
many lovely types of bread, of sweetbread, of cakes, so many
delicacies, of khurma and sahina and alloo, to make. And soon
in front his store were people selling on payday weekends, guava
jams, tamarind balls, strainers for rice, rolling-pins, mortars, coal-
pots, khaki pants and khaki shirts. People were selling birdcages
and monkeys and parrots and various singing birds. People were
selling squirrels and tropical fish and swizzle sticks and dog
chains. They were selling framed pictures of Joe Louis in fighting
pose, of Haile Selassie in the uniform of Emperor, of Vishnu and
Hanuman and Marcus Garvey.

Inside his store, too, he delighted in moving among the items
for sale and taking them up and manipulating them. He loved
the simple technology of scissors, of pliers, the feel of the equipment and the smell of sawn wood, of painted furniture, of the
screws in the wood. He had for sale every type of can opener in
the island, and he would show them to customers, Look at it!
Look! and he would open a can or cut through a piece of cloth
or drive in a nail just to show how the thing was working, his
wife and, later, his children looking at him out the corner of their
eye in case they had to run and rescue some piece of cloth or
wood or tin from ruin.

His delight was the seamless lines of well made furniture, of
things done with patience, with taste. Sometimes an item would
attract him and he would pick it up, Look at this! Look, and he
would run his hand down the line of the wood in a kind of
wonder and praise and blessing; but shoddy workmanship
brought out the worst in him, chairs with the nails showing,
benches with one foot shorter than the other where you had to
put a chock under one side to keep it from rocking. He offered
to buy them for spite, but for a price so ridiculously low that
the sellers would realize that it was better to redo them, then to
sell them.

That was the world to him, everybody making something.
When he went to buy stock for the store his wife had to be right
there with him for fear that he would run amok and buy things
that nobody but he wanted. When she saw salesmen coming she
rushed to bar their way before they got to him, so that the
salesmen themselves before they came in used to send out spies

to see if the coast was clear to make sure they got to show him their wares. He bought envelopes and writing paper and clips, novels of W. Somerset Maugham and Edgar Rice Burroughs and Marie Corelli and *The New Yorker Magazine*, he had comic books and the framed pictures of Mary and Jesus and Lakshmi and Vishnu, tennis racquets and tennis balls when nobody in Cunaripo played the game, golf balls. He had everything. And that was the fame he had for miles around. Anything you can't get anywhere else, try Moon for it. If it not inside the store, it on the pavement outside. So he had grown, this growth giving him the idea of himself as a benefactor.

On Saturday mornings when the old and infirm of the village passed through the town to collect alms, he would station himself at the door with a bag of coins to give out to them. In order that his children maintain this tradition and have the respect he felt they should for people, he involved each one of them in this ritual, so that they took turns each Saturday morning, one of them, he, his wife or one of the children having the bag with the money to give to poor people.

In 1946 when he was aged fifty-one, he saw Gopisingh going up for election to the Legislative Council, and he decided to run too, as an independent. He already had his message: EVERYBODY COULD MAKE SOMETHING. It was that simple. Seventeen people were going up for the seat that year. He printed thousands of posters and handbills with his picture in jacket and tie and a dhoti. Mr Bissoon, his campaign manager, then twenty-two years old, wanted him to take out the picture barebacked, like Mahatma Gandhi, Bissoon's hero and the only man that Moon really admired; but he knew Trinidad too well to expect them to fall for that, so he made a compromise, jacket and tie on top and dhoti below; East meets West, but in the end it didn't matter because the photographer, Mr Lee, had his own ideas of what was proper and did not focus the camera below his navel.

Eventually, his campaign came to be a contest to best Gopisingh. Gopisingh gave a feast with rum and roti; Moon gave a feast with rum and roti. Gopisingh played Indian music at his campaign; Moon played Indian music too. Then Gopisingh daughter got married to a big fella from Tunapuna and he had one big wedding for her, with people coming from every part of

223

the island, cars and vans blasting chutney and music from the soundtracks of Indian films. Food: paratha and buss-up shot with delicacies from chataigne and baigan and bhaji to feed the whole of Cunaripo and Cascadu. Moon played his last trump card.

Moon decided to give credit on easy terms to his customers. No down payment. Just come in and talk to me and sign the papers. His wife didn't like the idea, but Mr Bissoon, Moon's campaign manager, convinced them that by that tactic they would be able to distribute the thousands of leaflets supporting Moon. And so it was. People flocked to his store. He gave out leaflets with his picture to every customer: Pass them on, said Ezekiel McKnight, who now doubled as town-crier and election-eering announcer. Mr Bissoon, his campaign manager, wanted him to print more posters. To get into every household in the constituency. He printed more posters. And it was only after the results of the election in which the winner got 8,056 and he got 97 that he understood how devious people were. But he had beaten Gopisingh, who got 43. And that was not the worst part. The people to whom he had extended the 'no down payment' disappeared. Some of them had come from as far away as the far ends of the island: Cocorite, Cedros and Cap-de-ville. He had no way of contacting them. He made no complaint. He got Reynold Persaud, artist and sign painter, to draw a picture for him and he put it up in the store in a space right near to the cash register where everybody could see it. Framed in glass was the picture showing one man whose name was given as Credit, with an upraised knife about to bury it into the back of the other man, Trust. He didn't tell them anything else.

In 1950 he ran again, not so much with the intention of winning as to do two things. The first was to embarrass the people who had taken credit from him and absconded without voting for him in '46. The other was to use the election campaign as a forum for his ideas on people working, people making things. He spent his time on the platform talking about birdcages and bamboo and wood, about corraili and bhaji and baigan, about scrubbing-boards and dog chains, so that the majority of people walked away from his meetings and those who remained did so only because they felt entertained by his utterances.

After he lost that election, by pretty much the same margin, he sat more often on a bench in front the store. Now and again he would take the loud hailer and speak to the town over the music, pre-dating the deejays that were to become popular twenty, thirty years later. He would speak less about the wares he was selling and increasingly about things that were happening, the scores at the cricket Test Match, wherever it was playing, about romance and dancing, about caring for babies, everything that his wife didn't believe he knew anything about; and he would play records to the town, playing along with chutney songs and Indian music, calypso, and, for Christmas, parang. Sometimes too, but very infrequently, because his children didn't want him to do it, he would play requests for people who were buying in the store or for family or friends and he would talk a little about the old days, about love, about meeting his wife, about how to rear children.

In these days too, he would put on a hat of a type he was selling or the galoshes. He liked to put on the tall boots and join Ezekiel McKnight on the bench in front the store and wait for the old customers to come in, and they would talk about the '46 elections and all the changes that were taking place, all the sadness, all the talk about race, and he would smile at all of that because he had begun to notice that his hair was white and so was Ezekiel McKnight's, and when they cut it short you couldn't tell what was their race. That was the greatest joke that he would tell again and again, how all babies resemble and you can't tell their race and how old people you can't tell their race. He didn't have no conclusion to these observations, he just made them and laughed. There was one other thing he talked about. It was something his wife and children didn't want him to talk about. And anytime she heard him talking about it the wife Dularie would ask her son Chote to go and turn up the music loud. But Moon talked about it anyway. It was about the people who ate his roti and drink his rum and take his things on credit without down payment and didn't vote for him.

'Come in,' he said. 'I want you to come in. I would like to talk to you about it. I ain't vex or anything, I just think it would make a good discussion.' And, really, he held no grudge. If anything, he had a kind of admiration for those people, for their crookedness, and, really, he would have been happy to have them come and speak with him, for him to salute them, for him to say, 'You ketch me. You get me good.' What choked him wasn't grief, it was wisdom.

One day when his children were about to close the store they couldn't find him.

'Chote, all you see allyou father?' his mother asked.

Eventually, Chote looked behind the folding of the half-closed front door. Moon was sitting there, barebacked like Mahatma Gandhi, his head wrapped in a white cloth, with his favourite tall boots on his feet and a pair of binoculars in his hands. He had a smile on his face.

'What you see that so sweeten you, old man,' Chote asked. 'Come, go and put on some clothes, you not accustomed to this barebacked business like Mahatma Gandhi, you will catch cold.' And when he got no answer, Chote nudged him to wake him from what he thought was sleep. Moon's head lurched forward, and even as he shook him to waken him, Chote knew that he was dead.

In the years that followed, Chote never tired of telling about the wake they had for Moon, right there in front the store, with the whole of Cunaripo and Cascadu gathered, and people from far off, makers of birdcages and people selling squirrels and parrots, joiners who remembered how he touched the grain of their furniture, married couples who were lovers back then and became married after he played a request in his store from one to the other of them, Baptist and Shango and Hindu and Presbyterian and Muslim. The Nine Nights was nearly as big, with bongo dancing and card playing and fellars drinking rum and Ezekiel McKnight dress up in the costume that he and Moon used to share. And then the Forty Nights with people they didn't even know and never see before coming in and talking about the kinda man Moon was.

'And you know,' said Chote, 'I think he went maybe two times to Port-of-Spain.'

After his death, it was Sonan's father, Chote, who steered his mother into a direction which he knew that Moon, with his instinct for modernity, would have approved. Motor cars were becoming plentiful in Cascadu and Cunaripo. There was need

226

for car parts. Dularie had watched the business grow, with every-thing packed together. She didn't want to add motor-car parts to the confusion. So, for the sake of order, they agreed to divide the building into two, one side to remain the Hardware, to which she added books and records and, many years later, to profit from the short-lived boom in blue movies, videos for rental; the other to sell motor-car parts.

It was while they were making the division that they came upon a trunk bulging with handbills and posters which Moon had printed when he was running for the election in '46. At first they thought to use these leaflets to wrap nails and other small items, but seeing Moon's fierce eyes staring back from the leaflets, they became aware of the irreverence of that operation. They couldn't throw them out or burn them, and it didn't look good to keep them in the house doing nothing; so it was that the idea came to Chote that one of his sons would have to use them. To do so he would have to become involved in politics.

'Which one of you is the one?' Chote asked. They all looked at Sonan.

As the one who resembled his grandfather most closely, Sonan was chosen to be the one, thought there was Sonan's sister Maya who even then at thirteen was already smarter, more rigorous in her thinking, more correct in her grammar and more understanding of the business world than any of her brothers. Of her, Chote was both proud and uneasy. He was certain she would win a scholarship. But what kind of life would she lead with all that education.

His other two sons, Saagar and Bal, were young men and they were given the parts place to run. Later it would be in that place that Sonan, the one who so resembled his grandfather, would go to join them, fresh from high school, with the wiry build and wild interrogating eyes that in his grandfather had been masked by his fund of mischief and humour, but which, with Sonan's innocence, had him appearing to be looking at people as if he wanted to pry out from them the truth they wasn't telling – Detective was the name his school fellows gave him – so that when many years later he got involved in politics, the committee screening candidates to run for the position of County Councillor for the Democratic Party found Sonan quick, intelligent, witty and combative, but were scared to nominate him lest he frighten away people with his interrogating eyes. And when after much deliberation they finally decided in favour of him, it was on condition that he wear dark shades at least to his political meetings.

From small, Sonan was passionate about cricket, begun in the backyard with his brothers Saagar and Bal and later on with Hindu School, making his debut when he was still only in Third Standard. When he went to Fourth he blasted the ball to every part of the ground in an innings against Government School that everybody was to recall because it was only due to lack of support from the other members of the team that Hindu School did not beat them for the first time in the twenty years of their meeting.

In the following year, scenting victory, all the Hindu School parents came to see the match. Sonan who everybody depended upon was a failure. He had looked good at the beginning, but he turned out to be mediocre, and that was how he continued through the years in Hindu School and later in Naparima College, doing well at practice, but when the big game was played, his legs wouldn't move, he couldn't keep his eyes on the ball, his mind wandered. He heard it being said that he couldn't play fast bowling. He heard it said that the big occasion overawed him. None of that was correct. Sonan knew he could bat. What he came to realize was that batting for himself, he was all right, but faced with the hopes of Hindu School or Naparima, he was batting no longer for himself but for them. He was not just a batsman, he was an Indian. That was the burden that weighed him down. Other people had bigger problems. Sonan's one problem in life was that he couldn't find a way to bat up to his potential.

Still trying to work out his problem, he came to the car-parts store with an extravagance of gesture as if he was on the cricket field, throwing up the part he was selling, juggling it behind his back, catching it again and then hurling it over the counter – over the bails – for the startled customer to drop or catch depending on the state of his reflexes, Sonan looking up, delighted at the accuracy of his throw, either to compliment the customer on his dexterity or to pick the part up from where it had fallen. This went on for months, until it dawned on his father that this was not the place for Sonan, cooped up here.

No. Go and play cricket, his father said. Go over to the other store, to which, capitalizing on Sonan's passion and expertise, he would now add cricket implements, bats and balls from India and Pakistan as well as the more expensive ones from England to the stock of things sold.

Ventures, the club that he joined, gave him every opportunity to play. They put him to open the battihg. They sent him in one down. They put him in the middle; but this thing was on his shoulders and the paralysis set in. All the cricket books he read couldn't help him and he remained a batsman of promise until the politics that was his destiny claimed him.

It happened one night in the elections season. He was going with his brothers Bal and Saagar to see Marlon Brando in *On The Waterfront* when he encountered the National Party having a meeting. He became so engrossed in it that he told his brothers to go on, that he would catch up with them.

When cinema was over, they came and met him at the same spot they had left him. On the following night he set out to see the same movie, this time he found at the Junction the Democratic Party having its meeting. He couldn't move. That was the beginning. From then onward he would leave off going to cinema to go to places where they were holding political meetings, leaving Cunaripo and going Arima, San Fernando, Port-of-Spain, Couva. In the store now, no longer retelling the story of the movie, but repeating the political speeches verbatim.

'We of the National Party come to you with an understandably unmatched record of public service. We have fought for your self-government, we have fought for your Independence and we have fought for your education, we have fought for your religious freedom. Tonight we are here to let you know that there are still more battles to be fought – and won . . . What concerns us is your welfare, your happiness, your freedom, your security . . .

'Our country is not constitutional reform and parliamentary caucuses and commissions of enquiry, it is people working, people having food to eat and shelter for their families and freedom of opportunity, it is freedom of opportunity, it is equality before the law, it is protection by the police . . .'

He liked the sense of theatre, the Ministers with the remote air of recently painted buildings set in the midst of slums, triumphant like people coming back from a funeral. He watched them watching their wristwatched hands, their foreheads creased with importance, their smiles of condescension, the confidences between them, their whispers, the breath of life. He watched the gestures of hands clasped against hearts, the index finger pointed and wagged. But the words; the words:

'The future welfare of the constituents lies in the future welfare of the educational system. If we succeed in the task we have set ourselves, we shall in our own small way be demonstrating that the Caribbean countries can rise above their history of dependence, degradation and self-contempt and create worthwhile societies, independent economies and self-respecting people.'

Soon Mr Bissoon began to come over to the store to discuss politics with him. One day Mr Bissoon came over to tell him that the Democratic Party wanted him to contest the County Council elections. He hesitated.

There was a lot of his grandfather in him. He was an Independent at heart. But the day of the Independent was done and he knew that if he was to enter politics it had to be as member of a Party. There were still only two parties to choose between. One, an Indian party with a few Africans, in the opposition; and the other an African party with a few more Indians, only because, Mr Bissoon said, it was the party in power in the government.

Sonan wasn't sure.

'Don't let them put you in that trap,' his sister Maya advised. 'Choose one of those parties and you either make yourself an Indian or people see you as a traitor to your race. Look for options.'

By that time Maya was enrolled as a student at the University of the West Indies and it was there she advised him to go to seek the new politics that was emerging, that would do away with all this race stupidness.

And that was how Sonan came to find himself at the University, where the new parties were being born, to meet in turn, each of the three potential prime ministers, each one with a PhD, each one addressed as Doctor, each with his own bearded face and his unlistening eyes, each with the habit of remaining speechless long after Sonan had spoken, as if what he had to say was of such little worth that no comment was needed, or that he had said something wrong that he needed to re-present after making corrections. And Sonan, responding to this insinuation, would begin the rephrasing of what he had already said, and when he was in full flow of his adjusted statement the future prime minister would begin his own speech in which he would restate what Sonan had meant to say and then, having provided the question, go on to provide the answer. Each one welcomed him with open arms, each one gave him the newspapers and leaflets of his organization for him to sell in Cunaripo. He felt really great to be among these scholars, these bright wise people, but he felt a little out of his depth and ill at ease until his sister introduced him to her heroine, Reena Loutan, who lived on her own, who wrote articles that were published in the newspapers, who came to these meetings with her long swirling skirt and pleading eyes giving him the mistaken impression that she wanted to be rescued.

'From what?' she asked him when he eventually got the opportunity to sit with her one evening after one of the meetings. 'You mean from all these black fellows?' And she had patted his cheek, as if he could not understand. She was doing her research paper on the Indian Woman and Politics. Her thesis was that women were being kept out of power by a macho and insecure male, made largely impotent under enslavement and colonialism vis-à-vis the whiteman and who consequently harboured a residual sense of shame at having been so exposed in the presence of his woman, the Indian male even more vulnerable because he perceived African political power as a new threat, so he felt the need to keep the Indian woman hidden away, unexposed, cocooned by whatever means available to him.

'I am afraid of you, you know,' she said.

'Of me?'

'Of you?' – shocking him with the knowledge that he who wanted to protect her was the one she felt she needed protection from. He had to be careful with her. But he kept on looking for her at these meetings at which she appeared and disappeared just as unexpectedly, leaving him to wonder where she had come from, where did she disappear to and with whom? needing her but cautious, afraid.

It was about that time that Alford George claimed the headlines by his fasting, and it was out of curiosity that at first Sonan went to see him. What attracted him most was Alford's uncertainty, his willingness to listen. And Sonan was content to play along with Alford and later Kennos and Carabon especially as their meetings gave him the sense of being involved without really committing him. And he was comfortable even when Alford resisted the pressure from Kennos to form a political party. But when Alford became involved with the National Party, *to work from the inside,* Sonan had felt a sense of betrayal. What it meant to him was that Alford had gone back to the original African fold; and what was suggested was that he, Sonan, should likewise go back to the Indian party. So when Mr Bissoon approached him again to run for County Council, a course fully supported by his mother who saw it as the opportunity to get rid of the trunk of Moon leaflets his grandfather had left, he decided to take the plunge. To his sister, it was the worst choice he could make. It showed him as no different to the males of Reena Loutan's thesis.

Mr Bissoon, who had elected himself his campaign manager, had come up with what proved to be the most rewarding plan of his career in politics. It was to distribute the leaflets with Moon's picture all over the county and to present Sonan as Moon's grandson. The theme of the campaign was simple: REMEMBER MOON.

On the day of the voting there was never such a sight. Old people had come from every nook and cranny of the district on crutches, with walking sticks, trembling, deaf, half blind they were led into the polling booths to vote for – and this nearly killed him, this touched him so much – to vote for Moon grandson. They were the people who years ago had eaten Moon's food and drunk Moon's rum and taken Moon's furniture on hire purchase without any down payment and who didn't vote for him in two elections, now had taken this opportunity on this occasion to pay something back, to vote for his grandson. It touched Sonan deeply. And when he entered the County Council, having beaten his nearest rival two to one, he did so with a sense of his own individuality, with the knowledge that it was Moon and the simple contrary beauty of people more than the workings of The Democratic Party that was responsible for his election. And it was this as well as the nettling by his sister that continued to keep him a little apart, a little more objective, with his eyes open for something better for who were now his people.

County Council politics disappointed him. One thing only redeemed it for him. He was the lone member of the Democratic Party in a nest of National Party people and therefore he was The Opposition in the Council and for that reason had the opportunity to make a contribution to every matter. But the Council had no power. Except for a few traces and sporting grounds, almost everything had been put in the hands of the central government.

He tried to get Cunaripo cricket ground graded. He tried to get access roads for farmers in Cascadu. Everything ended up in indecision, in waiting – on funds from the central government. What he was left with was his attendance at the various festivals on the national calendar. In Cunaripo and Cascadu, he was given the opportunity to light the first deya at the opening of the Hindu festival of Divali and submit himself to being doused in abeer at the Phagwa celebrations, and, in the absence of the Minister of Festivities, who couldn't make it to every festival in every part of the island, to give out prizes at the calypso singing competition or to crown the Carnival queen of Cunaripo.

On the occasions he was called upon to speak in public, he tried to point to the possibility of the new world, to give some sense of that vision fashioned in his discussions with Alford and Kennos and Carabon, and, later in talks with his sister and to some extent Reena Loutan.

A number of his colleagues in his party were unhappy with his offering. They accused him of upholding the myth of racial harmony projected by the National Party and not giving attention to the fact that they had been kept out of power for the entire life of the country. He did not express the grievances of Indian people, nor uphold their religion and their family values and their exemplary conduct in civic affairs and their untiring economic efforts that had brought prosperity to the country. Most of them would have left him to rot in the County Council in

Cascadu. But there were others who believed that far from becoming narrower and focusing only on Indian questions, in order to seriously compete for power in the national arena, the Democratic Party had to express a national vision that would encompass everybody. In this cause they believed Sonan invaluable and invited him to join the Democratic Party platform preparing for the next general elections.

At a meeting in Cunaripo he was uncomfortable. He had looked óut at the audience. It had fellars he had played cricket with in Hindu School, fellars from Government School. He saw fellars from Ventures Cricket Club, customers from the store, old people who had voted for him in the County Council election because he was Moon grandson. And although he knew he was Democratic Party, he felt that he was more. And that is how he spoke to them, as people who knew him and whom he knew. He talked about his grandfather Moon, about his cricket. He talked about his search to find an alternative to the politics of mash-up-ness, of division. Seeing Harris there in the crowd, who years ago bowled him first ball that year he went to play for Hindu School, he talked again of batting. He talked of his anxiety over having to bat just for Hindu School. So afraid that if he got out Hindu School would collapse.

What he had learned from that was that he had to bat for something bigger no matter who he batting for. And that is why now, as he is called upon to bat for the Democratic Party, they mustn't expect him to bat for some little idea, some Indian people alone. 'If I am called upon to bat for the Democratic Party the best way I can do that is to bat for batting. Because,' said he, quoting the poet John Donne: 'No man is an island entire unto itself. Every man is a piece of the continent, a part of the main. Any man's death diminishes me. Because I am involved in mankind and therefore never let me send for whom the bell tolls, it tolls for thee.'

To some it was his most impressive performance and when people met him afterwards they sighed and said, 'For whom the bell tolls,' which they remembered as a picture starring Ingrid Bergman and Gary Cooper. People in Cascadu and Cunaripo started calling him For Whom The Bell, and after that simply Bells. But Mr Bissoon was puzzled.

234

'What is this talk you talking about batting?' Mr Bissoon asked. 'The Democratic Party is who you representing.'

'I don't like it,' he told his brother Saagar.

'You don't like being Indian?' Saagar asked.

Sonan didn't know how to explain.

'I understand what he saying,' his sister Maya said.

Sonan was grateful to her. To give a balance to his references, at other meetings, he quoted from the Sanskrit poet Kalidasa:

> Where the wind from the Sipra river prolongs the shrill
>   melodious cry of the cranes,
> at early dawn from the scent of the opening clouds,
> and like a lover, with flattering requests,
> dispels the morning languor of women and refreshes their
>   limbs.

He quoted from the anonymous poet of seventh-century India:

> Why are your limbs so weak, and why do you tremble?
> And why, my dear, asked her lord, is your cheek so pale?
> The slender girl replied, It's just my nature! and turned away
>   and sighed,
> and let loose the tears that burdened her eyelids.

He quoted from the movie *Panhandle*, starring Rod Cameron:

'Seems like you got wet, Mister Sands.'

'Not as much as the men outside.'

He quoted from calypsos by Shadow, and from the chutney songs of Anand Jaikaran and Sundar Popo.

He quoted from the scene in *Billy The Kid* when Doc Holliday asks, 'Why didn't you draw?' And the Kid answers, 'I changed my mind.'

As the crowds warmed to him, his humour, his sincerity, his hesitations, his as his sister put it half-assed jokes, the feeling came over him that he was on the right track. He had seen the same movies, listened to the same songs, danced to the same music, had drunk the same water, breathed the same air, lusted after the same women. His uncertainty was put finally to rest when at a meeting at Penal, before one of the largest crowds of the campaign, Gopisingh, at seventy-eight and the Democratic Party's candidate since 1946, embraced him after he was finished speaking. Gopisingh had known Sonan's grandfather Moon. He had run against him in '46 and again in '50 and had been beaten by him. He would be damned if he would run now and take the chance to be beaten by the grandson. The time had come for him to stand down and give his full support to this young champion as the Democratic Party candidate for the constituency of Cascadu in the upcoming general elections.

Sonan was elated by the widespread and enthusiastic acceptance given him. But he was bent on becoming a real contender and not the ritual sacrifice that previous Democratic party candidates had been. This was not just idle dreaming. True, the National Party had held the Cascadu seat since Independence; but a lot was changing in the country. The National Party's lengthy and unchallenged stay in power had begun to work against it. There were accusations of corruption, there was the disaffection of some of the members and slowly as well, because of changes in the boundaries of the constituencies, many seats that were previously securely National Party could, the polls predicted, be won by the Democrats if they could get more widespread support.

It was in this connection that Sonan began talks with Joshua Little, former Liberal Party activist, member of the Cascadu Carnival Committee and trustee of the Rose of Sharon Friendly Society, to help him bring into the party group members of the African community. His sister Maya was immediately supportive:

'This is the first sensible proposal I hear you make since you in this politics,' she said to him.

Mr Bissoon didn't like it. 'You now start and already you ready to throw off your own people,' he said. 'Once you start to mix up the politics, you begin to mix up the people. And that is when trouble start.'

'Tell me, Mr Bissoon,' Sonan said. 'How can we win an election without people?'

'This not going to stop at politics. This will get at our religion,' Mr Bissoon said, 'our strength.'

'Our women?' Maya prodded.

'Yes, our women,' Mr Bissoon said.

'I know that is what frightens you men,' Maya said.

Her most recent declaration was that she was against marriage, and she had been giving hints that she was going to shack up with a young man from St Augustine. Who he was, none of the family knew and her father, Chote, was afraid even to ask.

On the other hand, Mr Bissoon's fears were real. Mr Bissoon's own nephew Basdeo had gone and joined Dr Kennos in the Church of Fellowship and Joy. And another nephew, Bal, had for the last two years been bringing out a Carnival band with an abundance of half naked Indian women.

Sonan saw all these things not as backsliding, but as evidence of growth, as the settling in of the community into which he was born. He was looking at what was happening on the larger public stage.

The Standard newspaper was running a series on corruption in the country, accusations flying concerning multimillion-dollar deals, foreign bank accounts, and kickbacks. A government minister so nettled by the charges had astonishingly shouted publicly his admission of the widespread nature of the corruption: 'All of we thief.' Hindu priests were praying for the country. The Archbishop was calling for a return to the morals of yesterday, the Ecclesiastical Congress of Spiritual Baptists was holding daily vigils in Woodford Square to bring divine guidance to bear on the Prime Minister, the Old Mas Bands Association wanted one of their members to be elected to the Senate to represent culture, the Chamber of Commerce was calling for the privatization of national enterprises, editorials in *The Standard* asked for more consultants from the developed world to set up monitoring devices to avoid corruption. Kathleen Hope of Prizgar Lands, Laventille, in a huge revival meeting in the Savannah was thanking Pastor Glendell Prue for saving her from the clutches of sin and damnation. Nurses were clamouring for more pay and better working conditions. Bank workers were threatening strike action. Bus workers were being retrenched. Unemployment had reached twenty per cent of the population. Early rains had flooded the central plains and destroyed crops and flooded houses. Mother Earth, one half of her face painted white, descended from the forest of Matelot to warn people of the fire that was coming.

After much thought, the country decided that they should hold the National Party responsible. The country was ready for change. The task of the Democratic Party was to be ready for the country.

On the first Friday of that May, Mrs Cassandra Pilgrim, a seamstress of Westmoorings, was on her way down St Vincent Street to the office of the Justice of the Peace to sign an affidavit to swear that she was the same Cassandra Pilgrim, seamstress of Westmoorings, in order to get her birth certificate which she had lost along with her husband Stanley Pilgrim in a fire of unknown origin that burnt their house down.

Mrs Cassandra Pilgrim was approaching the office of the justice of the peace when she thought she heard somebody calling her name. As she turned around to see who it was, out of the corner of her eye she saw a pigeon flying towards the roof of the Red House.

She was just about to look away when she saw the pigeon alight on the weather-vane, which was shaped like a dragon. She saw the fire flick out of the mouth of the dragon and next moment right before her eyes the extraordinary sight of the dragon grasping the pigeon in its jaws. As if the dragon sensed her looking, it turned its blood-red eyes threateningly upon her, lifted its wings and was about to leap upon her when she reached for her rosary and began to scream.

Mr Garth Villafana, aged sixty-two, a night watchman and spiritologist from Valencia, employed at Naim Aboud & Sons, was making his way from St Vincent Street to Woodford Square when he heard her scream. He had travelled from Tacarigua where he had that morning gone to exorcise evil spirits that were attacking seventeen-year-old Girley Chong. He had found the walls of the house oozing blood and an incessant rain of stones falling upon the roof with no visible person throwing them. He had managed to stop the stones and had quieted the girl, but the blood in the walls was beyond his powers. He was on his way to Woodford Square to get help from an exorcist, the Roman Catholic priest Father Bean who worked ministering to the spiritual needs of the growing army of vagrants who roamed the Port-of-Spain streets, casting out evil spirits that had found it easy to enter the bodies of people who were homeless and hungry.

Mr Villafana was running to give aid to Cassandra Pilgrim who had fainted immediately after she screamed when the head of the dead pigeon fell directly at his feet. When he looked up he saw the dragon on the weather-vane looking away from him —in the direction opposite to how the wind was blowing. With his experience, he knew right away that the dragon was the culprit and that the spiritual wickedness in high places had reached a level that had now put the people of the city at great peril. He would confirm this just a few moments later when someone from the crowd which had gathered around him and the fainted woman reported that the commentary on the Test Match between the West Indian and the English cricket teams had been interrupted to flash the news that a series of mishaps was taking place all over the island. In La Romain, a fire had just consumed two young children and that at that same hour also in the waters of the sea at Mayaro two Indian girls floating on the innertube of a motor-car tyre had been washed away into the currents, had panicked, let go and drowned. A band of vagrants had attacked Father Bean. Garth Villafana did not have to hear anything more. This was clear evidence that the National Party had departed from the ways of righteousness. His triumph was that he had identified the symbol of their corrupt and endangering rule. It was the dragon on the weather-vane of the Red House, the seat of government. The Dragon had to be removed. This was the opinion given first by Garth Villafana, and taken up immediately by Pastor Glendell Prue and other knowledgeable spiritual people in the island. The Dragon must come down. The National Party must go. Corruption must stop.

The National Party tried to fight back. They invited important leaders from Africa and from India to pay State visits to the country. They unveiled plans for a Performing Arts Centre with a space for a Carnival Museum and a Museum of Calypsos. They published the artist's sketch of a remodelled South Quay which they planned to rename The Avenue of Unnamed Heroes, on which they were to erect statues of heroes for every race and nationality in the island. They began a beautification programme in Port-of-Spain, which involved planting flamboyant trees and removing the vagrants from main thoroughfares and allowing them to roam on designated streets. They offered prizes to children in primary and secondary schools for essays on 'My Beautiful Country' and 'The Independence Journey'. Garth Villafana along with Pastor Glendell Prue and his assembly of pastors wanted the dragon removed from the Red House. For the first time in its history the country began to look beyond the National Party for its leadership.

As if fate had turned against the ruling Party, Dr Eldridge Slocombe, the Minister of Festivals and Public Holidays, was hospitalized as a result of lacerations to his back and buttocks inflicted upon his person by two lashes from a bull pistle wielded by an irate husband, Dunstant Joseph, a crane operator from Saint Madeline. Mr Joseph had returned home unexpectedly and found him in bed with his wife, a runner-up in one of the local Carnival queen competitions. As reported, MP Slocombe had stood at attention when he received the first lash. At the second lash he had walked with great dignity to his car parked in front the house, got in and, still naked, driven to the Maraval police station, got out, still naked, and gone to the desk to ask the constable on duty for a snowcone. 'Sorry, sir,' said the constable, thinking to make it into a joke to ease the embarrassment. 'We have no ice.'

'OK, Constable, I will take it without ice,' MP Slocombe was reported to have said.

On the very next day the PM announced that he was setting out on a trip to Singapore to see the economic miracles of that land and to bring back capital for investment into the various new industries they had been planning to set up during the last fifteen years. The plane was delayed and rather than waiting at the airport, the PM decided to pay a visit to his old office. There he found Alford George sitting in his, the PM's, chair. Furthermore, it was revealed, Alford George had embarked on a campaign to give out government lands and to make purchases of private lands to give to members of his constituency, against the democratic principles of the Party that since Independence had kept the country stable and its various races living in harmony. This was the real issue. Every Tom, Dick and Harriet wanted to be PM. But he wasn't going to stand for it. He had a mandate to govern from the young, from the ordinary people from Barrackpore to Cap-de-Ville. He was going to bring in new people. This election there was to be a totally new slate of candidates.

But even the rattling of the PM was not enough to drown the chorus asking for the dragon to be removed from the Red House and calling for the government to resign. Nor did it obscure the fact that for the first time in its history the country was looking beyond the National Party for leadership.

Galvanized by the unexpected possibility of an election victory, the Democratic Party put its electioneering machinery into high gear. At every meeting they emphasized the shortcomings of the National Party, they repeated the rumours of corruption, the scandals, and declared themselves ready to take over the government and give positive, honest and imaginative leadership to the country.

Sonan was swept along with this tide, but even so he saw this as the opportunity for something larger. It was at this time that Sonan received the call from Alford George inviting him to appear with him on the rostrum at the Independence Day celebration in Cunaripo. The first time he mentioned Alford George's invitation to Mr Bissoon he was practically rebuked.

'So you want to give the creole and them land? You feel that go make them vote for you? Look, don't let them frighten you. If they give the creole land, they have to give the Indian. This election we have the numbers to win, we have a good candidate, we have the issues. This is our time.'

Sonan felt stumped.

'What happen to your liberation philosophy now?' his sister Maya asked him. 'What happen to your national ideas? What batting you batting for now?'

'This is our time now,' Mr Bissoon crowed.

On the day of the Woodford Square meeting Sonan joined the motorcade to Port-of-Spain in El Dorado, with hundreds of cars and loudspeakers blasting chutney music and calypso, blaring Indian songs, with van loads of men beating tassa drums. He watched the towns go by – Tunapuna, Curepe, St Joseph, San Juan, Barataria, Laventille, into Port-of-Spain, feeling the excitement growing as the motorcade picked up support, the gleeful Mr Bissoon beside him in the car, beaming without even having to say it, the pride. This is our time. And then he was on the podium before the sea of faces as the chairman called his name, Sonan Lochan, one of the young brigade, the young lions that would take the party to victory.

Once again his mind went back to Hindu School, to cricket, to batting against Government, coming in one down. And he knew Hindu School wanted to beat Government School. They wanted to win. They were depending on him. Nobody didn't talk about race or anything. But he could feel their pride, their desire to win, to be respected. And he was the one to make the difference.

Around him was the noise of tassa, of tabla, of dholak, of dhantal, the iron, the music of drumming and singing rose as a background to the introduction. There wasn't really need for speeches, what they wanted was their presence, these sounds, the need to go on, the need for victory, the chant of triumph.

'Don't give a big speech,' Mr Bissoon warned. 'You don't even have to talk.'

But as the chairman introduced him Sonan could hear the chime of the iron, the heave of the drumming and the roaring noise of human voices. Not knowing what else to do to still his trembling, he took off his dark shades. He could see everybody in the crowd. Every single face.

And he struck the microphone, tock tock tock. 'Can you hear me?'

The noise rose up. He saw Bissoon looking at him. It came to Sonan that all he had to do was to pitch his speaking to the mood and rhythm of the calypso/chutney/tassa beat.

'Can you hear me?'

'Yeah!' they shouted. The music was carrying him. It was taking him over. He was going deep down inside it. Out of its depths, to his surprise, he heard the sound of his mother's singing, a bhajan, a sacred song. The words came to him, and he repeated them:

Do not leave everything on God.
He has blessed you with wisdom.

242

Perform your wise and noble thoughts.
Be the creator of your destiny.

And he heard himself telling the story of Moon, his grandfather, of his arrival in Cascadu, and the part that he had always
left out – out of sensitivity – of coming to this place, of finding
these creole people, of their misunderstandings, of the need to
welcome each other. He talked about his cricket, that he had
learnt that the best way to bat was to bat for batting.

In the crowd, he saw Mr Bissoon's eyes widening with what
he realized later was horror at this change of rhythm, this other
note. He saw irritation on Bissoon's face as he, Bissoon, turned
to his side and Sonan's father Chote and said what Sonan learned
soon afterwards, 'Oh, Lord. He mess it up. We lose this election
again.'

But as Sonan continued to speak, he saw a big smile spread
across Mr Bissoon's face as Bissoon raised his two hands triumphantly with what Sonan at that time thought was his
response to the cheering of the crowd. And it was only afterwards that he realized that the reason for Bissoon's surprising
exultation was that, with all the noise in the square, nobody was
hearing a word he, Sonan, was saying. What he was saying
was drowned out by the chutney tassa calypso music, coming
from the enthusiasm of a people who would not be denied the
victory they were scenting for the first time.

13

Independence Day

The night she thought would be her last in Alford George's bed, Florence poured avocado oil in the palms of her hands and massaged his naked body with a thoroughness she had not employed since the early passionate days when in the idle leisure of their affection they went though the ritual of the rubdown as a necessary movement in the prelude to their lovemaking. Now her hands roamed over his skin, not vi-ki-vy as of late, but with the lingering emphasis of the farewell that she had in mind, kneading first the muscles of his shoulders, back and waist, then going straight to his toes and moving teasingly up from them to his calves, his thighs, up, until the sleeping animal awakened and he stretched his hand behind his back to find her with a tenderness that surprised her, that sliced a moist flame through her flesh and had her learning all over again how to exhale.

After they made love, she fell asleep and dreamed that she was climbing from a dinghy up a rickety ladder into a schooner with its sails up ready to leave the harbour, stretched out before her a sea of furrowed silver underneath a white and blinding sky, behind her, on the shore, Equimilado Millette, the apprentice carpenter whom years earlier she had left on another shore when she was seventeen and he was eighteen.

He had come to the little nursery school that she held in the Community Centre of Cascadu to repair some benches for her and had worked silently, seriously, with his cap pulled down over his forehead and a pair of dark shades on, looking a bit like a henchman, with his hair teased out, tall and woolly on his head, in the Afro style of the time. That job done, he had returned a week later to bring her the first of his gifts, a windmill carved out of wood bark and shaped like an aeroplane, the propeller, anchored in the soft winged seed that had floated down in that dry season from the cedar tree, set in motion by the slightest breath. On another day, he brought her a boxcart of his own making, just big enough for her to fit inside, with a steering-wheel and lines of wire connected to the axle to steer it. He had remained to show her and the children how to work it, watching as the children took turns to ride in it. Later, he brought her a rose that he had assembled from wood shavings and painted red. This is for you alone, he had said, and stood beside her, slim, long-legged, in a pose of elongated nonchalance, while she looked admiringly at the rose. Feeling him breathing quietly beside her, she said, 'Why don't you take off those dark shades so I could see your face.' He took off the shades shyly and she saw with alarm and pity the tender uncertainty of love in his eyes, that filled her with the consciousness of a power she thought she had only over the children.

Softened and confused by that power she had reached out to him, to help him, but he was already falling and together they yielded to the hard softening power. Before she knew what hit her, she had his ring on her finger and she was at his house, with his mother telling her whom they should invite for the wedding, who was to make the cake, what dress she should wear, what church they were to get married in, and Equimilado standing before her like a little boy agreeing to everything, as if he had settled for a world no bigger than his mother's dreams. It was then she had heard the high-pitched kya-kya laughter from her cousin Marjorie who sat on the steps in front their door, with her legs spread open, without a ring on her finger nursing the younger of her two children, alternately cursing Roxy for going to the States and not writing, and dreaming of the day he would send for her.

And all at once I wake up and realize that I only have seventeen years, I never even been to Port-of-Spain, never play mas' in a carnival band, never sit down on a plane to go as far even as Tobago, the island just twenty miles away. And if I was saving Equimilado from his mother, what was I saving myself from? And the voice inside my head screamed, Run, girl. Run! You too young. Run!

And I tell Marjorie, Girl, I have to go and do some shopping tomorrow, please God, just stay with the children for me, and I put some things in my grip and I take off so fast that before I finish catch my breath I was looking out the window of a bus headed for Port-of-Spain, the engagement ring that Equimilado mother find so expensive and pretty in an envelope that I leave for my mother to give him.

She saw him on the shore, still eighteen, with the pathos of his pulled-down cap and his dark shades, his affected seriousness, and his muffled power. Beside him in the dream was her aunt Maisie whose doorsteps she had arrived upon when she left Cascadu and who had stood barring the way to her door, saying already, even before she shifted ever so slightly to allow her to enter, 'You can't stay here long, you know. This is really not my house. I have to get permission from Ely.' And who after Florence went past her at the door had turned and followed her sullenly, her face swell up already with accusation and reproach as if all Florence had come with was her short skirt, bare arms, innocent little hoity-toity country manners and the curves of her melodious body to arouse her envy and send up the blood pressure of the man she was living with, Ralph Ely, a lumbering heavy-set man with bloated belly and a careless belch, with the title of Road Engineer, who had made a name for himself in a Public Works department, faced with the impossible costs of repairing potholed roads, by coming up with the idea of painting a white circle around each of the shallower potholes on the roads and of sticking a branch in the deeper ones, so that motorists would be alerted to the route they ought to take in the effective navigation of the streets.

By diverting materials consigned for use on the repair of the road to sites of his own choosing, Ely had built three houses of his own, one in Belmont, one in San Juan and another in Santa Cruz, in each of which he had installed a mistress with whom, on a rotational basis, he shared his days; except for the Christmas holidays, when he had the delightful punishment of having to eat at least one meal at each house. To keep Ely's presence ever before her, Maisie had photographs of him everywhere: Ely on the beach, Ely on the road with a gang of road workers, Ely posed in front his house in Santa Cruz, his mistress looking through the window.

Maisie was always washing or ironing his clothes or putting them on hangers or putting them away in presses, or sunning them on lines. All about the house was the smell of Ely, established by his shoes, his caps, his hats, his medicines, his purgatives, the Epsom Salts, the Andrew's Liver Salts, the Eno's Fruit Salts, his Vick's Vapour Rub. The whole house suffocated with neatness, the cleanness of a museum visited by no one, not a thing out of place, everything used washed and put back in its place. You drink from a glass you had to wash it, everyone functioning as a servant preparing the place for an absent master that Florence had assumed must be Ely, yet when Ely came nothing changed. He too drank out of plastic cups and heavy shop glasses, while put away were the finest of mugs, jugs, teacups and saucers.

'Summertime' was the song Florence sang that year, in the be-bop style of Sarah Vaughan, as she washed and cleaned and tried to keep out the way of Maisie and her man.

Florence awoke with 'Summertime' in her head and with the sense of the past she had left behind her, with Alford lying asleep inside her, recounting in her mind those days in the city, the marches of Black Power, the sight of people marching with their flags, their tall hair, the scraping tramp of their feet, the noise, the voices trying not to scream at last, of people breaking a silence they had lived in, speaking of the astonishing insult they had endured all these years, this wondrous exhalation of freedom, as they sought to reclaim name and dress and colour and life. She couldn't find a job, until – Praise God! – one day, coming back from another fruitless search, she found herself in front of this hairdressing place and was about to go past it when a vaps hit her. She said to herself, To hell with everything, let me go and do my hair and look nice and go to a fête somewhere. She had her last money in her purse.

'No,' said Bernice, the hairdresser, when Florence asked to straighten her hair. 'No. Look at your face.'

'How I should do it, then?' asked Florence.

'Siddown and let me,' Bernice said.

When I get up from the chair and look in the mirror I see my own real face looking back at me, and for a moment it frightened me: That is me? That is me? she asked Bernice. That is you, Bernice tell her. And when I open my purse and go to take out the money, she stop me and ask if I know anybody who could braid hair, since, with Black Power kicking hell in Port-of-Spain, Blackpeople didn't want hot comb in their hair. Black was Beautiful. If I know anybody what? And she got the job braiding hair. That was her beginning. She had a job; now she had to find a self to go with her hair.

In the beginning, she was not in no Black Power business, no fighting against Whitepeople or whatever ideology the people was talking. I just liked the style. It just suit me. I just see me, see how my hair and my nose and eyes and the colour of my skin all fit and flow.

That year, with the encouragement of Bernice and her friend Valerie and her boyfriend Roger, she played mas' with George Bailey's band, Egypt. She really didn't have the money, but when she see the Cleopatra costume the pores of her skin raised. She see herself. And when she hold the cloth of the costume up to her body, Valerie look at her and say, Yes, that is you. That is you.

And that was she. She played Cleopatra with George Bailey with her beaded braids falling down over her forehead and after that it was hell. Because now she couldn't go back to being nobody. And that is when her problems begin: because she really was this different person. Men watched, her and none of them don't know what to do with her. They find she was too picky, too demanding, like she feels she's a queen or something; but she couldn't turn back. It was not that she believed she was a queen really. It was not that. Is just that she was more person, more somebody who was not quite somebody, and she felt that the man she wanted would be somebody to help her hold on to that self. But where was he? Loneliness overtook her, but she couldn't go back. And then she started on this search and waiting for the man who was to meet her on her sister's veranda, sifting through the parade of males passing in the road in front the house until Alford came and saw her and out of her belief that he was the man in her future she had allowed herself to go for the lessons and write down the minutes of their meetings and wait for him to see her.

His carelessness had set in almost from the beginning. All the tenderness was from her. He was busy. He had his politics to attend, the world to save, and he acted as if he was doing her a favour to make love to her, to hold her after their lovemaking. And she had put up with it, out of her own shame, out of her own hope, out of her fear that she would be seen as fickle, she waited, not knowing how to tell him that she was the woman he was looking for.

For nine years they faced each other with little more to link them than their lovemaking, undertaken with a sense of duty as something through which they could lay claim to whatever hope they saw in each other. Anytime she thought to leave him he would do something to open another window of hope in her heart, she to the possibility that she believed resided in him and he out of a kind of habit that had him constantly waiting also for her to change into the woman he wanted.

The call to politics in the National Party and his election campaign had kept them both busy and his victory left her shaking because between them so little really had been built that she began to think that she would lose him. It was not something that she wanted to show or to feel since between them, in place of commitment there was this sense of freedom: You do what you want, I do what I want, except that she was less concerned with her own liberty than with appearing to be imposing herself on him.

But suddenly there he was, the centre of all this attention, all these women circling around him.

'And you frighten one of them grab him up?' Valerie asked.

And, yes, that was a source of worry, but, more than that, it was Port-of-Spain itself. Alford didn't know the city life, the intrigue, the cleverness, the deceit, the bluffers. He didn't know town. He didn't know who was who. They would chew him up and spit him out, she told Valerie.

'And why you don't warn him?' Valerie asked.

She watched him enter his new position with his invincible smile and his country sense, making promises he couldn't keep, inveigled into positions that upon second thought he should have abandoned but out of his idea of principle felt himself forced to honour.

This new world mesmerized him. It was a place he wanted to conquer. It was a holy place he wanted to be admitted into. He wanted people there to like him, to acknowledge him at least. These were his challenges. All he had was the confidence in his own righteousness, in the virtue of his own goodwill.

She watched him, shy in the tumult of an importance that was new to him, performing before his secretaries, the press, the Party, trying without success to present the plans of a quickly fading and frustrated vision, the sense of action transmuted into possibilities that became more remote as he moved to make himself one of the amnesiac élite whom political power had made infallible and invincible. It was as if suddenly he discovered that he did not belong anywhere, not to the ordinary people who had voted for him, not to the corpulent wielders of power, not to the white people, the French Creoles they called them, not to the Indians nor to the Chinese. She saw him one day in the Catholic church among the white saints and Jesus, images that made him a stranger. It was ludicrous to see him speaking to a Chamber of Commerce where his was the only black face. Did he understand what was happening to him, into what milieu he had ascended? She watched him as he changed into striped shirts to enhance his appearances on television, as he put on his Nehru jackets, his Orisha dashikis, the better to relate to the racial diversity in the country, his hair cut in the latest fashion, with his party tie, his new gold ring. Everything new, everything changed, as if before coming to the House he was never anybody. His speeches which used to have, even in their confusion, a sense of wrestling with some truth, became easy, trivialized by the statistics that were supposed to make them more credible.

'He not doing nothing different than what the others doing,' Valerie told her.

'No, he is not,' she said. But she was afraid. He was not only seeking to change himself. He wanted to take her with him.

Unknown to him, she had visited Mother Ethel for help. There were potions that Mother Ethel could give her to give him. There were things she could put in his tea, things she could cook up for him to eat with his food. But this was a case where she had to watch him.

'Watch and pray,' said Mother Ethel. 'Is the newness. Is the place, is the kind of power, it is the kind of power that they have there.'

'Is not another woman?'

'No,' Mother Ethel tell her. 'The woman he looking for is you. But he don't know it.'

'For me, the woman?'

'Yes. You must help him.'

And how to let him know it was me he was looking for? How to help him to find me? She settled for lighting candles in churches at Mt St Benedict and Cascadu, for the judicious burning of incense in her house on Friday evenings. And she watched as he went alone to the many functions he felt it necessary to attend, his reason for leaving her behind (which she was careful never to ask for) some fuzzy propriety, of their not being married, a concern that vanished later in the evening with his call to 'come and rescue me from the boredom of these people. I will send my driver for you.' And she went, in the beginning, on tiptoe in her high heels with her braided hair, wearing fashionable clothes that hugged her melodious body with such intimacy as to bring her to the attention of everybody, and he'd come over to her, a little cautiously, almost as if she were a stranger, and stand beside her in such a way as to suggest that perhaps he had just met her, and introduce her around a bit uncertainly or not at all until the time came for them to leave and he would drop her off at her house or more often take me to his place and she'd listen to his post-coital musings on the ambitious Members of Parliament jockeying for the limelight with the PM who played one against the other, the Cabinet an ongoing circus of musical chairs, men echoing and reflecting the PM's moods, smiling when the PM smiled, scowling when he scowled, laughing when the PM laughed, and he himself feeling increasingly out of it.

Feeling the insecurity of his position and the need for an ally to fight beside him, he began to take her with him to functions; but she could see that he was uneasy. It was her hair, her dress, her perfume, always something about her was not quite right, needed to be adjusted, and he only relaxed when they arrived at wherever they were going and he found that she fit in with what other women were wearing.

To avoid the agony of being under his constant scrutiny, she began to decline his invitations to his new world and moved closer to Valerie and Roger, going with them to another world: to the Shango feasts, to public dances ramcrammed with people, with sweat and the rhythm of calypso, to excursions once more, to the beaches, to Best Village plays where hundreds of villagers came on stage to dance and sing with the scent and rhythm of a blackness that she had not known. But, in every place, her elegance left her unmolested, as if she had shown herself to be too grand for them, too black to be so *black*.

In his first year in Port-of-Spain, they had played mas' together, he and she, the two of them sweating under the burden of their wings. This year she left him to play by himself while she went with Valerie and Roger in another band. As the band crossed the Savannah stage, he appeared from nowhere, wearing the costume of his own band, and put an arm around her. She was happy. But, even as they danced in the arms of each other, she felt resentful that he believed he had rescued her, that somehow the better world was the new world that he had been trying with such passion to enter.

'What it is you want?' Valerie asked her. 'I don't think you yourself know.'

But she was sure that there was another place, another world where she could be herself, that self that she felt wanted to come out and be a self.

She had remained in this limbo place between the two worlds, looking to him for rescue, finding herself wary with him as with someone who would lead her into that comfortable nowhere, still with a belief in him, still believing that what he was doing was what he thought was the best, but not wanting to give him support for a course that she believed would drown them. And yet she was drawing away from him, this drawing away tinged with ambiguity because it wasn't as if he stood in her way of becoming independent. In fact it was he who had helped her to get a new place and who had supported her when she decided to move from hairdressing to dressmaking and, later, from making the dresses herself to what she discovered she had a knack for, designing. Still, she found herself thinking of leaving him.

In all the years they had been together, she had slept over in his house on only one occasion. She had never allowed him to sleep until morning in hers, believing that such a development would move them from friending to living. They had discussed it only in passing and there was no serious indication from him that he wanted it to go beyond what it had become; and she remained someone he could call upon in the middle of the night to come to someplace and join him, and he to her the ever-diminishing possibility of this new world. But she remained. There was no one he could trust around him. He had been cut off from his father, from his brothers. He had surrounded himself with new friends. Somebody had to remain with him in this new place until he discovered what exactly he was doing. She had remained. Now she was going to leave him.

When he told her that the PM was reluctant to endorse his nomination as representative of Cunaripo/Cascadu, she was glad for the opportunity it would give him to review his relationship with the party. And it happened; as one by one his friends distanced themselves from him. He was exposed, alone. But she was afraid that he was using Bango and the people of Cascadu as chips with which to bargain.

Alford left for his unfinished house in Cascadu with the clear understanding that if he stood against the PM he would stand alone. Ethelbert B. Tannis had made this clear to him. All he had to do to get the nomination was to drop the matter of land for Bango and the business of appearing on the same platform with Carabon and Lochan and the PM would reconsider.

But when Florence got to him she realized that he was not going to call the PM. She found him instead going over the notes of the speech he proposed to give at the March Past on Independence Day. He was waiting for calls from Lochan and Carabon, he said.

Nobody called that first day, and in the evening the sentry who stood guard in front his house was called away. That night it was on the news: Alford had been removed as Minister and Cabinet member.

Now he had to decide whether he wanted to remain in the parliament as a back-bencher or resign from parliament and party, or join the opposition or move to begin his own party.

'Take your time,' she told him. 'Maybe this move is just to frustrate you.'

The next day he cleared his things out of the office he had occupied as Minister. The same evening he sat with Florence drinking rum punches and playing calypsoes, among them the tape of the calypso Ethelbert B. had written for his election campaign, which he played over and over again. That night he wrote out two letters of resignation: one to the secretary of the National Party and one to the Speaker of the House. He had opted to resign from party and parliament. It was chilly there at his house. Florence tried to talk to him about his future; but he had no ideas other than writing articles for the newspapers and perhaps setting up a private school in Cunaripo. One thing he was going to do was to take the salute and give the feature address at Bango's march on Independence Day. And then Florence knew that she could now afford to leave him. There was no call from either Lochan or Carabon. Strangely, this did not disturb Florence. It really did not matter. To her, Alford had arrived. He had found his way. To her the question was not whether Carabon or Lochan would join him; it was that he had arrived at a self. There was no longer any need for her to protect and guard him. The irony of it was not lost on her. She was going to leave the man she had been looking for now when she had found him.

Her awakening must have roused him. As he made to roll off her belly, she held him to her breast, keeping him there.

She said to him, 'Listen, man, I'm not coming back here like this. I'm not getting up in the morning alone any more.' She said it not with anger nor resentment but as a statement of fact, with a sense of triumph even. With this new man she felt she wanted something more suitable. This wasn't suitable. 'No, I'm not coming back like this. No. We have to do better.'

As if she had communicated a new excitement and warmth from her body to his, she felt him swelling inside her and she held him close, sadly and sweetly; for this was going to be the last time, this night. At the edge of her brain, she felt a thrill of release, a surprising and sober grandeur, as if in giving him himself she had begun to reclaim her own.

She dozed off once again. This time the dream was clear. She had come to the house and opened all the doors and the windows and taken down the curtains and turned over the beds and turned the mirrors and the pictures to the walls. There in the house she saw herself dressed in a long African dress with her plaited hair under a huge headtie of African cloth in the same style as Mother Ethel. Around her were all these African women with lothars of flowers and water to sprinkle in front the house and censers of incense to smoke out the house. In another room, she saw drummers drumming and men playing cards and in another part of the house her father and Bertie and Bango singing hymns. Outside in the yard people were beating bamboo and dancing bongo. The women were getting ready to pray. Mother Ethel said to her, 'Go and get some coffee to give out to people.'

In the dream, still, just as she entered the kitchen to get the coffee, she awoke quite groggy with the dream, trying to call it back and feeling it dissolve. The part that alarmed her was that in the dream she did not seem concerned at the death.

She was in his arms. He was holding her.

'I dream something,' she said. 'Death.'

'What does it mean?'

She said the first thing that came to her mind: 'You have to have a Thanksgiving feast to ward off death.'

'How you do that?'

But she felt she didn't have time to tell him the details of her dream, because she remembered that it was late and it was time to be leaving. And she thought she would get up now and put on her clothes. She had to leave and he had to get up and drive her over to her house.

She tried to untangle herself from his embrace. 'Get up,' she said.

'Wait.' He held her. 'Stay with me.'

'No,' she said. 'Listen. You free.'

'You, listen,' he said.

'I have to go.'

'Stay with me.'

She tried to hold herself stiff, erect, and not to cry, but she felt herself, this big woman, crumbling. As if he knew of all that he had put her through, there in the dark the fingers of his other hand found their way to her face to wipe away the tears that were silently rolling down her cheeks, and long after the tears had ceased to flow he continued wiping them away with the calming tenderness of an anointing, making her feel herself someone discovered, someone new and precious that he wanted to cherish and to heal.

He said, 'Let us hold the Thanksgiving feast.'

255

She lay down beside him.

On Independence morning Alford awoke to find Florence not with him. For a moment there panic struck him and he jumped out of bed and rushed out the room to find the doors of the house open, and village women, their heads tied, wearing the costumes of their faith, with mops and brooms, sweeping the house and scrubbing the floors. Florence was with them. She had brought them in, she said, for the Thanksgiving feast on account of her dream. He himself was to bathe and change, then he was to come into the living-room. Alford obeyed. He took a shower and put on the white clothes Florence had lain out for him and came out to find incense burning, the women standing in a circle, holding hands and praying. They motioned him to join them, and he joined the circle and shut his eyes.

He was back to being a child of seven when he was part of the ceremony to get him to talk, beside him his mother, before him Mother Ethel large in her dress of many layers of cotton, her hands in his, her breathing bosom heaving out her mothersmell, the smell of scented oils under folds of cotton and of the colour blue and the smell of the wax of burning candles. As the praying went on, he felt himself taken back past that past, beyond the mysteries of that ceremony to the edge of a chasm he could not cross. Africa was out there. Out there was part of his self that all at once he longed to recover, to reclaim and so reclaim a wholeness for himself. He strained to reach back to that child, to that past that he felt belonged to him. And he could feel it, sense it, right there behind a wall, behind Mother Ethel and the Orishas, behind Ogun and Damballa and Yemanja and Shango. It was there, out there, with Africa, out of reach. It was so pitiful.

The praying stopped, and Alford turned from that far near distance and walked out on to the veranda alone, thinking still of that self beyond his reach in a faraway place, as a loss, as something he had been deprived of. But how do you feel the loss of a self that you did not have to lose? How can you lose an Africa you did not know? But that was what he felt: the loss of not having had that loss to lose.

Later that morning, as he stood on the podium of Cunaripo recreation ground, the sense of that loss came back, flooding him, as he heard in the distance the sound of the steel band, soft, muted, metallic and the faraway tramp of feet. Bango and his troops were on the march. He felt for home, for family, for the people he had never really got close to. He looked out among the crowd hoping to see Carabon and Lochan coming. He looked out among the crowd to see if any of his brothers was there. And then he heard the cheering, and over on the other side of the ground, he saw Bango, all in white, his flag held aloft, on his shoulders his epaulettes, on his chest the medals that he had won in wars no one but he himself had recorded, at the head of his troop of soldiers and the children he had costumed to represent the different races in the island. As the marchers passed before him, their eyes turned right to take the salute, their out-turned palms across their foreheads, in front their eyes, at the side of their ears, with the pathos of their ragged and delightful disarray, Alford lifted his hand to salute them. Suddenly, he felt small before Bango. And all at once it hit him: Bango had kept the self that he, Alford, had lost. Bango had crossed the chasm into that past to link up with JoJo, to carry still his sense of violation after the granting of the 'Emancipation' that neither acknowledged his injury nor addressed his loss.

And then he felt shame, at himself and his community that had left it to Bango alone to be outraged at the indignity its people continued to live under. It was of this shame he spoke. It was of his own loss of a sense of loss, of the blotting up of the outrage he should feel at the insult and indecency that had made their way from the past into their living from day to day. He wanted himself to feel the outrage. He wanted the whole community to feel outrage at injustice and indignity and cowardice.

How can you free people? he asked. When every move you make is to get them to accept conditions of unfreedom, when you use power to twist and corrupt what it is to be human, when you ask people to accept shame as triumph and indignity as progress? What is power if power is too weak to take responsibility to uphold what it is to be human?

He did not belong on the podium. He did not belong in the stands as a spectator. He had to find his way back to the people

257

from whom he had stood apart from the beginning, from whom he had tried to escape, to embrace his shame, to claim his outrage and so lay claim to a future of dignity. He had been too long underneath the limbo pole erected for him to pass under in order to be admitted into that other world that had for too long been the world. He was grateful now to have arrived here to find people waiting for him to join them to remove the guilt and shame we had our people labour under ever since Columbus landed and begin to construct the new world that we had been waiting on ever since Guinea John flew back to Africa.

At the end of his speech, the steel band struck up, the soldiers came to attention, Bango shouted the command and they began their march out of the ground. Alford George left the podium and joined in behind them. Other people joined in too. I ran ahead up Main Street the better to see the size of this new march. At the corner directing traffic was Corporal Aguillera, immaculate in his dress uniform, some fellars in white going to play cricket and families with baskets waiting for the bus to take them to the beach. There was not a lot of people in the march; but for a beginning it wasn't too bad. My mother, Pearl, my father, Michael, the neighbours, parents of children, Florence and the women, Miss Ramsingh, Moxy, Kenny. They were all there with Bob, Kennos, Leroy, Raoul. I saw Walt and Che and Lulu and Miss Maya with a space around her and her arms spread open like a Carnival queen. Robyn was holding Tiy. And in the crowd was Jean and Miss Marjorie and Margaret and Sara and Jazzy and Smithy and Wasa and Lawrence and Jenny and Pico and Lyris and Hoda and Mizzi and Funso and Sister Lillian and Talbot and Lloyd and Bernie and John and Judy and Nadine and Sharon and Asad and Christine and George George, and John De John the novelist from Matura, Einton and Merle and Norvan and Warner. It wasn't bad for a beginning. I got in behind them and we marched all through the town. Just as we were leaving Cunaripo, at the corner was a National Party election campaign meeting. The speaker was one of the new people the party had brought in from the business world. He was speaking about the march. I stopped to listen.

'Alford George has begun his campaign of political revenge. It is against the National Party that has governed in the interest of the people. Since we took office we have maintained a stable society that is the envy of any in the world; now Alford George has taken the forum provided by innocent and patriotic people to celebrate nationhood, to invoke the spectre of racial division by claiming reparation for Africans.

'There is nothing original in what he is proposing. All that it shows is the depths to which political outcasts will go to gain popularity. Like so many before him, Alford George is not going to succeed in dividing this community. He will do well to remember that our watchword is Tolerance. It is this that has enabled us to live with such goodwill despite our different histories.

'It will be useful also for him to note that the call for reparation is being mouthed by persons who are themselves just as corrupt as those they accuse of sinning against their people.'

'Our Africans,' the speaker said, 'are quite happy to claim this as their homeland along with our Indian, our European, our Chinese and the many other ethnic communities that make up the population of this island. Ask them and they will tell you, all of them, that hard as it has been here, they all feel that they have been fortunate to escape the poverty and corruption in the lands from which their parents originate.'

I turned away feeling somewhat sad. How didn't he understand? Then I saw it clearly. The tragedy of our time is to have lost the ability to feel loss, the inability of power to rise to its responsibility for human decency. As I made my way back to the march, I was far from without hope. I suppose what I have learned is to not despair because of our errors or to be afraid to try again. I thought of my uncle Bango and of Miss Myrtle, of Alford George and the lifetime it had taken him to get to here. I was thinking that if what distinguishes us as humans is our stupidity, what might redeem us was our grace.

I rejoined the marchers at Hibiscus and we went on through Deep Ravine and Mile End, travelling the same road Alford had taken as a child, past the fields of the Carabon plantation into which his father Dixon had poured his pride. And I was hoping that Carabon and Lochan would join us somewhere on the way. Once more I worked my way through the crowd up to the front where Miss Myrtle was now at the side of Bango, who was marching with a sad stateliness and a sense of distance as if he

259

was keeping his strength in reserve, making me feel that this march of his was for all our own lives and had to be carried on, even if it took us to the very end of time. I got in beside them.